# ALFRED HITCHCOCK'S
# GRAVE SUSPICIONS

# ALFRED HITCHCOCK's GRAVE SUSPICIONS

Edited by Cathleen Jordan

The Dial Press
Davis Publications, Inc.
380 Lexington Avenue, New York, N.Y. 10017

FIRST PRINTING
Copyright © 1984 by Davis Publications, Inc.
All rights reserved.
Library of Congress Catalog Card Number: 76-43201 (Alfred Hitchcock's Anthology #19)
Printed in the U.S.A.

All the stories herein were first published in *Alfred Hitchcock's Mystery Magazine*. Grateful acknowledgment is hereby made for permission to reprint the following: *To Catch a Big One* by Robert Edmond Alter; copyright © 1958 by H. S. D. Publications, Inc.; reprinted by permission of Larry Sternig Literary Agency. *My Daughter, The Murderer* by Eleanor Boylan; copyright © 1977 by Davis Publications, Inc.; reprinted by permission of the author. *Murder in Miniature* by Nora Caplan; copyright © 1962 by H. S. D. Publications, Inc.; reprinted by permission of the author. *Strange Prey* by George C. Chesbro; copyright © H.S.D. Publications, Inc., 1970; reprinted by permission of the author. *No Fish for the Cat* by Neil M. Clark; copyright © 1965 by H. S. D. Publications, Inc.; reprinted by permission of Scott Meredith Literary Agency, Inc. *This Day's Evil* by Jonathan Craig; copyright © 1964 by H. S. D. Publications, Inc.; reprinted by permission of Scott Meredith Literary Agency, Inc. *Mr. Reed Goes to Dinner* by Ed Dumonte; copyright © 1964 by H. S. D. Publications, Inc.; reprinted by permission of Larry Sternig Literary Agency. *The Forgiving Ghost* by C. B. Gilford; copyright © 1961 by H. S. D. Publications, Inc.; reprinted by permission of Scott Meredith Literary Agency, Inc. *Monkey King* by James Holding; copyright © 1966 by H. S. D. Publications, Inc.; reprinted by permission of Scott Meredith Literary Agency, Inc. *Nice Work If You Can Get It* by Donald Honig; copyright © 1962 by H. S. D. Publications, Inc.; reprinted by permission of Raines & Raines. *Jurisprudence* by Leo P. Kelley; copyright © H. S. D. Publications, Inc., 1968; reprinted by permission of the author. *The Weapon* by John Lutz; copyright © H. S. D. Publications, Inc., 1969; reprinted by permission of the author. *Police Calls* by Carroll Mayers; copyright © 1976 by Davis Publications, Inc.; reprinted by permission of the author. *A Dash of Murder* by Jack Morrison; copyright © 1963 by H. S. D. Publications, Inc.; reprinted by permission of the author. *Never Trust a Woman* by Helen Nielsen; copyright © 1957 by H. S. D. Publications, Inc.; reprinted by permission of Scott Meredith Literary Agency, Inc. *A Voice from the Leaves* by Donald Olson; copyright © 1976 by H. S. D. Publications, Inc.; reprinted by permission of Blanche C. Gregory, Inc. *Dead Drunk* by Arthur Porges; copyright © 1959 by H. S. D. Publications, Inc.; reprinted by permission of Scott Meredith Literary Agency, Inc. *Till Death Do Not Us Part* by Talmage Powell; copyright © H. S. D. Publications, Inc., 1975; reprinted by permission of the author. *Smuggler's Island* by Bill Pronzini; copyright © 1977 by Davis Publications, Inc.; reprinted by permission of the author. *Piggy Bank Killer* by Jack Ritchie; copyright © 1967 by H. S. D. Publications, Inc.; reprinted by permission of Larry Sternig Literary Agency. *The Return of Crazy Bill* by Frank Sisk; copyright © H. S. D. Publications, Inc., 1969; reprinted by permission of Scott Meredith Literary Agency, Inc. *The First Crime of Ruby Martinson* by Henry Slesar; copyright © 1957 by H. S. D. Publications, Inc.; reprinted by permission of the author. *The Crazy* by Pauline C. Smith; copyright © 1975 by H. S. D. Publications, Inc.; reprinted by permission of the author. *The State Against Sam Tucker* by William M. Stephens; copyright © 1960 by H. S. D. Publications, Inc.; reprinted by permission of Larry Sternig Literary Agency. *Funeral in a Small Town* by Stephen Wasylyk; copyright © H. S. D. Publications, Inc., 1973; reprinted by permission of the author. *The Night of the Sea Serpent* by Thomasina Weber; copyright © H. S. D. Publications, Inc., 1970; reprinted by permission of the author. *Hit or Miss* by Edward Wellen; copyright © H. S. D. Publications, Inc., 1974; reprinted by permission of the author. *Sweet Remembrance* by Betty Ren Wright; copyright © H. S. D. Publications, Inc., 1968; reprinted by permission of Larry Sternig Literary Agency.

# INTRODUCTION

In the twenty-eight stories that follow, only one thing is certain: grave suspicions about the goings-on in any of them are appropriate. Anybody at all might have designs on the life or loot of someone else, and it's no easy matter to unmask—and then outwit—the thieves and murderers that crowd these pages.

Not that you'll be alone. Assorted detectives, professional and amateur, are on the scene as well, from country lawyer Rube Claggett, to resourceful—even on her wedding night—Prudence Buckram, to a young man who makes invisible things. Even so, however, one must be on one's toes: the crimes (and criminals) are various indeed, and detectives of perspicacity are needed.

What is one to make, for instance, of the problem of the tree house in Donald Olson's "A Voice from the Leaves"?

Or the eerie dollhouse in Nora Caplan's "Murder in Miniature"?

Or the *empty* house in Donald Honig's "Nice Work If You Can Get It"?

What, exactly, are the clues in Bill Pronzini's "Smuggler's Island"?—there are more than are apparent.

How did it come to pass that justice was done in C. B. Gilford's "The Forgiving Ghost," or in Thailand in James Holding's story ("Monkey King")?

What do sea serpents have to do with justice, pro and con—for the answer, see Thomasina Weber's tale—and what mystery lurks in a mausoleum in Louisiana?

There's a be-spectacled youngster with more savvy than cash (total assets: twenty-seven dollars and fifty-six cents), possessed of an unruly uncle; a case wherein a man knows too much—about everything *except* crime; a man who can only save himself if he doesn't; and a blackmailer who knows no sins. There are weapons like sharks, cut ropes, and bicycles.

Some of the latter, by the way, lead, literally, to grave results. And that can be—often is—pretty chilling. But throughout there are stories full of humor and mystery in addition to that somewhat earthy side to life, and characters whose company one likes. There are, of course, all kinds of satisfying resolutions. The tales collected here, in short—all from the files of *Alfred Hitchcock's Mystery Magazine*—are ones that, whether you can unravel the crimes or not, we hope you will enjoy. (We might even say that, if not, we will be gravely disappointed.)

**Cathleen Jordan**

# CONTENTS

The Night of the Sea Serpent     *Thomasina Weber*   11

The State Against Sam Tucker     *William M. Stephens*   22

To Catch a Big One     *Robert Edmond Alter*   40

Never Trust a Woman     *Helen Nielsen*   52

Piggy Bank Killer     *Jack Ritchie*   62

No Fish for the Cat     *Neil M. Clark*   77

The First Crime of Ruby Martinson     *Henry Slesar*   92

Till Death Do Not Us Part     *Talmage Powell*   104

Mr. Reed Goes to Dinner     *Ed Dumonte*   116

The Return of Crazy Bill     *Frank Sisk*   130

A Dash of Murder     *Jack Morrison*   139

Strange Prey     *George C. Chesbro*   148

Sweet Remembrance     *Betty Ren Wright*   188

A Voice from the Leaves     *Donald Olson*   194

This Day's Evil     *Jonathan Craig*   209

The Forgiving Ghost     *C. B. Gilford*   221

The Crazy     *Pauline C. Smith*   233

Police Calls     *Carroll Mayers*   240

Funeral in a Small Town     *Stephen Wasylyk*   246

Hit or Miss     *Edward Wellen*   265

Murder in Miniature     *Nora Caplan*   271

Smuggler's Island     *Bill Pronzini*   281

Monkey King     *James Holding*   296

Nice Work If You Can Get It     *Donald Honig*   303

The Weapon     *John Lutz*   312

Dead Drunk     *Arthur Porges*   321

Jurisprudence     *Leo P. Kelley*   333

My Daughter, the Murderer     *Eleanor Boylan*   340

# ALFRED HITCHCOCK'S
# GRAVE SUSPICIONS

# The Night of the Sea Serpent

## by Thomasina Weber

**E**verybody knows there's no such thing as a sea serpent, especially my husband. He's the most down-to-earth, unimaginative person on the west coast of Florida. Still, ever since that glamorous divorcee next door insisted that she had been attacked by one, Jack has been out on the beach with her every night, waiting for it to come back.

I suppose I ought to be out there helping them because it's pretty hard to see at night, but I never go out on the beach after sunset. The mosquitoes bite me something fierce and I swell all up. Besides, I'm usually busy with my embroidery or the mending. Actually, I don't often go on the beach during the day, either, because I burn and peel and shed skin for a week after. Jack is usually pretty happy surf fishing by himself.

He hasn't done much fishing since Wilma Paine rented the other half of our duplex on the beach, though. There's always some little thing that has to be done after work at Wilma's place. Jack says it's the least he can do, since poor Wilma doesn't have a man around, and, after all, he is her landlord. It isn't Wilma's fault that the house is old. When we bought it five years ago, right after we were married, it was pretty rundown, but Jack spent a lot of time and money fixing it up.

Not a lot of money, really, because we don't have much. Jack works as a maintenance man in a six story office building. He's had the same job for twenty-nine years. He got it when he quit school to support his sick mother. When she died, she left him a little bit of money, and with what he had been saving, he had enough for the down payment.

The night of the sea serpent was two weeks after Wilma moved in. I was re-covering a chair while Jack was getting ready to go surf fishing. We both heard Wilma yell and Jack was outside faster than I ever saw him move. The moon was bright and he went galloping across the sand to where she was splashing out of the water. I can't figure what color that bathing suit was—as a matter of fact, I wonder if she—but then, I'm quite nearsighted.

Anyway, he brought her up to the house. She had on a terry cloth robe by that time. Her shiny black hair was piled neatly on top of her head the way she usually wears it. It wasn't the least bit wet, so I guess the sea serpent hadn't dragged her under.

"Can I get you some coffee?" I asked after she had told us what happened.

"No, thanks, Sophie," Wilma replied. "I think I'll go home and go to bed." She turned to Jack, who was standing there sort of glassy-eyed. "I don't know how to thank you, Jack."

"Yeah. Well." Jack isn't very good at conversation. In his job, people don't talk much to the maintenance man. Half the time they don't even see him, he says.

Jack didn't say another word for the rest of the night, but he made up for it the next morning. "You burned the toast, Sophie."

"The toaster doesn't pop up any more. Remember I told you about it three months ago?"

"Well, why don't you fix it?"

"It's worn out."

"If it's been broken for three months, how come this is the first time you burned the toast?"

"I guess I wasn't watching it."

So I watched it very carefully after that.

When Jack asked me how much longer I was going to keep mending his old shirts, I went out and bought him six new ones. I was glad I did, too, because he looked so nice in them. He really has a marvelous build for a man of forty-five. I wouldn't tell him, though, for it would only embarrass him. I guess he thinks he'd embarrass me if he ever gave me a compliment, but I wouldn't be embarrassed a bit. It would please me no end. But I suppose there's just nothing about me that's worth complimenting.

I'm not complaining. I consider myself lucky to be married at all, especially to Jack Conmar. He's very handsome, only he doesn't have the kind of job where anyone notices it. He was thirty-nine years old when his mother died, and if you ever saw a lost soul, Jack was it. I used to cook at the diner where he ate lunch every day, but he never had much to say to me. I felt so sorry for him after he lost his mother, but the only thing I could do was give him extra-large portions of everything. I guess it worked, though, for he began to smile at me.

I wasn't kidding myself. It was no head-over-heels love affair. I could never hope for one of those. I was already forty-four years old—five years older than him, I found out—and when you've got all that against you besides being short and dumpy and nearsighted, well, anything goes. He needed somebody to take care of him and I needed somebody to take care of, and that's all there was to it. He thinks it was his idea, of course, and I'll never tell him different.

After Wilma moved in, she started coming over every day to have coffee with me, but since the night of the sea serpent she doesn't do it as often. She did come over one afternoon, though, to model a new bathing suit she had bought.

"Thirty-seven fifty I paid for it," she said.

"For—*that*? But there isn't half a yard of material in it!"

"It's the design that costs, honey. And you've got to admit this is an extremely strategic design." The words didn't mean much, but I got the general idea. "I've never seen you in the water, Sophie."

"I can't swim."

"Oh, that's too bad. Jack swims, doesn't he?"

"He's a real good swimmer. He likes anything that has to do with the water. If it was up to me, I'd rather live in the mountains."

"A man likes someone to share his interests."

"I do the best I can."

She gave me a funny up and down look. "You must be a good cook," she said as she left.

I noticed she had forgotten her cigarettes. I picked them up and dropped them in the trash can. Then I started to bake a batch of brownies, but I guess I wasn't watching those, either. They burned and I had to throw them away.

There is this little island off to the south of us. I suppose it was a sandbar at one time and some mangroves washed up on it during a storm and took root and began to grow. Pretty soon the sand built up and the birds started to visit it and then there grew some Australian pines and some sea grapes. Anyway, it must be a couple of miles around by now. It's too far to swim to, but you can get there easily by boat.

King Charlie lives on the island. He thinks he owns it, so that is what he calls himself. Nobody knows where he came from or how old he is, because of that bushy white beard and thick mop of hair. He looks like a giant to me, but when you are only five feet tall, everyone looks big. Jack says he's way over six feet, though. He could probably pick up his little boat if the engine conked out and carry it to the mainland under his arm.

Most people are afraid of Charlie. I guess it's because he has a voice to match his size. When he laughs, you hang onto your chair so you don't fall off. Everybody has his own ideas about Charlie. Some people say he is a rich eccentric who ran away and buried his fortune on the island so his greedy relatives wouldn't get it. Others say he's a political refugee or a disguised writer or a no-good bum. Whatever he is, he keeps pretty much to himself, coming to the mainland every so often to sell fish or clams he has collected. All the housewives buy them because they are afraid not to. Not that he has ever threatened anyone, but you just never know what he's going to do next.

Wilma was sitting in my kitchen one morning when Charlie clomped up the steps, strode into the room, and slung a sack of clams onto my table, leaving without saying a word.

"What was *that?*" asked Wilma, sitting up straighter.

I told her about King Charlie. "People think he's crazy because of the things he does. Like leaving stuff. If he likes you, he won't sell you his fish—he'll give them to you. He used to leave me so much fish I finally had to beg him to stop."

Wilma's mind must have got stuck about halfway through my story. "Do you think he's really got a fortune buried out on that island?" she asked.

"Of course not. Where would Charlie get a fortune?"

"You're as bad as your husband, Sophie. No imagination at all. I can think of a million places he could get it. And I can think of a million places to spend it."

The next day was Saturday, Jack's day for doing chores. I expected him to clean out the garage, but Wilma came over and said she was having trouble with her refrigerator. I didn't see Jack again until lunchtime.

"Garage needs cleaning," he told me between mouthfuls of crab salad.

"I thought you wanted to do it."

"I haven't finished Wilma's refrigerator yet."

When I finished cleaning the garage, I went inside to take a shower. When I finally came out to the kitchen, I found a note on the table from Jack saying he had driven Wilma to the store because her car wouldn't start. The store had been closed for two hours by the time they got back. Jack didn't have much to say, just mumbled something on his way to the shower about a flat tire and no spare and no gas stations open. He must have had to do a lot of walking. He looked worn out.

I decided to sit on the beach the next morning while Jack fished. I put on a longsleeved muu-muu and a floppy straw hat to protect me from the sun. I was sitting under the umbrella, my face smeared with suntan lotion, when Wilma appeared. She was wearing the thirty-seven fifty bathing suit. I still couldn't see that much money in it, but I guess Jack appreciated it. He went right over to talk to her. I watched them, feeling like a beached whale.

All of a sudden Wilma bent over, her arms across her stomach. Jack dropped his fishing pole and grabbed her. By the time I could get to my feet, he was halfway to the house with her in his arms. She seemed to be in pain.

It was quite a day. I phoned for a doctor, who came and said it was a touch of ptomaine, nothing serious. Jack, meanwhile, was charging around her apartment in a frenzy.

"Your wife's going to be all right," the doctor assured him. I tried not to laugh, picturing the doctor's face if I should tell him Jack was only her neighbor.

Wilma, weak and exhausted, told us from her bed that she had eaten some fish she found in her refrigerator.

"You *found* it?" asked Jack.

"Yes. Somebody must have left it for me when we were in town yesterday."

"Who would do a thing like that?"

"King Charlie often leaves fish for people he likes," I said.

"*Tainted* fish?" asked Jack.

"Maybe it wasn't spoiled when he left it," I replied. "You said the refrigerator wasn't working, didn't you?"

"Oh, that's right," said Wilma.

"Well, no harm done," I said, getting to my feet. "I'll bring you a bowl of soup, Wilma."

We were having supper a couple of nights later when Wilma burst into the house, waving something above her head.

"Look at this!" She slapped it down on the table between us. It was a small cloth doll with shiny black hair piled on top of its head and it was dressed in a bikini. From the center of its chest protruded a long pin.

"What's that?" asked Jack.

"It's a voodoo doll! I found it on my bed."

"It's cute," said Jack.

"*Cute!* Don't you know what a voodoo doll is? Somebody is trying to kill me!"

"It's probably a joke," I said. "Sit down and have a cup of coffee."

I could tell that Wilma disturbed Jack. He had never had much experience with dependent women. Although his mother had been an invalid, she had always managed to fend for herself and take reasonable care of her son. Maybe if she had spared herself more, she would have lived longer.

Jack has had a hard life and I do my best to make up for it. I cook everything he likes and keep the house real clean, and Jack never has any buttons missing. I make all my own clothes, and that's a big saving. Of course, they don't look like those gorgeous shifts Wilma wears, but then I don't look like Wilma, either. How she can sit in the sun all day and still look so beautiful is beyond me. Maybe if I spent as much time on myself as she does—oh, there I go again. I just don't have the material to work with in the first place.

The next day Wilma asked if she could use the outboard. "I'd like to see what the island looks like."

"King Charlie doesn't care much for company," I told her.

"I don't think he'll mind me," she said.

I sat down on the porch and watched her shove off, slim and tanned, in a bathing suit I hadn't seen before. It was black, all in one piece, but with a lot of see-through places in it. I wondered if I'd ever have the courage to wear a suit like that, if I was ever lucky enough to be as slender as Wilma.

I saw her beach the boat and throw the anchor up on the sand. I was glad Jack had bought such a good pair of binoculars. It was the first time I had used them. Wilma disappeared into the trees and I put the glasses down. She would probably spend a nice afternoon getting acquainted with King Charlie.

But she didn't. About fifteen minutes later she came flying out to the boat, snatching up the anchor on the way. King Charlie followed and stood at the water's edge watching her struggle to get the engine started. She must have thought he was chasing her, but if he wanted to catch her, all he had to do was step into the water and pluck her out of the boat.

She jammed it into reverse, making a sharp turn that almost capsized the small boat, and came toward the mainland so fast it looked as though she was skimming over the top of the water.

"That old goat!" she gasped when she finally got back. "That lecherous old goat!"

"I told you King Charlie didn't go for company."

"That's what you think! He went for me! Like a four alarm fire!"

"Maybe you shouldn't have worn a bathing suit like that."

"How was I to know? I assumed he was civilized."

"Did he tell you where the money's buried?"

She gave me a funny look. "What kind of a crack is that?"

"Isn't that why you went out there?"

She reared her head back and looked down her nose at me. "Sometimes I wonder if you have any brains at all, Sophie Conmar!"

The nights were getting hotter and Jack was coming home from work more cranky and tired than ever. The hot weather always affected him this way. He used to come home, take a shower, and sit out on the porch after supper in an old pair of shorts until it was cool enough to go to bed. But this year he took up night swimming, staying out till eleven, twelve o'clock. I worried about him at first, but I guess I shouldn't have. Jack is a good swimmer and I'd be sure to hear him shout if anything went wrong, like getting a cramp or something. So I just put it out of my mind and kept busy with my needlework.

But the swimming was doing something for Jack. It was relaxing him and putting him in a better mood. I wondered if it was relaxing him too much; sometimes he didn't even hear me when I spoke to him.

I had fixed him some cocoa one night after his swim and he was just sitting down at the table when a shriek from next door lifted him right out of his chair. I followed him into Wilma's apartment.

She was standing by the bed staring down at something. Jack hurried to her side and I looked around them to see a carving knife buried in the mattress.

"Right where I would have been if I was in bed!" wailed Wilma.

"When did it happen?" I asked.

"I don't know. I came in and there it was." She turned and laid her face on Jack's shoulder. She's as tall as he is, so she didn't look too graceful. I guess she wasn't too comfortable either, because she lifted it again and looked into his eyes. "What am I going to do, Jack? Someone's trying to kill me!"

"Take it easy," Jack said, pulling her close to him. He saw me watching, so he patted her back awkwardly. "She's all upset," he told me.

"Have you noticed how nothing ever happens to her in the daytime?" I said. Only when you're around to pat her shoulder, I thought.

For the next three days and nights a storm hung in the air. The water was restless, and Jack said the bad weather would soon reach us. The days were humid with heavy air that pressed around me like a blanket. I didn't think Jack should go night swimming with the water stirred up like that, but he shrugged and went anyway. Once in a while I could hear him laugh out there in the dark, depending on if the wind was blowing. So I'd sit in the house and stitch faster on my embroidery. I had three-quarters of a rosebush done before I discovered I had used brown thread.

On the fourth night the storm still hadn't come and Jack and I were in bed, but neither of us could sleep. He kept tossing and turning and I stayed as close to my edge as possible so as not to disturb him. Finally he lay still. I hardly dared to breathe. My leg was cramped, but I wouldn't have moved it for anything. At least I thought I wouldn't have. Then all at once the room seemed to fill with sound. In the first second or two I thought the storm had broken, but I must have been half asleep myself because I soon realized that it was King Charlie's thunderous laugh, and a shrill scream from Wilma. Jack and I leaped out of bed just as a lamp crashed to the floor next door—six ninety-eight at the five and ten—and a door slammed.

"What are you afraid of?" roared Charlie.

We got to our living room just as Wilma plunged through the door, her long black hair falling down her back, and her nightgown—my eyes popped. No wonder Charlie had been roaring. I went back to my bedroom to get her a robe. Jack just stood there, his hair all mussed up, his mouth open. I wondered if he was awake yet.

"He's after me!" said Wilma as I helped her put on the robe, though she might as well not have bothered since she left it hanging open. "Charlie's the one who's trying to kill me!"

"Charlie?" said Jack, regaining consciousness. "Why should he want to kill you?"

"Because I called him an old goat! Because he's crazy!"

I heard Charlie's outboard start up. "Charlie wouldn't kill anybody," I said.

"How do you know?" demanded Wilma. "You said he was a nut. He left me that fish, didn't he? And he could have made that voodoo doll."

"Charlie is clever with his hands," I admitted, "but I still don't think—"

"You can't tell about someone like Charlie," said Jack.

"Well, he's gone now," I said to Wilma. "You'll be all right."

"I won't be able to shut my eyes."

"I'll sit on your porch until you're asleep," said Jack.

The storm never did come, and by Saturday Wilma had calmed down enough to polish her nails, set her hair, and ride into town with Jack to do some shopping. They came back before noon and Jack carried Wilma's bundles inside for her. I was washing my kitchen windows when I heard Jack's voice.

"Say, somebody left you a note."

"They did?" Wilma laughed, a tinkly, musical sound. I wondered how long it had taken her to learn it. "One of my admirers, no doubt."

There was silence. I could imagine her standing there reading it, with Jack looking over her shoulder. Then I heard her say, "Jack—do you think—it's a joke, isn't it?"

"It doesn't look like a joke to me, Wilma."

"But it's got to be! It's too ridiculous to be serious! 'Be out of town by two o'clock this afternoon or you're dead.' Who would believe a thing like that?"

"But so much has been happening, Wilma. And maybe Charlie isn't—I mean, we don't really know anything about him."

"Why, your own wife said Charlie wouldn't hurt a fly!"

"Don't pay any attention to Sophie. She's not much better than Charlie."

I wrung my rag out so tight it ripped. It was too bad if Jack felt that way about me, but I didn't think it was very nice of him to tell other people about it. I always did the best I could. Someday he might really look at me and see beneath the surface.

"Maybe you better go somewhere for a few days, just to be on the safe side," said Jack.

"Why, Jack baby, you aren't trying to get rid of me, are you?"

I was setting the table when Jack came in. "Was the traffic heavy?" I asked. "Usually is on Saturdays."

"So-so." Which meant he hadn't noticed. "Wilma wants to go fishing this afternoon."

"That's nice."

"I said I'd take her on account of she doesn't want to take the boat out alone."

"She's taken the boat out alone before."

"She's afraid of Charlie."

I sat on the porch and watched them go. It was five minutes to two when they anchored over the rocks halfway between the mainland and the island. It was exactly two o'clock when the rifle bullet slammed into the side of the boat. Jack dropped his pole, grabbed Wilma and pulled her with him into the water. They must have surfaced close to the boat because I couldn't see their heads in the water.

Then I saw them. Actually, the first thing I saw was the splashing. I wondered what was going on. I went inside for the binoculars and got back in time to see Jack sock Wilma on the chin. Then he heaved her into the boat and climbed in himself. He must have dropped to the floor beside her. They waited about ten minutes, probably to see if there would be any more shots. Then Jack started the engine, pulled up the anchor, and headed for the mainland.

As soon as they were close enough, Wilma was out of the boat and running toward the house full tilt. She didn't even say hello to me. Jack ignored me, too, as he followed her inside.

"Look, I told you I was sorry," he said. "I had to sock you. You were hysterical."

"*I have had it!* When people start taking potshots at me, you can be pretty sure they're not kidding."

"But, Wilma, I told you we'll go to the police."

"Oh, sure! And can you prove one bit of it? Did you see Charlie leave the fish or the doll? Did you see him try to stab me or shoot me? Did you?"

"Well, no, but—"

"Okay. So they can't touch him. So goodbye."

"But Wilma, what about me?"

"What do you mean, what about you?"

"Just that. How about—us?"

"Jack, you're just about as dumb as your wife. You two deserve each other."

"But I thought you loved me!"

"Did I ever tell you so?"

"Well, no—but words aren't everything."

"And neither are actions, Dad. You were an amusing diversion, but it won't take me long to find another one. And this time I think I'll stay in the civilized world and leave nature all to the primitives."

Jack was pale under his tan when he came in. Wilma hadn't even said goodbye to me, but I didn't care. Jack was here now and that was all that mattered.

"I'm making pot roast for supper," I said.

"Okay."

"And would you rather have apple pie or pudding for dessert?"

"Doesn't matter." He took a long shower before supper and he looked more like himself when he sat down at the table.

"I decided to serve the pie," I said.

"Okay."

I was wearing a new dress I had made last week and my hair was combed a little different. I saw him looking at it. He finished his meal and sat back. "You sure can cook, Sophie."

"Thank you, dear. That's only one of my talents."

He scraped at the tablecloth with his fingernail. "Wilma's gone," he said, not looking at me.

"I know."

"Sophie, there's something I ought to tell you. About Wilma and me."

"Yes?"

His face got red. "She, uh, kind of liked me."

"I know."

"And I liked her, too. Not the same as you, of course. I mean, she was different from you. She was—beautiful—and she needed me. At least, she acted like she needed me. She was sort of helpless. She made me feel—different."

"I understand, Jack."

"You always do." He smiled at me and I felt good all over.

"Would you like to take a walk on the beach?" I asked.

"What about the mosquitoes?"

"I'll take my sweater." I went to the closet to get it, I glanced at the rifle standing in the corner, as if it hadn't been moved for years.

He took my hand as we stepped outside. I haven't seen such a lovely night in months. The moonlight is bright on the water. Jack is still holding my hand. I wouldn't be a bit surprised if we end up looking for sea serpents.

# The State Against Sam Tucker

## by William M. Stephens

**T**hat's the trouble with you, Charley," Rube said to me. "You believe every dadgum thing a client tells you. Me, I don't trust nobody. I don't give nobody a chance to hornswoggle me." Rube Claggett shook his head vigorously, and his sandy hair flounced like the strings of a busy dust mop. He kicked his swivel chair backward and propped his big brogans on the desk. "No, siree, I don't trust nobody. Right, Ellie?"

Ellie Day looked up from her typewriter. "That's right, boss." She winked at me. "It's been at least a week since your friend Abner Gribble walked out of here with a twenty dollar bill. He only wanted five, but you told him to take the twenty and get it changed at the drugstore."

Rube's feet hit the floor. "What?" he roared. "You mean that scoundrel never brought the change back? Why—I'll take it out of his hide!" He chewed viciously on his unlit cigar. "He'll pay through the nose the next time he needs a lawyer!" He glowered at me, then chuckled. "That old reprobate." He pulled open a desk drawer with his foot, lifted a pint bottle, and took a swallow.

The staccato rhythm of Ellie's typewriter stopped in mid-sentence as her pert nose sniffed the air. "Mr. Claggett," she said severely, "I'll thank you to take that bottle out of here. It's not good for business to have this office smell like a distillery."

Rube held the bottle up to the light. "Mighty near empty," he grinned. He drained the bottle and lobbed it into a wastebasket. "Come on, Charley, let's check up on your thievin' client." He bowed to Ellie. "We'll be at Higley Farm Supply, Miss Blue Nose."

On the sidewalk, I said, "I wish you'd talk with Sam. He tells a pretty straight story. I don't believe he stole Mr. Higley's money."

Rube's eyes glinted under his heavy eyebrows. "Ain't Sammy Tucker the boy that Oscar Spivey accused of car-stealin' a while back?"

I nodded. "It was all a misunderstanding, though. Sam borrowed Spivey's jalopy and hit a tree. When the car wasn't back the next

morning, Spivey reported it stolen. He dropped the charges after
Sam agreed to pay the damages."

Rube grunted. "Tucker's always been full of wild oats 'n' vinegar,
but he never impressed me as the thievin' kind. How long's he been
sellin' tractors for Hump Higley?"

"About three months. Most people figured Hump hired Sam just
to keep him out of town—away from Daisy. Sam's been courting
Daisy Higley since she wore pigtails, and her uncle never did approve."

"Hump Higley never approved of nobody," Rube muttered. "So
Sammy's charged with stealin' from his sweetheart's guardian?" He
bit off the end of his cigar and spat it into the gutter. "You got a
tough row to hoe, Charley."

He wasn't just whistling Dixie. That's why I wanted help on the
case. I'd only been out of law school a year, and even though a year
in Rube Claggett's office is probably worth more than several years
of active practice, I didn't feel ready to handle a tough case by myself.

We crossed the street and cut through the courthouse lawn, passing the Saturday morning crowd that talks politics and plays check-
ers on the iron benches. Rube spoke to nearly everybody: "Mornin',
Mr. Marks. . . . 'Lo, Purvis. . . . Howdy, Jake, you keepin' sober?"

Through the barred windows at the rear of the courthouse I saw
a white face. Sam Tucker, I figured. As far as I knew, there wasn't
anybody else in jail. "Want to stop in and see Sammy?" I asked Rube.

He glanced toward the jail and scowled. "Reckon we oughta find
out what Higley's got to say first—though I don't relish the job."

Higley's office was empty except for Ezra Sharp, whose skinny
shoulders were bent over a big ledger. He carefully ignored us until
Rube leaned over his shoulder and said in a low voice, "What's
this—the spare set of books you keep for the auditors?"

Sharp closed the ledger and smiled thinly. "Can I help you gentlemen?"

"I reckon so," said Rube. "What about this Sam Tucker trouble?"

The bookkeeper slanted a look over his bifocals. "I think you'd
better wait for Mr. Higley. He'll be back soon." His thin fingers
drummed the table. "What's your interest in the matter, Mr. Claggett?"

"Can't rightly tell. I 'spect we'll be representin' Tucker."

"I see." He studied his fingernails. "He'll plead guilty, I suppose?"

"Can't say right now," said Rube. "Do you think he should?"

Ezra shrugged and turned back to his work. "I told Mr. Higley he shouldn't hire that crook."

The door opened and Humphrey Higley moved ponderously into the office. Lowering his bulk into a wide swivel chair, he loosened his collar and patted his perspiring jowls with a handkerchief. "I figured they'd have hung you before now, Claggett," he said. "To what do I owe the honor of this visit?" He raised his hand. "Wait. I have it. You're defending that nice young man everybody's picking on." His beady eyes glittered. "Do I win the big bananas?"

"That depends," said Rube. "The judge appointed Charley on the case. I may help if he needs me."

Higley snorted. "That's a polite way of saying you'll help if there's a fee, isn't it? You're out of luck, Claggett. The only money Tucker's got is what he stole from me. And he won't have that long."

"I thought maybe you'd help out on the fee," drawled Rube, giving me a sly wink. "Sam's practically a member of your family, ain't he?"

Higley's face flushed, and he doubled his meaty fists. "You listen to me, Rube Claggett. I'm not responsible for the mistakes of that niece of mine. She's wild and unruly, just like her mother was. But Daisy's going to grow up to be a decent woman if I have to beat that devilment out of her." He stood up, wheezing. "She's sure not going to marry a jailbird. She's not going to marry anybody!"

"I hear she's wearing Sammy's engagement ring," I ventured.

He swung toward me angrily. "Not in my presence, she's not. And I'd better not catch her wearing it."

"I guess he won't help us, Charley," said Rube.

"I'll tell the world I won't!" Higley said. "I wouldn't spit on Sam Tucker if he was burning to death!"

There was a twisted smile on Rube's face as he stood up, and his eyes were like agates. "You win the prize bag o' bananas, Higley," he said. "I'm representin' Tucker."

After we got outside, Rube said. "If anybody ever murders that man, I'll take the case for free."

We walked back to the jail to see Tucker. Sam was twenty-one, with a wiry build and dark, brooding eyes. He told us he'd sold a used tractor to Leland Dauber, a farmer on Iron Mountain, two weeks before, and had collected five hundred dollars as a down payment. "That's what they claim I stole," he said. "But I turned it in. I'm bound to have."

"But you don't remember when?" Rube asked.

Sammy stared at the barred windows. "I can't remember, not for the life o' me. I had the money in an envelope. I must've left it on Mr. Sharp's desk."

"Was there a contract coverin' the sale?"

"No, sir. We sold those ol' clunkers for whatever we could get. When I'd get a down payment, I'd take a note for the balance. The office girl would type up a contract later. Mr. Sharp says he got the note, but not the money."

"Now, Sam," said Rube, "tell us what happened the day you were arrested."

"Well, I'd been over to Pine Valley all week calling on farmers. When I came back and walked in the office nobody said pea turkey. Then the sheriff came in and arrested me."

"Did they ask you what you did with the money?"

Sam shook his head. "They claimed they knew where I hid it." He looked up at Rube. "How can they know? I didn't hide it anywhere."

Rube chewed savagely on his cigar. "Sammy, let's get one thing straight. We can't help you if you hold back. If you stole that money, I want to know. Otherwise, God help you, 'cause I sure won't."

Sam looked away, then shrugged. "What can you do anyway? They're not gonna trust my word against Mr. Higley's. Ever since I got in trouble over Mr. Spivey's car, people act like I got a stripe down my back." He looked at Rube, his eyes angry. "I didn't steal that money, Mr. Claggett. I swear I didn't."

Rube said softly, "What about this girl of yours—Daisy? Did you buy her a ring?"

"What's that got to do with this?"

"Nothing—unless you bought it with stolen money."

Sam's lips tightened. "I bought that ring at Stein Jewelers. I paid a hundred and twenty dollars, and it wasn't stolen money."

"Speaking of money," said Rube, "you'll need a court reporter at the trial; and a bondsman—'less you wanta stay in jail. Also," he smiled, "lawyers like to get paid a little something."

"I've got about a hundred in the bank. Is that enough?"

That wasn't enough for the court reporter and bondsman—not to mention a fee—but it wasn't my place to speak up. Rube was the one who had to pay the rent. "I reckon we can make out on that," Rube said.

"It's in my savings account in Knoxville. Tennessee National Bank. How can I get it out?"

"You can sign a power of attorney. We'll get the money."

Rube and I returned to the offfice. After Ellie typed up the power of attorney, I took it back for Sammy to sign. Coming out of the jail, I ran into Daisy Higley. She'd been crying, I could tell, but she was still one of the prettiest girls you'll ever see.

"What do you think about the case, Charley?" she said anxiously.

"I don't know," I said truthfully. "Mr. Claggett's working on it."

"Sammy's not guilty. I know he's not. You've got to believe that." Her intense blue eyes held mine. "They can't take Sam away from me, Charley. He's all I've got. We plan to get married next month."

I swallowed. "Sure hope you don't have to change your plans." I shuffled my feet. "Your uncle doesn't like Sam much, does he?"

Her face clouded. "He hates him. He says he'll disown me—turn me out in the street—if I go on seeing Sammy." Her eyes were defiant. "Well, let him!"

"Mr. Higley's your legal guardian, isn't he?"

She nodded. "My mother died when I was born. And my father—" she looked away, embarrassed "—well, I don't even know who my father was. My uncle knows, but he won't tell me."

It's funny how people in trouble tell these personal things. Helps to relieve the tension, I guess. You don't have to be a lawyer very long to learn about family skeletons.

When I told Rube about my conversation with Daisy, he looked thoughtful. "I remember her maw," he said. "Pretty as a picture. Rosebud Higley. I last saw her back in forty-two, before I left for the army. She was running around with a paratrooper from Fort Bragg."

Ellie said, "I've heard my mother mention Rosebud Higley. Wasn't her husband killed overseas?"

"Husband?" asked Rube. "Where'd you hear that?"

"That's what Mother said. We were talking about it last night."

Rube shook his head. "The things these women remember."

"My mother knows the history of every family in Boone County," Ellie declared.

"Well, don't sic her on the Claggetts. I come from a long line of horse thieves." He waved his arm in a gesture of dismissal. "I ain't payin' overtime this week. Get lost, you two. I wanta cogitate."

Rube left for Knoxville on Monday and was gone several days. On Tuesday the grand jury voted a true bill against Sam and fixed his bond at twenty-five hundred dollars. The case was set for the first day of the summer term—the following Tuesday. I filed a motion to reduce the bond and got it cut down to fifteen hundred dollars, but I couldn't find anybody in Boone City who'd make his bond.

"Thanks for trying," Daisy said with a wan smile. "If there's any way we can repay you—" She pulled off her ring. "This is all I have. Apply it to the fee."

Before I could object, she was gone.

When Rube got back, I showed him the ring. He shook his head firmly. "We've got our fee, Charley."

"A hundred dollars?" I said scornfully.

He grinned. "There was a little more in Sam's bank account than he thought. We wouldn't take that girl's ring, in any case."

"She wants him out on bond in the worst way," I said. "Could we pledge the ring with a bondsman?"

"Nope. You take this ring back to Daisy. Then tell Joe Kemp I'm signin' that bond. When he turns Sammy loose, send him over here."

Sheriff Joe Kemp was mighty surprised when Daisy and I walked in to get Sammy. "I hope Rube's got fifteen hundred dollars to lose," he said. "I got a hunch that boy's gonna take off like a big bird. I reckon I would, in his place." He looked Daisy up and down. "And I'd take this little gal with me."

When Sam came out, Daisy grabbed him like she was scared he'd melt. They started across the street to see Rube while I went to the courthouse to look up some deeds.

Next day Hump Higley came charging into the office like a wounded rhino, with the sheriff riding his coattails. "Where's my niece?" Higley roared.

Rube was sprawled across two chairs dictating an answer in a dogbite case. He glanced up, motioned for silence, and went on dictating, while Higley snorted and fumed and the sheriff stared at Ellie's knees.

Rube finally finished and pulled a flask from behind Volume Two of the Tennessee Code. "Care for some nerve medicine, gentlemen?"

"Where's my niece, Claggett?" snapped Higley.

"Why, I haven't got your niece," Rube said amiably. He took a swallow from the flask and smacked his lips. "Good for what ails you. Want one, Joe?"

The sheriff looked longingly at the bottle, then shook his head. "Rube, you're in trouble. Daisy Higley didn't come home last night. Looks like she run off with Sam Tucker."

"Why tell me about it?" Rube asked. "I'm not Daisy's guardian."

"I'll tell you why!" Higley sputtered. "You made bond for that scalawag. You gave him money for a getaway. I'm holding you responsible. Tucker stole my car and kidnaped my niece."

"Kidnaped?" said Ellie. "You couldn't have pried Daisy loose from Sam Tucker with a crowbar."

Higley whirled. "You stay out of this, young lady. Yes, I said kidnaped. My niece is a minor, Claggett. She's below the age of consent. My attorney says that makes it kidnaping. Furthermore, if that scalawag takes her across a state line, he's headed for Alcatraz. And you, Claggett, are guilty of criminal conspiracy as well as aiding the escape of a felon."

"My word," said Rube. "Sounds pretty bad, don't it, Charley?"

I nodded nervously. It did sound bad.

"This ain't no joke," said the sheriff. "We got proof. You drove Tucker and the girl to the Higley place yesterday. They stole Higley's car and got a check cashed at Shorty's gas station—a check written by you. They asked Shorty for a Georgia road map." He shook his head. "You've pulled shenanigans before, but I never thought you'd help corrupt an innocent girl."

"Oh, has she been corrupted?" Rube asked. "How'd you find out?"

"We're figurin' that. And we're figurin' Tucker has jumped his bond. You better be ready to cough up fifteen hundred dollars."

After they left, Rube chuckled. "Higley's a mite upset."

I wasn't sure I blamed Higley. "Did you help those kids skip town, Rube?" I asked.

He held up a hand. "It only takes two to make a conspiracy, Charley. The less you know, the less you've got to worry about."

Ellie said. "But what about this bail business? Can they make you pay the money?"

"Not if Sammy's here for the trial. He can go to Timbuctoo if he wants to, as long as he gets back here for the trial."

"He is coming back then?" I asked.

"Dear God, I hope so," he said fervently.

That week I paced the floor plenty and gnawed my fingernails down to a nub, but on Monday—the day before the trial—Sam and Daisy walked into the office.

"Meet the missus," Sam grinned. "We got married in Georgia. There's no waitin' period down there."

"Congratulations, you lucky young scoundrel," said Rube.

"I hope you'll be very happy," said Ellie.

Before I could even kiss the bride, the sheriff came in, followed by Attorney-General Ambrose Switgall and a dapper gentleman with a fancy briefcase. The attorney-general because of his military brusqueness had acquired the title of general.

"Samuel Tucker," said Joe Kemp, "I hereby arrest you on a charge of larceny of an automobile."

"Oh, Sammy!" cried Daisy.

Rube said, "Well, I reckon you'll have to spend the night in jail, son. You should've stayed gone till tomorrow." He turned to the sheriff. "What about them other charges? Gonna pop 'em one at a time or all together?"

General Switgall said, "Before we're through, Rube, you'll have charges running out of your ears. We're starting with larceny. We know we can make that stick. Later we may have a few things to say to the grievance committee of the Bar Association."

The man with the briefcase spoke to Daisy. "Miss Higley, I'm Benjamin Blackerby of Knoxville, your uncle's attorney. My instructions are to take you home."

Daisy gasped and moved closer to Sam. "But I'm married now. I want to stay with my husband."

"Your husband is going to jail, my dear. And I imagine he'll be there quite a while. You're only eighteen. Mr. Higley is responsible for you, and he's asked me to begin proceedings to obtain an annulment."

"But I don't want an annulment," she cried. "I love my husband."

"I understand, my dear. But I have no choice in the matter. I must turn you over to your guardian."

Rube stepped forward. "Lay one hand on this girl and I'll shove that pretty briefcase down your throat. Daisy's not goin' anywhere."

General Switgall cleared his throat. "Rube, this is a civil matter and not within my jurisdiction, but I want to remind you that this young lady is a minor. She's Mr. Higley's ward."

"You're right, Ambrose," said Rube. "This is outside your jurisdiction." He glared at Blackerby. "Now, git, before you raise my dander."

"You're skating on thin ice, Mr. Claggett," the lawyer said.

Rube turned to Sammy. "Don't worry about Daisy, son. She'll stay with my secretary tonight." He scowled at the others. "If there's any more objections, let's hear 'em."

"Let's go, Tucker," said the sheriff, pushing Sammy toward the door.

At nine o'clock next morning Judge Daniel Webster Venable, lifting his robe like an old woman crossing a briar patch, entered the courtroom and took his seat.

The clerk rapped for order. "Oyez, oyez, the Circuit Court of Boone County is now in session. State of Tennessee against Samuel Tucker."

"Is the State ready?" inquired the judge.

General Switgall stood up. "Ready, Your Honor." He cleared his throat. "In view of a new charge against this defendant, however, the State will not object to a continuance so that both cases may be tried together at a later date."

"We haven't asked for a continuance," said Rube. "On the contrary, we're ready for trial on both cases. We move the court for a joinder of the charges."

"But the larceny case isn't on the docket, yet," objected the attorney-general.

"Mr. Claggett," the judge said, "what's to be gained by trying the cases together? Do they both relate to the same set of facts?"

"We expect to prove, Your Honor," said Rube, "that both charges arose from the same conspiracy. They fit the same frame—very neatly. The prosecution wants the second case for insurance—to keep this young man out of circulation even if he's acquitted of the embezzlement charge. They want to keep him locked up, Your Honor, while they go into Chancery Court and take his bride away from him."

"I deny that charge!" shouted Ambrose Switgall.

"Oh, you're just a pawn, Ambrose," said Rube. "The knave is over there at your table."

The lawyer from Knoxville, livid with rage, pounded the table while Switgall spouted like a broken fire hydrant. The judge banged his gavel. Then he said. "Those are serious charges, Mr. Claggett. I doubt the wisdom of making such allegations in open court. On the other hand," he added, "since the charges have been made, it might be best to let the jury hear all the facts and decide for themselves." He looked at Switgall. "How long will it take the State to prepare the larceny case?"

Switgall glared at Rube, then went into a huddle with Higley and Blackerby.

Rube said, "I think we can simplify things, Your Honor. The new charge is that the defendant stole a 1960 Roadliner sedan, Motor Number KHL128891. We'll stipulate that the defendant took this car, as alleged, without the knowledge or consent of the plaintiff, Humphrey Higley."

General Switgall stared. "You're pleading guilty?"

"Absolutely not. We're admitting the facts. We don't admit that these facts constitute larceny."

The judge looked puzzled. "If there's no issue of fact, general, the State should be ready for trial."

Scratching his bald spot, Switgall whispered to Higley, who nodded vigorously and displayed a paper. The attorney-general turned to the bench and shrugged. "We're ready, Your Honor," he said, "in both cases."

Judge Venable nodded, then looked toward the jury panel. "Will twelve of you people take seats in the box? Any twelve. The attorneys will question you."

The box was soon filled.

Rube walked in front of it. "I reckon you folks are already tired of hearing us lawyers fuss, so I won't ask you a lot of foolish questions." His eyes swept the twelve faces. "You all look honest to me. We'll accept the jury, Your Honor."

Switgall glanced coldly at Rube, then turned to the jury box. "I think you people are honest, too, but the State doesn't pay me for my opinion. My duty is to check your qualifications."

He spent an hour satisfying himself that none of the jurors were Rube's cousins, drinking buddies, or clients, and that they were not prejudiced against public servants, farm supply companies, or Roadliner sedans. Finally, he said, "The jury's satisfactory," and sat down.

The clerk swore the witnesses.

"We'd like the witnesses put under the Rule," said Rube.

The judge nodded. "All witnesses will leave the room with the bailiff. Read the charges, Mr. Attorney-General."

After the indictment was read, the attorney-general called his first witness, Leland Dauber, who testified he had bought a used tractor from Higley Farm Supply on June 13th and had given Sam Tucker five hundred dollars in cash as a down payment. Later that day, Dauber couldn't make the engine run, and he tried without success to start it every day that week. The evening of Monday, June 20th, he went to Higley and demanded the return of his money. Higley looked up the account and, finding no record of the down payment, asked Dauber to telephone Ezra Sharp, the bookkeeper, on the following day.

"So I called the next morning," said Dauber, "Tuesday morning, and learnt that Sam Tucker had stole the money. I said that weren't no concern of mine, and I still wanted my money. Mr. Higley gave it to me."

"Your witness," said Switgall.

"Now, Mr. Dauber," said Rube, "who told you Tucker had stolen the money?"

"Mr. Higley."

"But didn't you say that Higley told you to call Sharp?"

"Yes, sir. I asked for Mr. Sharp, but the lady that answered, she said he wasn't there. So Mr. Higley come to the phone 'n' told me about the theft."

Rube frowned. "What time of day did you telephone?"

"Around ten o'clock. I'd just come in from the fields."

"All right," said Rube. "Step down."

"Ezra Sharp," called General Switgall.

Sharp testified he had worked for Higley for five years. He learned of the missing money after reporting to work on Tuesday. He immediately checked the records and determined that the money had not been turned in. Then, suspecting Tucker of having taken the money, and knowing that Tucker did his banking at Tennessee National, Sharp telephoned the bank and learned that five hundred dollars had recently been deposited in Tucker's account.

"Just a minute," interrupted Judge Venable. "That's all hearsay, general." He looked at Rube. "The defense is not objecting, but . . . "

"He can't afford to object," said Switgall, grinning. "He knows the money was put in the bank—because he went there the other day and drew it out."

The judge looked sharply at Rube. "Is that true, Mr. Claggett?"

"That's correct, Your Honor."

"Do you have any explanation to offer?"

"I'm not a witness in this case," Rube said. "If Your Honor wants to put me under oath, I'll testify. But I'll reserve the right to cross-examine myself on anything material to this case."

The judge frowned and rubbed his chin, then turned to the court reporter. "Let the record show that five hundred dollars was deposited in the defendant's bank account and was later withdrawn by the defendant's attorney." He paused. "Is the State through with Mr. Sharp?" Switgall nodded and the judge said testily, "Cross-examine, Mr. Claggett."

Rube sauntered forward, his hands deep in his pockets. "Mr.

Sharp, you say you learned on Tuesday that the money was missing?"

"Yes, sir. After Mr. Higley told me of Mr. Dauber's complaint."

"What time did you call the bank?"

The witness hesitated. "I'm not sure of the exact time."

"Was it before ten, or after?"

Sharp twisted his fingers. "After."

"So, at ten o'clock neither you nor Mr. Higley knew the money was in Sam Tucker's account?"

"We didn't know till I phoned."

Rube paced slowly, studying the floor. Then he whirled. "Who'd you talk to at the bank?"

Sharp jumped and his Adam's apple bobbed. "I'm not sure. The cashier, I think. I can't remember his name."

"You can't remember his name," Rube said disdainfully, "but he was a mighty nice fellow, wasn't he? Since when have banks been so free with information about depositors' accounts?"

Sharp smiled thinly. "Mr. Higley is a director of the bank, and they've always been most cooperative with us."

Rube snorted. "Did you make the call from the office?"

"Yes, sir."

"Then the telephone company will have a record of the call?"

Sharp licked his lips. "I guess so."

"What time did you get to work that day?"

Ezra swallowed. "About nine, I think."

"What?" Rube shouted. "What?" Jaw thrust forward, he moved closer. "Don't you know you were in Knoxville Tuesday morning, and you were seen entering the Tennessee National Bank at a few minutes past nine?"

Sharp's face turned ashen and his lips quivered. He opened his mouth, but nothing came out.

Rube towered over the witness. "You went to the first teller, didn't you? A young brunette with glasses? You gave her five hundred dollars to put in Sam Tucker's account. Isn't that right?"

Sharp shrank in his chair and his eyes shifted from side to side. "No, sir," he said hoarsely. "No, sir."

Switgall stood up, frowning. "Your Honor, the State would like a short recess."

Judge Venable looked irritated. "I don't like to break up a lawyer's cross-examination. However," he glanced at the clock, "it's close to lunchtime. Will you need this witness much longer, Mr. Claggett?"

Rube's eyes narrowed as he looked with contempt at Sharp. "I haven't even started on this witness yet, Your Honor," he said.

"All right. The court will be in recess until one o'clock." He turned to the witness. "You be back here at one, Mr. Sharp."

"Yes, sir," said Sharp and jumped from the chair and scurried out the door.

Rube stuck a cigar in his mouth. "Pretty good timing," he said to me in an aside. "I was runnin' outa steam, but didn't wanta turn Sharp loose. Right now he thinks he's gonna be burned at the stake this afternoon, so he may bolt. If he does, we're home free."

I was puzzled. "Rube," I asked, "who saw Sharp go into the bank?"

He shrugged. "How would I know? I only said somebody saw him. In a big city like Knoxville, somebody must've seen him."

"Then you were bluffing?" I asked.

"Sure," he grinned. "But I had a good bluff. Sammy didn't deposit that money, or he wouldn't have been so willin' to give us the power of attorney. I went to the bank to draw out Sammy's money, thinkin' it was about a hundred dollars, and derned if the balance wasn't over six hundred. So I got 'em to show me Sam's deposit slips—with the power of attorney, they couldn't refuse—and I learned that a deposit of five hundred dollars was made at 9:06 A.M. on Tuesday, June 21st, to teller number one, a brunette with glasses. After the testimony came out that Sharp hadn't been at work that Tuesday morning, I figured he must've made the deposit."

We went to the cafe for lunch, and I thought about the developments in the case. Finally I said, "Rube, why would Ezra Sharp frame Sammy?"

"Good question," he grunted. "Maybe to take the heat off himself."

I mulled that over. "Why would he steal the money in the first place if he planned—?" Then it hit me. "Say! Maybe Sharp was stealing all along. He couldn't afford to have an audit run on his books, so when Higley discovered that the five hundred was missing, Sharp had to do something fast. He rushed to Knoxville Tuesday and put the money in Sam's account, then told Higley he'd learned about the deposit by telephone. By putting the finger on Sam, he'd keep himself in the clear and protect the money he'd stolen before. He was willing to sacrifice the five hundred to prevent an investigation of his books."

"Not bad, Charley; but there's one gap in your theory. How'd Sharp know Dauber had been to the office the evening before?" He paused.

"There's only one way he could've known. Higley." He looked up. "Speak of the devil."

I saw Higley and the Knoxville lawyer approaching our table. "May we join you?" Blackerby asked pleasantly.

Rube shrugged. "We ain't choosy. What'd you do with Sharp?"

Higley reddened and said gruffly, "We all make mistakes, Mr. Claggett. It seems I gave my bookkeeper too much credit. It wouldn't surprise me to learn that he and Tucker were working in cahoots all the time."

"It'd surprise me a hell of a lot," Rube said dryly.

"Oh, I grant you Sharp may have been the prime villain. We're planning an audit of his books. In the meantime I have a proposition that will convince you of my good faith in this entire matter."

"This we've gotta hear," said Rube.

Blackerby broke in. "Mr. Higley's only concern is for the welfare of his niece. He feels no personal enmity toward Tucker. He is therefore willing to dismiss the embezzlement charge. In the larceny case, he will ask the court to give Tucker a suspended sentence." He smiled expansively. "The boy won't have to serve a day."

Rube's face didn't change expression. "And what's your price for this show of generosity?"

"Tucker must leave the state immediately and make no effort to contact Daisy. Furthermore, he must submit to an annulment of the marriage."

Rube shook his head. "No dice, counselor. We're going whole hog."

"Be sensible, man," said Blackerby. "We're offering Tucker his freedom. He might get ten years on the larceny charge even if he beats this embezzlement case."

"We're greedy," said Rube. "We want a lot more than a suspended sentence."

Blackerby raised his eyebrows. "I understand," he said softly. He leaned forward. "We will also arrange a substantial attorney's fee for the services you gentlemen have rendered."

Rube's neck muscles tightened, but his voice was calm and even. "You're bound and determined to get that fancy briefcase shoved down your throat, aren't you?" He nodded to me. "Come on, Charley, let's get some fresh air."

When court reconvened, the witness stand was vacant. After waiting fifteen minutes, the judge issued a warrant for the arrest of Sharp as a material witness. Then he said, "All right, general. Call your next witness."

"Humphrey Higley," Ambrose Switgall called to the bailiff.

Higley's testimony varied substantially from Sharp's. After Dauber came to the office demanding his money, Higley said he'd telephoned Sharp and summoned him to the office. The bookkeeper denied knowledge of the missing money, but hinted he could prove that Tucker was guilty. Next morning Sharp wasn't at work. About ten o'clock—just before Dauber's call—Sharp telephoned from Knoxville and said he'd learned that Tucker had deposited five hundred dollars in the bank. "I had no reason to doubt Ezra," said Higley, "so I swore out a warrant against Tucker."

I leaned over to whisper to Rube. "He's in the clear, isn't he?"

" 'Fraid so," he said. "He's been coached on the weak points in Sharp's testimony. If I'd had 'im on the stand before lunch, I'd've punctured him like a balloon."

General Switgall said, "That's the State's case on the embezzlement charge, Your Honor. On the larceny count, the defense admits the taking of the property, so we'll only establish ownership. Mr. Higley, state whether or not you own a 1960 model Roadliner sedan, Motor Number KHL128891."

"I do. Here is my certificate of title." He handed a paper to the attorney-general.

"We'd like to introduce this as an exhibit," said Switgall.

"No objection," said Rube.

Switgall bowed slightly to Rube. "You may ask him."

"Where'd you buy that car, Mr. Higley?" asked Rube.

Higley smiled. "Munson Motors, in Sweetwater."

"That's what I thought. You wrote a check for $3057.19, didn't you?"

Higley's smile looked a little strained now. "That sounds like the figure. I'm not sure."

"Oh, that's the figure, all right." He walked toward the witness. "Tell me, Mr. Higley, how'd you sign that check?"

The smile disappeared and the witness glanced quickly at Blackerby. "I signed my own name, Mr. Claggett," he said. "What else would I sign?"

"What else *did* you sign—that's the important thing. You wrote the word 'Trustee' after your name, didn't you?"

Higley's jowls glistened with perspiration, and he darted another look at Blackerby. Rube said, "He can't help you now, Higley. Answer the question. Did you write that check on a trust account?"

The witness swallowed, then answered in a harsh whisper, "Yes, sir."

"Are you losing your voice, Mr. Higley? Now, answer this question loud and clear. Speak up so that young lady in the back row can hear you. Who's the beneficiary of that trust fund?"

Higley's jaws worked. Then he sighed and his shoulders slumped. "My niece," he said hoarsely. "Daisy Higley."

Rube looked at the perspiring witness with contempt. "So you spent your niece's money for that car?"

"I bought it for Daisy's benefit," Higley stammered, "I let her use it."

"You let her use it!" Rube said scornfully. "But you didn't tell her she owned it, did you? Instead, you swore out a warrant against Sam Tucker for driving Daisy to her own wedding in her own car!"

Higley avoided Rube's eyes. "I was looking out for Daisy's interests," he whined. "I'm her guardian."

"You *were* her guardian. According to the terms of the trust, the guardianship ended when she got married and the money became hers entirely. That's why you were so anxious to get Tucker out of the way and have that marriage declared void, isn't it?"

The witness looked at the floor and didn't answer. Rube turned to the judge. "Your Honor, I don't think it's necessary to argue the merits of these trumped-up charges. The defendant moves for a directed verdict in each case."

Switgall stood up. "With considerable embarrassment, Your Honor, the State joins in the motion. We also move the court to issue a bench warrant for this witness's arrest. Nothing is more reprehensible than to use the courts of justice for personal gain, or to maliciously prosecute an innocent man."

That night, before Sam and Daisy left on their honeymoon, we had a party at the office and Rube filled us in on the case.

"What I can't figure out," said Sam, "is how you knew about the trust fund."

"Well, I'll tell you, son," Rube grinned as he poured himself three fingers. "You can put it down to long years of diligent study, a keen eye for detail, an inquiring mind, and—" he winked at Ellie "—a secretary that loves to talk."

He pulled a cigar from his pocket and propped up his feet. "Ellie said that Daisy's maw had married a soldier, so I checked the Bureau of Vital Statistics. Sure enough, Lieutenant Wallace Montague married Rosebud in Knox County in 1942. Rosebud died giving birth to Daisy at Knoxville Hospital, and Montague was killed in the South Pacific. I did a little checking and found that Montague had been the last member of a wealthy Middle Tennessee family. When he died, his entire estate went to Daisy, his only heir. I searched the Knox County court records and learned that Higley was appointed Daisy's guardian and the trustee of her estate, to serve until she married or became twenty-one. Higley never told Daisy about the trust fund, or even that her legal name was Montague, and I reckon he figured he could ride the gravy train for several more years. All he had to do was keep you single, young lady," he said to Daisy.

There was a knock at the door and Ambrose Switgall came in. "We caught Ezra Sharp," he said. "He's been embezzling money for years, but he claims it was Higley's idea to frame Sammy. Since Higley had the goods on Sharp, I guess he figured he was in the clear no matter which way the ball bounced. If Sam got convicted, Higley'd still have a club over Sharp's head. If Sam was turned loose, Higley could pin the rap on Sharp."

Switgall scratched his bald spot. "One thing bothers me, Rube. How'd you know that Higley paid for the car with trust funds?"

Rube shrugged. "That wasn't hard to figure out. The court had limited Higley's guardianship expenditures—for Daisy's support and welfare—to five hundred dollars a month. He could draw that much without anybody's say-so. Knowin' Higley, I figured he wouldn't be satisfied with that—not when the fund had a balance at the last accounting of more than thirty thousand dollars. So I got to figurin' the different ways he could justify takin' the money. Everybody knows Higley buys a new car every year—and, for some reason, he always buys these cars out of town. His latest car had a Sweetwater tag on it. I checked Munson Motors in Sweetwater and found that Higley paid cash for the car. That was enough to convince me he'd used Daisy's money—Higley's business ain't that prosperous. So I went back to Knox County courthouse and examined the chancery petitions with a fine-tooth comb. Six months ago, Higley petitioned the court and got permission to spend $3057.19 for a new car for Daisy."

Switgall slanted a look at Sam and Daisy. "Did these kids know the car was Daisy's—or did they think they were stealing it?"

Rube grinned. "They just followed their lawyer's advice. I told Sam he wouldn't be breakin' the law—but I reckon he doubted my word when the sheriff slapped him in jail. I didn't tell anybody the whole story for fear it'd leak back to Higley. I wanted him to stick his neck out so far he couldn't wiggle free."

Switgall shook his head. "Rube, you could fall in a cow pasture and come up smelling of dandelions."

"It's all in livin' right." Rube lifted a glass. "To crime."

"Crime," mused the attorney-general. "That reminds me. You made one mistake, counselor. You took five hundred dollars from Tucker's bank account. Technically, that makes you guilty of receiving stolen funds."

"Why, Ambrose," said Rube. "I got that money under a legal assignment from my client. Sammy didn't steal any money; so the money he gave me couldn't have been stolen."

Switgall scratched his bald spot, shook his head, and walked out.

"That money was stolen," I said. "Wasn't it proved, Sharp—"

"Why don't we just consider it a fee," said Rube, grinning, "paid by Messrs. Higley and Sharp."

# To Catch a Big One

## by Robert Edmond Alter

omething waited for Bent on the other side of the horizon: something with a soundless voice called to him. I thought of that every time I saw him alone on the deck of our schooner, as he watched the sea with brooding, unsatisfied eyes, his face a dark pool of intensity, every splinter of thought reflected there like a dart of light. I don't know where it might have ended, but it doesn't matter now; Harvey Wolfe saw to that, Harvey and his wife Lorry.

Bent and I were professional skin divers. We worked the Indian Ocean; we put amateurs through their paces, and charged whatever the traffic would bear. We hired out to oceanography groups, to independent movie companies, worked lagoon bottoms for pearls and mother-of-pearl shells, we trapped rare fish for any nation's aquariums, chartered underwater excursions. We were businessmen who lived from day to day. I was content, this was my life, the way I wanted it, but I knew Bent wasn't content. He seemed to expect more from the sea: fulfillment, or an answer.

Bent got on to Harvey Wolfe while we were in Galle, through Charlie Hall, a guided-tour man. "He's a rich boy," Bent said with a wry smile. "An amateur sportsman. We can jack the price up to a new high."

I nodded; this was his end of the business, I never infringed. "How many in the party?" I asked.

He turned away, his face indifferent, casual. "Just Wolfe and his wife," he said.

Too indifferent, too casual; I knew Bent. And suddenly I was sorry that Harvey Wolfe had come along, Harvey—and his wife. Women turned simple when they saw Bent. No man who doesn't have it will ever know what it is, and no woman will ever tell him. But Bent had it and he knew it. He could be the only man in a crowded room, the only man on a busy street, the only man in the world, as far as women were concerned. They looked at Bent and they forgot how old they were, or how young; they forgot husbands, lovers, boyfriends, and the moral code. And Bent liked it that way; it was the only weapon he had against the soundless voice that called from the other side of the horizon.

We were standing in the cuddy of the schooner, it was late afternoon and the shadows were heavy, hardly disturbed by the square beams of light falling from the skylight. On deck the drone of Malay chatter and soft laughter went on; the crew were at their ritual game of Fan-Tan. Bent turned from the deal table and bathed himself in the deep shadows by the sideboard. He picked up a snorkel tube and stared at it as though it interested him.

"This Mrs. Wolfe," I began, and I hit the Mrs. hard. "What's she like? Pretty?"

The little white ball in the snorkel rolled in its cage. Bent watched it with unblinking eyes.

"Yeah. Yeah, she's all right. You'll see tomorrow."

"Bent—" I began again.

But he wasn't going to be caught. He threw the snorkel back on the shelf with a jerk of his hand, and turned away. "I think we'll run them down to the Maldives." His tone was loud now, as though he wanted to drown out all sound but his own. "That should please them."

He was at the door when I stopped him. "And Mrs. Wolfe," I called. "Does *she* want to spear fish?"

He paused, looking down at the deck, his hands on either side of the doorframe. "No," he murmured. "I don't think she does."

I had Wolfe pegged before he left the quay; he was the forever playboy, the last of that lonely breed who were still hanging on desperately in a world that had lost interest in the antics of their type.

He had a little boy's face, and must have been fifty. His face had that whimsical, self-contained look that said: "See how cute I am? Women want to mother me; I can't help it." Whisky and nightlife had given him a slackness and a pallor, but there was a weakness about the edges of his mouth, the movement of his eyes, that I think he was born with.

We met them at the gangway. Bent made the introductions and we passed hands around. There was a lingering between Bent's hand and Mrs. Wolfe's that hastened me to say to Wolfe, "Captain Bent has a nice cruise planned for you, sir. Have you ever been to the Maldives?"

Bent relinquished her hand and exchanged a smile with Wolfe;

then it was my turn to hold her hand. She offered it as though I were a doorman accepting her gloves. She was beautiful. Her face was like a delicately rounded porcelain face. Her eyes were of a black transparency; when I looked in them, I saw how empty she was. She gave me a smile that meant nothing, and took her hand back.

Tani, our Malay boatswain, hurried past us to collect the Wolfes' luggage. Bent led us aft, we had an awning stretched there over the cockpit. Masart, who doubled as steward when we had clients aboard, stood in an immaculate white jacket by a tray of iced drinks. We sat down, raised our glasses "for a fair wind," and proceeded to become acquainted. This seemed easy for Bent and Mrs. Wolfe. They just looked at one another and smiled.

"Call me Lorry," she said to him, and her languid eyes seemed to imply that he might call her anything, anything at all. She didn't make the same offer to me; so I continued to call her Mrs. Wolfe. She didn't object.

"There's two things I want to do," Wolfe said to me, and he turned in his chair and glanced at Bent.

Bent smiled at him, but his eyes were far away. Wolfe smiled, too, and looked back at me.

"I want to prowl around a sunken wreck," he said. "It—well, it's just something I've always wanted to do." He almost seemed embarrassed. He looked down at his glass and smiled as though he were amused with himself.

"Of course," I said. "That's easy. A tanker went down near the Ari Atoll four months ago."

He looked up and his eyes seemed to suggest that he had been patiently waiting for me to stop talking, as though the sunken ship idea had just been a preliminary.

"And I want to get a shark," he said with his little boy's smile. "I want to catch a big one."

Bent looked at him, and then flicked an "Oh, dear me, aren't we something" look at me.

Lorry moved in her chair with a sudden turn of her long body. It startled me because it seemed out of character for her. "Oh, for God's sake, Harv," she said, and her eyes were annoyed. "Who are you trying to impress?"

Wolfe said nothing. He rattled the ice in his glass and smiled at me. Bent shifted in his chair; he leaned forward. He looked at Lorry when he spoke. "I think we can arrange that, Mr. Wolfe. I can't promise how big."

Wolfe didn't look at him, his eyes watched me over the smile. "Oh, call me Harv," he said and then he looked at his wife.

Her eyes narrowed and darkened, and her lips formed a thin, vivid line. She made a soft contemptuous sniff and her eyes melted lazily. She looked back at Bent. "Oh, yes," she said, "he's a great hunter. We went on safari last year in Kenya. Harv shot an antelope from a moving car. Actually wounded the animal with only four shots."

I wanted to get up and walk away. I wanted to tell Bent to throw them off the schooner. But I went on sitting there, feeling sick to my stomach, and watched Wolfe rattle his ice cubes under his smile.

But she hadn't dug the hook in deep enough; she watched and some of the languid mockery left her eyes. "He's so good," she said slowly, "that he even shot down the safari hunter. Of course, this was an accident, or he would have missed."

The ice cubes in Wolfe's glass tinkled like strips of Chinese glass hanging in the wind. He turned the smile on his wife and looked at her as though he had a secret that only he could enjoy. She stared back at him as though she had seen a glint of that secret.

She turned abruptly and leaned suggestively toward Bent. Her voice became husky, promising. "What are the nights like out here at sea, captain? Is there romance?"

Bent's head moved imperceptibly in a nod. "You'll never forget them," he said.

She smiled and raised one eyebrow higher than the other. I could hear her breathing.

The ice tinkled. Wolfe was smiling at me again, watching me from behind the innocent barrier of his little-boy face. And I smiled too and I thought, You fool! Can't you see? You poor blind fool!

All the way down to the Maldives the sea was like a field of broken glass. Its reflected brilliance hurt the eyes, and its constant choppy motion made me restless. Once I snapped at Tani for leaving a bucket on the foredeck. He looked at me with surprised, hurt eyes, and I stomped off aft, hating myself.

We made our first stop near Miladummadulu Atoll, in a wide mirror lagoon. Bent said it would be a good place to start Wolfe. The transparency of the water was unbroken, the schooner seemed to be floating in air. The jeweled coral bed lay four fathoms under our keel. I felt relaxed for the first time in days. It would be good to slip down into the blue world and forget for a while the human jungle that existed above.

Lorry appeared in the cockpit in thonged sandals, shorts, and tight halter. Her cropped hair framed her face like black smoke. Beautifully tanned, she moved like a cat, graceful, effortless, secure. She stretched out luxuriously on a deckmat and riffled the pages of a fashion magazine. She was the most beautifully bored female I had ever seen.

Bent looked up from the compressor and watched her. The Malays paused in their work and stared at her askance. I turned away and looked at Wolfe; he was smiling at me.

We put him over with fins, face plate, lead waist weights, deflated Mae West, and aqualung. "If anything goes wrong," I told him, "inflate the Mae West, it'll snap you up to the surface. Don't be afraid if your breath is hard to get. It's always like that. Just keep sucking. Stick close to me, I'll guide you."

He looked down at the vivid bottom, smiled, and bit thoughtfully at the rubber nipples of the mouthpiece. "Will we find sharks?"

"I don't think so. Don't worry about that now. Hold your face plate with your hand and dive in. Okay?"

He went in like a lump of lead, stomach first. I watched him floundering in a fathom of water for a moment, and then he clawed his way back to the surface and spat out the mouthpiece.

"Anything wrong?" I called.

He grinned and shook his head. "No, I'm all right now."

I turned to Bent, who was looking aft. "He'll do all right," I said. Bent nodded and licked at his lower lip. I lost my patience. "If you want to stay on board, say so," I growled at him.

Bent turned a grin on me. "Take it easy, Mack. I'm with you."

Wolfe did fine. He enjoyed himself immensely. He chased little reef fish, trying to catch them with his hands, stopped to inspect every curiously humped form of madrepore, proceeded to execute fantastic underwater ballets for my benefit, and would dart off suddenly on mysterious quests into the bluer depths. I would follow after and bring him back.

Every time I thought of something new, I would hustle him up to the surface. "Stay away from the coral," I would tell him, "it's poisonous." Or, "That fat little orange fish with the long spines, don't chase him any more. That's a lion fish, poison." And, "Stop running off into the depths. I'll tell you when you're ready for deep water."

Finally, he spat out his mouthpiece and grinned at me good-naturedly. "For God's sake, Mason," he said, "stop babying me. When are we going to spear fish?"

I realized for the first time that Bent was missing. I looked toward the schooner. The valves of his lung glinted silver sun at me from the edge of the cockpit. But the cockpit was empty; only the Malays moved on deck.

"We'll spear them when I tell you!" I growled at Wolfe. "Now do what I say. That's what you're throwing your money away for."

He smiled and raised the mouthpiece in a salute. "Aye, aye, skipper."

In the afternoon, we brought out the spearguns and had a lesson on the maindeck. Bent sat with his back against the companionway and watched us. He told us that he had developed a cramp in his leg that morning, or he wouldn't have left us. I had nothing to say, and Wolfe only smiled.

I showed him the harpoon with its steel line, and placed it in the projector, then I wrestled with the propulsion unit until I forced the heavy spring to compress. "One shot," I told him. "Make it count."

He nodded, smiling. "I will."

In the quiet hush of mid-afternoon, we skimmed into the sunken vault again. Bent begged off, using his cramp for an excuse. "I must be getting old," he said to Wolfe, and grinned.

"Perhaps you can amuse my wife," Wolfe suggested. "I'm afraid she's a little bored with all this."

"I'll do my best," Bent replied, and he looked at me.

I led the way through a fantastic petrified forest of madrepore, and then, because Wolfe was following me with a loaded speargun, and because he had never used one before, and because a certain white hunter had been shot by accident in Kenya last year, I motioned him up front and fell behind. I thought it was a smart thing to do at the time, but I was wrong; just as wrong as when I had told him I didn't think we would find any sharks.

We were skirting the base of a coral reef when a movement in the shadows ahead woke me up. It was a school of blue shark, five or six of them. The leader shot out of the shadows, the myopic eyes bugged curiously. It was a twelve foot, barrel-shaped mama shark taking her tads for a stroll. Two prison-striped pilot fish trembled above her nose. Mama decided that we were up to no good. She jackknifed and headed back for her brood.

I forgot where I was and started to shout at Wolfe; he was going after her. Mama became a little rattled. She led her offspring into a coral trap. The pink walls rose sheer to the surface. She took one popeyed glance at Wolfe, thrashing his way after her, and then she doubled back, darting low to the floor. The brood followed after, their eyes big with terror and confusion. Wolfe changed direction, cut down to head off the procession. The last shark, a baby of six feet, spread his pectorals in sudden panic, and turning, bumped his nose against the coral wall.

Wolfe had him fenced in. He raised the gun and pumped in closer. I was right behind him, reaching for him, when the shark opened his mouth and charged with all the fury of ignorant fear.

There was a blur, the backwash slapped me, shoving me aside. The water trembled and then fell clear and undisturbed. The shark was gone, but Wolfe was hanging suspended, his head bobbing sickeningly at the end of his taut neck. His mouthpiece was out and splaying up a jeweled collection of fat, silvery bubbles. I grabbed him, jammed the mouthpiece back in, and tugged him up to the surface.

Bent rowed over in the skiff and picked us up.

"Don't ever," I said to Wolfe, when we were back on the schooner again, "corner a big fish like that. Even if they don't bite, they can knock you senseless. Their backwash is terrific."

"I thought he was scared," he said. "I thought I had him buffaloed." He was still smiling, but he looked cowed.

"He was like a rat in a trap," I told him. "Hereafter, Captain Bent or I will tell you what to shoot and when. Stay away from big sharks. If we should run into a tiger shark, lay low. Don't do anything. The blow from the tail of a tiger shark can kill a man."

"All right," he said. "I'll remember that."

I was down in my cabin drying off when Bent came in. He leaned against the doorframe with an unlit cigarette in his mouth and looked at me. I had a fifth standing uncapped on my table and a shot glass. He nodded his head toward it. "Building back your courage?"

I looked at him and threw the towel on my bunk. "What have you been building?" I asked him.

He grinned slantwise and pulled the cigarette from his mouth. "Don't get nasty, Mack. I'm just trying to keep the passengers amused—both of them."

I filled the shot glass, emptied it, made a face, and started pulling on my dungarees. "Why don't you forget her, Bent, and wait until you get back to shore? There's plenty of girls on the beach. Give Wolfe a chance. He's not a bad guy."

"You're tearing me apart," Bent sneered. "Any moment now I'll have to run for my hanky." He crumpled the cigarette in his hand and threw it down on the deck. He looked at me, his face as emotionless as the wall locker by his side. "You've dished out a lot of free advice today, now have some of mine. Keep your snout out of my business." He said it flatly, without anger or feeling.

I paused with my shirt in my hands. "Why don't you take a walk," I suggested, "before I take a crack at that girl-killer face of yours?"

He merely grinned and left.

The sky was a great expanse of blackness, sprinkled thinly with silver dust. Straight above the masthead, the moon hung like a Persian's fat crescent. It was the type of night that Bent had promised Lorry she would never forget. Dinner had been another game of cat-and-mouse. Wolfe had sat there with the secret smile, drinking too much whisky, while Lorry had dug at him with her mocking eyes and honeyed, double-meaning words. And Bent had sat at the end of the table, watching, smirking, raising his eyebrows at me.

I strolled aimlessly along the starboard rail, wondering if I wanted to go below and get drunk, or jump in the skiff and go prowl on the lonely atoll. The soft sound of hushed voices whispered back to me from the bow. I paused, wondering, because it wasn't Malayan.

"Something could happen down there, couldn't it? It's happened before, hasn't it?" That was Lorry; I knew her particular type of purr.

"Yes, but Mack'll be there; he's an old hand; he'd know better." That was my good old partner, the lady killer, building me up, telling her that her husband was perfectly safe as long as old Mack was there.

"Well, then, couldn't something also happen—"

"No." Bent's voice rose slightly, and then waned. "Forget it. That's out."

I turned away and went back aft. I didn't want to eavesdrop on their clandestine meeting. The tinkle of ice floating in a glass reached me and I stopped short. Wolfe was standing on the other side of the companionway, just beyond the glare of the cockpit light. In the gloom I saw the gleam of his teeth as he smiled.

"Mr. Wolfe," I said, because for the moment I couldn't think of anything else. Then—"Have you been on deck long?"

"No, I just strolled up to see the moon. Romantic night, isn't it?"

"Yes, sir," And then, because Bent was my partner, I turned and shouted into the darkness. "Tani! Fetch a deck chair for Mr. Wolfe." I nodded to Wolfe and stepped into the lighted cockpit. "Good night,"

I said. And all the way down the steps and into the saloon I could hear the tinkle of his ice cubes rocking against the circle of his glass.

It took us two days of easy running to make Ari Atoll. The *Penn Warren*, the tanker, lay there amidst the coral, eighty feet down. When the tide ebbed, her truck, the tip of her mainmast, was but a few feet below the surface. I was in the lead and reached the truck first. When I looked down into that incredibly clear water, I grew instantly dizzy, and had to clutch the mast for fear I would topple and fall the fifty-some feet down to the deck of the wreck. The illusion was complete, it was as though the old tanker was still plowing across the familiar blue ocean. I grinned at myself and shoved clear of the truck. In a moment, Wolfe appeared and reached for it with a casual hand. When he glanced down, he dropped his speargun and grabbed the mast with both hands.

I laughed silently behind my mouthpiece.

Bent took the lead then, spiraling down to the marled top of the deckhouse. He found Wolfe's gun and handed it to him. Wolfe turned and winked at me through his face plate. We formed up and coasted slowly forward toward the lonely wheelhouse.

Every dead ship has a personality of its own. Some are mere mounds of deceiving coral, others are brilliant flower gardens and fish sanctuaries; many are gaping, twisted, dark hulks whose very aspect warn the diver to be on the alert for something uncanny, unhealthy.

But the *Penn Warren* wasn't any of these; she was like a large toy scuttled in a clear fishpond. Except for the fine film of marl dust on her decks, her paint was still fresh, her shrouds whole, her varnish gleaming. Her death wound was along the bottom, hidden from view. Droves of green parrot fish sported about the open wheelhouse. A blue-striped grunt wavered near the idle wheel, grunting his displeasure at my entrance. I waved the spear at him and he fluttered off in a huff.

We spent about fifteen minutes inside the deckhouse, drifting down the silent, gloomy passages, poking into lonely cabins, and peeking into drawers. Bent found a woman's black compact and stuck it inside his trunks. I looked away, wondering if Wolfe had noticed.

We went back to the deck and finned our way toward the forecastle. Halfway across the cargo deck a heavy shadow fell on the hatch cover, wavered, and edged off. We looked up and saw an eight foot blue shark gliding effortlessly above our heads. Wolfe looked at me and I nodded. We started after him with Bent in the lead.

The shark must have seen us coming; he gave a swish of his tail and vanished in the dark blue void. We sank back down to the floor of the bay and paused there for a moment to look at the wreck. From this vantage point, she appeared fake—like a movie shot of a sunken ship. She didn't belong there.

Wolfe saw the shark first and reached out for Bent's arm. I turned and looked off across the bay's floor, aft of the wreck. It wasn't the blue shark returning; this was the king of the Indian Ocean, who had been led out of his depth by the guiding pilot fish. It was a twenty foot tiger shark, a massive chunk of barrel-like tanned muscle. His skin was a pale yellowish-brown, with dark brown transverse bands. His nearsighted saucer eyes bugged out in suspicious awe as he glided silently across a bed of purple sea rods, following the fluttering pilot fish that rode secure above his great snout.

I was a little ahead of Bent and Wolfe; I turned and motioned them down. Bent was already pulling Wolfe behind a huge, umbrella-humped madrepore. A large, spreading red fan of king coral was growing at the foot of a staghorn forest. I crouched down behind the plant, holding onto the brittle staghorns to remain stationary.

The tiger shark was coming toward us seemingly without motion. He moved with a sort of dreamy rhythm as though he might suddenly close his great staring eyes and drift to the bottom asleep. But I knew better. I knew he was a gliding charge of TNT waiting to be touched off. He was way off base, belonging out in the open sea. As a consequence, this bright, clear shallow water confused him; he was edgy and angry, and didn't know why. If he spotted us . . .

He drifted through a break in the madrepore and blacked out the turquoise of the bay before me. I held my breath as he started out across the staghorn field. His great smooth belly was less than a fathom above the topmost horn. The slow shadow fell across the king coral plant, turning the orange-red to a deep rust. I gripped my speargun and watched the shadow. I didn't have the heart to look up. The shadow passed; the plant brightened. I looked up, feeling the constriction in my chest relax. Now if he overlooked Bent and Wolfe . . .

He turned, the great body curving in a slight arc. I started breathing again; he wasn't even going to pass over them. Then I realized that there was something wrong in the picture, but for a moment I couldn't believe what my eyes were watching. My brain wouldn't accept the fact that Wolfe was swimming cautiously out of his shelter, moving but an inch or two above the coraled bottom. His speargun was held up slantwise, aiming into the broad belly of the shark passing over him.

Bent moved into action before I could. He straightened up, reaching for Wolfe, but he was too late. I heard the *paazzzing* of the projector, saw the flash of the harpoon, and then—blurred color. Everything went out of focus. The shark, Wolfe, and Bent disappeared in a flurry of movement and brilliant color. The backwash struck me like a sledgehammer, and I toppled over backwards through the crumbling staghorns. Far above me, the shimmering silver of the surface, under the sun glare, quivered and whirled away from me. I remember reaching out as if to grab it, to steady myself.

Wolfe was all right. He was lying on the bottom, half senseless, but his mouthpiece was still in and he was breathing. There was nothing I could do about Bent. He was half floating over the umbrella madrepore, his air tube bobbing before his face like a heavy branch in the wind, the air bubbles forming a glistening halo above his head. He must have caught the brunt of that driving tail full in the face and across the chest. All I could do was take him up.

I was glad Lorry was down in the saloon. Bent wasn't nice to look at. I turned him over to Tani and Masart and looked at Wolfe. He smiled vaguely and said he was all right, all he wanted was a drink. Funny, but at the moment that's all I wanted from the world, too.

Lorry wouldn't believe it at first. She said Wolfe was a liar. She stood by the sideboard, a half finished drink in her hand and looked at us in turn with full black eyes that figuratively sparkled red in the centers. I didn't know why I should have felt sorry for her—I'd never liked her—but I did. I certainly didn't like what was happening to her face.

"I'm sorry, dear," Wolfe said quietly, and he sat down with his drink and smiled slightly, sadly. "But it's true. Mr. Mason was there."

She didn't say anything else; she just stood and watched him. I wondered if she were going to fall and started to move forward, but Wolfe rattled the cubes in his glass slightly, and then she straightened up.

"This time," she said in her peculiar husky voice, "you won't get away with it. I'll see to that, Harv."

Wolfe said nothing. He didn't look up, just smiled his sad, secret smile and looked into his glass. She turned and started for the door.

"It was an accident, Mrs. Wolfe."

Her gaze held me for a suspended moment, as though she wanted to impress my features forever in her mind.

"Fool," she said tonelessly, and she was gone.

I walked over to the sideboard, rubbing wearily at my face. I looked back at Wolfe, still sitting with his smile, not moving, or drinking, just sitting.

"I'll have to report this just as it happened," I said, finally. "It needn't have been."

He nodded. "Of course," he murmured. "I want you to."

I set my glass down; suddenly, it didn't taste good. "I told you not to try for a tiger shark," I said to him. "I told you what they could do. I warned you about the backwash and the slap of their tail."

He was silent for a moment, and then he shook the ice cubes gently and spoke through his smile.

"Yes, I remember what you told me."

# Never Trust a Woman

## by Helen Nielsen

**A**man who is foolish enough to marry a woman named Prudence should know what to expect. A name like that is to a woman what certain names are to a man: she has to live it down. Now, a man named Joseph Buckram, Sales Representative, Anderson Electronics, didn't have to live down a thing except a wife named Prudence, whom he'd been careless enough to acquire on a trip to the coast—that could double as a honeymoon if the head office never found out.

It was nearly eleven o'clock when they checked into the hotel on Hollywood Boulevard. Joe, who'd made the trip enough times to know his way around, took charge of the registration.

"We have a nice double with twin beds, Mr. Buckram."

"Are you crazy?" Joe said.

After he got that straightened out, he looked around for Prudence, who was shoulder high, built like a tomboy with a few, to be expected, differences, and had large brown eyes that hadn't missed a thing since she'd first hoisted herself eye-level with the playpen about nineteen years earlier.

"The Fandango Room—gathering place of the stars," she said, quoting the wishful thinking from a sign directing guests to the bar and grill. "Joe, do you suppose—?"

Back in Kingman, Arizona, where Joe had found Prudence on the working side of a counter that served coconut cream pies like Mother used to make before she got a television set, girls were apt to make a ta-do about celebrities. Joe was an understanding guy, but this was their wedding night.

"Propaganda," he said. "Movie stars couldn't eat in this hotel. It's too expensive."

"Is it too expensive for us?"

She gave Joe those big eyes and his hat shrank at the temples.

"Tonight nothing is too expensive for us," he said with expression, "absolutely nothing!"

Which was the kind of reckless talk that got them joined in holy matrimony·in the first place.

They could have had room service, though Joe wasn't hungry. They'd already had dinner in a cosy little place on the highway, where nobody tortured jazz out of an organ as it was now being done in the Fandango Room. And the smoke hadn't been so thick that he had to squint, as he was now doing to make sure it really was Prudence across the table in that upholstered booth. But it had to be Prudence; only the petite ones ate so much. When she tore into her steak, it occurred to him if he ever married again it would be to some diet-conscious matron who never ate anything more expensive than watercress. Then he found Prudence's hand through the smoke—the one that didn't have a fork in it—and was glad she wasn't matronly, even if he'd have to ask the boss for a raise.

Prudence peered at the shadowy figures around the bar.

"I wonder if Errol Flynn is bald on top," she mused.

"It's getting late," Joe said. "I've got a nine o'clock appointment with Aero-Dynamics."

"No, that isn't him after all. Or is it he? I never remember."

"It's a hot night," Joe said. "Nobody important goes anyplace on a hot night. They stay home in their swimming pools."

But Prudence went on peering.

"There's a woman in that booth across the aisle who looks a little like—no, she's too old and too fat. Now, that's strange. Why do you suppose she's crying?"

"She probably wants to go upstairs and turn in for the night," Joe said.

"Joe, be serious . . . ! It's that man with her. He's making her cry. I don't like him at all. He's wearing a flashy suit, and he's got a sneaky face and a mustache."

"Men have hung for less," Joe said.

It was impolite to stare at people, especially at bars, but nothing would do but that he look where Prudence was looking. He finally located what held her attention—a woman, not old and fat, but thirtyish and well developed, and a glutton for punishment to be wearing a fur coat on such a warm night. With her, a man in a flashy suit who had a sneaky face and a mustache. The woman dabbed at her eyes with a handkerchief while the man pleaded with her across the table. It was impossible to hear what he was saying, for the organ had just broken into what sounded like a rock-and-roll arrangement of "The Old Rugged Cross."

"Don't worry about it," Joe said. "It's their anniversary and he's asked the organist to play their song."

"It's not that kind of crying," Prudence argued. "I think she's afraid of him."

Joe looked again.

"You're right," he said. "It's not that kind of crying. It's the 'one drink too many,' or 'I've had such a hard life' kind of crying, and she's too far gone to be afraid of anything."

"Maybe that's his scheme. Maybe that's why he's forcing drinks on her."

It was like forcing taxes on the government. The woman clutched her glass as if it were a lifeboat in a stormy sea. For a moment, it required her complete and undivided attention.

"Look," Prudence cried. "Look at him now!"

The organ struck an exuberant passage that covered her outburst, but not before Joe involuntarily obeyed. What the man was doing was taking a quick, furtive peek at the contents of the purse his thirsty companion had left open on the table.

"That only proves it's their anniversary," Joe said. "When we've been married that long, I'll probably have to hit you for enough to pay the check."

He said it tenderly, hoping to remind her of the vows they'd exchanged before a justice of the peace a little after dawn.

"He's a thief!" Prudence insisted. "And they can't be married. They don't match."

It was as stupid an observation as Joe had heard, but he hadn't married Prudence for her brains. He tried to signal the waiter to get his check before she took such an interest in any of the other customers, and that was just when the lady with the big thirst suddenly took affront at what was being confided to her across the table.

"You called me a tramp!" she shrieked. "How dare you call me a tramp?"

The organist had run out of music. So this lady's outburst had an instant audience of every ear in the room.

"I won't sit with you when you talk to me that way . . . ! And you can take your lousy coat back!"

"That's an awfully careless way to treat mink," Prudence observed.

It was rather careless, the way she peeled off the coat and draped it over the man's head, but that wasn't what made Joe uneasy. In the smoky darkness, he couldn't tell a mink from a French poodle. Maybe Kingman, Arizona, wasn't as remote as he'd imagined. That thought and all its disturbing implications upset him so much he almost missed the next round. Obviously, the man with the coat on his head wouldn't take it lying down. He was already on his way to the bar where his lady friend was beginning to free-lance.

"You called me a tramp—" she whined.

He wrapped the coat around her shoulders and whispered in her ear. It must have been mink. She didn't whine long. A few minutes later, she was staggering off to the powder room to replace her face, and the man, looking pleased with the world, was calling for his check.

Joe also looked pleased with the world.

"So you've seen a real night-life drama," he remarked, "complete with happy ending. Now we can go—"

"I'll be back in a minute," Prudence said.

Joe watched Prudence march off to the powder room, and now he wasn't pleased with the world at all. She'd never been so difficult before. Maybe it was the city that upset her—the lights and the noise and that lobby swarming with strangers. Prudence had never spent a night in a hotel before. And then Joe saw the light. She was nervous—the poor kid was nervous! The thought pleased him. He began to feel very proud and tolerant. No wonder she was making such a fuss over nothing. No girl wants to admit she's nervous when she's married a man of the world. Smiling over the thought, Joe lit a cigarette. After all, how did he want her to be—brazen, like one of those ladies of the evening hovering around the bar?

The waiter brought the check and Joe signed with a flourish. Still smiling, he lit a cigarette. The waiter looked at him strangely and went away. Then the lady with the reclaimed mink emerged from the powder room and went out with her sneaky-faced friend. She wasn't in condition to see much of anything, but she looked at Joe strangely as they passed. Seconds later, Prudence returned. She looked at him strangely, too.

"Joe, why are you smoking two cigarettes?"

Joe coughed out both cigarettes and ground them into the ashtray.

"Have they gone?" Prudence asked. "She was awfully sick in there."

"And you nursed her, I suppose."

"I didn't go near her, but I could hear. She's still careless, too. She dropped her mink coat on the floor and left her purse lying open on the makeup table. Her name is Leona Muller."

"I thought you didn't go near her." And then Joe had a horrible thought. "You didn't—"

"It was just lying there open. The catch wasn't caught."

"But ransacking another woman's purse!"

"I didn't ransack anything. I just found the identification card and wrote it down for the police." Prudence had a small piece of pink paper in her hand. She held it under the table lamp and began to read: "Leona Muller, 1221—"

"The police?" Joe echoed.

"In case something terrible happens. I have a feeling, Joe. There's something wrong. That expensive mink coat and a shabby old purse—they don't match."

"So she likes to economize!"

"And I don't think she should go off with that man tonight. I don't trust him."

"Look, honey," Joe said. "I'm an understanding guy, but this has gone far enough. I'm your husband and I order you to forget Leona Muller, her mink coat, and all of this silly business once and for all. We're getting out of here right now!"

Gently, but masterfully, he grabbed her wrist. It was the wrist of the hand that clutched the small slip of pink paper. He looked closely at the slip of pink paper. It had perforated edges.

"Prudence—"

Joe tried to hide the tremor in his voice.

"Just one question. Where did you get this paper to write the name and address on?"

Prudence looked at him unblinkingly.

"I looked in my purse, but I didn't have anything to write on. Only a pen—"

"So you took this slip of paper from Leona Muller's purse?"

"It's just a little piece."

It was just a little piece until Joe took it from her hand and unfolded it. Pink, perforated edges—yes, it had to be. Joe sat down again and buried his face in his hands. The little piece of pink paper was a check made out to Leona Muller for the sum of twenty-eight thousand dollars.

When a man has married a woman who steals twenty-eight thousand dollars on her wedding night, he must take drastic action. Joe sat with his head in his hands for fifteen seconds. Then he stood up.

"Come on," he ordered.

"Are you going to call the police?" Prudence asked.

"Not unless you want to postpone our honeymoon for about ten years. Those two went out of the street door. They must have a car in the parking lot."

"But, Joe—"

"And when we catch them, I do the talking, understand? You *found* that check on the powder room floor—understand?"

"But, Joe—"

Joe wasn't the top west coast representative of Anderson Electronics just so he could argue with a five foot brunette who couldn't keep her hands out of another woman's purse. He was practically dragging her behind him when they reached the street. The man and the woman had a start of several minutes on them, but with the woman in such a fluid state, they couldn't move very fast. The hotel parking lot was just around the corner of the building. The lights were burning brightly. About halfway down the center row of cars, a man in a plaid suit was trying to pour his female companion into the front seat of a light green midget sedan. At first Joe wasn't sure—

"You called me a tramp! I haven't forgotten you called me a tramp!"

Joe was sure then. He ran forward.

"Hey!" he yelled. "Hey—you!"

"Joe, be careful!" Prudence cried.

This was the one time she lived up to her name. The man had his mind on what he was doing—and both hands—until Joe came on the scene. He didn't seem to appreciate interference.

"Who asked you to butt in?" he demanded. "Can't a man have a fight with his wife, without a buttinsky butts in?"

"I'm not butting in," Joe said. "I've got something for you—"

"And I've got something for you!"

Joe didn't even have time to duck—much less explain. Sneaky-face was in a terrible hurry. A fist had shot out of nowhere, a car door slammed, and above the plaintive wail—"You called me a tramp—" the midget motor sputtered alive. When Prudence reached him, Joe was seated in the middle of the asphalt drive and the little sedan was nosing its way toward the exit of the parking lot.

Joe muttered in an ancient tongue, native to bootcamps and locker rooms.

"I told you not to trust that man," Prudence said.

Joe looked up at Prudence and, for one ghastly instant, he had a wild desire to slug her.

Never could Joe have done what he did then if he hadn't been so angry. Nobody but an exceedingly angry man could pull a car out of a lot that fast, miss tearing off anybody's fenders, ignore the protests of a bewildered brunette clinging to the edge of the seat, and make it to the street just as the little sedan was pulling away from the boulevard stop at the corner.

"Keep your eye on him!" Joe ordered. "Don't let him out of your sight!"

"Joe, are you hurt?"

"A guy tries to do a guy a favor! A maniac like that shouldn't run loose!"

"Joe, the light—"

Joe didn't have time for lights. The only red he could see was in his own eyes, and the boulevard was nearly empty at this hour anyway. Up ahead, the taillights of the little sedan were bobbing over the pavement like a pair of skipping fireflies. Joe ground his foot against the gas pedal and the fireflies were a lot nearer.

"That motorized kiddy-car! I'll run it clear up on the sidewalk! I'll put it in the trash can!"

"Joe, there's another light—I mean, there was another light!"

It was a fine time for Prudence to be getting cautious. This was all her fault anyway. Joe hadn't forgotten that for a minute.

"Damn the lights!" he said. "I've got to get that idiot before he reaches the freeway."

"But the police—"

"I told you, I don't want the police. I'm going to give Leona her twenty-eight thousand dollars if I have to stuff it down her husband's throat!"

"I still say they aren't married," Prudence said.

Prudence didn't say any more.

She never had a chance. By this time they had come alongside the little sedan, and Joe wasn't kidding about running it up on the curb. He veered his car toward the midget; the midget veered toward the sidewalk. The man with the sneaky face yelled something out of the window and Joe yelled something back; and then, as Joe swung toward the little car again, it leaped the curbing, shuddered, and came to a stop in the doorway of a florist's shop.

The driver's door was open by the time Joe reached the sidewalk.

"You stay away from me" the man yelled. "Stay away or I'll let you have it!"

Joe heard the words, but they didn't register. As far as he was concerned, he'd already had it. He had to slug somebody, and Prudence was too small. The man backed toward the shop window, one hand stuck out in front of him. The lights from the little car glinted off the object in his hand, but Joe was too far gone for caution. His fists began to whirl in front of him like a pair of crazy propellers. The gun clattered to the sidewalk as useless as a toy. Somebody screamed. There was a loud thudding sound, and then the window shattered as if it had been struck by a heavy body—because it had been.

When the glass stopped tinkling, there was a moment of awful silence; then brakes screeched and a blinding light stabbed through the darkness. Joe whirled about, blinking.

"The police—!" he gasped.

Prudence picked her way toward him across the broken glass.

"That's what I was trying to tell you in the car," she said, "when you ran the lights—"

Joe didn't say anything. He groaned.

It was nearly two o'clock when they got back to the hotel. The police were very understanding after Prudence explained everything. That was after they'd pulled the sneaky-faced man out of the potted camellias and throttled Leona Muller's wails when they took away her mink coat.

"Tha's my wedding present! We're going to Las Vegas to get married, an' tha's my wedding present!"

"You see!" Prudence said. "I knew they weren't married."

And then the policeman who was in charge of the sneaky-faced man turned his flashlight on his sneaky face and said. "Well, if it isn't Duke McGinnis! Getting married again, Duke? Where did you steal the bait this time? And how much is the lady's dowry?"

"Twenty-eight thousand dollars," Prudence said. "My husband has the check which I found in the powder room and we were only trying to return—"

"My house money!" Leona Muller exclaimed. "That's my house money!"

It was very confusing for a while, especially after Leona finally realized that McGinnis had given her a hot mink and was only trying to marry her for the twenty-eight thousand dollar check she'd just received for the sale of her old rundown bungalow at the edge of Beverly Hills. It all had to be straightened out at the police station with the owner of the florist shop bawling about his broken window and uprooted camillias, and the police looking at Joe and shaking their heads.

"Your husband is an excitable man, Mrs. Buckram," the desk sergeant said.

And Prudence gave him a smile that could melt the gates of San Quentin.

"He's really very sweet, but tonight he's a little nervous. You see, we were only married this morning."

After that the police were very understanding.

Back in the hotel—in their own room at last—Joe had a few words to say.

"I'm not angry any more," he said. "I'm willing to forget the whole thing and never mention it again. I won't even ask if you knew that piece of pink paper was a check when you lifted it from the purse."

"No woman should carry anything that valuable around with her when she's out with a man who's deliberately trying to get her drunk," Prudence said.

"I won't," Joe added, "even ask if you knew that mink was stolen—"

"It didn't have any labels in it," Prudence explained. "I looked when I was in the powder room. If I had a real mink coat, I'd have the furrier's label and my name embroidered in gold."

"—stolen," Joe repeated, "and given to Leona to lure her into a phony marriage long enough for McGinnis to get her check cashed—"

"Imagine a flashy-looking man like Mr. McGinnis going for a fat old woman like Leona Muller. They don't match!"

"Like the mink coat and the cheap handbag?"

"Exactly the handbag McGinnis couldn't keep his hands off because all he was really interested in was the check tucked away inside. Joe—!"

Prudence didn't have twenty-eight thousand dollars, but Joe had her in his arms. And he didn't want to hear any more explanations, or to be told how brave he was for knocking an armed man into the camellias even if he had been too angry to recognize that it was a gun McGinnis had stuck in front of him, or to engage in any kind of conversation at all—because it was two o'clock in the morning, and he had an early appointment at Aero-Dynamics, and some people did match—perfectly.

Joe, finally, made this all clear to Prudence. And they were just getting cosy when a shrill, female voice drifted up from the parking lot below.

"You called me a barfly! You take your hands off me! You called me a barfly!"

Prudence raised up.

"Joe—listen!"

Joe was on his feet in an instant. He made it to the window in one leap and slammed down the sash.

"But, Joe, it'll get warm in here—"

Joe came back toward Prudence with a determined glint in his eye.

"I wouldn't be surprised," he said.

# Piggy Bank Killer

## by Jack Ritchie

"**A**re you a professional killer?" he asked.

"Of course," I said.

He was a boy of about twelve and he wore glasses and a clean but obviously aging jacket. "Good," he said. "I'd like you to murder my great-uncle on my father's side, James Rawlins. I can pay you twenty-seven fifty." He looked past me at my cluttered study-living room. "Actually I have twenty-seven fifty-six, but I thought you'd prefer to deal in round numbers."

"I suppose you were saving for a bicycle?"

"No. Webster's International Dictionary. Third edition. Despite what people say about it."

I let him in and cleared a chair of some books. "Why do you want your Uncle Rawlins killed?"

"He's interfering with my mother's education."

I began filling one of my straight pipes. "Perhaps you could elaborate just a little bit?"

"The situation is simple," he said. "My mother is a widow. My father died when I was three. His parents—my grandparents—were killed in an automobile accident when he was ten, and Uncle James took over his rearing. Uncle James is quite rich. However, since he did not approve of his nephew's marriage, we were left penniless when Father died. Uncle James—who has never bothered to see me, by the way—has grudgingly been keeping us going these past nine years with a small amount of money each month, but now he threatens to discontinue that entirely unless Mother quits college."

I had the feeling the boy could have written *War and Peace* on the back of a postcard. "Your Uncle James disapproves of higher education for women?"

"I don't think that's it," he said. "I believe it's because through all these years he has derived a certain sadistic enjoyment in our dependency upon him."

"And this will end if your mother is educated?"

"Naturally. My mother accepted his charity—rather than get a job—because she felt I should have her undivided attention during my crucial childhood years. However, I am now twelve and about to enter high school, and Mother believes that now it is safe for her to finish her education. She was a junior when she left college to get married. It is her intention to become a teacher and thereby achieve our independence."

"Why doesn't she just declare her independence right now by getting a job?"

"That is what she is going to do if she can't go to college. But I don't think that's at all wise. What kind of a job could an untrained woman of thirty-two get? Especially in view of automation."

"What is your name?"

"Donald."

"Well, Donald," I said, "has it ever occurred to you that your uncle's monthly payment, small as it is, will cease entirely if I kill him?"

"Yes. But on the other hand I am his only blood relative and I rather think that I would eventually get some portion of his estate, whether I am mentioned in his will or not. I would imagine his beneficiaries would prefer a settlement to a court fight."

Apparently the boy had thought of everything. "Donald," I said, "let's go back to the beginning. What made you think that I would murder anyone at all for twenty-seven fifty?"

"I didn't. That was just a gambit for your sympathy. I thought you might do it for nothing. *If* you did decide to kill Uncle James."

"I'm glad you emphasized the 'if,'" I said, "because that brings me to my second point. Whatever gave you the idea that I'm a professional killer?"

He smiled. "You said so, didn't you?"

"My dear boy," I said, "when I hear a knock at my door and find a small boy who blithely asks me if I am a professional killer, what would you expect a man of my acerbic temperament to answer?"

He grinned. "Exactly what you did."

I flushed slightly. "Donald, when you attend college, in what field do you intend to specialize?"

"Psychology."

I was not the least surprised. "Since there are any number of people in this world, why did you knock on my door? And how did you know about my temperament?"

"My mother happens to be in your Comparative Literature class."

I thought about that. Oh, yes. Madelaine Rawlins. Straight A student. I remembered her October thesis, "Why Women Don't Read Hemingway."

"But surely she has other instructors and professors? Why did you come to me?"

"You're the one she talks about."

Naturally I was curious. "Favorably?"

"Yes and no," Donald said. "But anyway, I don't know any adult males and so I had to turn to someone."

I sighed. "Just what in the world do you expect me to do?"

"Well, I thought you might go to see Uncle James. Reason with him. But if that doesn't work, and it probably won't, you could tell him that I tried to hire you to kill him."

"Why not tell him yourself?"

"He wouldn't take me seriously, but coming from an adult, he might believe it. You could even pretend that you're considering taking the job."

"And you imagine that such a threat coming from an assistant professor would throw him into a fit of abject terror?"

"You don't have to mention about being a professor. You could sort of leave that up in the air. Let him think just whatever he likes."

"That I really am a professional killer?"

"Why not?"

I shook my head. "Donald, when you attend your psychology classes, please don't go to sleep. You have a lot to learn. I sympathize deeply with your mother's problem, but I haven't the slightest intention of threatening anyone."

I expected him to press his point, but he merely smiled and rose. "I guess I'll be going."

I let him get to the door before I spoke again, "Donald, if you really could hire somebody to murder your uncle, would you?"

His face hardened. "Yes, I would."

The next morning while lecturing to my Comparative Literature class, I sought out and noted the regular features and rather attractive brunette coiffure of Donald's mother. Near the end of the period I interrupted my discourse to say, "Mrs. Rawlins, would you please remain a few moments after the bell?"

When we were alone, she looked at me expectantly. "Yes, Professor Weatherby?"

"Mrs. Rawlins," I said, "did your son tell you that he came to see me last night?"

She lifted her eyebrows. "Why, no."

"He offered me twenty-seven fifty to murder his Uncle James."

She smiled slightly. "Did you accept?"

I cleared my throat. "He informed me of your particular predicament. Do you intend to quit the university?"

"I imagine I'll have to. Though I do wish I could have at least finished this semester."

"Your husband's uncle seems to have very little contact with you. How did he manage to discover that you were attending college?"

"I write to him about once every six months—more or less as a duty, though he never replies—and I mentioned it. I thought he would be pleased at the prospect of soon having us off his hands. Apparently he wasn't. I received word from his lawyer to that effect."

"Your son mentioned that you were considering taking a job rather than continue to accept the allowance?"

"Yes. If I can find one."

"Donald seemed to think that I could do something about it. Besides killing his Uncle James, I mean."

The gray eyes studied me. "Can you?"

I was slightly uncomfortable. "I don't see what influence I could possibly have."

"Did Donald have any suggestions for a course of action?"

"Well . . . yes. He thought that I ought to see his uncle and try to reason with him. And if that didn't work, then. . . . "

She smiled again. "Yes?"

My collar was definitely tight. "But the whole thing is ridiculous. I am a perfect stranger to you, to Donald, and to his uncle."

"Of course," she said. "So there's no need for you to get involved." She glanced at her watch. "Do you mind if I go now? I wouldn't want to be late for my next class."

When she was gone, I sat down in one of the student chairs and engaged in the process of thinking. I eventually sighed my way into a decision.

I arrived at Rawlins Tool & Die at approximately two thirty.

James Rawlins' secretary was narrow-eyed and appeared to have a headache. "Which company do you represent?"

"None," I said. "My business with Mr. Rawlins is personal."

"Mr. Rawlins is an extremely busy man. Perhaps you could give me some idea what this personal business is?"

"No," I said. "I couldn't."

She regarded me coldly. "Take a chair. I'll let you know when—and if—Mr. Rawlins will see you."

Perhaps it was her idea, but I was kept waiting forty-five minutes before she condescended to show me into his office.

James Rawlins was large and gray-haired, but tanned and obviously fit. He probably took great pride in defeating tennis opponents thirty years his junior.

He glanced at his memo pad impatiently. "Mr. Weatherby?"

"Yes." I decided to get directly to the point. "Mr. Rawlins, I have been offered twenty-seven dollars and fifty cents to kill you."

He looked up. "That's the most original touch I've heard yet. Am I supposed to offer you thirty dollars not to?"

"No."

"And who made you this munificent offer?"

"Your grandnephew."

His eyes hardened. "Just who *are* you?"

"Weatherby," I said. "But you have that information already. Anything else is extraneous." My attention was momentarily distracted by a bookcase containing a number of trophies celebrating his prowess at tennis, golf, and sailing. "Mr. Rawlins," I said, "for the past nine years you have been sparingly supporting your grandnephew and his mother, but now at the prospect that your overwhelming generosity will no longer be needed, you seem to object."

"That's my business."

"In any event," I said, "it appears that Madelaine Rawlins would prefer getting a job to continuing to receive money under your terms."

He flushed angrily. "What kind of a job can she get? Waiting on tables? All right, let her."

"It seems to me that you are, in essence, still punishing your nephew for choosing to disobey your wishes regarding his marriage partner."

His color was still high. "Why the devil did my grandnephew choose to go to you with his miserable twenty-seven fifty?"

"He thought I might be able to help him."

He studied me, and wariness slowly crept into his eyes. "And just how did he think you could help him?"

I reached toward my inside coat pocket for my tobacco pouch. The movement seemed to trigger galvanic electricity in his veins. He flinched and waited tensely.

I hesitated, evaluating the situation, and smiled with a certain significance. I removed the hand from my coat empty—for now, the motion seemed to indicate.

Rawlins tried a weak smile. "Of course you wouldn't kill anybody for twenty-seven fifty?"

"Naturally not," I said. "However money isn't everything." Really now, Weatherby, I told myself, why ever do you say such things?

He licked his lips. "And naturally you wouldn't kill anybody in his office when he is surrounded by literally hundreds of employees?"

I'm afraid I showed teeth. "I understand that the safest place to murder anyone these days is in Grand Central Station during a rush hour. No one has the initiative to interfere, and the thousand witnesses will tell a thousand different stories."

Rawlins now was perspiring.

I pulled myself together. Somehow I had taken a wrong turning and now—in the interests of continuity, at least—very little remained except for me to kill him.

Retreat was obviously in order.

My eyes searched the room for inspiration. They fastened upon a framed photograph of a football team, vintage 1920's. Rawlins was undoubtedly in one of the rows.

"Mr. Rawlins," I said, "you have never seen your grandnephew?"

"No. Never laid eyes on him."

"Or talked to him?"

"No."

I glanced at my watch. Yes, it was just about the right time. "Mr. Rawlins," I said, "I want you to come with me."

He was not at all happy.

"You will be perfectly safe," I said. "You have my word."

My word obviously meant nothing to him but, on the other hand, he decided that he had no choice. He sighed and rose.

Outside the office, he stopped at his secretary's desk and cleared his throat. "Dora, if I'm not back in one hour I want you to call my cousin Horatio and tell him I can't make it today."

Oh my, I thought, since Donald told me that he was James Rawlins' only blood relative, then obviously this cousin Horatio bit is a plea for help.

His words, and possibly the tone of his voice, had alerted Dora. She stared at me, and I had the uneasy feeling that she might be memorizing my features for a police lineup.

I smiled. "What your employer means, specifically and absolutely, is that you are to call no one—no one at all—for at least one hour.

Otherwise our business deal might terminate unsatisfactorily." I turned to Rawlins for confirmation.

"Yes," he said hastily. "Don't call anybody or talk to anybody for one hour." He took a stab at optimism. "I should be back by then, shouldn't I?"

"Of course," I said.

Five minutes later, we drove away in my car. I selected the Stevenson High School at random and parked at the football practice field. The first and second teams were engaged in daily scrimmage.

"What now?" Rawlins asked.

"Just watch," I said.

After about ten minutes, one of the backs succeeded in breaking through tackle and scampered thirty-five yards for a touchdown. He was a tall, goodlooking boy, and he grinned as he tossed the ball back upfield.

"That's your grandnephew," I said.

Rawlins stared at the boy for a full minute. A tight smile appeared on his face. "So he's big and strong and knows how to play football. What am I supposed to do now? Run to my lawyer and change my will?"

"That might help," I said. "But for the present, I simply suggest that you continue sending your regular allowance to Donald's mother and withdraw your objections concerning her college attendance."

His eyes went back to the boy.

"There is one other thing," I said. "I don't want you ever to talk to him or see him again. I think he'll be much happier that way."

"That's an order?"

"Yes." I turned on the ignition and pulled away from the curb. "By the way, I wouldn't bother going to the police about any of this. In the first place, it would be just your word against mine. And in the second, I don't think you would enjoy the publicity of having a grandnephew who offers twenty-seven fifty for your death."

"And if I don't follow your suggestions in all respects, you would . . . take care of me?"

I smiled—rather like a cold-eyed killer, I thought—and said nothing.

Frankly, I was enjoying myself, both for performance and accomplishment.

At Sixth and Wells, I stopped for a red light, directly opposite the central police station. Evidently a change of shift period had just occurred. Dozens of uniformed policemen were descending the wide cement stairs.

Rawlins quickly opened the door on his side and stepped out.

Naturally I was alarmed. "Have you forgotten what I said about going to the police?"

"No, I haven't forgotten and I have no intention of telling the police. However, I like having them around me because it gives me the safety to inform you of two facts. First of all, that wasn't my grandnephew."

I frowned. "You said you'd never seen him before."

"I haven't. Not personally, that is. But every year his mother seems to make it her business to send me a snapshot of him, so I am perfectly aware of what he really looks like."

He smiled, but without humor. "And secondly, before I entered this car I memorized the license number. I intend to write a full account of what happened and deposit it, along with your license number, in a safe place. If anything should happen to me, the police will know immediately who is responsible." He slammed the door shut.

The traffic light had turned to green and there was nothing for me to do but go ahead. I do not know whether I was more embarrassed or more depressed, but whichever took precedence, I still came to the reluctant conclusion that it was my duty to inform the interested parties of my failure. I stopped at a drugstore telephone booth to look up Madelaine Rawlins' address.

When I arrived there, Donald opened the front door of the one-family dwelling at my knock. "Oh, hello, professor." He showed me into the comfortable living room.

"Where is your mother?" I asked.

"She's out shopping. At the supermarket, I think."

I sat down. "Donald, I'm afraid I've made things even worse than they were."

When I finished telling him about my meeting with James Rawlins, Donald smiled.

I flushed slightly. "Well, I tried my best."

"That's all right," he said. "You got a lot further than I thought you would."

"Then you *expected* me to fail?"

He shrugged. "I just thought it might be pretty hard to reason with Uncle James."

I studied him with renewed interest. "Donald, something has just occurred to me. When you came to me with your story, what would be my most obvious first action?"

"I don't know."

"But I'm sure you do. The first thing I would do would be to see your mother and talk to her. Isn't that right? And possibly be impressed?"

"I guess so."

I smiled. "Donald, I have the strange feeling that when you came to me, you had in mind a solution to your problem which you did not mention."

"Did I?"

"Yes," I said. "How does it happen that your mother never remarried?"

"I don't know. I guess it's because intelligent men are few and far between."

His eyes went to the clock. "I *think* she went shopping." He rose abruptly and went to the French secretary against one wall. He opened the top drawer and seemed relieved. "Yes, it's still there."

"What is?" I asked automatically.

"The gun," Donald said.

I got out of my chair and walked over. The butt of what appeared to be an automatic protruded from the drawer of tightly packed books. "Is it loaded?"

"It shouldn't be," Donald said. "I emptied the clip."

I reached into the drawer. The weapon seemed to be stuck and I pulled. The automatic fired.

I closed my eyes for a moment. "Evidently it was loaded." I removed the clip and examined it. "It's full now and apparently someone put an extra bullet in the chamber."

Donald removed a few of the books. "No harm done. It just went through a few of these and stuck in the last one."

"Donald," I said, "you were worried that your mother had taken the gun? Why?"

He put the books under his arm. "I'll get rid of these. There's no need Mother has to know about this." He smiled faintly. "She might think you weren't very intelligent."

He evidently went down into the basement because I heard the sound of a furnace door being opened.

Through the front window I saw Madelaine carrying two bags of groceries up the path to the house.

Had all this talk about killing James Rawlins given her the idea of personally solving her problem by . . . I glanced at the automatic in my hand. Out of sight, out of mind. I shoved the gun under the davenport.

I would have to talk to Madelaine alone. If that wasn't possible now, I would speak to her at the university tomorrow.

Madelaine opened the front door. "Why, hello, professor. It's nice to see you."

Donald returned from the basement and I re-told my encounter with James Rawlins.

Madelaine shook her head. "You really shouldn't have taken all that trouble. I'm sure things will work out." She moved toward the kitchen. "Would you care to stay for supper?"

"Well . . . " I said, and was easily persuaded.

In all, it was rather a pleasant evening and reclaimed the day. I did not leave until after nine.

The next morning, after my first class, I found two men waiting. They showed me their badges and identified themselves.

"We'd like you to come with us to headquarters," Sergeant Waller said. "Last night at approximately eleven thirty, James Rawlins was shot to death."

I experienced sudden, overwhelming dismay. Why hadn't I made it a distinct point to speak to Madelaine last night? Perhaps I could have prevented her from . . .

Waller continued. "This morning when his lawyer heard about the event, he came to us with a sealed envelope which Rawlins had given him earlier in the evening. We read all about the twenty-seven fifty and so we came here."

"You traced my license number, I suppose?"

"We didn't have to take the time. Donald Rawlins told us where to find you."

"The letter can be explained," I said. "I am not a professional killer. Not even an amateur, for that matter."

"Maybe not," Waller said noncommittally, "but we'll talk about that at headquarters."

I cleared my throat. "I can understand why I am a suspect, of course. Do you have any others?"

He thought about it for a few seconds before he decided to answer. "Naturally we're talking to the boy."

"Utterly ridiculous," I said. "He wouldn't harm a fly." I tried to make the next question casual. "Any suspects besides the two of us, like a genuine public enemy?"

"Not yet."

Good, I thought. Perhaps Madelaine was safe after all. I almost felt cheerful.

In their unmarked police car, I said, "Well, gentlemen, I've never been taken in for murder before. What is the procedure?"

"We'll ask you some questions," Sergeant Waller said, "and if we don't like your answers, we'll take your fingerprints and give you a paraffin test."

"Paraffin test? Oh, yes. For powder grains?" Then I remembered and laughed slightly. "As a matter of fact, I think you might find powder grains on my right hand."

Waller looked at me.

"It was an accident," I said. "I happened to be handling an automatic in Mrs. Rawlins' house when it discharged. If we could stop there for just a moment, her son could explain everything."

"We won't have to stop there," Waller said. "He's at headquarters."

At headquarters, Waller took me to a room where Madelaine and Donald were waiting.

"Donald," I said, "will you please tell the sergeant here how I happen to have powder grains on my hand?"

Donald's face was blank. "Powder grains? What powder grains?"

"The ones I got when that automatic accidentally discharged in your living room yesterday."

He shook his head slowly. "I don't remember anything like that happening."

I blinked. Why did the boy lie?

"Donald," Sergeant Waller said, "you *did* offer Professor Weatherby twenty-seven fifty to kill your uncle, didn't you?"

"Well, yes. But it was sort of a joke and I admitted it to him."

"But why did you make the offer in the first place?"

Donald looked at the floor. "Well, my mother's in one of his classes, and from the way she talked about him I knew that she was very impressed."

Madelaine colored faintly. "Donald!"

He continued. "So I just thought that if the two of them got somehow introduced . . . I mean talking to each other . . . well, maybe nature would take its course and our problems would be solved." He sighed. "I guess things just worked too fast and too strong, and he thought he was doing us a favor by killing Uncle James."

The door opened and a plainclothesman appeared. "The boys just found a gun on the grounds of the James Rawlins place. It looks like the murder weapon and it's got some fingerprints on it."

I was about to caution Madelaine not to say a word until she had seen a lawyer, but then I looked at Donald. I closed my eyes. The computer section of my brain neatly sorted facts and came up with a conclusion: I had stepped into a little boy's fiendish pit and the walls were dead vertical.

Waller tapped my shoulder. "Professor Weatherby, would you come with me please?"

I attempted a riposte with the straw of reason. "Sergeant, if I murdered someone, I most surely would not conveniently leave the weapon with my fingerprints in the neighborhood."

The plainclothesman had the answer. "There are a couple of acres of woods and underbrush around the Rawlins house. The way I figure it is that after the killer shot Rawlins he ran out of the house into that tangle and stumbled. The gun flew out of his hand and because it was dark and no moon, he couldn't find it again. Besides, he didn't have the time to do much looking. The servants heard the shot and were calling the police, so he decided to get himself out, hoping that maybe we wouldn't find the gun, or maybe he could get a chance to come back later and look for it."

I was taken to the fingerprint department and after that to another room where I waited with Sergeant Waller.

Yes, it was quite ingenious and I was . . . I blushed . . . the patsy. Donald had anticipated everything. He had come to me with his fantastic offer and, naturally, my next logical move had been to see his mother. Just as logically—since she *was* an attractive, intelligent woman—I had been impressed and reacted by endeavoring to help her. That had taken the form of my visit to James Rawlins.

At that point, Donald could not have been absolutely certain of what I would say or do, but evidently he had had high hopes and I had not disappointed him.

There had remained only the process of getting my fingerprints on the automatic and powder grains on my hand. He had booby-trapped the gun in the drawer in such a manner that when I pulled, it would fire. So, last night Donald had taken care not to unduly disturb my fingerprints when he used the gun to kill James Rawlins. When that had been accomplished, he had left the automatic on the grounds for the police to find.

Another thought tugged at me. Had it been *entirely* Donald's idea? That bothered me almost more than my present predicament. I had almost surrendered to utter resignation when the door opened and a laboratory technician appeared.

"Those aren't the professor's fingerprints on the gun," he announced cheerfully.

To say that I was surprised was to whisper.

Waller frowned. "But it was the murder weapon, wasn't it?"

"Sure. That much checks out. But not the professor's fingerprints. As a matter of fact you could almost tell from the size alone. I'd say they were the prints of a woman or a boy."

Sergeant Waller gave the necessary order. "Fingerprint the woman and the boy."

When that was done, Waller and I went to see them.

Who *had* killed James Rawlins? I wondered. Donald? Or Madelaine?

"Donald," I said, "my fingerprints were not on the gun."

He sighed. "Not even one?"

"Not even one."

He looked at Waller. "Did you check the clip?"

Waller nodded. "When we look for fingerprints, we don't miss anything."

He looked at the floor again. "I was hoping that . . . whoever . . . used the gun would have sense enough to wear gloves. That way some of the professor's fingerprints would still be on the gun. The clip especially."

Waller's eyes were narrow. "Are you trying to tell us that you were trying to frame Professor Weatherby?"

Donald rubbed his neck. "I was going to wait a week or so—until his motive for killing Uncle James was stronger, so to speak—and then commit the crime. I would have left the gun with the professor's fingerprints behind."

Waller leaned forward. "But you decided to kill him last night? Why?"

"Donald," I said, "don't say another word. Not another word."

But the damage had already been done, and Sergeant Waller had evidently re-examined some of Donald's previous words.

"Just a minute," he said. "You said that you hoped that 'whoever' used the gun would have had enough sense to wear gloves. Does that mean that *you* didn't shoot your uncle?" His eyes went irrevocably to Madelaine.

"Donald," I said again, "not another word until we've seen a lawyer."

But Madelaine shook her head. "No, Donald. I want you to tell the sergeant everything. Do you understand?"

He seemed to agree. "I guess I might as well since they've got all our fingerprints anyway." He sighed. "It's one thing planning a murder—even fun—but it's another thing actually committing it. Last night I thought things over for a long time and decided that I really couldn't go through with it after all."

Waller nodded. "Go on."

"When you came to our house and told us that Uncle James had been murdered, I knew that *I* hadn't killed him, and I was almost positive that Professor Weatherby hadn't, so when I looked in the drawer where the gun was supposed to be and found that it was gone, well . . . "

Madelaine smiled faintly. "You thought that *I* had killed Uncle James? And you tried to protect me by implicating Professor Weatherby?"

Donald's eyes went to me. "I'm really sorry. I've kind of gotten to like you, but still I would have preferred that you go to jail rather than . . . " he swallowed, " . . . somebody else."

The laboratory technician appeared. "Their fingerprints aren't the ones on the gun, either."

Madelaine was the only one of us not surprised. She smiled. "Of course I didn't kill Uncle James. I don't think murder is the solution to anything. Especially if you do it yourself. We're all agreed on that."

Donald was immensely relieved, but still puzzled. "But why should someone carefully wipe the professor's fingerprints off the gun, and how did the killer get hold of our automatic in the first place?"

"I haven't the slightest idea," I said. "The last time I touched the .45 was when I shoved it under the davenport in your living room."

Sergeant Waller frowned. "A .45? The murder weapon was a .25 caliber. A Beretta."

"In that case, Donald," I said, "your automatic is probably still under the davenport and has been all this time."

Sergeant Waller surveyed us with a trace of irritation. "Well, if none of you did it, then who the devil did?"

I thought about that, too. "Sergeant, it seems to me a remarkable coincidence that the killer should choose the precise time when my license number was put into an incriminating letter. Clearly someone hoped I would be blamed. Did his lawyer know what was in the letter?"

"No. Rawlins just gave it to him with instructions to give it to the police if he died violently."

I pondered that. "If he didn't tell his lawyer, the chances are pretty good that he told no one else. Still . . . " I saw a light. "Was the letter possibly typewritten, sergeant?"

"Yes."

"Neatly and without errors?"

"Yes."

I nodded. "Rawlins was a businessman, but I doubt if businessmen are good typists. He undoubtedly dictated the letter. I suggest you get the fingerprints of his secretary. I believe her name is Dora." I smiled with justifiable satisfaction. "I hope *that* will teach her to keep me waiting forty-five minutes."

We read about it in the newspaper the next day.

Dora had been led to believe for quite some time that she would become Mrs. James Rawlins. When she had finally realized that matrimony was definitely not on his agenda, she had plotted murder and suicide. However, after my encounter with Rawlins, she had decided that perhaps suicide was not really necessary after all. It would be preferable to have a professional murderer take the blame for his death—and professional murderer she thought I was.

As for Madelaine, at the end of the semester she received an A in my Comparative Literature course. There have been some sly hints from faculty members that I exhibited favoritism, but there is no truth to that whatsoever.

My wife earned her grade.

# No Fish for the Cat

## by Neil M. Clark

Fishing was the principal subjèct on Sheriff Joram "Ram" Webster's mind as he waited on the station platform to board the *Nancy Lou*. The law was on holiday, badge and holster belt nowhere in sight. All the way up in the jeep Ram had been prospecting, not very successfully, for lines for a new song about a corpulent fish with an itch and a wish to be eaten at six in a china dish. Memories of big rainbows, which had battled him vainly in other days in the fast waters of the San Vicentes, had induced him to abandon his yellow tomcat Theodore Roosevelt, his beer-guzzling burro Predacious, and the duties of office for a brief binge. Faithful Effie Bates, telephone operator at the county seat, knew about it, but it would have taken a catastrophe to make her tell.

The high air was tonic. The narrow-gauge engine, not much bigger than a tin lizzie, huffed and puffed up front, bragging that it had made it up those four percent grades thousands of times and could do it again. Ram's bulk occupied considerable space, and a man, hurrying to be one of the first aboard, bumped into him and pushed past without even a friendly grunt. Glimpsing his cleft chin and clipped ear, Ram had a sudden sinking in the metabolic regions. "Oh no!" he thought. "It can't be—not on a fishin' day!"

He moved ahead less joyfully. Wayland Booth, wearing gray corduroy pants, a brown jacket with brass buttons, and a blue conductor's cap, stood by the bottom step of the passenger coach, big gold watch importantly in hand. "Hi, Ram," he said.

"Howdy, Way."

"Lookin' for somebody in these parts, sheriff?"

"Yes," indicating his fishing gear, "fellow named Trout. Know him? Supposed to live up-river a piece."

Way grinned. "He's been moved out. Didn't you hear? Couple dudes from Denver came and got him a week ago. Too bad, Ram."

"Well, it's pretty country to dream in, anyway." The downstate sheriff ducked and stepped into the last century.

The *Nancy Lou* was a living fossil. Its like went out in most places years ago, along with knickerbockers, slit skirts, and hand-cranked cars. But *Nancy Lou,* a durable damsel in corsets and high-button shoes, round-tripped into the tortured San Vicente mountains several times a week, providing the only regular transportation in that up-and-down country for some high-valley ranches and two moderately active mining towns. It was a magnet for steam-railroad buffs, who came hundreds of miles for a Gay Nineties train ride.

The coach was nearly full when the train pulled out, and something like a cheer rose as the engine strained, got the mixed batch of cars rolling, and soon reached its maximum speed of fifteen miles per hour. Not more than six or eight passengers, Ram judged, were local people. Most of the others were railroad eager beavers loaded with cameras, curiosity, and enthusiasm, and they showed no signs of sitting still to enjoy the jerky ride. The conductor gave Ram a quizzical headshake after he finished collecting tickets.

"Nuts!" he said. "Know where two of 'em are? On the cow-catcher."

"You make your trips too interestin', Way."

"I know. There's a female in levis hanging on the bottom step of this coach; claims, by jingo, she's goin' to spit a thousand feet straight down. I told her she sure could if she stayed there. Three or four, maybe more, are parading on the catwalks of the box cars, singing 'Hail Columbia.' One fellow, a philosophy professor from the University of Texas, he comes every summer, is riding in the cab of the pickup we've got on the flat car for the X-L."

"You got one passenger," Ram remarked, nodding at the man a few seats ahead who had bumped into him, "who doesn't act restless."

"I noticed. Sedate. We get that type, too."

"Who is he?"

"No idea. Seems to have ridden before. Wants to get off close as he can to Ragweed Gulch."

"Well, that's real lonesome country. Doesn't seem to be a fisherman. Wonder what he wants there."

"I never know what these gedazzlers want. Probably," disgustedly, "he's training for the Peace Corps in Tibet. If he wants off at Ragweed Gulch, heck! we stop and let him off at Ragweed Gulch. Contented customers we got to have." The conductor gave Ram's shoulder a friendly twitch, and passed on cabooseward.

Left to himself, Ram picked his teeth for the fourth or fifth time since breakfast, and rummaged around in the attic of a retentive memory, only to find unhappy confirmation for his original hunch. He got up and walked to the front end of the car, triggered a drink at the water fountain for which he had no use, then sauntered slowly back toward his seat, managing unobtrusively a good look at the passenger for Ragweed Gulch. It was exactly as he thought; the fellow did have a cleft chin, and the lobe of his left ear was clipped in a new-moon shape, not too obviously, but plain to be seen if one looked for it.

"First ear-marked human I've seen," Ram mused. He didn't stop at his seat, but went on to find the train boss. "Way," he said, "suppose you had an emergency along here sometime—"

"Have 'em regular, Ram. You figure to commit one?"

"Might." The sheriff eyed the conductor shrewdly. "Suppose it was needful to call in some extra troops. What would you do in a case like that?"

The conductor looked out and noted where the train was. "Probably walk up the track a piece, Ram."

"Where to?"

"Place about a mile from here."

"What's there?"

"Telephone. Belongs to the Forest Service. I'd call Georgetown, tell my troubles, and they'd send at least a colonel and a bat boy."

"They got a hand car there?"

"Motor car. Track crew's."

"If a doctor was needed, say, or somebody like that, not on the railroad, could he catch a ride on it to where he was wanted?"

"Could."

"Way," said Ram, "I've got a wish to employ the use of that telephone."

The conductor shot him a curious look, but asked no questions. "Can do," he said, and gave the necessary signal.

Ram took his time putting through a call on the instrument, which he found inside a wooden box nailed to a ponderosa pine tree. After finishing his conversation, he loitered some. When he finally reached the train, considerable time had elapsed; and he was glad to see still more delay caused by the railroad buffs, who had scattered like quail, examining the train inside, outside, even underside. Time and whistle-tooting finally got them all back on board again. Meantime, Ram explored his wallet and found a five-cent postage stamp. He handed it to the conductor. "Tell you what I wish you'd do, Way . . ."

Neither animal, man, bird, nor shack was in sight where Ram Webster, several miles farther on, climbed off the train with his modest handful of fishing gear. The spot he had chosen was half a mile short of Ragweed Gulch. The frowning cliff on his left looked ready to topple over on him. To the right was a gorge whose bottom he couldn't see.

"We'll be looking for you on the way back," the conductor called out as Ram stepped off. "Hope you catch that big one."

"Aim to!" Ram held his rod high and waved.

The little engine worried the train into motion again and disappeared around a bend on a roadbed that looked about as wide as the brim of a bracero's sombrero. As soon as the caboose was out of sight, the man who had been hiding behind a huge boulder stepped out.

"Webster?"

Ram nodded.

"Wright here." He held his badge for Ram to see. It said "deputy." A quick glance, and Ram saw a man half a head shorter than himself, perhaps half his age. He was disappointed not to see the sheriff, Peter Townsend, but supposed Wright was a good man or Townsend wouldn't have him. "Glad one of you could make it," he said cheerfully, adding, "we've heard about Sheriff Townsend downstate. Hear he's a smart officer."

Wright nodded. "He was out when you called. Didn't want to waste time hunting him." Ram was aware he was being carefully looked over. "What do you figure on doing, Mr. Webster?"

"Ram is the handle for short, son. I'm in your territory up here, clean out of my bailiwick, and your troubles are no business of mine. But I thought, seeing as I spotted this fellow—"

"The Federals are on that, you know. It's an FDIC job."

"Suppose so. They got anything?"

"Done a lot of looking. No results."

"Ain't that the way! Don't suppose you'd mind catching him yourselves if he jumped into your arms, huh? I read the circular you or somebody sent. The marks noticed on your robber were pretty special-peculiar, and when I saw this fellow on the train who looked like the spittin' image, and found he was headed here, I thought it was only decent to ring up and let you know."

The officers made good time up the track in the direction taken by the *Nancy Lou.* The deputy seemed to be the bashful type. At least, he had little to say. Ram, however, knew he was being carefully studied. It suited him just as well to hold his own tongue.

"You ain't wearin' a gun," Wright remarked presently.

Ram's grin came and went. "Don't show, does it? I could find one pretty quick if I had to. Why?"

"Wonderin', that's all. Didn't see it. When *I* go huntin' somebody I'm always—"

"Me too, son. Don't feel dressed without a weapon. But in strange country on a fishin' trip, that's why I'm here, I don't advertise." Ram let his eyes wander. "This is sure the goldangedest up-and-down country I ever did see. That train is a crackerjack."

"First trip up?"

Ram took time to spit. "Might say." He had no good reason for hiding the fact that he had been coming to these mountains on and off since he was big enough to straddle a frog's knee. But the deputy wasn't giving. Why should he?

They reached the point where a trail of sorts left the railroad and disappeared downward. "This what we're looking for?"

The deputy nodded. Ram gave it the once-over and ventured the opinion that only a mountain goat would call it a superhighway.

"Worse than it looks, too," Wright said. "I've been thinking—" the deputy hesitated.

"Yes?"

"Could this be a false tip? It looks screwy to me."

"Why?"

"A man so easily recognized, would he be likely to show himself so public?"

"Might have reasons. How long ago did it happen, the holdup?"

"Six weeks ago, about. Six or seven. Even supposin' he did come back, why would he come to this forsaken spot?"

"You tell me. It's your country. What's down there? Any houses?"

"Nothing. Rocks, scenery, river."

Ram looked at the deputy with interest. "Is that a fact?" He could have mentioned one or two interesting things he knew of down there. But he didn't. All he said was, "Makes it all the more curious, don't it? Why tell the conductor to let him off at a place like this?"

"That's what I mean. Did he? I mean, he might have said it and still not get off here. We don't know where he got off. Lots of places are more likely."

"Such as?"

Wright shrugged. "One of the ranches, maybe. There are some mighty lonely ones. That train stops for anybody anywhere."

"He told the conductor Ragweed Gulch."

"Doesn't mean he didn't change his mind."

"What do you suggest doing?"

"Why don't we get hold of the conductor and see what he can tell us?"

"Wouldn't that give this fellow a chance to get lost again, supposing he did go down here?"

"He won't get lost far in a few hours."

Ram was puzzled. Did Wright have some reason for not wanting Ragweed Gulch looked into?

Ram had already established one fact which the deputy didn't know. On the side of a rail, where he had asked Conductor Booth to stick it if the stranger headed down the trail, he had seen his own postage stamp; he idly wondered whether he would ever succeed in reclaiming the nickel it had cost him. He decided not to mention this bit of evidence just yet. "You know," he said, "you could be right and me wrong. There is certainly no sense in both of us goin' on a wild-goose chase if there's no goose. Why don't you go to town and see that conductor, and find out what did happen after I got off and met you? I'll mosey down here, on a chance. I might not find your bank robber; kind of hope I don't. If there's one thing I don't have any special use for today, it's a bank robber. But I might find a fish down there, and that's what I really came for."

The deputy's grin was crooked. "Stubborn, ain't you?"

"Seem so to you?"

Wright wiped his nose with a long forefinger. "If you're set on going down here, Mr. Webster, I'll go. I just think it's a waste of time."

So the deputy didn't want him down there alone, either. Ram tossed his latest toothpick into the gorge and watched the wind catch it. Holler when you come to a brush pile, Ram often said; you never know what'll jump out. He tried it now. "Was you drug up in these mountains, Wright?"

"Few miles north. Been living in Georgetown five, six years, ever since they deducted me out of the army."

"You know where things are in this country, then. There was a question I meant to ask that conductor comin' up, but seeing this fellow made it plumb skip my mind. A man's relative told me about a place up here, and ever since I heard about it, I thought I'd like to see it if I ever got up here."

"What's the place?"

Ram scratched the back of his neck as if to help his memory. "Owl's Nest, is that it? Seems like that's what he called it."

"Thatcher's Owl's Nest." The deputy gave Ram a hard look. "Sure, I've heard of that. I've been to it. Interesting place, sort of. Why?"

"Is it handy to get to?"

The deputy's head was shaking. "You say you've never been up here? Never seen it?"

Ram's "Nope" was a truthful answer to part of the question.

"It'd take a lot of time to get to," Wright said. "It's a tough trip. You'd need a good deal more 'n a day or so, the way I reckon."

"How come?"

"First place, it's to hell and gone over beyond Baldy," pointing to a distant peak. "Next place, there was a landslide in there last year. Uranium prospectors tell me you can't get to the Owl's Nest now, short of a three-day pack trip."

Ram scratched a chin that still had yesterday's bristles on it. The sheriff wondered if the deputy told his Sunday School class fairy stories, too.

They had scrambled precariously more than halfway down the precipitous trail, when Ram called a halt. He was sweating to beat the band, and thought it would do no harm to let the deputy see that negotiating a trail like this was not exactly a downstate sheriff's idea of a nice fishing holiday. He picked a rock to sit on, and sat. "I'm not as young as you by a few years, Wright," he said. He got out his pipe and sucked on it, but didn't light it. "I'm used to the kind of country where most of the hills is flat. Sure is pretty here though, if you like your back yard on edge." He showed no hurry to get going. "This bank robbery of yours." He yawned. "Tell me about it. I only know what I read in the papers, and they didn't give too many details."

"Nothing special about it," Wright said shortly. "The fellow got a pile. Something over sixty thousand."

"That's a lot of money to be picked up in a small-town bank. How come it was so much?"

"There'd just been a big cash deal."

"It was a one-man job?"

"That's right. This fellow showed up at a time when the bank was almost empty. Herded the cashier and teller and two customers into a basement room, grabbed the cash, locked the doors to keep people from getting in, and left."

"How did he leave?"

"Nobody knows. We'd like to. Nobody saw him, or thought anything of it if they did. By the time those people inside got loose and turned in the alarm, the trail was dead cold."

"They did notice those two special marks on him—"

"For all the good they've done."

Ram flipped a pebble into space. It was a long time before he heard it hit. He gave his forehead a scrubbing with his big pocket handkerchief. "Wasn't there something thought curious about the robber's knowing exactly what time to show up at the bank, just when that big sum was to be there?"

"Papers said that. Plenty of people could have known."

"Such as who?"

"Anybody in the bank or mine office."

"Nothing suspicious there?"

"Not as we know of."

"Could just anybody around town have known?"

"Might, if they was told."

"Sheriff's office be likely to know? Would *you* know?"

The deputy shot him a sharp look. "Me? Hell, no! Pete might, the sheriff."

They continued down, Ram in the lead. He had reached an extra steep spot when the boulder was dislodged behind him. He heard it coming, saw it in the nick of time, and dodged, wrenching his leg getting out of its way. It whizzed past his ear, a hundred pounds or so of solid rock. The slope was so steep where it went that it only touched the cliff occasionally as it bounded down. If it had hit him, it would have taken him with it. Looking up quickly, Ram surprised a strange look on the deputy's face. "Where'd that come from?" he asked sharply.

"Golly! I—I just stepped on it. Sorry. Didn't think it was loose."

"Step a little softer, please!"

Ram went on, thinking hard, and limping noticeably on the leg he had twisted.

Ragweed Gulch, when they reached the foot of the trail, turned out to be tightly blocked in upstream. Nearly vertical cliffs came within a hundred feet of each other to form the river banks. The brawling stream rushed in a racket of rapids over boulders of all sizes. The water was too deep for wading. But it was possible in places for a fisherman, taking good care of his footing, to cross it, or to stand on one of the rocks and cast.

The trail debouched near the downstream end of this formidable gulch. From there on, the enclosing walls drew back a few hundred feet, permitting the river to widen and flow in more leisurely manner between banks which, at this season, had grown rank with ragweed not yet in the heavy pollen stage.

It was an awesome spot. In his first quick glance Ram saw fish in the clear water, big ones, any one of which would have looked fine in a china dish, nosing upstream against the current. Now and then one leaped, a streak of dark silver in the sun. The sheriff heartily wished he could stop there and give them something worth leaping at. But in a patch of soft dirt, half hidden in the grass, he caught sight of the print of a man's crepe-soled shoe. Only one. It looked fresh, made, he imagined, not more than an hour ago. It was his first certain proof that the man from the train had not only started down, but had arrived. His suspicion as to where he was bound now came close to being a certainty. In view of the deputy's fairy stories, Ram decided to keep his own counsel.

It was impossible for him to give the scenery his whole attention. He was limping badly.

"What happened to you?" Wright asked.

"It's this crocky leg of mine. I broke it once, horsewrangling. Least little thing still makes it go funny. When that rock came down, I wrenched it."

"That's too bad."

"The climb didn't help any either, I guess. I'm more tuckered 'n I expected to be."

Ram leaned his fishing things alongside a big rock at the foot of the trail, after getting his gun and holster out and strapping them on. "Just in case," he said.

"What do we do now?" Wright asked. He sounded surly.

"Good question!" Ram pushed his hat back and sighed. "Beats all what a little time added to a man's age can do to him. Few years back, I wouldn't have thought a thing of a climb like that." He tried putting his weight on the bad leg, and winced. "If you were a bank robber, mister, and found yourself down here, where would you head for?"

"Back up!"

Ram grinned. "Smart idea, likely." But that wasn't quite the scheme the sheriff was hatching.

He studied the cliff walls that closed in against them upstream. "Nobody could go that way," he mused. "If that fellow came here, he must have headed downstream. Guess we ought to take a little dally down that way and see what it's like. Not that I have much hope. You agreeable?"

Wright shrugged. "I still say it's no use." But he followed Ram across the river on boulder stepping stones. Ram, limping quite badly, slipped once on a wet rock. He barely saved himself from going in. "I can see I'm not going far on this leg," he said.

Around the first bend he looked up and caught sight of the snow-capped summit of Mt. Warden right where, from earlier trips, he knew he'd see it. This, he figured, was about the right place for him to stop. He hadn't been able to think up any very good scheme to give him a line on the deputy, and he knew that what he was thinking of now might or might not work. "Ouch!" he said, as he stepped the wrong way on a sharp stone. His leg suddenly seemed to be a good deal worse.

For some time he had been keeping a sharp eye on what he thought was a fresh trail of broken weeds. A deer could have gone that way and made it. Or a man. He called it to Wright's attention. "What do you think made that?" he asked.

The deputy took time to examine it. "Most likely a deer," he said.

Ram scrubbed a sweating forehead. "Damn this leg!" The sun poured into the walled-in gulch and made it like an oven. "I think we ought to make sure; see if it is a deer. There'd be droppings. It could be a man, you know. If we go as far as that farther point, we ought to be pretty sure which it is. How far is it to there, quarter of a mile?"

"More like a half. Could be more."

Ram shook his head. "I'll give this leg a rest, then I'll tackle it." He found a stone big enough to sit on.

"Do you know something, Mr. Webster?" Wright said thoughtfully. "That trail will be just as tough going up as it was coming down. Tougher."

"You think I hadn't thought of that?"

The deputy was rolling a cigarette. He said nothing more till it was lit. "Tell you what I think we better do and then call it a day," he said between puffs. "I'm in good shape. You set here and rest that leg." Ram shook his head. "Listen," urgently, "I'm thinking of that climb. I don't want to have to half carry you uphill."

"And I don't want you to."

"Rest your leg. I'll go down there. I shouldn't have to go far to find if we're on the trail of this man. Around that point the country opens up and is flat for a long ways. A good look is all we need."

It was just what Ram wanted, but he protested. "I feel like I'm bailing out on you."

"Shucks, I don't mind." The deputy seemed eager.

"If you're sure . . ."

Ram sat on his stone and watched till the deputy was around the bend immediately ahead and safely out of sight. Then he was on his feet fast, and off. The leg didn't seem to bother, now. He knew exactly where he had to go.

The first fifty feet were steep. After that the ground flattened out till it was nearly level. He was crossing a monolith of granite that thrust itself out from the cliff like a finger. The river goose-necked around the end of it. Ram picked his way quickly across the level part. In less than a hundred yards he reached the far side. Here the "finger" dropped down again toward the meadow bordering the river, which was flowing in the opposite direction over here. Below and beyond, Ram gazed out on what he had long considered the most spectacular view in the entire scope of the San Vicentes. A range of sharp peaks, white with snow even in midsummer, formed the far horizon. Foothills, like worshipping nuns, knelt at their feet. For grandeur, Ram didn't know where he could go to find anything to beat it. In their lower reaches the foothills were covered with aspen and pine. Knowing exactly where among the trees to look, the sheriff picked out the start of the faint trail which, from traveling it, he knew a jeep equipped with four-wheel drive could navigate, with some difficulty, while no other kind of car would risk it. The grades were sometimes ten percent, many of the curves were hairpin turns. In places the so-called road was on bare rocks little wider than a roof ridge between sheer drops. After many a tortuous mile, he knew, the track came out in the vicinity of Georgetown.

Directly below Ram was a roof; this was the Owl's Nest, which the deputy had said was a three-day pack trip away. Ram could almost have tossed a pebble and hit a chimney. It was not big but, like the mountains themselves, had been put up to last. The eccentric mining millionaire, Woodley Thatcher, had built it for a retreat and hunting lodge. He had died long since. Nobody, so far as Ram knew, had bothered to keep it in repair. Few except hunters or fishermen ever came near it any more.

But someone was there now. A wisp of smoke rose featherlike from the chimney at the kitchen end.

For ten minutes Ram lay hidden and watched. Nothing stirred. "I could have guessed wrong," he thought.

Suddenly he heard two revolver shots in quick succession. Echoes bouncing off a sheer rock face opposite made the shots sound like four. Ram wriggled for a better view. He saw the deputy. For a man who was positive there was nothing in Ragweed Gulch worth looking at, he seemed to have found something to do. He was waving a red handkerchief back and forth.

A man came out of the house. Ram recognized the ear-cropped stranger from the train. He was carrying a revolver, but did not fire it. Instead, he too pulled out a handkerchief and waved it. The deputy started for the house at top speed, running when the ground permitted.

Ram watched grimly.

The men greeted each other briefly and disappeared inside. For five minutes, perhaps ten, Ram saw and heard nothing more. Smoke continued to wisp lightly from the chimney. Once there was a muffled plop. It could have been a door slamming. A few minutes later the deputy left the house and set off fast in the direction from which he had come.

Ram scrambled to his feet, crossed the finger of land on the double, and when Wright appeared downstream, was sitting on the same rock as when the deputy left. He watched the other approach, and when he was in calling distance, said, "See anything?"

The deputy was puffing and sweating. "Not a thing. That trail *was* a deer trail. Droppings . . ."

"I was afraid it'd be like that."

"Leg better now?"

"Seems as if." Ram was tinkering with his gun. "Set down and rest your own self," he said. "You look hot."

Wright picked him a rock, put his hat down beside him, and mopped sweat with his bandana.

"Didn't I hear a shot down that way?" Ram asked. "Thought I did."

"Prob'ly did. More 'n one. I saw a porky in a tree. I shoot 'em every chance I get."

"Hit him?"

"He dropped."

"How far off was he?"

"Sixty yards, I'd guess."

"Do say! That's good shootin' with a handgun. What kind do you carry? Like mine?" Ram handed his own gun, butt to, to the deputy.

Wright gave it a casual glance. "They're about the same, I'd say. Mine's newer."

"Let's see."

Ram gave the deputy's gun a brief look. "Practically twins," he said. He handed the gun back and took his own. He now knew one more fact.

The climb back up to the railroad tracks was considerably stiffer than the climb down, but Ram, with his leg rested, stood it all right. "That rest was all I needed," he said. "Sorry I had to put you to all that extra work. You going back to Georgetown on the track car?"

The deputy nodded assent.

"Does it carry double?"

"Oh, sure."

"I'll go with you. My fishing is all shot; and I'd like to see that town, now I'm up here. I suppose I can catch the *Nancy Lou* there later for the trip down, can't I?"

In its day, Georgetown had been a flashy camp and for a while a rich one. It continued to furnish jobs for several hundred men in the two mines still operating. Ram inquired and found that the train wouldn't be leaving for some time, and told Wright he'd like to drop in and meet Sheriff Townsend, if that officer was likely to be in.

At the sheriff's office, which was housed on the ground floor in a corner suite of a hotel that had seen far busier days, the deputy introduced the two men. "Well, well!" said Townsend, "if it ain't old Dan'l Webster himself! Long time no see, Ram."

The deputy's surprise was plain. "I thought you two didn't know each other."

"Did I give that impression?" Ram said. "Guess I have that habit—" he grinned at Townsend. "I don't usually show all the teeth I've got till I know what I'm goin' to have to bite. Us two was together some little time on the Border. How long ago was that, Pete?"

"Before Korea."

"Right." He shifted slightly in his chair, and anyone acquainted with him would have noticed that his right hand didn't stray far from his gun. "Pete," he said, "I think I have some news for you."

"Good or bad?"

"Depends, I expect. Good for some, bad for others."

"Mind lettin' me hear it?"

"Thought I might. I believe I know where your bank robber is . . . *Don't touch it, Wright!*"

Ram had his gun out and pointed before the younger man could get a hand anywhere near his. "W-what are you talkin' about?" Wright asked.

"Pete," Ram ignored the deputy's words but kept a cold eye on him, "it kind of ain't none of my business perhaps, but if I was you, I'd put that young feller in a safe place till I had a chance to look into a few things."

"Why you—you—!"

"Hold it! Keep your hands right where I can see 'em. Pete, I'd advise you to take that gun."

Not knowing why, but knowing Ram, Townsend did.

"Does he usually carry it full loaded?"

"Supposed to."

"How is it now?"

"Three empties."

"I know for certain where two of 'em went. Believe I could guess pretty sharp where the third one is."

Ram quickly sketched the day's events. "I could be wrong on some of the points," he said, "but I'd risk a blue on the main particulars. This fellow and the one that did the robbing was in cahoots on the bank job. Wright found out when the money was to be there. I'd guess he bird-dogged the whole setup, passed word when the time was right, helped hide his boy friend before and after, and the cash too, and engineered the getaway, probably over the old jeep trail to the Owl's Nest. It'd be hard, way your trains run, and no roads worth anything much, to take the money out and not get caught. It was stashed at the lodge, I'd say. The pal was to come back for the divvy when it seemed safe. Wright arranged that, too. Today was the day. They had signals planned. I wasn't supposed to be present. If I'd been real troublesome, I guess Wright wouldn't have minded fixing me so I couldn't tell. Way it turned out, he prob'ly figured I didn't upset his applecart.

"Pete, it's my opinion you got more than an accessory to bank robbery working for you. I have a hunch he gulched his pal today. If you go down to the Owl's Nest and look, I wouldn't be one bit surprised if you found your crop-eared robber good and dead, and most of the money still hidden there someplace. This coyote thought it would be nice to have it all for his own self—"

It was a job for both of them to hold the fighting deputy, squirming like an eel, and to park him in a cell. The facts, upon investigation, turned out to be just about the way Ram had them figured.

The sheriff's jeep reached Ram's ranch home in the wee hours that night. Theodore Roosevelt, sitting up to admire a very large moon, met him, permitted a pat or two, then prowled the jeep from end to end. Upon finishing, he threw the sheriff a look of complete contempt. He jumped down and headed disgustedly for the hayshed, his half-mast tail saying as accusingly as words, *"No fish!"*

Ram shook his head sadly. "I'm sorry, Teddy," he called after the retreating cat. "I'm two and a half times sorrier 'n you are. But they wasn't biting worth a fidget today."

# The First Crime of Ruby Martinson

## by Henry Slesar

**M**y cousin Ruby Martinson is one of the most desperate criminals I ever met. He has what you would call a fiendish, diabolical type of brain, absolutely stripped of conscience or scruples. He is a real scourge of society, a gunman and a robber and a thief, a slick confidence man, a swindler, a holdup artist, an embezzler, and a blackmailer. No crime is too horrible for him to contemplate, but that's about all he does. Contemplate, I mean. He never actually committed a crime that I knew about, but from the way he talked, you knew he was only waiting for the opportunity.

We used to meet over at Hector's Cafeteria on Broadway every day after work. Over hot coffee and crullers, Ruby would fill me in on his new scheme for knocking over the Manufacturers Trust, or maybe rifling apartments over on Sutton Place, or lifting some art object out of the Frick Museum. That boy was really a mastermind, and I used to get so excited listening to his cleverly-laid plans that I would almost forget that I was an honest citizen.

Partly, I guess I was flattered, too. I wasn't quite eighteen, just out of high school, and working down on Seventh Avenue running hatboxes around the garment district. Ruby was about five years older, and an accountant working for a big firm on Madison Avenue. I kind of enjoyed the mental picture I had of Ruby, sitting up at a scrubby old desk in his shirtsleeves, bending over ledgers with his big eyeglasses on the end of his long nose, his shoulders no wider than his hips, his small hands writing tiny figures in the book. And all that time, that great criminal brain of his—working, thinking, plotting. If the guys he was working for only knew!

Sometimes, Ruby would scare me with his talk, but he also made my life exciting. I'd get mysterious notes in the mail from him, signed RED. (Ruby is a redhead, complete with freckles.) Other times, he'd phone me up at home and tell me to meet him at the rendezvous. (He meant Hector's.) Sometimes, we'd be walking down Sixth Avenue or someplace, and Ruby would shove me into a doorway and flatten out, as if a cop or rival gangster was in the vicinity. As for the police, whenever we'd pass a patrolman on the street, Ruby would start acting very casual and nonchalant, start telling jokes, or laugh like a fool. He acted so casual once in front of a cop that we were both picked up on suspicion.

Ruby went to the movies a lot, too, and read a flock of crime novels and magazines. The movies were all crime movies, naturally. I hated going to the movies with him because he'd always walk out just towards the end. He never wanted to see the crooks get caught. I guess he read books the same way.

"They put those endings on just for the censor," he told me. "That crime-doesn't-pay stuff. The only reason I go is to get new ideas."

Ruby had ideas, all right. Every one of them struck me as ingenious and foolproof. I thought he would be a big man in the crook department one of these days, and even though I was content to keep on what the crime magazines called "the straight and narrow," I couldn't help wishing Ruby good fortune in his enterprises.

The place I worked for was called Brett's Hat Company, and it wasn't much of a job. For one thing, the hatboxes I delivered were big and bulky, and my boss really piled them on. Here's how I got loaded up for delivery. I'd stand with my feet together and my arms stretched out at my sides. Then my boss would take a double stack of five hatboxes, all tied up with string, and slip the top string over one arm. He'd do the same with the other arm. If I was taller, he would have made it a six-box stack. Then I'd stumble out of the building, like some kind of batman. I had trouble with a few of my deliveries, on account of I didn't fit into some of the service elevators. Not even sideways.

Anyway, I was making a delivery on 45th Street one day when I saw Ruby coming toward me. I could tell it was Ruby without seeing his face, just by the way he skulked down the street. Once, when some guy bumped into him, I saw his hand dart quickly into his jacket, as if to draw out a pistol. All I can say is, that guy was lucky that Ruby didn't carry a gun.

I was about to greet him, but he warned me into silence with his eyes. He passed by me quickly, and shoved a note into my hand. Then he went on his way.

It was pretty annoying, not being able to read the note until I got rid of the hatboxes. When I did, all it said was:

MEET ME AT THE RENDEZVOUS,
5:30 SHARP, IMPORTANT.

I could hardly wait for the workday to be over. It must have been something urgent, since I'd been meeting Ruby at Hector's at the same time for months. Without notes.

When I got there, Ruby was at a table chosen strategically to face the doorway in case of trouble, and pretending to read the *Daily News*. I got us two cups of coffee and sat beside him.

"What's up?" I whispered.

"Quiet! Don't like the looks of that guy."

I followed his gaze, and saw that he meant a fat, greasy-looking man at the next table, who was breaking a Danish with clumsy fingers and dunking it into his coffee.

"Looks like Louis the Mule," Ruby said. "Let's move over."

We reencamped at another table, and then Ruby told me what was on his mind.

"This is it," he said. "This is for real, the big one, the payoff caper."

"Gosh," I said.

"No more dreaming, no more blue sky. This is it, Joey. It's gonna take a while to get it organized, but it's worth it. Now all I have to know is one thing. You in, or you out?"

"Huh?" I said.

"Not so loud. I asked a simple question. This is a two-man plan. Straight fifty-fifty split. What do you say?"

"Gee, Ruby, I dunno. I just don't have the nerve for this kind of stuff. I'm not built the way you are, real tough and all that."

"Argh," he said disgustedly. "That's what I get for mixing with punks. I never thought *you'd* chicken out on me, Joey. I had big hopes for you."

"You did?"

"Sure. What do you think I been telling you all this stuff for? I really had hopes. You're a smart kid."

Boy, that little piece of flattery made me feel great, coming from Ruby. He could have stopped talking right there, and I would have picked the pocket of the President of the United States. But he kept arguing about how foolproof his plan was, and how we wouldn't run any risk after he got through scheduling the crime with his diabolically clever accountant's brain. I was convinced in no time.

"Okay, Ruby!" I said enthusiastically. "Tell me the caper!"

He bent closer. "The joint's called the Savoy Delicacy Shop, over on 76th Street off Lexington. I first ran across it when some broad who lives across the street took me in there to buy some groceries."

I knew that he was talking about Dorothy, and I was shocked to hear him call her a broad. Dorothy was a nice quiet girl who went to Columbia. Ruby's father gave piano lessons, and that's how he met her. She was certainly not a broad.

"Now this joint isn't very big," Ruby said. "But they carry a lot of ritzy stuff. You know, caviar, turtle soup, rattlesnake meat, foreign foods, stuff like that. This guy who owns it, Leiberman, he really rakes it in. I figure they average maybe two hundred bucks a day. Once a week he takes the dough to the bank. That's when we move in."

My eyes were popping, and I was trying to multiply seven by two hundred.

"First thing we got to do is get things organized down to the tiniest detail. That's the secret of success. We'll make a complete timetable of Leiberman's movements. We'll set this thing up so that it goes like clockwork. Understand?"

I nodded my head.

"Tonight, I'll mosey around the neighborhood and get a picture of the area. Cross streets, traffic conditions, location of the police precinct, check the cop's beat, stuff like that. Tomorrow night, we'll both go down there, and you go in and buy something. Take a mental picture of everything you see. I'll go in a little later and make a cross-check. Then we'll compare notes. Got that?"

"Sure, Ruby." My head was swimming.

"Then we'll set up a stakeout, pin down his movements for a couple of weeks. Find out when he makes his trip to the bank and that kind of thing. It's gonna be a tough job, Joey, but that's the way you gotta handle these things."

I began to wonder if I was up to all this. Ruby was a mastermind, I told you that. I wasn't even so smart in school.

"In a few weeks, we'll be ready," he was saying. "Then we move in. Wham! Like lightning we strike. In a couple of minutes, we're walking off with the dough. How's it sound, kid?"

I swallowed hard. "Sounds great."

"Sure. But it all depends on—oh-oh." Ruby swiftly put the newspaper in front of his face as the fat, greasy-looking man came down the aisle. I watched the man waddle over to the cashier's and pick up a toothpick. Then he paid his bill and left. I had the feeling that maybe he wasn't Louis the Mule at all.

The next evening, I met Ruby at Hector's, and he was carrying a folded sheet of paper about as long as a walking stick. He unrolled it for me and I absolutely gasped when I saw how much work he had put into illustrating the layout of the Savoy Delicacy Shop neighborhood. The drawing was pretty crude, but boy, the detail! He had everything in there. Even the manhole cover in the street, and a funny little smudge I found out was a gray cat that sat outside the Savoy all the time.

I had told my mother that I would be eating out that night. She sure would have been floored by my menu. I got myself three pieces of apple pie and two cups of coffee, and that was it. Ruby was too excited to eat. Then we took a bus to 76th Street, and walked to Lexington.

The Savoy Delicacy Shop didn't look like much to me, but I guessed Ruby knew what he was talking about. I went in first, as Ruby had suggested, praying that I could come out with a detailed mental image of the interior. It was a small place, half-filled with a big glass refrigerator case that held sturgeon and smoked salmon and little golden fish with slit gullets and staring eyes. The aisle wasn't big enough for two people. The shelves were loaded with canned goods, most of them exotic and expensive.

Mr. Leiberman was a kindly old gentleman, not unlike my own father. That didn't make things easier. I got tonguetied when he asked me what I wanted, so I picked up a tiny jar from a display on the counter and handed it to him. He dropped it into a bag and asked me for two dollars and twenty-five cents. I almost went through the floor. When I got outside, I looked at my purchase. It was jar of red caviar.

Ruby started barraging me with questions right away. "Where's the cash register?" "Did you see a safe?" "Is there a door to the back room?" I just stood there stupidly, looking at the jar label and reckoning how many hours, at fifty cents an hour, it had cost me. I couldn't tell him where anything was, except maybe the caviar display.

Ruby looked disgusted with me. We walked around the block once, and then he went in himself. When he came out, that gigantic criminal brain of his had the interior layout down pat. He had bought something, too, but I didn't ask him what it was.

We did this kind of thing for about five days, and found out that Leiberman had only one clerk, a girl who took over for him on Friday nights, when Leiberman went to visit somebody in the Bronx. We found out a whole parcel of things, most of which had no significance, to my way of thinking. But Ruby figured everything was important, and we had it all jotted down in a notebook. The average number of customers between six and nine o'clock. The day Leiberman went to his bank. (Every Friday morning at ten o'clock.) The name of the cat. (Pussy). The direction Leiberman took on his way to the bank. His walking speed. Which arm he carried the money under. The kind of briefcase he carried it in. We even tested his vision one night. Ruby sent me in there with a shopping list, and I watched the old man squint at it. Conclusion: he was nearsighted.

About eight days later, Ruby met me at the cafeteria and he was holding a flat cardboard box. "Look," he said.

He opened it up. Inside was a leather briefcase, kind of cheap-looking and shiny. I said: "What's it for, Ruby?"

"Ah, you jerk, can't you tell? It's a duplicate of the briefcase Leiberman takes to the bank with him every Friday. We're gonna make a switch job out of this."

I looked at him with wonder and complete faith.

"Now here's the poop," he said. "The way I got it figured, we have to knock Leiberman down with a bicycle."

"A bicycle?"

"Sure. That's how we pull the switch routine. Now look at this—"

Ruby pulled out a thick batch of notes. "Here's the street plan, and here's the time schedule. Leiberman usually packs up the money around nine forty-five and leaves the store around ten. Then he walks one block east to Third Avenue, and two blocks downtown. He crosses the street at 74th Street, around ten minutes past ten. It's usually pretty quiet around there then. That's when you come along on your bicycle and knock him over. Not rough, you understand, just enough to separate him and his briefcase. Then I come out of the coffee and doughnut shop with *this* baby." He patted the cardboard box. "We pull the switch, and we're all set. I'll go over the plan in detail, but there's a couple of things we have to do first."

"Like what?"

"Well, we gotta age this bag. Kick it around, scuff it up. It's too new. Second, we gotta get ourselves a bicycle."

"I don't have any bicycle," I said.

"Well, we can rent one."

"But I don't even *know* how to ride—"

"Then you'll learn!" Ruby snapped.

I sipped my coffee glumly. I never liked bicycles or roller skates or horses, or anything that took my two feet off the ground. But Ruby insisted that this bicycle gimmick was the best way, so we rented ourselves a bicycle and I tried to learn.

I suffered, let me tell you. We went out to Central Park every morning before work, and Ruby tried to teach me. *He* couldn't ride the thing either, but he figured I shouldn't have any trouble.

Eventually, bruised and battered, and having broken the front wheel frame twice, I gained a shaky mastery over the two wheeler.

Meanwhile, Ruby had been getting the briefcase nice and scuffed-looking. But he wasn't satisfied. He walked around with it all the time, dropping it on the floor, kicking it, stepping on it, dumping it in the gutter, and generally acting like that briefcase was some kind of personal enemy.

Three weeks after we began casing the Savoy Delicacy Shop, we knew more about Mr. Leiberman's habits than he knew himself. I was just about ready to decide that crime was too much work, when Ruby announced that the day of action was at hand.

I got excited, and a little queasy in the stomach, when I knew the moment had arrived. On Friday morning, when I called Brett's Hat Company and told them I was sick, I was telling the truth.

When I left the house around eight thirty, my mother thought I was going to work. If she had known I was embarking on a major crime, I hate to think what her reaction would have been. My mother is a very emotional woman.

I have to admit here that I had my doubts. Not that I thought Ruby could have failed in anything he attempted, but there were three things that bothered me terribly. One was my own lack of iron nerve. The other was my uneasy confidence in bicycle riding. The third was Ruby's choice of a base of operations. The base was Dorothy's apartment across the street from the Savoy. Dorothy is the piano student I told you about, the one Ruby called a broad.

Dorothy wasn't in on the scheme, of course. She was going to be what you might call an innocent accomplice. I think she liked Ruby a lot, and would have been greatly upset to realize his true criminal nature. Some nights, when Ruby and I would go up to see Dorothy, and while Ruby kept her interested in the living room, I'd wander into the kitchen whose window faced 76th Street, and keep tabs on the activity at the Savoy through a pair of army field glasses. Also, Ruby had talked Dorothy into letting us keep our rented bicycle in the basement of her apartment building. I think she was a little mystified by our actions, but she wasn't the suspicious type. I mean, she really wasn't a broad or a moll or anything.

Anyway, I took the subway up to 76th Street that morning, and my stomach wasn't behaving in a normal manner. I arrived in front of Dorothy's apartment house at nine fifteen, and there wasn't any sign of Ruby. I was relieved when he finally showed up, coming through the front door pushing the bicycle ahead of him, the dummy briefcase under his arm. He was wearing a new topcoat, easily three sizes too big for him. I learned later that he had bought it just to conceal the briefcase under it during the switch. He looked terrible.

"All set?" he asked me.

All I could do was nod. We looked across the street at the Savoy Delicacy Shop, and everything seemed quiet. Pussy was out front as usual, licking her paws in a patch of sunlight.

"Then let's go," Ruby said. "Remember, after we pull the job, we head back here. I got it all set up with Dorothy. I told her you and me were going bicycle riding, and we'd be up in about an hour. We're coming up for a second breakfast." He chuckled unpleasantly, and we started down the street towards Third Avenue. I felt sorry for poor Dorothy.

It was a pleasant autumn morning, and I would have been a lot happier playing stickball or rowing in the lake or something. When we reached the corner of 74th and Third, we crossed the street and entered a coffee and doughnut shop, parking the bike outside. I ate doughnuts and watched the big clock over the counter until I couldn't eat any more. Then it was ten o'clock, and time for me to do my part. I slipped off the stool and headed outside. Ruby didn't say a word, just sat there cool as could be. I had to admire the guy.

I got on the bicycle and started to wobble off down the street. I zigzagged and careened up and down Third Avenue, and my stomach zigged with every zag. Once I hit a cobblestone and almost fell off. It was a nightmare. I was actually glad when I saw old man Leiberman come around the corner, carrying his beat-up old briefcase.

I circled around a pillar (the old El was still up then) and waited until he was halfway down the block, maybe ten yards diagonally across from the coffee and doughnut shop where Ruby was waiting with the duplicate briefcase stuffed with old school notebooks. I must have miscalculated a little, because the old man seemed to be walking faster this morning. Maybe it was the weather. Who'd figure he'd be feeling extra chipper? I had to put on a burst of speed to catch up to him.

He started to cross the street. This was it. I pedalled furiously, trying to reach him before he made the sidewalk, but I just couldn't keep the wheel straight. I wobbled crazily and almost hit a pillar.

For a moment, I thought the whole plan had gone up in smoke, just because I couldn't aim the wheel straight.

Then I got lucky. Old man Leiberman tripped over a loose shoelace, and that gave me time to catch up to him. I shut my eyes and pushed on those pedals, and the next thing I knew I was full of gutter dirt and aching ribs, and the old man was sitting down on the cobblestones and looking surprised, his precious briefcase about eight feet from him.

Ruby timed it beautifully. He was out of the coffee and doughnut place like a shot, and heading towards us, the briefcase under his floppy topcoat. My job was to distract the old man while the switch was performed, so I limped over to him and started to help him to his feet, burbling apologies.

"Crazy kid!" he said angrily. "Why don't you watch where you're going?"

"Gosh, I'm sorry, Mr.—" I caught myself from saying his name just in time, and began brushing at his soiled trousers. Out of the corner of my eye, I could see Ruby coming towards us, holding the briefcase out in front of him. The phony briefcase, of course. The other one, with all the money in it, was already stashed inside his coat. I hadn't seen the switch made myself. Boy, that Ruby was a slick article.

"You dropped this," he said.

"Thanks, thanks," Mr. Leiberman said gruffly, snatching it from his hand. He glared at me and said: "You don't even know how to ride a bike, you know that? You shouldn't be allowed on the street!"

"I know," I answered humbly. "I'm just a learner."

"Then learn someplace else!"

He stuck the briefcase under his arm and hurried off in the direction of the bank. Ruby was already strolling uptown, and I went to pick up the fallen vehicle. I couldn't believe that it was all over, so swiftly, so easily. I was so relieved that I didn't care about the fact that the wheel frame was bent again, for the third time.

I followed Ruby's instructions and walked quickly down to 73rd Street, pushing the crippled bike along with me. I made a circuit of the block and headed up Lexington once more. Ruby had told me to ride around for about half an hour before returning the bike to Dorothy's basement, but there was no riding it now. Instead, I took the damned thing for a long walk. I was plenty tired by the time I returned to the apartment house, and stuck it away in a dark room full of baby carriages and undelivered parcels.

I took the stairs to Dorothy's apartment on the third floor. Dorothy answered the bell, and she looked flustered when she saw me. I got the idea that she and Ruby had been doing a little smooching in the parlor. I was sure of it when I came in and saw Ruby on the couch, with his mouth all blurred with lipstick. For some reason, I felt angry with him.

"Come on in," Dorothy said, pushing back her hair. "You can keep Ruby company. I'm just going down to get some milk and bread. I thought I'd give you boys some French toast."

"That'd be great," I said weakly, thinking about the half dozen doughnuts I'd recently devoured.

When she left the apartment, I went to Ruby and said:

"You got it? You got it?"

He grinned. "You betcha, kid." He got up and went to the coat closet, returning with Leiberman's briefcase.

It contained three government checks amounting to about four hundred dollars, all of them endorsed to Mr. Leiberman. There was a savings account passbook listing some three thousand dollars. There was also sixty-five dollars in cash.

We both groaned when we saw the result of all our labors. The checks were worthless to us. The sixty-five dollars was far short of the thousands we had been reckoning on.

Ruby stared at the contents of the briefcase for a while, and I watched his thin face, hoping for inspiration from that giant criminal brain. Finally, he said:

"Gimme a pencil and paper."

I found a stubby pencil in a drawer, and he wrote on the back of a magazine cover for about five minutes. He wrote swiftly, knitting his brows intently, jotting down little figures in a long column. I didn't know what he was doing, but I expected something important.

He tightened his lips when he finished, and handed me the magazine.

"Take a look at this," he said.

I looked. It was a little hard for me to make out Ruby's cramped writing, but his numbers were nice and sharp. That was his accountant's training.

It read:

| | |
|---|---|
| Purchases at Savoy | $38.50 |
| Bicycle rental | 18.00 |
| Repairs on bicycle | 12.00 |

| | |
|---|---|
| Briefcase | 14.75 |
| Topcoat | 11.00 |
| Field glasses | 7.50 |
| Meals and incidentals | 8.00 |
| Total expenditure | $109.75 |
| Net gain | $65.00 |
| Loss | $44.75 |

I stared at the column of figures for a long time, afraid to look at Ruby's face. After all his talk about crime paying off, it must have been a terrible blow to him to realize that our caper had actually cost him money. I didn't even mention the two and a quarter I had paid for the jar of red caviar.

He sat there, deep in thought, chewing on his fingernails for about four minutes. Then he said to me:

"Joey, I'll tell you what I think. I think we ought to give old man Leiberman his money back."

"What? But Ruby—"

"Why get in dutch for a measly sixty-five bucks? I think you ought to go down to the Savoy and give him his briefcase back. Tell him you picked up the wrong one by mistake after you fell off your bike."

"Who, me?" I gulped.

"Sure. He'll be grateful as hell; he won't ask any questions. Give him back his old briefcase—"

Dorothy walked in just then, and Ruby jabbed me with his elbow. I clammed up. She got busy in the kitchen and made us some French toast. I didn't feel like eating and neither did Ruby. But she stood over us and tapped her foot and said:

"Now, you boys eat up. You need food after all that exercise. Come on, Ruby. Every scrap!"

Ruby looked at her kind of sheepishly, and ate every scrap. It was kind of funny, her talking that way to one of the greatest criminal minds of the age. I would have been amused, but I was too worried about the project Ruby had outlined for me.

I got up after eating, and he shoved the briefcase into my hand. "Do what I told you," he said.

So I took the briefcase into the Savoy. Mr. Leiberman was behind the counter, looking old and worried. I told him about the mistake, and his face lit up like a thousand candles.

"Let me give you something," he said. "A little reward—"

"No money," I said. "No money, Mr. Leiberman. I'll tell you what, though. How about one of these?"

I picked up a jar of red caviar, and he put it into a bag. Guess I was developing a taste for the stuff. I took it home with me and ate it after dinner. My mother thought I was crazy. She still does.

# Till Death Do Not Us Part

## by Talmage Powell

s constable of Grande Isle Parish, Louisiana (Jerem Jenks
is the name), I'll naturally stick to bald facts when I write
the official report. I've pieced together details of the killing
out at the Deveau place without much trouble. It was a simple,
direct act of violence. Once it was started, it had to end in blood. In
physical terms, we've never had a messier killing in the parish; but
it was tidy in one respect, leaving none of those wearisome questions
about motive and identity that cause a lawman sleepless nights and
a case of heartburn.

I'll write up the details with impersonal attention, the same way
I'd give directions to a motorist passing through our back-bayou
country, but I'm not sure the bare facts will tell the full truth or its
complete meaning. Ten dollars plus ten dollars equals twenty dollars—but that doesn't explain the latent power in the printed paper,
what the twenty dollars will buy. The significance depends on the
druthers and desires of whoever owns the twenty. The visible fact
of the money is only the beginning of the truth concerning it.

In my own mind, Robert Deveau's love for his wife had a lot to do
with what happened. Yes, I know that Robert died thirty years ago.
I know that my notion is fanciful, but I believe it. I don't think his
love died with his flesh. It was a part of her, always. It was there
when she needed it most. His devotion, through her undying memory
of it, steadied her, directed her; and an earthly portion of him protected her and kept her safe. . . .

The background of it all goes back quite a way, almost forty years.
Robert Deveau was a strapping, black-haired, sun-darkened young
man descended from those French Acadians who fled British rule
in Nova Scotia almost two hundred years ago and trekked all the
way into the Louisiana wilderness seeking freedom.

Robert's was a working plantation, and he was rarely seen lolling
on the verandah of his comfortable old colonial house sipping mint
juleps. His muscles were hard and his hands were calloused. He was
outgoing and generous, honest and compassionate. The way the par-

ish felt about him, he could have had any local political office for the asking.

He met Valerie during a business trip to New Orleans and spent every weekend down there until he married her a few months later.

They went to Europe for about a month, and Grande Isle awaited their return with the usual small-town expectancy and curiosity. They settled into married life on the modest Deveau plantation, and Grande Isle quickly had its answers about her. Robert Deveau couldn't have made a better choice. Tall, lithe, chestnut-haired, strongly beautiful, Valerie made Grande Isle her home with such a natural ease and unpretended warmth that folks soon disremembered she hadn't been born in the parish. I figure that Robert was the key to that. Robert was her home, just as she was his. The two of them could have been at home in Baltimore or Borneo, just so long as they were together.

About the eighth year of their marriage, they went up to the Great Smoky Mountains near Asheville for a short summer vacation. One night as they were returning to their rented cottage, his brakes faded on their car during the long drop down the steep mountain road. The car hurtled into a tight hairpin curve even as Robert reacted to the emergency. It plunged down the mountainside, rolling over and over with glass shattering, metal rending, and hot oil and water spewing from the engine's guts.

Robert was knocked out the first time the car turned over. When he groaned back to pain-filled consciousness, he knew he was badly hurt. His stomach, chest, and head felt as if a team of Louisiana mules had walked across him. From the numbness in his left leg, he suspected what his groping fingers confirmed. He had broken the left femur, the big thigh bone, just above the knee. The sharp, jagged end had punctured the flesh, and blood was coursing down his calf.

The first shock of pain began to build in the fractured femur, but it wasn't as important as the emptiness of the car.

"Valerie . . ."

He realized that he was lying awkwardly on his side against the top of the car. It had come to rest upside down. The door near his face had sprung open during the long and violent fall.

"Valerie . . ."

Had she been thrown clear, escaped relatively unharmed? With the prayer on his lips, he dragged himself out of the car.

He lay for a moment fighting off faintness, dwarfed by the hugeness of the moon-washed mountains and their desolate silence. He sucked at the clean air and found a little strength.

Raising his head, he saw her face, not a dozen feet from him; just her head and shoulders. The rest of her was pinned between soft, loamy ground and the curve of the topsy-turvy front fender.

He crawled toward her, the sight of the stillness of her features killing his own pain for a moment. His trembling hand touched her lips, her throat, the place where the fender pressed down on her.

He looked up the long, moon-spangled slope, seeing the trail of broken brush and shattered saplings the car had plowed. Against the heights was the dark band, like a black scar on the mountain's face, made by the road cut. Perhaps he had strength to crawl the distance up to the road. Maybe there'd be the luck of a passing car he could stop for help. He had a chance to save himself before he bled to death from the leg wound. A chance with strength and just the smallest bit of luck . . . but, he knew, he didn't have the time. If she was still alive at all, Valerie wasn't breathing under the weight and pressure of the fender. She couldn't wait for help. She was suffocating now.

He dug his hands into the earth under her shoulders and started tearing it away. Inch by inch he gave her room, somehow hanging onto consciousness and sanity. Each handful of dirt he grubbed out loosened the clamp against her chest a little bit more.

He heard a faint popping sound, the recoil of cramped muscles within her ribcage, and with a shuddering gasp, the first thread of air streamed past her lips and into her lungs. It was followed by a stronger gasp, and then another, and in a few seconds she moved her head a little and moaned.

She was trying to speak his name, and he said weakly, "I'm here, Valerie."

"Oh God, Robert . . ."

"Can you manage? Wiggle out?"

"I'm hurt, Robert. My arm . . . my stomach . . ."

"Try, Valerie. Work your way out. A little at a time. That's it. Keep trying. You'll have to do it . . . I'm plain tuckered. Give me a minute . . . just a minute . . . to rest. . . ."

His eyes closed slowly, and the last drops of life oozed through arteries and flesh sliced by the razor-sharp end of the broken femur bone.

When Valerie brought his body back, Grande Isle closed up for the day and joined her mourning. His service was held in the community church, and the long procession of cars wound its way the ten miles out to the Deveau place.

Robert was interred in the family mausoleum, which stood a hundred yards to the rear of the house in a grove of live oaks. The burial place was like a dozen others in the parish, a thousand others in our part of Louisiana where the nature of the swampy soil rules out below-ground burial. It was an almost-crude blockhouse built from stone. Weather had pitted and stained it and ivy smothered the walls. The sheet-iron door that was pulled open to admit Robert Deveau to his own niche in the dark crypt was blackened with rust. His father and mother were in there, his grandparents and their parents—and no doubt in that moment Valerie Deveau thought that in some distant day there'd be room for her. In keeping with custom, if it should be necessary, the bones of a long-dead Deveau would be pushed to the rear of a niche to make room for the new arrival.

Meantime, there were the pieces of her life to pick up, and she did so with the quiet brand of Deveau courage. She ran the business of the plantation on a reduced scale. She kept up old friendships. She drove into Grande Isle once a week for her volunteer day at the parish's small hospital. If her thoughts or wishes strayed beyond the plantation, she never showed any sign of it.

She might have married again, a dozen times. A lot of the parish bachelors made the try. As far as she was concerned, however, the male gender began and ended with Robert Deveau, before whose tomb she placed a basket of fresh flowers once each week.

The years burnished her hair to smooth gray, added wrinkles to the corners of her green eyes and full-lipped mouth, and tugged faintly at the animal beauty of her body; but she was structured not to grow old with bent back and rheumy eyes, and she remained a striking woman, even after thirty years of widowhood.

My mind was far and away from anything connected with the Deveaus the day Carlin Soulard drifted into Grande Isle. As constable, I didn't fancy his type. He was a hulking youth with hair like dirty frayed blond ropes hanging to his heavy shoulders. His stubbled face was brutish and habitually sullen. He wore dirty jeans tucked into run-over boots and a filthy green T-shirt with "Make War—To Hell With Love" stenciled across the chest. I figured he'd smoke pot and spit on the floor.

He came from beyond Chad Bayou, where the Soulards were a sizable interbred Cajun clan that existed on its knack for poaching, making moonshine, waylaying the infrequent stranger, and stealing from one another.

Once previously, Carlin had drifted into Grande Isle. His sojourn had stretched to sixty days in the local jail after a drinking bout with a home-grown tough had ended in a fist fight. This time, I hoped, he was just passing through, but on the third straight day that he chalked his cue in the Little Andy Poolroom & Beer, I decided to mention that our jail food had improved none at all, inflation being what it was.

He was crouched over the second table, running a rack of balls. He didn't see me right away, moving around the table, sighting his next shot.

He extended his left arm, bridging his cue stick, and I said, "Just make sure you won't end up behind the black ball, Carlin, the eight ball."

He jerked a dark look over his shoulder, then straightened and turned, fingering the heavy end of the stick. "Well, blast me! It's the oldtimer. Old friend Constable Jenks."

"Have some bad-blood trouble over your way, Carlin?"

"Now, whatever would give you an idea like that, Mister Lawman?"

"Just figured you'd had to make tracks to stay out of Chad Bayou for this long."

Half a dozen loungers in the place had perked up. They drifted over to lounge against the wall and take in the scene with a stirring of interest and curiosity.

"Stayed out once for sixty days," Carlin said. "Ain't forgot that, oldtimer."

"We aired the cell after you were gone, Carlin."

His eyes went a shade darker in their heavy sockets. Then he winked at one of the bystanders. "Real comic you got for a local fuzz. Real funny, ain't he?"

One of the loungers laughed, uncertainly. Carlin shot him a look and the laugh broke off in mid-note.

"Only I ain't letting him set me up." Carlin swung his gaze back to me. "Just shoot your mouth off all you like, old gray fuzz. You ain't egging me into giving you an excuse to invite me back into your lousy pokey. I'm a free citizen and I know my rights. That's a public street out there and this is a public place. Now get yourself a cue stick and stand the hell out of my way."

"Where you staying, Carlin?"

"The Bide-A-Wee Tourist Cabins on the edge of town. I registered right and paid for my flop. Don't get any ideas about vagrancy charges, high mucky-muck policeman. I got money. Here. Look." He fished a small roll of bills from his jeans and jammed them under my nose. "You want to count it, oh mighty chief of the gestapo? You got my permission."

I raised my hand and pushed his aside with my fingertips. "All right, Carlin. I don't need to count it, seeing as how there's nothing visible except a few singles. I wouldn't be surprised if you lifted it off a cousin or uncle and had to run like hell. In any event, I don't imagine you've got enough there to last you long—and I'd suggest looking for some honest work before you go broke in Grande Isle."

"I'll be right over and apply for the job of deputy constable, old-timer."

He thought that was rich, and I left him standing there laughing and slapping his thigh.

Late the next afternoon, as I pieced it together later during the investigation, Jeff Moseby showed up in the Little Andy. A lanky swamp cypress logger, Jeff had recently lost the first two fingers on his right hand in a sawmilling accident. Today, he'd had out-patient treatment and rebandaging of the finger stumps at the parish hospital. With a wave of his bandage, he offered to stand a round of beer for the half-dozen loafers in the Little Andy. The group included Carlin Soulard.

Jeff was fond of describing his accident in bloody detail, and today he had a spinoff bit of news. "Mrs. Deveau was doing her day at the hospital. She wrapped the fingers when the doctor was through. Made me a real interesting proposition, too."

Buster Toutain smacked the lips in his big, greasy-looking face. "She's still quite a piece, I bet. Play your cards right, Jeff-boy, and she might open the wall safe in her house for you. I hear it's loaded with a million dollars and a quart jar of diamonds. Just give her what she—"

Jeff's good hand shot across the pine plank table and grabbed the wrinkled collar of Buster's poplin shirt. "You hear a lot of crud because that's all you listen for, Buster. You could wash your mind in a sewer and it would come out twice as clean. You don't talk like that about Mrs. Deveau when I'm around, understand?

Buster sensed that most of the men at the table were in solid agreement with Jeff. Valerie Deveau was that little part of itself that Grande Isle didn't care to have dirtied.

"I didn't mean nothing," Buster muttered, straightening his collar as Jeff slowly released him.

"The hell you didn't—and one of these days cruddy talk is going to land you in trouble," Jeff's eyes swept the group about the table. "Fact is, Mrs. Deveau and me got talking about how hard it is to get help these days and how tough and dangerous swamp logging is. Nobody out there nowadays but her and the caretaker. Plenty of good land lying fallow, she says. Told me if I wanted to put in a cane crop, I'd keep the long end of the shares, her not needing money in particular."

Jeff paused to eye his bandaged hand. "I might just do it. Get me a small crew and quit making cypress stumps before I lose more than a pair of fingers."

Carlin Soulard took it all in. During the evening, when Buster was oiled with beer, Carlin drew him out about Valerie Deveau's lifestyle and the wall safe in her house. Then Carlin returned to his grubby room in the ramshackle Bide-A-Wee Tourist Cabins and did some long thinking. About daybreak, he slipped unseen out of Grande Isle on his batttered motorbike.

He hid the cycle in the weeds behind an old billboard on the county road and hiked across Deveau land until he had a wide, clear view of the house from the concealment of a thicket.

Carlin lay sweating as the sun climbed higher in the cloudless summer sky. At first he brushed off the swarms of insects that came to feed on him, then simply endured them while a growing thirst began to burn his throat. In a state of mild torment, he fueled a personal hatred for Valerie Deveau. It would make the robbery easier, and if he had to kill her, he could do so.

He watched the caretaker ride a power mower over the vast side yard. A stalwart, work-hardened, middle-aged figure, he broke the chore twice to walk to an outside faucet located against the north wing of the house and take long slow swallows of cool water. Cursing the man under his breath, Carlin held his impatience in check. He buoyed himself with the thought of the right moment, when she would be alone, when the safe would be open. Allowing for the exaggerations of gossip, Carlin was convinced that the wall safe would, at the least, contain the plantation's cash on hand, several thousand dollars. Even several hundred was more than he had any prospects of seeing in a lump during the rest of his life.

At last he saw her come out on the verandah with its tall, slender white columns. She called to the caretaker, who was finishing up the side yard. He got off the riding mower and walked across to stand in the shadow of the verandah. They talked for a moment, and the man returned to the mower and rode it out of sight around the rear corner of the house. She turned and went back inside.

With a ripple of tension passing through his muscles, Carlin crawled through the thicket, shaving the distance between himself and the grounds. He heard a car's engine surge to life and a few moments later a big blue station wagon nosed along the driveway, the caretaker at the wheel, alone in the car.

Carlin watched the station wagon follow the long curve of the driveway past the sheltering rows of tall Australian pines. Swiveling his head, he watched a distant humpback in the county road that was visible from his hiding place. In three or four minutes, the station wagon moved over the low rise and then was out of sight. Clearly, Mrs. Deveau had sent the caretaker to Grande Isle on an errand.

Crouching, Carlin snaked his way out of the thicket, ran across the side yard, and pressed his back against the side of the house. Breath was shallowing out now, eyes and ears straining.

He heard the soft, rattling slam of the back screen door. Running to the rear corner, he saw her walking toward the grove of live oaks a hundred yards away. She was carrying a basket of flowers, and he guessed she had been in the kitchen cutting and arranging them.

He turned and padded quickly along the side of the house, sprang up on the end of the verandah, and entered the house through the front door.

After the heat and insects, the foyer was a pleasantly cool invitation. He didn't pause, darting into the long, sunken living room. One by one he looked behind pictures on the wall, tested bookcases. At last he stood with fists clenched, teeth grinding. Was it just a made-up thing, this wall safe of hers?

He looked once more about the living room, his gaze stopping at the archway opening into the dining room. He hurried in, looking at the long table and arranged chairs, the tall bay with its soft draperies at the farther end of the room, the buffet closer at hand. Over the buffet hung an oil painting of a bowl of fruit. He crossed to it, touched the picture. It was hinged at the top, and when he swung it open, a soft laugh caught in his throat. An almost frenzied joy built in his eyes as he studied the dial of the compact and very secure-looking wall safe. He lowered the picture silently.

Slipping into the hallway, he hurried to the kitchen. He gave it a quick survey: cabinets, countertops, stove, refrigerator, walk-in cooler, large work table, the huge old copper sink with its sideboards cluttered with flower cuttings and a couple of gardening tools where she'd arranged the basket.

He looked out the rear window and drew in a thin breath. She was returning, only a few yards from the house, no longer carrying the basket.

He pressed himself against the wall beside the screen door and counted the approaching footsteps. He clenched and raised his fist, and when she stepped inside he slammed his knuckles against her cheek.

A small note of pain jarred from her. She reeled, twisted, tripped over her feet, and fell in an awkward heap near the sink. She was numbed for a moment. Then she pulled herself up, holding to the edge of the sink and looking over her shoulder at him. Her eyes were slightly glazed, more from shock and sudden terror than from the force of his blow.

"What do you want?" she managed in a hoarse whisper.

"Just open the safe, lady, that's all." He'd moved out from the wall and stood now near the center of the room, hands cocked on hips, staring at her defiantly.

She was perfectly still for a moment. Clearly, she was thinking, this could well be the last day of her life. She would live until she had opened the safe; but looking at his brutishness and the temporary loss of sanity in his eyes, she was certain that he wouldn't leave a living witness to his crime.

He mistook her silence. "Don't get crazy ideas," he warned. "You'll open the safe, one way or another. Easy or hard."

"I believe you," she said.

"And don't try to stall or con me. Won't do you any good to claim there's only some papers or something like that in the safe. I know what safes are for."

"No, I wouldn't try to lie to you about the safe."

"That's on the track, lady. Now let's get moving."

He stepped back and slightly to one side to make way for her to go ahead of him. She moved her hands, both of them, more quickly than he could blink. She grabbed flower cuttings, shears, heavy knife all in a motion from the sideboard and flung the lot of it at his face.

The wet stems, leaves, and petals showered against his cheeks;

the knife sailed past his ear; the heavy shears crashed against the bridge of his nose.

With a yelp of pain, he grabbed his face and stumbled backward a step. He heard the snap of the screen door. "Damn you! I'll really fix you now!"

He stumbled to the door, feeling the warm coursing of blood from his nose. He squinted his eyes back into focus and saw her running hard across the back yard toward the ivy-grown mausoleum and live oaks a hundred yards away.

Snorting out a spray of blood, he ran out to catch her, taking long strides, his mouth a confident and determined gash.

She was wearing workaday clothing, blouse, slacks, sandals, and she was much faster than he'd expected—a tough, hardy plantation woman.

He narrowed the gap between them steadily. Nearing the mausoleum, she cast a look over her shoulder, her mouth a wide hole laboring for breath.

He forced a little more speed. A few seconds now and he would trap her against the old family tomb. He could see the bright splash of color of the flower basket where she'd set it against the rusty sheet-iron door.

With a quick shift she darted around the mausoleum. Okay, he thought, but it wouldn't do her any good. Beyond the crypt he'd glimpsed only open fields of palmetto, sage, stunted brush that offered her no ready place to hide.

He burst around the rear of the mausoleum and stumbled to a halt. The fields yawned emptily. She'd disappeared, just like that.

He stood briefly, catching breath through his mouth and blood-encrusted nose. Then a cold smile crimped his lips, and he turned slowly. Simple, he decided. Since she didn't head across the field, she had to duck around the tomb, hoping to beat it back to the house.

He ran to the front of the mausoleum, looking toward the house and seeing no sign of her in that direction, either. Again he halted, more indecisively.

He scanned in all directions carefully, even among the lower branches of the spreading oaks. A tremor of anger and frustration ticked the corner of his mouth. He tilted his head, straining his ears for the cracking of a twig, the rustle of a sage clump, sounds that would tell him that she was now in back of the mausoleum. Round and round, he mused, while she keeps the vault between us . . . but it wouldn't work, of course. He'd charge, overtake her, or reverse directions suddenly and have her come charging around a corner straight into his grip.

Then a slow frown began to creep between his eyes. He had the feeling that he was seeing something he shouldn't. A wrong detail. Something out of place.

The basket of flowers! His breath caught. The basket was tilted over on its side now—and the door of the mausoleum was slightly ajar.

"Well, I'll be diddle-damned!" he breathed to himself. His gaze inched over the weather-blackened sheet-iron door. Her only hiding place . . . She'd slipped around, ducked inside, hoping that he'd search the fields and give her a chance to get back to the house, a telephone, a gun.

He let out a laugh. Bending, he picked up a small pebble, threw it, and listened to it ring against the sheet-iron door.

"You heard that, lady, that little old rock?" he called out. "It means you're not so smart after all. You've blown the deal. It means I'm coming in and drag you out. This time I won't fool around. I'll whip so much hell out of you, you'll be begging to open that safe."

He grasped the ragged edge of the door and swung it back hard, and lunged at the indistinct form of her there inside the dense gloom of the mausoleum.

His fist was raised to start giving her the message without any more question marks. As his hand came smashing down, he glimpsed a countermovement that she made. His eyes were still focusing from the brilliant sunlight outside, but he saw that she was holding something. A weapon.

As his weight crashed against her, the weapon in her hand was driven home, straight through the wall of his stomach, biting deep into his entrails.

His scream shattered against the stone walls. He fell back, grabbing at the sudden fire in his guts. He collapsed outside the mausoleum and lay thrashing in the sunlight.

Her half-incoherent phone call brought me to the Deveau place in record time. When I arrived, she was sitting on the front steps, her body bent far over, her arms wrapped around her shins, her cheek pressing against her knees.

She heard the police car skid to a stop on the driveway gravel and struggled to her feet as I got out of the car and ran over to her.

A sob racked her body. She reached toward me for support. "Constable Jenks . . ."

"It's all right now, Mrs. Deveau." I put my arm about her shoulders. "It's all over. Everything's under control, and Dr. Simmers is on his way."

Physically she was unhurt, but she needed Doc's help to get through the aftermath of shock.

As if on cue, Doc's dusty car rolled up, and when he took over with Valerie Deveau, I hurried around the house, crossed the back yard, and came to a halt a few yards from the Deveau mausoleum.

Although I expected it, the sight of Carlin Soulard's corpse stopped the breath in my throat. His death anguish had twisted his body out of shape, jutted his eyes, peeled his lips far apart.

My unwilling gaze was held by the pattern the blood had made on his shirt and pants as it had spurted from his abdomen. His dead hands still clutched the weapon protruding from his belly.

I forced a movement of my eyes and ventured a look inside the crypt. The scene of violence took shape in my mind, the way it must have happened. She slipped inside the crypt, hoping Carlin Soulard would search for her out across the fields. . . . But if he didn't, if he cornered her, she was desperate for a way to defend herself. . . . She lifted the lid of Robert Deveau's coffin a few inches. . . . Her fingers closed on the left femur bone with its lower end broken to jagged razor sharpness on a mountainside thirty years ago. . . . And when Carlin hurled himself on her, she used the bone as a strong and desperate woman would have used a sharp dagger. . . .

I stood for a hushed moment, just thinking about it. Why'd she hide in the crypt? For the logical reason that it was the only hiding place? Or because the memory of Robert was strongest there, to strengthen and steady her? And the weapon—had she thought of it for the logical reason that it was the only available weapon? Or because the suggestion came from an unseen source?

I shook the questions out of my head and started toward the house. My mind was made up on at least one thing: Doc Simmers—not the faithful constable of Grande Isle—was going to have the job of removing the weapon from Carlin Soulard's body.

# Mr. Reed Goes to Dinner

## by Ed Dumonte

The Heathertons' weekend guests were gathered in the glass-walled front room of the mountain lodge to await dinner. Although it was nearly eight o'clock, an early moon lighted the snowy slopes outside the window in royal blue and sparkling white. Inside the room, individual lamps made pools of yellow light which encompassed small groupings of the assemblage.

Henry Heatherton and George Endicott, taking advantage of the few minutes before dinner to continue their business talks, were bent over a writing desk examining ledgers and account books. Across the room Heatherton's daughters, Katherine and Joanne, sat on the arms of a chair and tried to make conversation with the young man slumped in the chair. Alice Heatherton had twisted the bulb and reflector of a goose-neck lamp to shine on a pile of abstract paintings stacked against the rear wall of the room. When Florence Endicott entered the room through the double door leading to the dining room, she joined Alice to inspect the paintings.

"I don't know why Jason is always making such a fuss about how difficult abstract art is to understand," Alice said, gesturing to indicate the canvases against the wall. "I understand these perfectly."

"You understand this hodgepodge Reed has been trying to sell you?" Florence Endicott was a tall, blonde woman, recently dressed for dinner. The effect of her perfect makeup was somewhat marred by a faint dew of perspiration at her hairline; her hand trembled slightly as she lit a cigarette. "For instance, this mess called, for some reason, 'Motion Study 21.' You understand that?"

"Of course. It's really very simple. You see this orange splotch in the corner? It's a train, a steam engine. And this smear that looks like someone drove a bicycle across the canvas before the paint was dry? Well, that's it! And this dribble of green ending in a blob? It's a bird in flight."

"What kind of a bird, dear?"

"A seagull, I think," Alice bent closer to the painting to examine the green blob. "Or maybe a sandpiper . . ."

Florence shrugged her shoulders, and walked over to join her

116

husband and Henry Heatherton at the account books. Atkins, the butler, opened the dining room door, paused briefly to search out Alice Heatherton, then crossed the room to speak to her.

"Pardon me, Mrs. Heatherton. I have something to tell you about tonight's dinner."

"Oh, Atkins, I'm so glad you're here. You seem to know about everything. What kind of bird would you say this is?"

"An albatross, madam. Definitely an albatross."

"An albatross, of course!" She inspected the picture again. "I've never seen an albatross before."

"About dinner, Mrs. Heatherton. I'm afraid it will be late."

"Late? Oh dear, and we were all so hungry," Alice sighed under the burden of being dinner hostess. "What's the matter, Atkins? Is Cook drunk again?"

"She is, Mrs. Heatherton, but that's not the trouble. Mr. Reed is lying on the dining room table with a knife in his chest."

"Lying on the dining room table!" Alice gasped. "But that's not like Jason at all. Is he playing a game?"

"No, madam. He's dead."

"Dead? Oh, what a shame! And before having his dinner, too."

"May I have your instructions, Mrs. Heatherton?"

"Well . . . " Alice's mind worked furiously to sort and arrange the facts as she saw them. "Can the food be kept warm a while longer?"

"Yes, madam. I had Cook place the hot dishes in the dumbwaiter and turn on the heat before I left the kitchen."

"Then there's just one thing to do, Atkins. You'll have to set up a buffet and serve us in here."

Atkins bowed himself out of the room to make the arrangements, and Alice announced the change in plans to her guests.

"Listen, everybody," she called. "A surprise! Instead of a formal dinner tonight, Atkins is going to serve us a buffet in here. No complaints now—I warned you we were going to have to rough it while we were here."

Reluctantly, Alice turned off the light and left her abstract paintings, which she understood, to speak to her daughters, whom she didn't.

"How about it, girls, are you ready for dinner?" she asked. "Katherine, is your young man going to eat something tonight? Or is he going to drink scotch, as he did for breakfast?"

"I don't know what he's going to do, Mother; I haven't been in communication with him lately." Katherine was a striking, raven-haired woman in her late twenties. "But if this is the best I can do in the Starlight Room, I'm going to take my patronage to another saloon."

"I haven't been in communication with him since you brought him up here," Alice said. "Not sensible communication. I don't even know his name."

"His name is Percival Jeffers, Mother, and he writes mystery stories," Joanne, the younger of the girls, said. She had all her sister's attributes, but several sizes smaller, or perhaps just less experienced. "Not just ordinary mystery stories, but mystery stories with social significance." She added, with a touch of awe in her voice, "He's almost a genius."

"Oh, yes? Well, that's nice," Alice said. "But I do hope he sobers up long enough to see how pretty our mountains are, all covered with snow and ice and things."

"Speaking of being covered with snow and ice," Katherine said, "where's my ex-husband? I haven't seen him around lately."

"Mr. Reed won't be taking dinner with us tonight, Katherine," Alice explained. "I don't think he's hungry."

"Jason not hungry? He must be dead."

"Well . . ."

"I think Mr. Jeffers is waking up," Joanne announced. "He's opened an eye."

"Either that or he's burst an artery," Katherine said, looking into the eye. "Well, I don't care if he gets both eyes open. He hasn't been any use to me this weekend, and I'm bored with him. Why don't you try your luck, kid?"

With a gesture, Katherine gave Jeffers to her sister and turned to walk away. Alice took her daughter's arm and went with her.

"Really, Katherine," she said, "I'm going to have a long, motherly talk with you sometime. In my day a young lady never picked up anything less than a concert pianist. Discriminate a little."

"Are they gone?" Jeffers asked when he got the other eye open. "They were talking about me like something they had pinned to a board."

"Maybe they had some cause," Joanne told him. "Our houseguests don't usually demand scotch for breakfast."

"Man, I must have been looped. I never drink anything but rye for breakfast."

"How about dinner? Do you feel like eating anything tonight?"

"Just lay a piece of rare roast beef in front of me and turn me loose," Jeffers said, and turned faintly green. "But first, I think I'd better make a quick trip to the bathroom."

He struggled to sit up, and waved his arms in a futile, swimming motion to get away from the chair.

"Can I help?" Joanne asked, taking his arm and pulling him up.

"Young lady, I've been going to the bathroom alone for years," he told her in an injured tone. "I spend half my life walking to and from bathrooms."

He started to walk away from the girl, but stumbled at the first step and saved himself from falling by grabbing her shoulder.

"But you may walk along beside me, if you wish, to see that nobody steps on my fingers," he placated.

Leaning against each other, they made their way across the room. Joanne opened the door to the dining room and switched on the light. Turning, she saw Reed's body on the table and gasped. Jeffers stumbled and dropped to his knees.

"Good heavens!" Joanne moaned. "It's Jason Reed!"

"I know I ordered my meat rare, but this is ridiculous!"

Joanne turned and ran back into the front room. Jeffers, forgotten, continued to the bathroom, mumbling to himself. In the front room, Joanne went directly to Alice.

"Mother, there's a body on the dining room table!"

"Yes, dear. It's Mr. Reed."

"But, Mother, you can't just leave him there!"

"Well, I'll invite him to dinner if you want me to," Alice said, puzzled. "But I don't think he'll come."

"No, no. I mean you've got to do something!"

"Now, dear, you're excited and you're not thinking. If he's dead, there's really nothing I can do about it, is there? And there's certainly no reason to disturb our dinner over something we can't help."

Alice pushed her daughter into a chair and patted her shoulder. "You just sit here a few minutes and breathe deeply. Atkins will be here with something to eat in a little while."

Atkins was there immediately. He pushed a serving cart into the room and set up a folding table before the fireplace. When he had an assortment of foods laid out on the table, he filled two plates and took them to Alice and Henry Heatherton. The rest he let serve themselves.

Alice filled a second plate and took it to Joanne. "Now don't just sit here and brood, dear. You've got to have some dinner. Eat your cold turkey before it gets warm."

At that moment Jeffers returned to the room. His eyes had cleared somewhat, and his head was damp from having been held under a water faucet. He crossed the room to Alice and Joanne.

"I'm sorry to have to tell you this, but there's a dead man on your dining room table. You know about it?"

"One couldn't very well *not* know about a body on one's dining room table, could one?" Alice asked reasonably.

Katherine joined the little group and tapped Alice on the shoulder. "Mother, I went to my room to get cigarettes from my handbag a few minutes ago," she said, "and on my way through the dining room I noticed that the centerpiece was bleeding all over your dining room table."

"Yes, dear. It's Mr. Reed," Alice and Joanne and Jeffers said.

"Yes, I know it's Mr. Reed," Katherine told them. "I was married to him, remember? What I want to know is, what are we going to do about it?"

"My goodness, don't young people have anything to talk about any more!" Alice exclaimed. "When I was a girl we talked about books and music and sex. Now all I seem to hear about is dead bodies on the dining room table."

Alice was prevented from continuing her reminiscences about the good old days by a roar from her husband, who emerged from the dining room. He was followed by George Endicott, visibly shaken and leaning on his wife for support.

"Alice! What is the meaning of this? Why is Jason Reed lying on our dining room table with a knife in his heart?"

"Oh, dear," Alice sighed. "It's just impossible to keep a secret in this house."

"Keep a secret!" Heatherton shouted. "Why in the world would you want to keep it secret that a man has been murdered?"

"It sounds so wicked, the way you say it, Henry," Alice reproached him. "I just thought—it happened so close to dinnertime—it would spoil everyone's appetite to learn about it right away. I was only going to save the news until it was more convenient."

Heatherton threw up his hands in mute despair. When he regained his voice, he spoke very softly to his wife. "We have all finished dinner," he said. "And we all seem to have discovered the body independently. Now, if you don't have any more inconvenient news for us, like the name of the person who pinned Reed's sport shirt to his chest with that knife, perhaps we could call the police and get him off our dining room table."

"Yes, of course, dear," Alice said sweetly. "If that's what you think right."

Atkins, who had stayed to help serve the food and collect the dishes afterward, overheard Heatherton's remark. "If you'll pardon me, Mr. Heatherton, I believe I was the first, sir, to discover Mr. Reed's . . . remains. After reporting the information to Mrs. Heatherton, I took the liberty of phoning the village authorities."

"Well done, Atkins," Heatherton said. "I'm glad someone in this house has some sense. We can expect the police, then, any minute?"

"No, sir. I was told they would be here, perhaps, in the morning."

"There! You see, Henry?" Alice remarked triumphantly. "The police not only wanted us to have our dinner, but get a good night's sleep as well."

"I'm sorry, madam. Their reasons weren't so humanitarian. It appears there has been a snowslide near the base of the mountain, and the road is closed. Work crews won't be able to clear it until morning."

"Does that mean we're expected to spend the night in the same house with that corpse?" Katherine asked. As the thought occurred to her, she added, "Not to mention the person or persons who made it a corpse?"

"Oh, dear, I hadn't thought of that," Alice said. "But you must be mistaken, Katherine. I know I didn't murder Jason, and I'm sure everybody else feels the same way."

"The fact remains," said Heatherton, "that Reed's body is on our dining room table. Go on, Atkins; did the police give you any instructions as to what we were to do until they arrived?"

"Yes, sir. I was told we were not to move the body until they had a chance to examine it. We may, however, cover it with a tablecloth, if we are so inclined."

"I think we are so inclined," Heatherton decided. "Is that all, Atkins?"

"No, sir. The person I spoke to was the sheriff. The telephone line went dead while I was speaking to him, but before it did, he deputized me to act in his absence."

"Why, Atkins!" Alice exclaimed. "Then you're a deputy sheriff, like on the television programs."

"Yes, madam," Atkins said miserably. "I'm afraid so."

"Well, that's fine. Then we know the matter is in capable hands, and we don't have to worry about it any more."

"Just a moment, Alice," Heatherton said. "I want to find out more about this. Atkins, are you going to solve this murder?"

"Oh, no, sir! I sincerely hope not!"

"No, of course not. Forgive me for doubting you, Atkins. But just what were your instructions?"

"I was to see that no one left the house, sir, until the proper authorities arrived."

"That means we'll all be under suspicion when the police get here," Jeffers told them. "I've written about situations like this a hundred times, and I know." He turned to look at Atkins to finish his statement. "And in the books I write, one particular person almost always turns out to have committed the murder."

"Yes, sir. Unfortunately this is real life, not farce."

"Now see here!" Heatherton interrupted. "We can't go around accusing each other of murder. Most of us had no reason to do it. George and Florence, for instance, didn't even know Reed until I brought them up here to the lodge."

"It didn't take long to learn to hate Jason, Father," Katherine said. "And if you want reasons for murder, I've got three hundred and sixty-five of them. One for every day of the year I was married to him."

"No, Katherine, that isn't right," Alice said. "You were married to Jason in 1960. That was a leap year. Three hundred and sixty-six."

"Thanks, Mother, for keeping the record straight. I hope you'll be available to say a few words for me at the execution."

"Of course I will, dear," said Alice, on whom sarcasm was lost. "What are mothers for, if not to speak up for their children?"

"Well, you can deal me out of this," Jeffers said. "I didn't even know Reed existed until I met him on the dining room table. He was on it. I was under it."

"Oh, but you did, my sweet," Katherine purred. "You met him Friday night, soon after we arrived. And the one meeting was ample reason for murder."

"I don't remember meeting him. But, come to think of it, I don't remember Friday night, either."

"Jason met us as soon as we came in the door," she told him. "He said something disparaging about the side of the street I was currently working, and then he recognized you. It seems a new book of yours is being published soon?"

"Yes, *Sweet Pterodactyl of Youth*. My first serious novel, after a bunch of mystery stories."

"Hmmm. Anyway, Jason was a sort of free-lance critic, and on the board of editors of one of the smaller book clubs. When he recognized you, he told you that it was his review of your book as 'the auto-biography of an adolescence that shouldn't have been lived, let alone written about' that kept the club from accepting the book. He added that the review was going to appear in the New York papers."

"Yes, I can see what made you think I might have murdered him. In fact, I just might stick another knife into him right now. But I must say I don't remember having done it before."

"I don't think the law requires that you remember committing the act, to be guilty," Katherine said. "Or even enjoy it. But in Jason's case, it would be a shame if you didn't."

Katherine and Jeffers stood together at one side of the fireplace. While they talked, the others had formed a semicircle around them to listen. After a moment of silence, Joanne left her place in the circle and went to stand with her sister and Jeffers.

"If you're looking for people who had a reason to murder Mr. Reed," she said, "I guess I had one, too."

"You, Joanne?" Alice asked. "Ridiculous! Why, you hated Jason from the moment Katherine brought him home. Surely nobody would kill someone she hated; it's so obvious."

"And besides," Jeffers put in, "it would have been impossible for a little girl like Miss Heatherton to commit this murder. It takes considerable strength to push a knife into a man's chest."

"Oh, let her confess to murder if she wants to," Katherine said. "I'm anxious to hear what Jason did to my little sister that made her think she wanted to kill him."

"It wasn't anything he did to me."

"I might have known. Jason was a bounder, but he was a selective bounder."

"It was something he did to Mother."

"To me? Oh, dear," Alice giggled. "I wasn't even aware that he looked twice at me," she amended.

"Mother, you've got a dirty mind," Katherine said.

"Will you please listen to me?" Joanne said, stamping her foot angrily. "I learned just last week that Jason has been cheating Mother for years.

"Jason Reed has been selling paintings to Mother ever since Kath-erine first brought him home," she explained to Jeffers. "Mother didn't know anything about art, but she understood abstract paintings. So Mother bought the paintings she understood from Jason, who got a commission for selling what he thought was junk. But the pictures she bought invariably turned out to be good and increased in value. Then Jason bought the pictures back, giving Mother a small profit, and resold them for exorbitant prices. Over the years, he's cheated Mother out of thousands of dollars."

"I think that's a pretty good motive for murder," Jeffers said. "Not only for Joanne, but for the whole Heatherton family. And that means the only ones in the house without a reason for killing Reed are the Endicotts."

George Endicott cleared his throat.

"No, George, don't!" Florence pleaded, putting her hand on her husband's arm.

"I might as well, Flo," he said, shaking her off. "It seems to be a night for confessions. Besides, I don't want anyone to think I'm the sort of man who wouldn't want to murder Jason Reed."

"Henry was only half right when he said we met Reed for the first time here at the lodge. I'd never met him before, but Flo had. When my electronics plant started making money, Flo and I moved out here and bought a house. Flo hired someone to help her decorate the place, and the someone turned out to be Jason Reed. He filled the house with a lot of expensive, uncomfortable furniture he called antique Early American. We learned later that he has a small factory upstate that turns out antiques to order for him. He clipped us for plenty, and I would gladly have strangled him."

"Well, it seems we've come full circle," Jeffers said. "When we started out, none of us had any reason to murder Reed. Now everybody has at least one reason."

"Maybe we ought to draw straws to see who gets the honor of hanging for the job," Katherine suggested.

"Mr. Heatherton, if I may be permitted to offer a suggestion . . ."

"Yes, Atkins. Please do," Heatherton said. "You seem to be the only one here who takes this matter seriously."

"I believe, sir, it is the custom of the police, in a case like this, to ask innumerable questions of everybody present. Perhaps your family and guests could be spared some inconvenience by preparing the answers in advance. Establishing an alibi, I think it's called."

"Good idea, Atkins," Endicott said. "If, for instance, we could learn what time Reed was killed, perhaps a few of us could eliminate ourselves from the list of suspects by not having had the opportunity to murder him."

"I believe I was the first to discover Mr. Reed's body," Atkins said. "That was shortly before eight o'clock. He . . . or it . . . was still quite warm at the time."

"Now you're talking my language," Jeffers said enthusiastically. "I happen to know that a body cools quite rapidly after death. If Reed was still warm when Atkins found him, he must have been murdered not more than fifteen or twenty minutes before eight."

"Wait just a minute!" Heatherton said after considering Jeffers' statement. "We all went upstairs to change for dinner at seven tonight. Endicott and I were back here in fifteen minutes, and the women came in shortly after. By seven thirty, at the latest, we were all in this room together."

"Well, thank goodness that's over," Alice said with a sigh.

"Thank goodness what's over?" Endicott asked, puzzled.

"Why, this silly murder business, of course. Henry just said we were all in here at the time Jason was murdered; therefore none of us could have done it, and it must have been a tramp or burglar. Now we can put the matter out of our minds and play parlor games, or something."

"Pardon me, Mrs. Heatherton," Atkins said, "but the local authorities may not take that attitude. They may even suggest, forgive me, that someone is not being completely accurate as to his whereabouts at the time of the murder."

"I suppose that's true," Heatherton said. "And I suppose we'll have the sheriff and his men—no offense, Atkins—hanging around our necks until they reach some conclusion."

"Yes, sir. I'm afraid so."

"Then why don't we just do what Katherine suggested in the first place?" Alice said. "If the police are going to come here and make a nuisance of themselves with questions and murders, why don't we just draw straws and pick someone to give them? Wouldn't it save us all, most of us, that is, a lot of trouble this weekend if we just made up a story to tell the police? Reached a conclusion for them, so to speak?"

"Mother!" Joanne exclaimed, aghast. "Are you suggesting we frame someone for murder just to keep from interrupting the weekend?"

"The way you say it, Joanne, makes it sound so barbarous. I really didn't mean it that way at all. I just thought if we gave the police someone to concentrate their attention on, it would save the rest of us a lot of inconvenience. After all, we know that none of us did it, and it would only be for a few hours, until the police caught the tramp or burglar who was responsible." Then Alice sighed and confessed her real reason. "Besides, it *would* get poor Jason off the dining room table."

"It sounds completely unethical," Katherine said. "But amusing."

"I must admit I'm thoroughly confused by this whole business," Heatherton said. "But in the twenty years Atkins has served me, his judgment has always proved sound. And since he represents the local authorities here, I'm going to leave the decision to him."

"Very well, sir, if you wish," Atkins said. "As a longtime retainer of the family, it is my opinion that Mrs. Heatherton's suggestion has considerable merit. As a deputy sheriff, I must add that a . . . subject . . . and a story should be chosen with great care. The police are known to possess a certain animal cunning which will make them difficult to deceive."

"Oh, Atkins, it always makes me feel so good to know that you agree with me," Alice said. "Now, how shall we go about picking a subject? Let's see, who are we least likely to miss?"

All eyes turned to Jeffers.

"Now, wait a minute. . . ."

"We might as well give them him," Heatherton said. "I don't believe he said a word to anybody until this Reed business came up."

"I'm sure he would have been friendlier," Alice said in Jeffers' defense, "if he'd been sober."

"I brought him up here," Katherine said. "But he hasn't been any use to me. I'm done with him."

"Well, I'm not," Joanne pouted. "In fact, I haven't even had a chance. I want to keep him."

"Now, now, baby; don't get excited," Alice tried to soothe her daughter. "It's only for a little while. We'll give him back to you when this is over."

"Please, ladies and gentlemen," Atkins broke into the discussion. "If I may say it, Mr. Jeffers is a bad choice. I don't think the police could be made to believe he killed Mr. Reed."

"Oh? And why not, I'd like to know?" Jeffers asked.

"Murder is an audacious and forceful act, Mr. Jeffers. Frankly, sir, you don't have the character."

"Oh, yeah? Why you . . . butler, you . . . I'll have you know I've got character enough to murder half a dozen like Reed."

"Well, Atkins is the authority around here," Katherine told him. "If he says you're out, you're out. Better luck next time, kid."

"That's all very well to say," Heatherton grumbled, "but now what are we going to do for a suspect to give the police officers?"

"I've concocted a story I think the police may believe," Atkins said. "The story is based on two facts: the first, that Mr. Reed's body is dressed in casual clothes; the second, that I saw Mrs. Endicott enter this room shortly before I discovered the body."

"You're mistaken, Atkins," Endicott said. "No one was out of this room between seven thirty and eight o'clock."

"Why, yes; I seem to remember . . ." Alice started. "While I was looking at pictures tonight, Florence stopped to . . . But maybe I shouldn't mention it."

"Nonsense, dear," Florence said. "I wasn't going to deny it. I . . . left my compact in my coat pocket and went out to the entry way to get it. But the light was out in the dining room as I passed through, so if the body was on the table then, I didn't see it."

"Of course not, Mrs. Endicott. I wouldn't have suggested it. It was just that having seen you gave me the idea for the story."

"Perhaps you'd better explain yourself, Atkins," Heatherton said quietly. "I don't understand this at all."

"In carrying out my duties as butler," Atkins began, "I could not help overhearing that Mr. Endicott has been trying to sell stock in his electronics company. Now, if we were to tell the authorities that the additional funds were not merely for expansion, but were a matter of life or death to the company . . ."

"Ridiculous!"

"Of course, Mr. Endicott. But the police might be led to believe it. And since it is common knowledge that Mr. Reed has for years made the better part of his living by selling paintings to Mrs. Heatherton, we might also convince the police that it was typical of Reed's character to boast to Endicott of being able to tie up all the available Heatherton cash by selling the pictures he brought up to the lodge."

"Not a doubt in the world," Katherine murmured. "It's Jason all over."

"That might give Endicott a motive," Jeffers said, "but still not the opportunity. If Reed was murdered shortly before eight . . ."

"But perhaps he wasn't. That's why Mr. Reed's casual dress is significant. It seems to imply that he was murdered before he had a chance to change for dinner. Therefore, closer to seven o'clock than eight."

"Remember that the body was still warm when you found it, Atkins. You pointed that out yourself."

"Yes, sir. But we have an electrically heated dumbwaiter that runs from the kitchen downstairs to the sleeping quarters upstairs. If someone, and for the purposes of our story we are assuming it to be Mr. Endicott, murdered Reed shortly after seven, he could place the body in the dumbwaiter and turn on the heat. Then his accomplice, we are assuming it to be Mrs. Endicott, could remove the body from the dumbwaiter and, using the serving cart to remove it, place the body on the table a few minutes before eight o'clock and it would still be warm.

"Mr. Endicott's alibi would be that he was in here when the murder was, apparently, committed. Mrs. Endicott, of course, would not have had the strength to do it alone."

There was a moment of silence while everyone fitted the pieces of Atkins' story together. As each convinced himself of the logic of the story, heads turned slowly to George and Florence Endicott.

"That's a pretty 'iffy' story, Atkins," Heatherton said at last.

"Of course, sir, since it's only a story. But it ought to give the police something to concentrate their attention on, until they turn up the real murderer."

"That's right," Alice said brightly. "It is only until the police find the tramp or burglar who really murdered poor Jason."

"I see there's a full bottle of gin and a damp vermouth cork on the coffee table," Katherine said, matching her mother's tone. "Would anybody care to join me in a mess of martinis?"

"I think I'd better," Florence said, "while I have the chance. But go light with that cork."

"And we'd better get to work and close this deal," Heatherton said to Endicott, "If you're going to be . . . ummm, tied up . . . for the next couple of days."

The group around the fireplace broke up into twos and threes and slowly spread to other parts of the room. Joanne stayed with Jeffers, and together they intercepted Atkins as he was about to leave.

"That was awfully clever of you, Atkins," Joanne said.

"Yes, it was," Jeffers agreed. "But of course, having seen Mrs. Endicott in the dining room was just blind luck, and anybody could have worked it out from there."

"Thank you, Miss Joanne, but I did no more than my duty," Atkins said. "Mr. Jeffers, I thought you, of all people, would see through my little deception. I didn't see Mrs. Endicott in the dining room, of course. But once I was sure of the other parts of the story it followed, logically, that she had to be there about the time I said she was."

"Hmmm. Yes, I thought it might be something like that," Jeffers lied. "You know, Atkins, if this new book of mine is as bad as Reed, and everybody else I've talked to, says it is, I may give up serious writing and go back to mystery stories. With your imagination and deductive skill, you ought to do pretty well in the mystery field. What say we get together and collaborate on a couple of things?"

"Thank you, sir, for suggesting it. But I'm afraid our stations in life are too far separated to permit any such collaboration.

"Yes, sir. I've spent forty years of my life working and studying to become a butler. To turn to writing now would be a step down the social scale that would break my poor old mother's heart. If you'll pardon me, sir, this unfortunate interlude has put me behind schedule and I must get back to work."

# The Return of Crazy Bill

## by Frank Sisk

As I drink a second cup of coffee, my eyes rove idly through the inside pages of the morning paper. Whatever I may have expected seems to be there: a quick recipe for marshmallow brittle, a speculative piece on the long range effects of LSD, an interview with a hundred-year-old man who has never drunk anything more intoxicating than dandelion wine, the bannered bargains to be had in chuck roast and honeydew melons at the local supermarkets. . . .

Torpidly I notice a straight news report datelined Bern, Switzerland. It concerns an inquest into the death of a woman I have never met, but as I read the several scraps of evidential matter thrice over, I find myself in a swift descent down the years—thirty of them—back to the days of my childhood when my world was bordered on the east by Indian Falls and High Ridge, on the south by Fournier's Meadow, on the west by Smith's General Store & Post Office, and on the north by the infinity of the future. Looming large in this world for a time, larger even than my parents, was Crazy Bill.

By our standards, Crazy Bill was old—forty at least. He had a scraggly graying beard and great popping green eyes, one of which was glass. He wore a high-crowned straw hat with a wide, wavy brim. He finally lost this hat, as you will see later.

Except for a fringe of gray hair that grew over his ears and joined the beard, he was bald. He always wore a checkered shirt open at the collar. His throat was scrawny. The sleeves were rolled halfway up his forearms, showing on the right one a tattoo of a snake coiled around an anchor. Invariably he wore a pair of faded blue overalls suspended from his sagging shoulders by pieces of rope. In one of the overall pockets high on his chest he carried cigar butts salvaged from around the steps of Smith's General Store. He broke these butts up and smoked them in a corncob pipe. His shoes were the thicksoled, yellow kind with leather loops at the back, and when they wore out, he threw them away in the woods and stole another pair from somewhere.

He roamed the woods, of course, and lived in a cave amid the ledges and fissures that flanked Indian Falls. Crazy Bill's Cave, we called it.

High Ridge, elevation three hundred feet, cannot be compared with the towering 3285 meters of Col Supérieur du Tour mentioned in the Switzerland news report, but we considered it in those days the steepest height on earth.

By "we," I mean myself and my younger brother Charlie, Roger Oliver and his little brother Austin, Fred Lyons, and Red Dacey. There were several others whose names I don't remember offhand, but those I've listed are still pictured in my mind as clearly as if I'd seen them only yesterday.

My brother Charlie is all freckles and ears. (He doesn't look like that now; the freckles have become floridity in a worried round face that neutralizes the ears.) Fred Lyons is undersized for his age, with a dimpled chin receding slightly. Roger Oliver is blond and blue-eyed and possesses a daredevil smile I secretly admire. His brother Austin, also blond, is possibly the quietest boy in the county, never venturing much beyond a monosyllable. And Red Dacey—well, he's somehow the color of sand: sandy hair, pale yellow eyebrows, a glint of ocher in the retina; and he bites his fingernails when things don't go his way. Red is the one who first called our attention to Crazy Bill; first learned about him from some mysterious source; first saw him in person, it seems.

We were blazing a trail, I remember, in the woods behind Indian Falls. Red Dacey's father had given him a birthday gift of a hunting knife in a beaded leather sheath, an impossible gift for the rest of us whose parents were dead set against knives. So there we were, doing as the Indians did, single file behind Red Dacey, who was nicking little chips off the saplings all the way across Fournier's Meadow and up the woodland slopes to the rockier ground until we came at last to the topmost cliff of High Ridge. Below us was a jagged gray drop, and off in the distance were the identifiable roof-tops of our family homes. The din of Indian Falls was so loud that we had to shout to be understood.

"The shortest way home is straight down," Roger Oliver yelled.

"What do you mean?" I yelled back.

"With a rope tied to this tree," he pointed to a gnarled dogwood, "we could let ourselves down the face of the cliff easy. If we had a rope, a long enough one."

"It's easier to walk around by the old path," Charlie piped up.

"Easier. Sure. And about three times longer. Besides, it wouldn't fool anyone who might be following us."

Austin Oliver nodded solemn agreement.

And Fred Lyons asked: "Who's following us, Roger?"

"Nobody that I know of. I mean *if,* that's all. *If* somebody was on our trail, they'd lose us right here. Like we'd walked off into thin air."

We found the concept intriguing, like so many of the ideas that Roger had, and we were beginning to speculate about acquiring a rope when Red Dacey broke in.

"You'd get killed," he said.

"Not if I had a strong, long rope," Roger replied.

"The rope don't matter any. By the time you were halfway down, Crazy Bill would reach out and grab you."

"Who's Crazy Bill?" I asked.

"Reach out from where?" from Charlie.

"He's got a cave halfway down the cliff," Red said.

"Crazy Bill?" Fred Lyons said nervously. "A cave?"

Red turned to Roger. "You mean you've never seen him?"

"I never even heard of him," Roger said.

"Well, it goes to show you ain't as smart as some people think you are," Red said. "Follow me. I'll show you the cave."

As we wended our way down the old path, I felt sure I was not the only skeptic present. Red had a habit of throwing a monkey wrench in the works whenever Roger came up with a new angle on adventure. I figured this was just one more scene-stealer.

Ten minutes later we arrived at the familiar clearing beside Ice Water Brook and, through squinting eyes, started a slow study of High Ridge's craggy face. We had all seen it a dozen times before and had never seen anything in particular because we had never been looking for anything like a cave.

"Well, there it is," Red said, pointing a finger.

"Where?" I asked.

"Halfway up to the left there. Where there's a ledge sticking out like a porch."

"I don't see it," Roger said.

"Look where I'm pointing and you will," Red said.

We bunched up behind him and took aim along his extended arm.

"I think I see it now," Charlie said. "Like a big crack in the cliff."

"That's it," Red said. "That's the entrance. And inside there's a room as big as a cellar."

I don't think I really saw anything, but I imagined I did and nodded my head. Red became a lawyer later in life, and I've heard he had a magic way with juries.

"I think I see it now," Fred Lyons said uncertainly.

"I still don't see a darn thing," Roger said.

"That's because you probably need glasses," Red said.

"Bushwah."

"All right, wise guy, but the last kid that Crazy Bill caught alone in the woods—well, he disappeared forever."

"Who was that?" Roger demanded.

"Billy Sneider."

"He moved to Syracuse. *Everyone* knows that."

"His *parents* moved to Syracuse. Not Billy."

"I never heard that before."

"It's true, though. The Sneiders moved away because they couldn't stand to live in a place where Billy just got lost."

"And you think it was Crazy Bill caught him?" Charlie asked, eyes wide.

"I can't prove it," Red said. "But I'm pretty sure."

"How come you know so much about all this?" Roger wanted to know.

"My father told me," Red said positively.

For the moment that ended the argument. In our young world a father's testimony was final. As I say, this all happened thirty years ago, before the coming of flower children.

A bit later, as we were beginning to wander back home, Red let out a hoot. "There he is. Up there on the ledge. Look quick."

We all turned fearfully.

"Did you see him?" Red asked excitedly. "He was standing there just as plain!"

"I think I saw him," Fred Lyons said.

"His face is all whiskers," Red said. "You saw him, didn't you, Austin?"

"Yes," Austin said.

"No, you didn't, Aussie," Roger said.

"Yes," Austin persisted.

"You're seeing things," Roger said. "There's nothing up there in those rocks. I'll prove it to you tomorrow without any question."

"How?" Fred Lyons asked.

"Wait and see," Roger said, smiling like a daredevil.

By some unspoken agreement we met the following morning after breakfast under the crabapple tree in Fournier's Meadow. I carried a bamboo cane. Charlie toted a baseball bat. Red wore his new knife and sheath. Roger had a hank of frayed rope (a discarded clothesline) looped over his shoulder. In a sense, we were armed against the contingency of evil.

"What are we going to do?" Fred Lyons asked apprehensively. He was equipped with a hammerless cap pistol.

"That's what I'd like to know," Red said, with a challenging look at Roger.

"I'm going to lower myself down to that cave with this rope," Roger said. "Let's go."

"You're crazy," Red said.

"We'll see who's crazy. You coming along?"

Again single file (the safest way to travel in the wilderness), we made our way up the summer slopes, where a few of Mr. Fournier's cows were ruminating, to the previously blazed trail that took us in about fifteen minutes to our goal. In unaccustomed silence we watched as Roger unshouldered the rope and tied an end of it to the dogwood tree. This rope didn't look long enough or strong enough to do the job, and finally I said so.

"Maybe you're right," Roger said. "I'll test it."

He found a boulder twice the size of a football and turned the rope around it twice and secured it with an impressive combination of knots. The boulder must have weighed more than a hundred pounds because it took two of us—Charlie and me—to nudge it along the ground to the edge of the cliff. Roger paid out the rope while Fred, Red, and Austin watched.

"Ready, get set," I said.

"Give me a hand with the rope, somebody," Roger said.

Austin jumped to his side.

"Not you, Aussie. You're too light."

Red was the heaviest, but he didn't move.

Fred Lyons, not much heavier than Austin, finally came forward and cautiously took some of the slack rope in both hands.

"Ready?" I asked.

Digging his heels into the stony ground, Roger nodded.

Charlie and I pushed the boulder over the side. The rope grew taut and began to pull Roger and Fred quickly forward. Fred was more hindrance than help. I grabbed the moving rope myself and reared backwards. That stopped the boulder's descent. Roger heaved a sigh.

"Now," he said, after a few seconds, "easy does it."

Together we began paying out the rope, a hand's width at a time. One-two, one-two, one—And suddenly we were flat on our backs with an end of the rope snapping at the air above us.

"Look at that rock bounce," Charlie was yelling.

I can hear it to this day, and especially well this morning, as it slams its way downward from outcropping to ledge until at last it concludes its bruising course in a muffled thud, which means it is half buried in the sod near Ice Water Brook. (The news story from Switzerland reports that Miss Miriam Ryman, falling a thousand meters from a glacial precipice, was found to have broken every bone in her body when recovered two days later from a snowfilled moraine.)

The next afternoon, we found one of Crazy Bill's shoes. It happened as we were engaged in one of our recurring expeditions to learn the source of Ice Water Brook. We never did find this source, as I recall, but each exploratory trip always carried us a little farther upstream and into a new realm of speculation.

"I bet it begins up on Sachem Hill," Charlie was saying.

"How far is that?" Fred asked.

"Five or six miles, at least," Charlie said.

"Hey, take a look here," Red called from a thicket of cattails.

We hastened to his side. There amid a lush crop of skunk cabbage was a mildewed shoe with a big hole in the sole. It was a man's yellow work shoe, a leather loop at the back, and somehow it seemed to menace us by its very emptiness.

"Crazy Bill's," Red said in a whisper.

We kept staring at that shoe in horrified fascination.

"I bet he's watching us," Red whispered again.

Peering into the alders and birches that surrounded us, we expected to see wicked green eyes (one of which we now knew to be glass, for Red Dacey had been intermittently describing Crazy Bill in minute detail) taking our measure before an all-out assault. Then we were running headlong downstream, except for Roger, who limited himself to a rapid walk, though he looked suspiciously from side to side.

A couple of days later we found the straw hat in Mr. Fournier's apple orchard. The apples were still green and hard. Again it was Red who identified the old hat as Crazy Bill's.

Roger contested the claim. "It's just any old hat. Probably belongs to one of the men who were spraying here last week."

"It's Crazy Bill's," Red said smugly.

"How can you tell?" I asked.

"I've seen him wearing it."

"Where?"

"Down at Smith's."

"He goes to Smith's?" Roger asked scornfully. "Leaves his cave and goes down to Smith's?"

"Every Saturday morning," Red said.

"I'd just like to see that," Roger said.

"When's Saturday?" Charlie asked.

"Tomorrow," Fred Lyons said. He was the only boy around who kept track of time during summer vacation.

The next morning we were loitering, not too inconspicuously perhaps, in front of Smith's General Store & Post Office. To pass the time we were chewing jawbreakers that stained our lips along the chromatic scale from bright red to nauseous violet.

A little after nine, when the mail was officially up in the rental boxes, this old man—all of forty—drove a slow-moving, slack-backed horse with wagon to the high curb in front of Smith's. He was hatless and his head was bald. He had a beard. His checkered shirt was open at the throat to a puff of gray hair. In short, he was exactly as I have described Crazy Bill earlier, even to the tattoo on his right forearm.

"Is that him?" Fred Lyons asked through orange-colored lips.

Red Dacey nodded, obviously pleased with himself.

Crazy Bill climbed down off the wagon and hung a feed bag over the horse's bowed head. His glass eye glittered fiercely.

"Gee whiz!" Charlie said in a low voice.

Crazy Bill gave the old horse an affectionate pat, then entered Smith's.

I remember wondering why he should like horses and hate kids. Another incongruency half came to mind also: where would a cave dweller keep a horse and wagon like that?

"I'm going to buy a brand new rope," Roger Oliver was saying.

"Yes," Austin said.

"What for?" Red asked.

"To lower myself down to that cave," Roger said. "If there's any such thing as a cave."

"You'll find out," Red said.

"I'll find out a lot of things, maybe," Roger said.

"Like what?" Red said.

"Like the truth," Roger said.

"Oh, yeah?" Red seemed to be getting mad about it. "A lot you know about the truth. Besides, a good rope'll cost you probably more than a dollar."

"I got two dollars saved up," Roger said, and without further argument he left us on the run to get his savings.

We hung around a while longer, the rest of us, and pretty soon Crazy Bill came out of Smith's with a few pieces of mail in his hand and nosed around the stone steps until he found a cigar butt of suitable length, which he pocketed. Then he took the feedbag off his horse and, as he climbed aboard the creaking wagon, we scattered to the four winds, full of the mysterious depravity that we had seen close up.

Early that evening, just after suppertime, Mr. Fournier and his beagle found Roger Oliver's broken body at the foot of High Ridge. The state police came and investigated. They even asked Charlie and me a few questions and they smiled when we told them about Crazy Bill. In the end, Roger's death was attributed to the accidental breaking of the rope.

We kids knew better. We knew Roger would never spend his hard-saved money on a rope not strong enough for the job.

A few Saturdays later, my father and I were coming out of Smith's when Crazy Bill drove up.

"There he is, Pa," I whispered excitedly. "The man I've been telling you about."

"You mean Jim Punch?"

"Crazy Bill we call him. He's the man who killed Roger."

My father's face grew stern. "Stop that nonsense, boy. The man on the wagon is Jim Punch. He lives with his crippled old mother over in Palmerston. A bit simple, perhaps, but he wouldn't hurt a fly."

"But he lives in a cave in High Ridge," I insisted.

"He lives on a hardpan farm in Palmerston," my father said.

"But *somebody* had to cut the rope," I said. "It was new. It wouldn't just *break*, would it?"

"Don't you remember what the police said, boy? The rope was likely cut by the flinty edge of the rock formation. Either that or it had a flaw."

That's what the police said. They said it thirty years ago, before investigatory techniques had attained certain refinements quite commonplace today, and intuitively I have always felt the police were wrong.

The inquest into the violent death of Miss Miriam Ryman proves how right I was. For instance, a microscopic examination of the broken strand of nylon rope found around Miss Ryman's waist convinced the Swiss authorities that a sharp knife had performed the severance.

Suspicion that Miss Ryman's death might not be accidental was first aroused, according to the news story, when her fiance, Leonard Hull, a junior partner in the New York law firm of Dacey & Mitchell, went to the police with a tale of passion and jealousy.

Miss Ryman was the private secretary to the firm's senior partner, W. R. Dacey, who had conceived an ungovernable passion for her. Though married himself and the father of three children, Dacey would not listen to reason. Upon hearing of Miss Ryman's betrothal to Hull, he flew into a fit of jealous rage, but several days later, apparently reconciling himself to the inevitable, he had suggested a combined business and pleasure trip to Switzerland. The pleasure consisted of skiing and mountain climbing and ended for Hull with a broken ankle.

"I was in a cast that fatal day Miriam and Bill decided to try conquering Les Trois Cols," Hull allegedly told police. "We were to leave for Paris the following morning. Knowing Bill's dog-in-the-manger complex, I should have . . ."

W. R. Dacey. William. Bill. Not until this morning did I realize this was Red's given name.

# A Dash of Murder

## by Jack Morrison

It was incredible that on such a clear, bright, innocent day Miss Helen Cranshaw, a somewhat dowdy, middle-aged spinster, should find herself suspected of murder. Such tragedies were usually accompanied by rain or dark clouds with, perhaps, a touch of fog. At least they always were in the detective stories she was so fond of reading. But nature in real life, it seemed, had no sense of atmosphere. No perspective, either.

Perhaps, too, if it had been anything but a delightfully bright summer day, Miss Cranshaw could have better accepted her predicament. As it was, she still couldn't believe in this awful thing that had happened to her. At any moment, she thought, they would come and tell her it had all been a macabre joke, a terrible mistake.

She sat in a small room, lost somewhere in the vast stone fortress that was City Hall, and stared in disbelief at the patch of blue sky just visible through the tiny barred window. They had left her alone to "think it over," as that Sergeant What's-His-Name had said. But they would be back.

Of course she had denied everything. How absurd it was that anyone would think she had poisoned her dear sister and her sweet little niece! All this talk about an affair with her sister's husband. An affair with that awful man, Henley Brooks? Why, it was simply incredible. She had never liked Henley. Well, not for many years anyway. She had opposed her sister's marrying him, but Ruth wouldn't listen to her.

Well, poor Ruth had made the best of a bad thing. And their little girl, Elizabeth. No sweeter child could be found.

She put her hands over her face once again to try to blot out the horrible picture that came periodically to haunt her—the picture of Ruth and the little girl sprawled there on the floor of their home—as she had seen them through the window last night. Was it only last night? Good Lord, it seemed ages ago. But then, she hadn't slept. They hadn't let her sleep.

She heard footsteps and muffled conversation in the corridor outside. Instinctively, she began fussing with her hair. It was sheer force of habit. Better to leave it alone, she thought, be what she was. Then, surely, they would understand that a dashing ladies' man like Henley Brooks wouldn't look twice at her.

The door opened and Sergeant Somebody-Or-Other and his assistant came in. The sergeant was still wearing his false smile as he sat down opposite her at the small table and placed a folder in front of him.

My case, she thought in a sudden panic, looking at the folder. *The case of the Commonwealth vs. Helen Cranshaw.*

The other man, who never smiled, stood by the door, his arms folded. As though she would made a break for it!

"Now, Miss Cranshaw," the sergeant said in a voice that tried to be pleasant but seemed to her to be edged with malice, "are you ready to cooperate with us?"

"I thought I had been very cooperative, Sergeant . . . Sergeant . . ."

"Halliday, ma'am."

"Yes, Sergeant Halliday. You asked me to tell the truth and I've told it. I really don't know what more you could want."

"Miss Cranshaw," Halliday said, hunching his big shoulders and leaning forward, "I hate to have to keep going back over the same ground, but I guess I'll have to. Now, let's go back to the beginning. You were with your sister yesterday afternoon. It was your regular Thursday afternoon visit, right?"

"That is correct."

"Now, you've told us you remember seeing the container of iced tea on the counter in the kitchen, right?"

"That's right. Ruth always made up a container of strong tea first thing in the morning these summer days so she could pour it over ice cubes anytime she wanted it."

"Okay. And you even admit knowing that the rat poison was in the cupboard in a green can, within easy reach, right?"

"Of course, but that doesn't . . ."

"All right, let's not get into another argument," Halliday said, holding up a hand as though to ward her off. "Let's go on. You left the Brooks home just before Mrs. Brooks and her daughter sat down for their usual four o'clock snack, right?"

"That is correct. I'm on a diet and, besides, I don't drink tea."

"And you went to the hospital to visit Brooks."

"Well, it was hardly a visit. Ruth had mixed up some cookies for him, but she hadn't baked them in time to take them with her when she visited him in the morning. She asked me to drop them off and I did."

"Then you returned to the Brooks home last night. Why?"

"I told you. I don't know why exactly. I—I just had an odd feeling, that's all—that something was wrong."

"An odd feeling, huh?" Halliday said with ill-concealed skepticism. He sighed and opened his folder. "Miss Cranshaw, we've determined that the poison was already in the tea when Mrs. Brooks and her daughter sat down to drink it at four o'clock. As far as we can discover, you were the only other person in the house before that time. And you're the only person we can find who had a motive."

"How dare you say that?" Miss Cranshaw snapped.

"You deny you were having an affair with Henley Brooks?"

"For the hundredth time, yes!"

Halliday picked up a sheet of paper from the folder.

"And you deny any knowledge of this letter we found in your home?"

"Naturally," Miss Cranshaw said, folding her arms defensively.

"Miss Cranshaw, I'm going to read this letter to you once again." He slipped on a pair of horn-rimmed glasses that made him look, Miss Cranshaw thought, quite owlish, and read:

" 'Dearest Helen—' " He glanced quickly at her for some reaction, found none and continued: " 'I have told you repeatedly that our situation is impossible. Ruth absolutely refuses to give me a divorce because of the child. You know I still feel the same way about you, but I think it best for all concerned that we try our utmost to forget about each other. There will be no more secret meetings. I can't bear them under the circumstances. Let this be the last communication between us. I love you. Henley.' "

"That letter," Miss Cranshaw said indignantly, "is an absolute fraud."

"It's in Brooks's handwriting and he told us he wrote it."

"Oh, of course he wrote it. Sergeant, I don't want to tell you your business, but I've read quite a few detective stories and I know a little about crime detection. Now, isn't it clear to you that Henley Brooks is the killer? He married my sister for her money in the first place, and he wanted to get rid of her so it would all be his and he could be free to chase his other women. He never loved my sister, and he hated his daughter."

Halliday sighed and glanced at the man by the door.

"Miss Cranshaw," he said in a weary voice, "can't you get it

through your thick . . . I mean, don't you remember that Henley
Brooks is in the hospital, has been since the automobile accident
two weeks ago, unable to move?"

Miss Cranshaw dismissed that minor fact with an impatient wave
of her hand.

"I know all that," she said, "but I'm sure you realize, sergeant,
that as the city's best criminal lawyer, Henley has all sorts of un-
derworld connections. It would have been easy for him to hire someone to plant that letter in my home and to poison my poor sister
and niece."

"Miss Cranshaw, we've been all through that. You told us yourself
the house was locked when you got there last night. We found all
the doors and windows locked securely from inside. And you also
said neither your sister nor her daughter was the type to let in
strangers. Now, how could a hired killer get in?"

"Well, really, sergeant, that's for you to figure out."

Halliday blinked at her.

"Okay," he said with resignation. "Here's another piece of information we just picked up. Isn't it true that you were once engaged
to Henley Brooks yourself? And isn't it true that after you broke up,
you never went out with another man again?"

Miss Cranshaw cupped a hand over her mouth.

"But, sergeant," she protested, "that was years ago. I was a foolish
young girl. But I finally saw through him. He was only after my
father's money. It was I who broke off with him. And then he went
after Ruth. Oh, I tried to warn her, but she wouldn't listen. As for
never going out with another man—well, I was just too busy, that's
all."

"But why didn't you tell us about it before, Miss Cranshaw?"
Halliday asked. "Did you think it would be too incriminating?"

"Not at all. I—I just forgot about it, that's all."

But she was flustered when she saw the narrow look of disbelief
come into Halliday's eyes. It made her angry. She leaned forward
and waggled a finger under the sergeant's chin.

"The trouble with you, sergeant, is that you lack imagination,"
she said, her eyes flashing with anger. "If everything isn't cut and
dried and black and white, you're lost."

"Now, wait a minute . . ."

"No, I mean it. You've deduced that I killed my sister and niece
simply because you don't have the imagination to conceive of any

other answer. You should read detective stories, sergeant. Then you'd know that the obvious answer is never the right one."

Halliday glanced again at his partner, sighing his annoyance.

"Thanks for the advice," he said sourly. He closed the folder. "Well, I see we're not going to get anywhere here. Get her coat, Joe."

"Where are we going?"

"For a little ride."

So that's what they're up to, Miss Cranshaw thought as the police car pulled up in front of her late sister's home. They thought they could rattle her by exposing her to the scene of the crime. Well, she would show them that she didn't rattle easily.

But, despite herself, she felt a little queasy as they entered the house. She struggled to get control of herself.

A man whom Halliday addressed as Roy came down the front stairs to meet them.

"Where's McGuire?" Halliday asked him.

"Upstairs checking around. He's going through the little girl's room now. Never saw so many toys."

"Did the lab men have anything to say before they left?"

"Yeah. There was enough arsenic in the iced tea to kill two horses. And they got some prints off the container—Mrs. Brooks's and her daughter's, as expected, but they also got one pretty clear one of somebody else."

"Oh, yeah? Whose?"

"Helen Cranshaw's."

Miss Cranshaw emitted a little gasp. The three men turned to look at her.

"Well, really, sergeant," she said, "what does that prove? Perhaps I did touch the container. I'm—I'm fussy that way. When I'm talking to someone, I'm constantly fidgeting, moving things about. It's—it's a habit."

"We'll talk about that later," Halliday said, scowling. "Right now, I want to try an experiment. We're going to re-enact your visit here yesterday. Okay?"

"Very well, but it seems a silly waste of time."

"Joe, here, will be Mrs. Brooks. You tell him what to do."

Miss Cranshaw felt very foolish. Joe didn't look a bit like her sister. But she acted out the charade.

Passing through the dining room on the way to the kitchen, Miss Cranshaw was appalled to find two chalked outlines on the rug where the bodies had been. She stepped carefully around them as one might step around a grave.

The large kitchen was spotlessly clean. There in a drying rack were the bowls, measuring cup, baking pan, and other utensils her sister had used to bake the cookies. At the opposite end, beneath a large window, was a table and four chairs.

A milk bottle was found to represent the iced tea container. Miss Cranshaw took up a position near it and directed Joe to stand by the sink.

"This is where we spent most of the time," she said. "Ruth was doing the dishes and checking the cookies in the oven while we talked."

"Did Mrs. Brooks leave the kitchen at any time?" Halliday asked.

"Not that I recall."

"Where was the little girl all this time?"

"Oh, around the house somewhere. No one had to worry about Elizabeth. She was an exceptionally well-behaved child. That's why Ruth was able to leave her alone in the house when she made those morning visits to Henley."

Halliday found a jar to represent the can of poison. He asked Miss Cranshaw to place it in the cupboard in the position in which she had last seen it.

By standing on her tiptoes and grasping one of the cupboard supports, Miss Cranshaw was able to place the jar on the shelf. But as she stepped away, she noticed something on the fingers of the hand that had held the cupboard support. She smelled it and then tasted it.

"Miss Cranswhaw," Halliday said, "what do you think you're doing?"

But Miss Cranshaw was silent. She was thinking.

"Miss Cranshaw, if you're ready we'll get on with it," Halliday said. He turned to Roy. "Is that about the spot where the poison was found?"

"Just about."

"Okay, now Miss Cra . . ."

But Miss Cranshaw had wandered over to the kitchen table. Halliday jammed his big fists into his hips and stood watching her in silent exasperation.

"I remember," Miss Cranshaw said, mostly to herself, "Ruth's saying she had made up the cookie batter before she left for the hospital. I'm sure she would have left it out. It would stiffen up too much if she put it in the refrigerator."

"Thanks for the cooking lesson," Halliday said. "I'll remember that next time I bake cookies." The two detectives chuckled. "Now, can we get on with the re-enactment, please?"

"In a moment, sergeant," she said.

She picked up one of the kitchen chairs and carried it to the cupboard. She placed it beneath the shelf that had held the poison, stepped back, and studied the scene carefully.

"Miss Cranshaw . . ." Halliday tried again to get through to her.

"Sergeant," she said, "you do want to solve this case, don't you? Then please give me a moment to exercise my imagination."

Halliday threw up his hands.

Miss Cranshaw walked into the dining room and he followed her helplessly. She stood staring thoughtfully about the room until her eyes lit on the telephone table. With sudden purpose, she strode up to it. On it, besides the phone, were two directories and a note pad and pencil. She stood staring down at the directories and then lifted the telephone from its cradle and looked it over.

"I believe," she said, "that my niece had a little toy doctor's set containing a pair of rubber gloves. Did your men find it, by any chance?"

"Yeah," Roy spoke up. "We did find a pair of kid's rubber gloves in a set like that."

"Gloves," Halliday said, looking first at Miss Cranshaw and then at Roy. "Say, what's going on here?"

"Oh, this is awful," Miss Cranshaw moaned and collapsed into one of the dining room chairs. "Simply awful."

"What's awful?" Halliday demanded angrily.

"It was poor little Elizabeth who poisoned the tea," she said, burying her face in her arms.

"What?" Halliday exploded.

Miss Cranshaw sat up quickly, her tear-filled eyes suddenly angry.

"That awful Henley Brooks," she said. "I always knew he was a terrible person, but I never thought he would stoop to this. He should be made to suffer the way poor Ruth and Elizabeth suffered."

"Miss Cranshaw," Halliday said, "will you kindly tell me what you're talking about?"

"Don't you see, sergeant," she said. "Henley must have telephoned here yesterday morning after Ruth left for the hospital. He told

Elizabeth to put the poison in the tea, probably telling her it was a special treat of some kind."

Halliday just stared at her.

"Then, I suppose," she went on, "he told her to put on the rubber gloves so she wouldn't leave fingerprints. He probably told her the stuff had to be handled with rubber gloves. But what Henley didn't know was that the cookie batter was in the kitchen. Elizabeth kept dipping her fingers in it as she went about following his directions.

"You'll find a smear of it on the inside of the cupboard and—" she lifted the telephone from its cradle "—there's some here on the phone, too."

"But . . . but . . ." Halliday stammered.

"And, oh yes, if you'll look at the topmost phone directory, you'll find the print of a child's heel, still quite clear. She had to put the directories on the kitchen chair to reach the poison. Oh, the poor dear!"

Miss Cranshaw appeared on the verge of breaking down and Halliday seemed uncertain whether to humor her or have her committed to a mental institution. He decided on the former.

"Now, now, Miss Cranshaw," he purred. "You've been through an awful lot in the last twenty-four hours. You need a rest."

"Hey, sarge," Joe said. "Maybe she's got something. It fits in. Brooks knew his daughter would be home alone yesterday morning, right? He also knew that Miss Cranshaw visited her sister every Thursday afternoon, right? And he knew Miss Cranshaw don't drink tea, so there was no chance of his frame-up blowing up on him. Get it?"

"Nuts," Halliday said. "Look, say she is right, just for argument. How we going to make a case like that stand up in court?"

"The sergeant is right," Miss Cranshaw said. "We need—what's the term?—a clincher."

Just then, heavy footsteps were heard on the stairs in the hall. The other detective—McGuire—came into the dining room on the run, holding aloft a small red book.

"Hey, fellows," he said breathlessly. "Look what I found in the kid's room!"

Halliday took the book. It was a diary.

"Read the last entry," McGuire said. "The one for yesterday."

Halliday riffled the pages to the last entry. There, in the painful scrawl of a child still mastering the art of writing, he found these words, which he read aloud:

"Daddy called with a surprise. I put Magic Dust from a green can in our tea. Daddy said it will make us very happy. He said not to tell Mommy."

Halliday looked at Miss Cranshaw.

"My God," he said. "You were right!"

"Read on, sarge," McGuire said, excitedly. "There's more."

Halliday read the rest of the entry:

"Then I put Magic Dust in Daddy's cookies. Now he will be happy, too."

They stood frozen, looking at each other, for a few silent seconds.

"Get on that phone, Joe," Halliday ordered. "Call the hospital. We've got to stop Brooks from eating those cookies."

But it was too late. As Joe soon learned from the hospital, Henley Brooks had enjoyed his wife's cookies for dessert at lunchtime and had shortly thereafter died in terrible convulsions, just as his wife and daughter had died the night before.

Joe replaced the telephone, Miss Cranshaw resumed her seat and stared blankly into space. It was just too terrible for tears.

Halliday walked past her and patted her clumsily on the shoulder. He dropped the little red diary on the table and started for the door.

"You fellows clean up here," he said. "I'm going downtown. And on my way, I think I'll stop off at a bookstore."

"What for?" Joe asked.

"I'm going to buy me a batch of detective books," he said. "I've got a lot of reading to do."

# Strange Prey

## by George C. Chesbro

"It is most difficult to know to whom we are speaking; in this troubled world the Civilized and the Savage wear identical trappings." *Senator Thaag, speaking before the U.N. General Assembly.*

It was starting again; someone was near.

Victor Rafferty looked up from the milky-blue water in time to see a squat, balding man with a limp emerge from the locker room at the opposite end of the pool. The man knelt clumsily in the gutter and grunted as he splashed handfuls of the cold water into his armpits and across his hairy chest.

Rafferty frowned with displeasure and stared down into the water at his own legs with their large, jagged patches of fish-white scar tissue that registered neither heat nor cold. He knew, of course, that the athletic club was open to any of its members at any time; yet this man had chosen a piece of the afternoon that Victor had come to think of as his own. The pool was usually deserted at this hour, enabling Victor to swim endlessly back and forth rebuilding his damaged body, savoring the silence in his mind that came only when he was alone and at peace.

There wasn't any pain yet. The man was still too far away. Now there was only the familiar pressure in Victor's ears as if he were ascending in a plane, an agonizing buzzing sound that seemed to emanate from a vast, dark abyss somewhere behind his eyes.

The man was swimming in Victor's direction, struggling through the water with a ragged crawl. He drew closer, and Victor pressed his fingers hard against the chlorine-bleached tiles as the noise and pressure were suddenly transformed into a needle-strewn veil that seemed to float beneath his skull, lancing his brain as it closed around his mind. It is so much worse with strangers, he thought as he waited for knowledge of the man, which he knew would come next.

"Swimming," the man said, spewing water and blowing hard. He was hanging onto the edge of the pool, a few inches away from

Victor. "Best all-'round conditioner there is. A man can't do enough of it."

Victor smiled and nodded through a haze of pain. The man pushed off the side and began to swim back toward the shallow end. Immediately the pain began to recede until finally there was only the residue of pressure and buzzing.

Rafferty knew the man was an accountant, suffered from hypertension, and had a headache that had been with him since early in the morning. He was also worried about his wife.

Madness, Victor thought grimly, rising and reaching for his towels.

He paused inside the locker room and stared at his naked image in one of the full-length mirrors that lined the walls. At forty, he was neither exceptionally handsome nor vain. It was not narcissism that held him motionless before the glass but rather fascination with the structure reflected there, the structure that housed his being; a body that should have been, by all the laws of probability, destroyed in the automobile accident four months ago. His hair was grayer now, and he was still too thin, but the swimming should remedy that; Roger had said so. At least he was alive.

But was he *well?*

Rafferty stepped forward so that his face was only a few inches from the glass. He reached up with his hand and slowly separated the hairs on the right side of his scalp to reveal a long, thread-thin scar that began an inch above the hairline and snaked down and along the side of his head and around to the base of his skull. He touched the wound, pressing on it with the tips of his fingers, first gently and then with increased pressure. There was no pain; there was hardly any sensation at all. Roger and his team had done a beautiful job of inserting the steel plate.

No, it was not the wound or the piece of metal that was causing the agony. He was fairly certain of that now. Other people; *they* were the source of his pain. In which case, Victor mused, he must indeed be going mad.

He stepped back but continued to gaze at his flat, scarred reflection. Perhaps it would have been better to die; better that than to suffer this ruptured consciousness that warped his senses and made even the close physical presence of his wife a fount of unbearable discomfort. Too, it was getting worse; his *awareness* of the man in the pool had been sharper, more distinct than ever before.

He knew now he should have told Roger about the pain and the images from the beginning. Why hadn't he? Victor wondered. Was it possible that he was so afraid of discovering the truth that he would wrap himself in his own silence before allowing himself to be told that his brain was permanently damaged . . . or that he was dying? Or was it a different fear, this ten-fingered hand that clawed at the inside of his stomach every time he even considered describing to anyone his symptoms?

Victor forced himself to walk away from the mirror. Then he dressed quickly. He lighted a cigarette and was not surprised to see that his hand was trembling. He was due in Roger's office in half an hour and he had decided to tell Roger everything, ignoring the possible consequences.

Victor wondered how the neurosurgeon would react when he was told his famous patient thought he could read minds.

It came as always; tongues of molten metal licking the scorched, exhausted sands of his mind; dagger thrusts that bled into a psychic pool of images and sounds that he could *feel* as well as hear as he approached the woman behind the desk.

"Dr. Burns will see you in a few moments," the receptionist said in her most professional tone. She'd spoken those words to him at least forty times in the last four months and her tone never changed. "If you'll be kind enough to go in and sit down . . . "

Victor thanked her and walked the few paces down the corridor into the large waiting room with its magenta walls and overstuffed, red leather chairs. He selected a magazine from a mahogany rack and tried to focus his attention on the lead article while waiting for the man who could hold the key to his sanity—or his life. He had barely enough time to finish the first paragraph before there was the soft click of a door opening and Victor looked up at the tall, lean frame of the man who had put his body back together after the accident. Roger was studying him through large, steel-rimmed eyeglasses that made his thin face seem all out of proportion.

"Come in, Vic," the doctor said at last, motioning Victor into a huge, booklined office. "It's good to see you; first interesting case I've had all day."

Victor strode quickly into the office, avoiding the other man's eyes. He automatically stripped to his shorts and sat down on the long, leather examination table. He studied Roger as the doctor glanced through the reams of charts and other papers that were the record of Victor's recovery.

He'd known Roger Burns for some time, even before the accident.

In fact, he had designed the award-winning house in which Roger and his wife lived. He knew Roger to be—like many great men—lonely and estranged, the victim as well as possessor of prodigious skills. Victor could understand that. Still, he resented the cold, clinical detachment which Roger brought to this new doctor-patient relationship, an attitude which he knew was prompted by Roger's concern about his condition. Victor would have discerned this even without the flood of anxiety that flowed from the other man's mind; it was written in his eyes. He'd probably been talking to Pat.

"How was your walk?" Roger had risen from the desk and walked across the room to a huge bank of filing cabinets. He drew a bulging file from one of the sliding drawers and began clipping X-ray negatives along the sides of a huge fluoroscope suspended from the ceiling.

"I didn't walk."

Roger's eyes flicked sideward like a stroke from one of his scalpels. "You should walk. The exercise is good for you."

"I've been swimming."

Roger nodded his approval and walked toward Victor, who lay back on the table and closed his eyes against the sudden onrush of pain.

"Elizabeth is giving a cocktail party Friday evening for one of the new congressmen," Roger said, glancing back over his shoulder at one of the X-rays. "You and Pat be sure to be there. I'll need someone to talk to."

Victor grunted as the surgeon's long, deft fingers probed and pulled at the muscle and bone beneath the fresh scar tissue on his arms and legs. Roger was bent over him, following the path of the thin, bright beam of light that was lighting the interior of his eyes.

Victor reached out and touched a thought. "Why are you thinking that my intelligence may be impaired?"

There was a sudden wave of anxiety that flowed across his mind like a cold wave as Roger shut off the light and straightened up.

"What makes you think I consider that a possibility?" Roger's voice was too tight and controlled.

Victor stared hard into the other man's eyes, very conscious of the beads of sweat that were lining up like soldiers across his forehead. There would never be a better time. "Just guessing," Victor said at last. The words tasted bitter on his tongue and he felt empty inside. "What *do* you think?"

The light came back on and the examination continued. Victor fought to keep his mind away from the pain and the noises.

"You're a walking miracle," Roger said, resuming his probing, and Victor swallowed a bubble of hysterical laughter that had suddenly formed in his throat. "I don't have to tell you how lucky you are to be alive. How many men do you know who've had half their skull crushed and lived to worry about their intelligence?" He paused and seemed to be waiting for some reply. Victor said nothing.

"Your most serious injury was the damage to your brain," Roger continued matter-of-factly. "You're obviously aware of that."

"And?"

"I don't know. Really. There's so little that we actually know for certain about this kind of injury. It's still much too early to know for sure how any of your functions are going to be affected." Roger hesitated, trying to read the expression on Victor's face. "I'm not putting you off," he said very quietly. "I really don't know. Every rule in the book says that you should be dead or in the terminal stage of coma."

"I owe my life to you," Victor said evenly, noticing the slight flush that appeared high on the cheeks of the other man. In a moment it was gone. "I think there's something you're not telling me."

"Pat tells me that you seem . . . *distracted* lately." Roger had returned to his desk and was writing something on one of the charts in his folder. "She says you've become very absentminded. I understand you haven't even been . . . close . . . with her since the accident."

"You need a record of my love life?"

"No," Roger said, suddenly slapping the folder shut. "I need information. That is, I need information if I'm ever going to answer your questions. Have you lost the desire to make love?"

"No," Victor said, searching for the right words. How could he explain how it hurt his *mind* to be so close? "I've been . . . upset . . . worried. You can understand that." He hurried on, conscious of the rising note of impatience in his voice, eager to leave the subject of his relationship with his wife. "You must know what parts of my brain have been damaged. And you must know what happened to others with the same kind of injury."

Roger was preparing to take X-rays. Victor rose from the couch and walked to the machine.

"Much of the left cortex has been destroyed," Roger said. His voice was low, muffled by the lead shield and punctuated by the intermittent buzzing of the machine at Victor's head. "Usually, the patient dies. If not, there is almost always a loss of coordination and speech. For some reason that I don't pretend to understand, you don't seem to have suffered any appreciable loss of any kind. Of course there's no way of knowing what damage has been done farther down in the brain tissue."

"You mean I could drop dead at any moment. Or I could be losing my mind."

The machine continued to click, recording its invisible notes. "I can tell you this: neurosurgeons all over the world are following your case. You may or may not be the world's greatest architect, but you're certainly the leading medical phenomenon."

Victor swallowed hard. "I—I wasn't aware that many people knew anything about it."

Roger came out from behind the shield and repositioned the machine. "I haven't published anything yet although, eventually, I'd like to if you'll give your consent. I need your permission, of course. I'll need more time to run tests and chart your progress."

"How did it get so much publicity?"

Roger looked surprised. "Vic, there isn't a major city in the world that doesn't have one of your buildings. You're like public property. Then there was the fantastic way you recovered from the injuries. Didn't you suppose people would be interested?"

"It never occurred to me . . . " Victor's voice trailed off, stifled by the thought of a world watching his disintegration; cold, dispassionate men examining him like a worm wriggling beneath a microscope. The machine had stopped. "Roger, I think I can read people's minds."

His voice seemed swallowed up by the large room. There was the sharp click of a match as Roger lighted a cigarette. The surgeon's face was expressionless.

"I tell you I can *hear* people *thinking,*" Victor said too loudly. He took a deep breath and tried to fight the panic he felt pounding at his senses like some gigantic fist. He searched Roger's face for some kind of emotion, but there was nothing; the other man was staring intently at a thin stream of smoke that flowed from his mouth. "It's true. I know it sounds crazy—maybe it *is* crazy—but I can feel you inside my mind right now."

"Can you tell me what I'm thinking?" Roger's tone was flat. He had not raised his eyes.

"It's not always like *that,*" Victor said quietly. He knew . . . and then he didn't know; not for certain, He knew it seemed as if he had been challenged and was coming up empty. Still, he felt more relaxed and at peace than he had for months; at last he had invited someone else to peer into his private hell. "It's not always definite words or sounds. Sometimes it's just a jumble of sensations. But they're not a part of *me*. Can you understand that? It's like I'm listening in on other people's conversations with themselves!" Victor paused and waited until Roger's eyes were locked with his. His voice gathered strength. "Right now you're fascinated; you'd like to pinpoint the damaged area of my brain that's causing me to hallucinate. You don't believe a word I'm saying."

There was the slightest flicker of surprise and consternation in the doctor's eyes. It was quickly masked.

"Let's not worry about whether or not I believe you," Roger said. "At least not right now. It's obvious that you *believe* you're reading other people's thoughts, and that's all that's important. Why don't you describe these sensations?"

"I'm not sure exactly when it started," Victor said slowly, taking a cigarette from the pack on Roger's desk and carefully lighting it. His hand was steady. "A week, maybe two weeks after I got out of the hospital. I began getting these headaches; but they *weren't* headaches, not in the usual sense, and God knows I'd had enough real headaches to know the difference. And there were noises that would suddenly spring up from nowhere. Sometimes there were words, but mostly it was just noise, almost like . . . static. And it hurt.

"It took me a while to realize that I experienced the pain and the noises only when I was near other people. I'd walk up to people and immediately there'd be pressure in my ears and behind my eyes. I'd walk away and it would stop. Lately, I've *seen* whole strings of words in my mind, words and sounds all floating around in my head. And pain that I can't describe to you. And I *feel* things—emotions—that I know come from somebody else."

"Has there been any change in the *way* you feel these things?" Roger's voice was even.

"Yes. The impressions are stronger, and the pain is worse. The more I know, the more I hurt."

"And you think these sensations have something to do with the thought patterns of other people?"

"I don't know what else to think," Victor said hesitantly. He was conscious now, more than ever, of how sick and foolish he must sound. The words were coming harder; he was pushing them out of his throat. "A few minutes ago, while you were leaning over me on the table, I thought my head would split. I kept *feeling* the word, *intelligence*. Over and over again: *intelligence, intelligence*. In some way that I can't explain, I knew that was *your* thought. You were wondering how much my intellectual capacity had been impaired by the accident."

Victor watched Roger light another cigarette. Now it was the surgeon's hands that trembled.

"Go on."

"It's like the words have teeth. There's just no other way I can think of to describe it; they sit in my mind and they *bite*. And just before they come there's a kind of pressure, a buzzing . . . a *numb* feeling." Victor hesitated. "All right," he said at last, "you still don't think it's possible. For a moment there, you were almost convinced; you were thinking about the Russian claim that they have a woman who can read colors with her fingertips."

Again Roger's eyes registered surprise but he spoke without hesitation. "Let's be realistic," Roger said, leaning close, inundating Victor with his thoughts. "It's *most* important that we be realistic. You've survived a terrible injury and it's to be expected that there's going to be some residual pain. You must understand that the mind plays tricks, even in a healthy individual, and you're still far from well. You're going to have to give your body, and your mind, time to *heal*. That's what you have to think about, Victor; that and only that."

"Test me!" Victor was surprised at the vehemence in his voice. It had cost him a great deal to come to Roger with his fears. He would not now be denied; one way or the other he would know the truth. "If you're so sure I'm imagining this, test me!"

"Victor, as your doctor, I—"

"Do it as my friend! Roger, I *need* this! Have you ever read anything about ESP?"

"Well, naturally, I've read the literature. But I don't think—"

"Good! Then you know the tests are fairly simple as well as statistically reliable. There isn't that much work involved."

"It's not the work that I'm thinking about," Roger said. He was wavering now, torn by uncertainty that was clearly communicated to Victor. "Maybe next week."

"Tonight!" Victor had to struggle to keep from shouting. He was intoxicated with the vision of an end of his nightmare. "You won't help me to relax by forcing me to wait a week," Victor said quietly.

"It won't be difficult to get the materials or set up the equipment. If I fail, well, I'll have all the time in the world to relax. Isn't that right, Roger?"

Victor gazed steadily back into the eyes of the tall man. "All right," Roger said, picking up Victor's folder and tucking it under his arm. "Tonight."

Victor paused in the lobby of the medical center and studied the knots of people moving past, crowding the sidewalk on the other side of the thick, glass doors. All his anger had been drained. In a few hours he would do battle with his fears in the neutral territory of a laboratory before the disinterested eyes of a man who believed he was hallucinating. It was all he asked. The tension and anxiety that had been steadily building over the long months was suddenly gone and in their place was an insatiable curiosity. Talking to Roger had brought him out of himself; his words had lanced the psychic wound that had festered in his silence. He was sure now that the sounds and images were real. Since he was not hallucinating, there was only one other possibility: he was telepathic.

*Telepath;* Victor rolled the word around in his mind, speaking it softly with equal parts fear and fascination. What if he could learn to control and interpret these sensations?

Victor pushed open the doors and strode out into the auburn glow of the late afternoon, plunging without hesitation into a small crowd of pedestrians who were waiting on the corner for the traffic light to change. Quickly, like a man pitching his body into an icy lake, Victor opened his mind and extended it out toward the man standing next to him. He remembered the time as a child when he had sought to prove his courage to a group of older boys by holding his arm over a campfire, holding it there until the soft down on his flesh had shriveled and fallen to the ground. It was like that now; his mind was suspended in the consciousness of another and he was burning. Still he hung on, struggling to stretch the words into sentences and trace the images and sounds to their source. A shaft of pain tore through him, erupting like a geyser.

Victor staggered back against a building, ignoring the frightened stares of the people at the crossing. The man whose mind he had touched was holding his head in his hands; he had dropped the briefcase he had been holding and was looking about him with a dazed expression. Victor pushed away from the stone facade and forced himself to walk the few paces to a phone booth which stood empty across the street. He half stumbled into the glass enclosure and slammed the door shut behind him.

Icy sweat had pasted his clothes to his body. Victor rested his head against the cold metal of the telephone and peered out from his sanctuary as he waited for the scream inside his head to subside. He had seen something inside the man's mind, something cold and dark which he did not understand and which frightened him; this time he had seen what before he had only felt.

I must practice, Victor thought; I must delve even deeper into this mysterious awareness which I now possess. Perhaps, in time, I could even learn to control the pain.

He hunted in his pockets for change, having decided to call Pat and tell her he would not be home for dinner, not until after he had seen Roger. Right now there was no time to waste; there was too much to learn.

Roger hesitated with his hand on the telephone as he tried to dispel a lingering uneasiness about the call he had decided to make. He finally picked up the receiver, dialed a number, and spoke in quiet earnestness for some minutes. When he had finished, he poured himself a tall drink from a bottle that had been a Christmas present and which had been around the office, unopened, for the past two years. He ground his knuckles into his eyes and groaned as pools of electric, liquid light darted and swam behind his eyelids.

Acting on an impulse, he had gone ahead and developed the latest series of X-rays, the set he had taken of Victor's skull earlier in the afternoon. He had not expected to find any significant change. He had been wrong. Now the entire surface of the large fluoroscope in his office was covered with negatives arranged in chronological order so as to provide, at a glance, a complete visual record of X-ray exposures taken over the past four months. Viewed in this manner, the effect was astounding.

On the left were the plates taken soon after Rafferty had been rushed to the hospital, more dead than alive. The carnage on the right side of the skull was indicated most vividly by small dots of light in a sea of gray, bits of bone imbedded deep in the tissue of the brain.

The next series of plates had been exposed three days later, after the marathon operation had been completed. The splinters of bone had been removed from the brain tissue and a metal plate inserted into the area where the skull had been pulverized. The rest of the exposures had been taken at two to three week intervals.

Now that he knew what he was looking for, Roger realized that the effect was evident, even in the early exposures: a tiny discoloration a few millimeters to the left of the injured area. Placed side by side, the plates offered conclusive evidence that the discolored region was rapidly increasing in size. It was almost as if the machine were not recording this area, but Roger had checked and rechecked the equipment and there was nothing wrong with it.

In the set of plates taken that afternoon the normal skull and brain tissue patterns were virtually nonexistent; the entire plate exploded in rays of light and dark emanating from that same tiny region just below the steel plate. It was as if the architect's brain had somehow been transformed into a power source strong enough to interfere with the X-rays—but that was impossible.

Roger licked his lips and swallowed hard, but there was no moisture left in his mouth. He turned off the fluoroscope and reached back for the wall switch before pouring himself another drink. In a few minutes there was the soft ring of chimes in the outer office. Roger glanced at his watch and rose to greet the first of the evening's two visitors.

Victor knew immediately that something had happened in the past few hours that made Roger change his mind; he could sense the excitement radiating from the mind of the neurosurgeon in great, undulating waves.

"Tell me again how you feel when you experience these sensations." Roger's voice was impassive, but his eyes glowed.

"Something like a second-grader trying to read *Ulysses*," Victor said easily. "You can recognize a few words but most of the time you haven't any idea what they mean."

His gaze swept the small anteroom where Roger had brought him. Shipping cartons, boxes of records, and obsolete equipment had been pushed back against the walls to make room for the two wooden tables that had been placed in the middle of the floor. Wedged between the tables and extending about four feet above their surfaces was a thin, plywood partition. On one table was what appeared to be a large stack of oversized playing cards, a pad, and a pencil. The other table was bare.

"I want you to sit here," Roger said, indicating a chair at one end of the empty table. He waited until Victor had seated himself. "I believe you may have been telling the truth this afternoon. Now I think we can find out for sure."

Victor felt as if he had been hit in the stomach. A few hours ago he would have given almost anything to hear Roger speak those words; now they stirred a reservoir of fear. He might have risen and left if it were not for the knowledge that, by doing so, he would be cutting himself off from the one person who might be able to return him to the world of normal sights and sounds.

"Let me show you what we're going to do," Roger said, fanning the cards out, face up, in front of Victor. They were pictures of farm animals. "I'm going to try to duplicate some of Duke University's experiments in parapsychology. There are figures on my pad which correspond to the pictures on the cards. Each time I turn over a card I'll signal with this," and Roger produced a small toy noisemaker from his pocket and pressed it several times. It emitted a series of distinct clicking noises. "You'll tell me whatever it is you see or feel: dog, horse, cat, or cow. At the end, we'll compute the number of correct responses. Any significant difference between your score and what is considered *chance* must be attributed to telepathy. It's as simple, or complex, as that."

"Fine. Just as long as it helps you to treat me."

"Victor," Roger said, shooting him a quick glance, "do you realize what it would mean for you to be proved telepathic?"

"Right now it means that I have a constant headache, occasional severe pain, and that I continually find myself knowing things about other people that I neither want, nor have the right, to know."

"Yes." Roger's voice was noncommittal. He disappeared behind the partition and Victor could hear him shuffling the cards.

It suddenly occurred to Victor that the other man was trying to hide something from him, concentrating hard on a set of words in what seemed an effort to mask an idea; the thought of *hiding* was floating in the other man's consciousness, soaring above and hovering over the other things on which he was concentrating. Why should Roger want to hide anything from him? Victor attempted to break through the curtain but Roger's will, and the pain, were too great. Victor let go and leaned back in the chair.

"Are you ready?"

"Ready."

Click.

" . . . Dog." He said it with far more certainty than he felt; there was nothing there.

Click.

. . .

"You're waiting too long."

"I can't . . . "

"Your first reaction!"

Click.

Victor said nothing. There were no animal words in Roger's thoughts. The words that were there were scrambled and totally unrelated to one another. Why would Roger want to ruin his own experiment? Unless there were no words except those that sprang from his own shattered imagination; unless he had been right in the beginning to suspect he was on the verge of madness.

Clickclickclick.

. . .

"You're not responding, Victor! Tell me what animal you see! Tell me!"

Nerves shrieking, Victor sprang from his chair and stepped around the partition, slapping at the cards, strewing them over the table and floor. Sweat dripped from his forehead and splattered on the wooden surface, the sound clearly audible in the sudden silence. Victor stepped back quickly, profoundly embarrassed. Roger was studying him quietly.

"I—I can't see anything," Victor said, his voice shaking. "For God's sake, Roger, I . . . I'm very sorry."

"Let's try it once more."

Victor reached for his handkerchief and then stopped, his hand in mid-air; there was a new emotion in the other man, almost a sense of elation. He waited for Roger to look up, but the doctor seemed intent on rearranging the stack of cards, pointedly ignoring Victor's questioning gaze. Victor returned to his chair and sat down.

"Ready?"

"Ready," Victor said weakly, cupping his head in his hands. He suddenly felt very tired.

Click.

Victor slowly dropped his hands away from his head; his heart hammered. "Dog," he whispered.

Click.

"Cat."

Now the clicks came faster and faster, and each one was accompanied by a clear, startling, naked impression. It was *there!* Roger's

mind was open and Victor barked out the words as the images came
to him.

Click.

"Cow."

Click.

"Dog."

Clickclickclick.

"Cowcatdog."

Clickclickclickclick.

Finally the clicking stopped. Victor could feel Roger's mind begin
to relax and he knew it was over. He sat very still, very conscious
of his own breathing and the rising excitement in Roger as the
results were tabulated. In a few moments the excitement had risen
to a sharp peak of unrelieved tension. Victor looked up to find Roger
standing over him, his facial muscles hanging loose in undisguised
astonishment.

"One hundred percent," Roger said breathlessly, repeating the
figure over and over as if unable to accept his own calculations.
"Victor, you *can* read minds. You're telepathic to an almost unbelievable degree. Here, look at this!"

Victor glanced at the pad on which his responses had been recorded. On the first test he had scored about one correct answer in
every four. *Chance.* On the second test all of the answers were circled
in red; the marks grew darker and more unsteady as they proceeded
down the page.

He looked up and was startled to find the neurosurgeon still star-
ring at him. It was unnerving; the man's pupils were slightly dilated
and his mouth worked back and forth. His thought patterns were
strange and somehow unpleasant.

"Let me guess," Victor said tightly. "You're looking for antennae."

"I'm sorry," Roger said, stepping back a pace. "I was staring,
wasn't I?"

"Yes."

"Well, you're a little hard to get used to. If you have any idea
what this means . . . "

"I'd rather not get into that."

Roger flushed and Victor immediately felt ashamed. Were their
situations reversed, he felt certain he would be the one staring.

"You were blocking me on the first test," Victor said easily.
"Why?"

"Control." Roger's fingers were tracing a pattern up and down the columns of red circles. "I had the cards face down on the first run. I didn't know what they were myself. The second time . . . Well, you saw what happened the second time."

"Where do we go from here?" Victor shifted uneasily in his chair. He had the distinct impression that Roger was already thinking in terms of *application.*

"I wish I knew," Roger said. "I wish I knew."

Victor's head was splitting and the nervous sweat in his armpits was clammy. He concentrated on shutting out Roger's thoughts; he wanted nothing more than to go home and sleep, but first he needed some answers. "How?" Victor asked at last.

"How what?"

"How does all this happen? What's going on inside my brain?"

Roger tugged at his lip. "If I knew that, I'd be famous."

"You already are famous."

Roger grunted and continued to tug at his lip. When he finally spoke, his tone was flat, his gaze fixed on some point at the far end of the room.

"It's been estimated that during our entire lives we only use fifteen to twenty percent of our total brain capacity," Roger said. "Nobody really knows what happens with the other eighty. For all we know, there may be a great source of power there, power that we never use. We never have need to tap that power and so it atrophies like an unused muscle. Maybe that power is there in reserve, to be used by some future generation; or maybe it's simply the difference between the ordinary man and the genius. It's just possible that in your case the energy, or whatever you want to call what's happened to you, was released as a result of the accident." Now Roger had risen to his feet and was pacing, lost in thought, his voice a beacon beckoning Victor to follow him through this thicket of ideas into which he had wandered. He fumbled for a cigarette, finally found one in a crumpled pack and lighted it. He couldn't sit down.

"We've always assumed brain damage to be disabling," Roger continued, dragging heavily on his cigarette. "The brain controls everything: coordination, thinking, reflexes. Different areas control different functions and when one area has been damaged, its function is almost always lost.

"We always assume that our present condition is the best. It never occurred to us that brain damage could be *beneficial* in any way." Roger stopped and looked at Victor. "You've shown us how wrong we were. Your injury somehow altered the function of your brain cells, releasing a power like nothing that's ever been recorded." He crushed out the cigarette. "I think evolution may have something to do with it."

*"Evolution!"*

"Yes!" Roger fairly shouted. "Now follow me on this: there are profound differences between the brain pans of, say, Neanderthal and Cro-Magnon man. Yet they are direct descendants! True, the changes took place over thousands of years; still, at least some Neanderthals must have had the seeds of change within their genetic makeup, a cellular plan that would someday transform them into Cro-Magnon man."

"I'm not a superman," Victor said cautiously. "I'm all of the things everyone else is; no more and no less."

"That's not true," Roger said, his excitement undiminished. "You were gifted—apart from other men—even before the accident. Now you're telepathic." He paused for emphasis. "The Cro-Magnons' forebears were not obviously different from their fellows; they lived, ate, drank, fornicated, and died just like the others. The differences were too small to be seen, at least in their own lifetime. It must be the same with us; to generations of men a thousand years from now, *we* will seem like Neanderthals. And some of us—you, for instance—are their genetic forebears. If I'm right, a freak accident triggered a mechanism inside your brain that most men will not know for dozens of generations!"

"But how does it happen?" Victor lighted a cigarette, his moves slow and deliberate, his voice completely noncommittal.

"All *thinking* involves a release of energy. Electrical impulses are triggered by certain chemical reactions within the cells that we don't yet fully understand; it's precisely those impulses that we measure in an EEG."

Roger sat down suddenly and began drumming his fingers on the tabletop. "In your case, the cells have been altered to a degree where the nerve endings not only pick up your own impulses but other people's as well. We've always suspected that there was a certain amount of electrical radiation or *leak* from the brain, just as there is from any power source. Besides, there are quite a few recorded instances of telepathic communication—but never anything like this. It's just *fantastic,* Victor! I wonder if you realize just how unique you are?"

Victor was gently probing now, looking for the meaning behind the words, trying to determine just what Roger planned to do with his newly acquired knowledge. He gave up when he realized that the neurosurgeon was effectively, if unconsciously, blocking him.

"All right," Victor said, concentrating his attention on a water stain just over Roger's shoulder. "How do we stop it?"

Roger blinked rapidly as if just startled by a loud noise or awakened from a deep sleep. "Stop it?"

"That's what I said, stop it! Do you think I want to *stay* like this?" Aware that he was almost yelling, Victor dug his fingernails into the palms of his hands and took a deep breath. "I'm an architect," he continued more calmly. "I used to build things and that was all I ever asked out of life; it's all I ask now. If you had any idea . . . but you don't. There must be something you can do, an operation of some sort; I want it."

"That's impossible at this point," Roger replied, passing his hand over his eyes. His voice was now slurred with weariness. "To attempt any kind of operation now is out of the question; I wouldn't even know what I was supposed to be operating *on*. Besides, another operation now would probably kill you."

"There may not be *time*," Victor said, tapping his clenched fist gently but insistently on the table. "I tell you it's getting worse; each day I know more about people I've never met, strangers I pass on the street. And my head hurts. For God's sake, Roger, sometimes I wake up in the morning and I don't—"

"Have you considered the *implications* of this thing?" Roger seemed unaware of the fact that he had interrupted Victor. "You can read men's minds, know their innermost feelings! There are all sorts of—"

"I've thought about the implications and I don't like any of them."

"Police work; imagine, Victor! You would know beyond any doubt who was guilty and who was innocent . . . "

"Some sort of mental gestapo?"

" . . . International relations, psychiatry . . . "

"Forget it, doctor," Victor murmured, half-rising. His voice was deadly soft. "If you won't help me, I'll find somebody else who will."

"I didn't say I wouldn't help you," Roger said, sobered by the intensity of Victor's tone. "I said I didn't think I *could* help you; at least, not yet, not until I know more. We'll have to conduct tests and *those* will be mostly guesswork. Even if I do operate, there's no way of knowing for sure whether it will do any good. That is, if it doesn't kill you."

"I'll take that chance. You can administer any test you want. The only thing I ask is that you do it quickly and that you keep this completely confidential."

"I'm afraid it's already too late for that, Mr. Rafferty."

Victor leaped to his feet, knocking over the chair. He turned in the direction of the voice and was startled to see a well-dressed woman standing behind him at an open door which he had assumed was a closet; now he could see the adjoining room beyond the door. The woman had been there all the time. She had seen and heard everything, and now Victor knew what Roger had been trying to hide.

Visual and mental images came at him in a rush: young and attractive but cold; high self-esteem, exaggerated sense of self-importance; fiercely competitive, slightly paranoid, habitually condescending. She concealed her nervousness well.

"Tell me, Mr. Rafferty," the woman continued, "don't you think the scientific community—your country—has a *right* to know about you?"

Victor turned slowly to Roger. "Who is she?" he asked very deliberately.

Roger's face was crimson. "Victor—Mr. Rafferty—I'd like you to meet Dr. Lewellyn, one of my colleagues."

"What the hell is she doing here?"

"Victor, I . . . I asked Dr. Lewellyn to observe. I value her opinion. I thought perhaps—"

"You had no right." Victor turned to face Dr. Lewellyn. "The answer to your question is *no*," he said tightly. "Neither you nor anyone else has any right to my life or my personal problems."

"Mr. Rafferty, I don't think you understand—"

"I mean it, Roger," Victor said, cutting her off, turning his back on her once again. "I expect this case to be handled with the utmost confidence. And I hold you responsible for this woman!" He hesitated, wondering why he suddenly felt so afraid. "If any word of this gets out, I'll deny the whole thing," Victor continued softly. "I'll make both of you look very foolish. Roger, I'll call you tomorrow. You can experiment with me all you want, but my condition *must* be kept secret. Is that clear?" He did not wait for an answer. Glancing once at Dr. Lewellyn, he walked quickly from the room.

"You've made a fantastic discovery, doctor," the woman said.

"Yes," Roger agreed, but there was no trace of his former enthusiasm.

"But he's terribly naive, don't you think? He must realize that we have certain obligations."

"I suppose so," the doctor said, crumpling the cards in his hands and studying their motions as they drifted lazily to the floor.

Pat Rafferty glanced up as her husband came through the door. She watched him for a moment, and her eyes clouded. "Victor," she said gently, "you smell like a brewery."

"I should," he said evenly. "I just drank a quart of scotch." He went quickly into the bathroom and splashed water over his face and neck. When he came back into the living room he was startled to find her standing in the same spot staring at him, her pale blue eyes rimmed with tears of hurt and confusion. Six years of marriage to the slight, blonde-haired woman had not dulled his love for her; if anything, the years had magnified his desire and need. It had been three days since the tests in Roger's laboratory and still he had not told Pat. It would have been hard enough, at the beginning, to tell her he feared for his sanity. Confirmation of his ability had only compounded his problem. How, he thought, does a man tell his wife she's married to a monster? "I'm not drunk," he said, turning away from her eyes. "I'm not even sure if it's possible for me to get drunk any more."

Pat continued to stare, dumbfounded at the words of this man who had, seemingly by intent, become a stranger to her. There was something in his eyes and voice that terrified her, robbed her of speech.

"You see," Victor continued, "I've made a remarkable discovery. If I drink enough, I can't hear other people thinking. I'm left *alone*. I . . . " Victor stopped, aware that his need had spoken the words his intellect would not. He turned away to hide his own tears of anguish. He did not flinch when he felt Pat's soft, cool fingers caressing the back of his neck. "I need your help," he murmured, turning and burying his face in his wife's hair.

Victor talked for hours, pausing only once when night fell and Pat rose to turn on the kitchen lights. He told her everything: the pain, his fear, the experiments in Roger's office. When he had finished, he drew himself up very straight and stared into her eyes. "Do you believe me?"

"I don't *know*, Victor. You've been acting so strangely for the past few months. I want to believe you, but . . . "

"The alcohol's worn off. Would you like me to demonstrate what I'm talking about?"

"I . . . "

"Think of a number. Go ahead; do as I say."

Victor held Pat's gaze and waited, probing, hunting for the numbers that he knew must eventually merge with the doubt and confusion he felt in her mind. When they came, he called them off with machine-gun rapidity, in a voice that never wavered. One by one he exposed every thought, every fleeting impression. He did not stop even when he felt the doubt replaced by panic. He could not escape the conviction that something terrible was about to happen. He needed Pat. Therefore, she must be convinced beyond any doubt that—

"Stop!" Pat's hands were over her eyes in a vain attempt to stem the tide of thick, heavy tears that streamed in great rivulets down her cheeks. "Stop it, Victor! Stop it! Stop it!"

Pat leaped from her chair and ran into the living room. Victor waited a few minutes and then followed. She was huddled on a far end of the sofa. He reached out to touch her but immediately stepped back as he felt her flesh quiver beneath his touch. In that moment he had felt what she felt and the knowledge seared him. He stepped farther into the darkness to hide his own tears. "I'm not a freak," he said quietly, and he turned away and headed back into the kitchen in an attempt to escape the sound of Pat's sobbing.

Her voice stopped him. "Forgive me, darling."

Victor stood silently, unwilling to trust his voice. He watched his wife sit up and brush away the tears from her face.

"I'm so ashamed," Pat continued in a voice that was steady. "I don't know what to say to you. All that time you were hurting so much . . . I *love* you so much, so very much . . . "

He went to her, folded her into his arms. They stayed that way for several minutes, each enjoying the renewed warmth and security in the touch of the other's body.

"You're afraid," Pat said at last.

"Yes."

"Why?"

Victor told her about Dr. Lewellyn.

"I still don't understand why you're afraid."

"They'll try to use me."

Pat pulled away just far enough to look up into Victor's eyes. "There's so much you could contribute, darling. Imagine what you could do in psychiatry, helping to diagnose patients. Think how much more scientists could learn from you about the human mind."

"They won't use me for those things," Victor said, surprised at the conviction in his voice. He had found the elusive source of his fear. "They'll use me for a weapon. They always do."

Pat was silent for long moments, her head buried once again in his neck. "We'll move away," she said at last.

"They'll follow."

"We'll change our names, start all over again."

"We'll see," Victor said, but he sensed that it was already too late.

Later, Victor lay back in the darkness and listened to Pat's troubled dreams. The orange-yellow glow of dawn trickled through the blinds of the bedroom window. He had not slept. If Roger was right, if his mind was, indeed, a window on man's future, what right *did* he have to keep that portal shuttered?

Pat was beginning to stir and Victor recognized the sharpening thought patterns that he had learned to identify as the bridge between sleep and consciousness. He slipped on his robe and went to the kitchen to make coffee. Pat joined him a few minutes later, kissed Victor lightly on the cheek and began preparing breakfast.

They ate in silence. Victor had poured a second cup of coffee and lighted a cigarette when the doorbell rang. He rose and kissed Pat full on the mouth, holding her close to him. He sensed, even before he had opened the door and looked into the man's mind, that the waiting was over.

He was a small man. His short arms and thin, frail body were in direct contrast to the strength Victor found in his mind. His face was pale and pockmarked, punctuated with a large nose that sloped at an angle as if it had been broken once and never properly set. He wore a thick topcoat and even now, in the gathering warmth of the morning, drew it around him and shivered as if he were cold.

"I'm Mr. Lippitt," the man said to Victor. "I think you know why I'm here."

"Come in," Victor said, surprised at the steadiness of his own voice. The man entered but politely refused Victor's invitation to sit. Victor glanced over his shoulder at Pat and waited until she had returned to the kitchen. "What do you want, Mr. Lippitt?"

The man suddenly thrust his hands into his pockets in a quick motion which served to break his wall of concentration. The dark eyes in the pale face riveted on Victor, measuring his reaction as he allowed his thoughts and knowledge to rush forth.

*He's too strong,* Victor thought; *too strong.* But he didn't react.

"If my information is correct," Mr. Lippitt said slowly, "you know what I'm thinking right now."

Victor returned the other man's gaze. He sensed pain, chronic discomfort that Mr. Lippitt went to great lengths to conceal. "Are you sure you have the right house?" For the briefest moment there was a flicker of amusement in Mr. Lippitt's eyes and Victor found that, in spite of himself, he liked the man.

"The people I represent believe you have a rather remarkable talent, Mr. Rafferty. Obviously, I'm not referring to your abilities as an architect. We know all about your interviews with Dr. Burns. We'd like to test and interview you ourselves. We would pay well for the privilege."

"No," Victor said evenly. "I don't wish to be tested or interviewed by anyone. Not anyone."

Mr. Lippitt's gaze was cold and steady. He hunched his shoulders deeper into his coat. "You understand that we could force you. We don't want that. Surely, you can see the necessity—"

"Well, I *can't* see the necessity!" Victor exploded. "What do you want from me?"

Lippitt's face registered genuine surprise. He drew his hand out from his pocket and gestured toward his head. "Don't you see?"

"I know who you work for," Victor said impatiently. "I can tell that you're not quite sure what to do with me and that I'm considered some kind of potential threat. The rest is very vague. Your training was very thorough; you're subconsciously blocking all sorts of information that you don't think I should have."

"You scored perfectly on a telepathic indicator test," Lippitt said, eyeing Victor curiously. "You can read thoughts like the rest of us read newspapers."

"It's not quite that simple."

"But it could be! I've heard the tapes of your conversations with Burns! You can control—" Mr. Lippitt paused and again Victor sensed his physical discomfort. When Lippitt spoke again his voice was softer and his breath whistled in his lungs. "We live in an age of technological terror. Both sides spend millions of dollars gathering information to assure themselves that they're not going to come out second best in any nuclear war."

"I'm not a spy, and I don't have the training or inclination to become one."

"Your mind makes conventional methods of espionage obsolete," Mr. Lippitt said, his eyes blazing. "Don't you see, Mr. Rafferty? You could gather more information in one hour spent at an embassy cocktail party than a team of experts could gather in a year! One drink with a foreign ambassador or general and you'd have the most valuable diplomatic and military information! There'd be no way for them to stop you. You'd know who was lying, what military moves were being considered, information that other men must risk their lives to get! In a way, you'd be the ultimate weapon. We would always be assured of having the most up-to-date and reliable—"

"Have I done anything wrong? Committed any crime?"

"No," Mr. Lippitt said, taken aback.

"Do you have the authority to arrest me?"

"No."

"Then my answer is still *no*," Victor said firmly. "I have a right as a citizen of this nation to be left alone."

"Have you considered your *duty* to this nation?"

"How would you know I was always telling the truth?"

"Ah, well . . . I don't have an answer for that; not now. I suppose, eventually, we would have to consider that."

"I don't want to work for you. I *won't* work for you."

Mr. Lippitt lighted a cigarette. Victor handed him an ashtray. Their eyes held steady.

"It's not that simple, Mr. Rafferty," Lippitt said. "It's just not that simple. No matter what you decided, you'd still need our protection."

"Protection?" The idea was there in Lippitt's mind but it was hazy and undefined.

"Our informant—"

"Dr. Lewellyn?"

"Dr. Lewellyn was more fervent than discreet," Mr. Lippitt said in a matter-of-fact tone that failed to conceal his embarrassment. "The channels she used to inform us of your existence were not, as we say, *secure*."

"You mean that in the spy business nothing stays a secret for very long."

"Not always," Mr. Lippitt said evenly, ignoring the other man's sarcasm. "But in this case we must assume that there's a possibility other powers may already know about you. If so, well, I think they'd go to great lengths to prevent you from working for us."

"They'd kill me?"

"Without a second thought. Unless, of course, they felt they could force you to work for them."

Victor was conscious of his wife moving about in the kitchen.

"You'd have to eliminate every trace of my existence," he said. "Otherwise, I'd be useless to you. And what are you going to do with Pat? Maybe she wouldn't care to undergo plastic surgery. Certainly, I'd have to."

"We'd handle everything. Would you rather risk having her see you killed? Or they might torture her if they thought it would do them any good. You know, their methods can be quite effective. You might have a more difficult time explaining to them that you simply choose not to use your skills for a dirty business like spying."

Victor's head hurt from the prolonged contact with Lippitt. His entire body ached and throbbed with exhaustion. "What if I decide to take my chances?" He no longer made any effort to mask his anxiety.

"I'm afraid that would put *us* in a difficult position," Mr. Lippitt said slowly, for the first time looking away from Victor. "You see, if you weren't working for us, we'd have no way of being certain you weren't working for *them*. They wouldn't hesitate to kill your wife or anybody else if it would force you over to their side." Lippitt's eyes hardened. "Or they simply might offer you a million dollars. Sometimes it's as easy as that."

Victor flushed. "Either way, then *you'd* have to stop me."

"Yes."

"Then I'm trapped."

"I'm afraid so, Mr. Rafferty. I'm sorry that it has to be this way."

Victor rubbed his sweating palms against his shirt. He was seized with a sudden, almost overwhelming desire to strike out, to smash his fist into the white face that looked as if it would tear like paper. He clenched his fists, but his arms dropped back to his sides in a gesture of resignation. Lippitt was right; on a planet covered with nations strangling on their own words of deceit and treachery, he was the ultimate weapon. He could determine truth, and he sensed that absolute truth and certainty would be a most dangerous possession in the hands of the wrong men. Had Hitler known the frailties of the men he fought, he would have ruled the world. On the other hand, a telepath could have prevented Pearl Harbor.

"Can I have some time to think about it?"

"What is there to think about?"

"Dignity. Allow me the dignity of believing I still have some freedom of choice."

Mr. Lippitt looked at Victor strangely for a moment before drawing a card from his pocket and handing it to him. "You can reach

me at this number, any time of the day or night. Call me when
you've . . . reached your decision." He paused at the door, turned
and looked at Victor in the same odd manner. "I meant what I said,
Mr. Rafferty. I am sorry that it has to be this way."

"So am I," said Victor.

The door clicked shut behind Victor with a terrible certainty,
muffling Pat's sobs, punctuating a decision Victor knew could not
be reversed. There was no turning back once he had begun running.
Never again could he be trusted, but he would be free.

Somewhere in the United States there had to be a place where he
and Pat could lose their identities and start over, perhaps a small
town in the south or the west. Victor knew he must find that place
and find it quickly. Then he would send for Pat. Perhaps it was, as
he suspected, a futile gesture, but it was something he had to attempt, the only alternative to imprisonment in a world of uniforms,
security checks, and identity cards. He knew, too, that he must
conserve his strength; already his arm ached from the weight of his
single suitcase.

He knew there was something wrong the moment he stepped down
from the porch. Victor felt the man's presence even before he spoke.

"Please stop right there, Mr. Rafferty."

Victor froze; he knew there was no sense in trying to run. Even
without the suitcase, which he needed because it contained his bank
book and credit cards, he realized that his physical condition would
never enable him to outrun the guard. He turned and stared into
a pair of cold, gray eyes. The man was short and stocky, very well
dressed, with close-cropped blond hair. Victor felt the man's mind
coiled like a steel spring.

"Who the hell are you?" Victor snapped, his frustration forming
meaningless words. He already knew the answer: Lippitt's man.

"I'm sorry, sir. I must ask you to come with me."

"Your boss told me I'd have time to think things over."

"I'm sorry, sir, but I have my instructions. I was told to bring you
with me if it looked like you were trying to leave. Will you follow
me, please?"

Victor shifted his weight back on one foot and then lurched forward, sending the suitcase swinging in an arc toward the man's
head. The guard stepped easily aside, allowing the weight of the
suitcase to carry Victor around until he was off balance. He moved
with the grace of a dancer, stepping behind Victor, knocking the

suitcase to the ground and twisting Victor's arm up behind his back gently but firmly, so that the responsibility for any pain would be Victor's if he attempted to struggle.

Victor acted instinctively, throwing back his head and closing his eyes in fierce concentration. He probed, ignoring the blinding pain, searching for some fear or anxiety in the guard's mind that he could touch and *grab hold of* with his own. There was something there, dark and shapeless, rough and rattling with death. Victor strained, probing harder and deeper, obsessed with the need to escape.

Now the guard was making strange, guttural sounds deep in his throat. Victor felt steel-hard fingers at his neck, pressing, searching for the nerve centers at the base of his skull. He was inside the guard's mind and there was pain there that he was causing; still the man would not let go. Victor probed still deeper, wrenching the sensations, magnifying the pain.

Then the fingers were no longer around his neck. Victor turned in time to see the man sink to the ground. The guard was moaning softly, writhing on the ground and gripping his head in his hands. The moaning stopped. The guard twitched and then lay still.

Victor knelt down beside the guard and was immediately aware of yet another presence. He threw himself to one side and missed the full force of a blow delivered by a second, larger man who must have been positioned at the rear of the house. The second man tripped over the first and sprawled on the flagstone walk.

This time it was Victor who attacked, swinging around and stepping close to the second guard who was just springing to his feet. There was already pain in the other man as a result of his fall, fear and uncertainty at the sight of his prostrate partner. Victor seized on both thoughts and concentrated, thrusting deep. The man slumped to the sidewalk without a sound.

Victor reached for his suitcase and looked up into the face of Pat, who had run out onto the porch at the sounds of the struggle. Her eyes wide with fear, the woman had jammed her knuckles into her mouth so that only her mind screamed in terror and ripped at Victor's consciousness. Victor threw aside the suitcase, turned and ran, away from the fallen men, away from the horror in his wife's mind.

Roger Burns was certain he'd turned off the lights in his office and laboratory. Even if he'd forgotten, the cleaning woman would have remembered. He'd had no way of knowing that sleeplessness and excitement over the Rafferty file would bring him back here to his office in the middle of the night. Now, someone had broken into the building. There was no other explanation for the shaft of light that leaked out from beneath his office door into the darkness.

Roger's hand rested on the doorknob. He knew he should call the police, yet the only phone was the one on the other side of the door. He could not wake up a neighbor at three o'clock in the morning, the nearest pay booth was three blocks away, and he did not want the intruder to escape. He was outraged at the thought of someone rifling through his highly confidential files, if that was it.

Anger triumphed over reason. Roger burst into the room and then stopped short, frozen into immobility by the sudden realization that the two men in the office were no ordinary burglars and that he had stumbled into a situation he was totally incapable of handling.

The light came from the fluoroscope. One man, an individual Roger had seen a few times at Washington cocktail parties, was taking photographs of Victor Rafferty's X-rays. The other had been microfilming files that Roger knew must also be Victor's. This man now had a revolver in his hand. The long, thick silencer made it seem ridiculously out of proportion, like a toy rifle.

Roger raised one arm and the gun kicked. There was a soft, chugging sound and a small, round, white hole opened in Roger's forehead, then quickly filled with blood.

Victor sat in a booth at the rear of the coffee shop, toying nervously with a cup of muddy brown coffee and staring at the front page of the newspaper he had spread out before him. He felt numb, dazed with guilt; the stories seemed to leap from the page, stabbing at his senses with twin fingers of accusation. So, Victor thought, I am responsible for the deaths of two men.

He was sure Roger had been murdered because of him; the guard, a man who had merely been doing his job, he had killed himself.

Some enterprising reporter had outwitted the dozen policemen outside his home with a telephoto lens. The picture showed the dead man on the walk. The second guard was just rising to his feet. Mr. Lippitt was standing off to one side, obviously unaware that the photograph was being taken. The picture had been captioned with a single, large question mark.

The waiter, an elderly man with dirty fingernails and a soiled apron, kept glancing in his direction. Victor wearily signaled for another cup. The waiter came to the table and wiped his hands on his shirt.

"Coffee," Victor said, not looking up.

The waiter pointed to the unfinished cup on the table. "You don't look so good, pal," he said. "Maybe you oughta get some food in your stomach."

"I'm all right," Victor said, aware that he sounded defensive. "You can get me some bacon and eggs. And orange juice."

The waiter swiped at the table with a damp rag and then shuffled off, mumbling to himself. Victor reached out for the sugar bowl and began rolling it back and forth between his hands. With the suitcase gone, he had little money and no place to go. In any case, Mr. Lippitt would have all the airports and bus terminals watched. It was too late to do anything and so it didn't bother him that he was too tired to think clearly; there was nothing left to think about. He wondered if they'd shoot him on sight.

He could still feel the *texture* of the guards' minds as he had entered them to twist and hurt; he could see their bodies lying on the ground. Most of all, he remembered the expression of sheer horror on Pat's face.

Victor stopped spinning the sugar bowl. He had been staring at it and it had suddenly come to him that he was seeing the object in an entirely different way, with more than his vision. He *saw* the glass he was touching with his hands; at the same time he could *feel* the mirror image of the bowl somewhere in his brain, elusive, ephemeral, and yet seemingly real enough to be grasped.

Victor slowly took his hands away from the bowl and touched the image in his mind.

The pain was greater than any he had ever known. Victor immediately released the image and gripped the edges of the table in an effort not to lose consciousness. The pain passed in a few moments, gradually ebbing away. He opened his eyes but did not have enough time to evaluate what had happened. The waiter, approaching his table with a tray of food, tripped over a loose linoleum tile. The tray and its contents came hurtling through the air. Victor reacted instinctively in an effort to protect his only set of clothes; he reached out and pushed at the tray with his mind. At that instant Victor felt his body bathed in searing fire. The walls and ceiling tilted at an odd angle and the floor rushed up to smash into his face.

The waiter stared, dumbfounded. His startled gaze shifted rapidly back and forth between the unconscious man on the floor and the eggstains on his apron. Something was wrong, he thought, something besides the man on the floor; there was something out of place. The old man's slow mind struggled with the problem of the flying tray and food as he hurried to call the police and an ambulance.

Now only the memory of the pain remained, like the lingering, fuzzy morning taste of too many cigarettes. Victor's mind and senses were clear at last, cleansed of their blinding crust of panic by the shock of coma. The sour, antiseptic smell in his nostrils told him he was in a hospital; the dull throb in his skull told him he was not alone. Victor kept his eyes closed and lay very still.

He recalled the incident in the coffee shop very clearly and he knew what had happened. He had seen the word in the textbooks: *telekinesis,* the theoretical ability to move objects by the intense focusing of thought energy. Except that telekinesis was no longer theoretical; he could do it. No matter that the crippling pain made it highly improbable that he could ever use it effectively; the very fact that he had exhibited the power made him that much more desirable, or dangerous, in the eyes of Mr. Lippitt and whoever had killed Roger Burns. Perhaps they had already decided that the risks of using him were too great. He had run. He had killed a man. He was a criminal. They could easily shut him away in some prison for the rest of his life to make sure, if he didn't work for them, he wouldn't work for anyone else.

In the meantime, Pat was in terrible danger. Whoever had killed Roger would be after her next; Mr. Lippitt had said as much. They would torture her, kill her, if they thought it could lead them to him. Victor was sure Mr. Lippitt had assigned men to guard her but that couldn't last forever. No, Victor reflected, he was endangering Pat by the very fact that he was alive.

The guard testified to the fact that he was caught. Probably the police or the hospital had called his home, and Mr. Lippitt would certainly have the phone tapped. Victor was surprised the thin man in the overcoat wasn't already at his bedside.

His was a prison with no doors and windows, a killing trap that was sucking his wife in to die with him, a problem with no solution—except one; only one. It was, as yet, only the embryo of an idea. First, he must escape the hospital.

"I'm feeling very well now," Victor said loudly, sitting up quickly and swinging his legs over the side of the bed. "Maybe you can tell me where my clothes are."

The policeman sat up as if stabbed with a pin. Startled, he fumbled for his gun and finally managed to point it in Victor's direction, but the asking of the question had been enough to implant the answer in the policeman's mind. Victor probed gently; the policeman was very tired; and his clothes were in the white closet at the far end of the room.

"You might as well just lay back there, mister," the policeman said, releasing the safety on his pistol as an afterthought. "I'm not even supposed to let you go to the head without keepin' an eye on you."

Victor crossed his legs on the bed. His lungs ached from the tension, but he managed to feign innocence. "Well, do you mind telling me why?" He must put the policeman off guard and there wasn't much time.

The policeman eyed Victor suspiciously. "I'm not supposed to talk about it."

Victor began to probe deeper and then stopped, sickened by the memory of the man he had killed outside his home. In that moment he knew he would not kill another innocent man, even if it meant his own death. Then, how?

" . . . damned silly."

"What's that?"

The policeman hesitated, and Victor probed, gently magnifying the frustration he found in the other man's mind. He smiled disarmingly. "I didn't hear what you said."

"I didn't say . . . Oh, hell, this whole thing is silly. Some little guy claims you turned a plate of eggs around in the air without touchin' them. 'Fore ya know it, I'm pullin' this extra babysittin' duty."

"That does sound pretty silly." Then he knows for certain, Victor thought; Mr. Lippitt knows I am telekinetic.

"Mind you, I was just on my way out the *door* when I pull this duty. As if that wasn't enough, I'm catchin' a few winks and this creep comes in and belts me in the mouth! He *hits* me, mind you! Weird little guy in an overcoat. Must be eighty degrees in here and this guy's wearin' an overcoat! I'd have killed any other guy did that and this creep's a *little* guy. But his eyes; I never seen eyes like that. Crazy, if ya know what I mean. Man, ya don't mess with a guy that's got eyes like that." The policeman sneezed and Victor sat very still. "Anyway, this guy says he'll have my job *and* my pension if I fall asleep again. Just like that! No, sir! Ya don't mess with a guy like that. And get this, he takes the key and locks me *in* here! He's gotta be some kind of big shot or he wouldn't dare do somethin' like that. Says he's gotta go someplace and he'll be right back." The man rubbed his nose and lips with an oversized red handkerchief, then blew hard into it and repeated the process. "I think he's some kind of spy," the policeman continued, studying Victor through narrowed eyelids. "I think maybe you're a spy, too. Spies are always makin' up screwy stories. Call 'em *cover* stories. See it all the time in the movies."

Victor choked back the strained, hollow laughter in his throat. "Did he say where he was going?"

The hand with the gun had relaxed. Now it tightened again and the barrel leveled on Victor's stomach. "You ask too many questions," the policeman snapped. "I ain't even supposed to talk to you. Maybe you're a *Russky* spy. Yeah, for all I know you're some kind of commie."

"It's all a mistake," Victor said very quietly, eyeing the gun. "I asked where the man went because I'm anxious for him to get back. I'm sure everything will be straightened out when he gets here. It's just too bad you had to get dragged into it, particularly when you didn't sleep much last night."

"Hey, how'd you know I didn't get much sack time?"

"Your eyes look tired. You were probably out playing poker with some of the fellas."

"Sonuvagun, you know you're right? Dropped twenty bucks and my wife's gonna be screamin' at me for a week!"

Victor began to concentrate on a single strand of thought. "You must be very tired," he said, accenting each word, caressing the other man's weariness. "You should sleep." The policeman yawned and stretched, and Victor glanced toward the door. Mr. Lippitt could enter the room at any time; he'd have other men with him. "It's all a mistake. You're free to go to sleep, to rest."

"I . . . can't do that." The man was fighting to keep his head up. The gun had fallen on the floor and he looked at it with a dazed expression.

"It's all right. You can sleep. Go to sleep."

The policeman looked at Victor with a mixture of bewilderment and fear and then slumped in his chair. Victor quickly eased him onto the floor before going to the cabinet and taking out his clothes. He dressed quickly and stepped close to the locked door. He bent down and looked at the lock, breathing a sigh of relief; it was a relatively simple, interlocking bolt type with which he was quite familiar.

Victor knew he must not think of his fear or the pain which was to come, but only of the consequences of failure. He sat on the floor and closed his eyes. He rested his head against the door, summoning up in his mind an image of the moving parts of the lock, each spring, each separate component. He knew he must duplicate his feat in the coffee shop; he must control the image in his mind so as to move the tiny metal bars in the door. Pat's life, and probably his own, depended on it.

The pain came in great, sweeping, hot waves, as it had in the coffee shop, and Victor recognized the wet, dark patches behind his eyes as the face of death. He could feel his fingernails breaking and bleeding as he pushed them into the wood, defying the agony. The lock *must* turn. His blood surged through his body, bloating the veins and arteries in his face and neck to the point where Victor knew, in a few seconds at most, they must burst.

The lock clicked.

Physically exhausted, Victor slumped to the floor. He sucked greedily at the cool drafts of air wafting in beneath the door as he waited for the fire in his head to cool. At last he rose and opened the door far enough to look out into the corridor. Empty; Mr. Lippitt had thought the locked door would be enough.

The policeman was beginning to stir. Victor hurriedly found the man's wallet and took out the money he needed. Then, summoning up his last reserves of strength, he stepped out into the hallway and headed for the emergency exit.

Pat Rafferty opened her eyes and stared into the darkness. She did not have to look at the luminous dial on the alarm clock to know it was the middle of the night; and there was someone in the room with her. "Victor?" She said it like a prayer.

"Yes," came the whispered reply. "Don't be frightened and don't turn on the light. I want to make love to you."

Pat felt a shiver run through her body. The voice was Victor's but it was different somehow, flat and sad. Resigned. His hand was on her body.

"Victor, I can't—"

"Don't think that, darling. Please love me. I need you now."

She felt her desire mount as Victor pressed his mouth against hers; his closeness and the need of her own body swept away her fears and she reached out to pull him down alongside her. In a few minutes they lay, spent and exhausted, in each other's arms; but Victor rose almost immediately and began dressing.

"Victor, please come and lie down again."

"I can't, darling. There isn't much time. I have to go."

Pat rubbed her eyes. Everything seemed so unreal. "How did you get in? There are men all around the house."

"I have my own built-in radar system," Victor said. "I can tell where they are." He moved closer to the bed so that Pat could just make out his shape in the darkness. She raised her arms but Victor moved back out of her reach. "I had to take the chance," he continued. "I had to see you to tell you I've always loved you. You see, I have to do something . . . terrible. There's no way to make you understand. I had to see you this one last time to say goodbye."

"Goodbye? Victor, I don't understand. Why . . . ?" She was suddenly aware of a numb, *thick* sensation in her forehead. Her ears were buzzing. "Victor," Pat murmured, "I feel so strange . . . "

"I know, darling," Victor said. His voice was halting as if he were choking on tears. "I know. Goodbye."

He stood in the darkness for a long moment, staring at the still figure on the bed. Once he started to walk toward her and then stopped. Finally he turned and went back the way he had come.

Mr. Lippitt sat at his desk in the specially heated office. His feet were propped up on his desk and he held a steaming glass of tea in his hand. His frail body was enclosed in a thick, bulky sweater buttoned to the mid-point of his chest. He sipped at his tea and stared off into space. He regretted the fact that the order had gone out to kill Victor Rafferty.

But what else could one do with such a man save kill him? Lippitt thought. He can read thoughts, move objects, and he can kill, all without lifting a finger. The military potential of such a man is too great ever to risk its possible use by a foreign power. Unlike the atom, there is only one Victor Rafferty, and whoever commands his allegiance possesses a terrible weapon, a deadly skill that was silent and could be used over and over again undetected, with virtually no risk to its user. I had always prided myself as a good judge of character, Lippitt thought. I would have sworn to Rafferty's decency and patriotism. Then why had he run?

Mr. Lippitt was interrupted in his thoughts by the buzz of the intercom. "Yes?"

"There's a message on an outside line, sir. I've already scrambled the circuit. Should I put him through?"

Mr. Lippitt's feet came down hard on the floor, jarring the desk and its contents, spilling the tea over a stack of multicolored, cross-indexed documents Lippitt had spent the day ignoring. He waited until he was sure he had regained control of himself and then picked up the receiver. "All right," Mr. Lippitt said, "cut him in."

There was a soft, whirring sound in the line, an automatic signaling device signifying that the scrambling device had been activated. "Lippitt here."

"He's in New York City," said the voice on the other end of the line. "He has a research lab in the Mason Foundry. He's hiding there. What are your instructions?"

Mr. Lippitt bent over and picked up the overturned glass. "What's your code name?"

"Vector Three," came the easy reply.

"Of course," Mr. Lippitt said, fingering the glass. "And I suppose that's where you are? The Mason Foundry?"

"Of course."

Mr. Lippitt hung up and shoved the revolver beneath his sweater, inside his waistband along the hard ridge of his spine. He jabbed at the intercom.

"Yes, sir?" came the quick reply.

"I want a jet to New York, *now,*" Mr. Lippitt barked at the startled secretary. "Arrange for helicopter and limousine connections. All top priority."

Mr. Lippitt was not surprised to find no agent waiting for him outside the building; neither was he surprised to find Victor Rafferty waiting for him inside.

"Come in," Victor said, leveling a pistol at Mr. Lippitt's forehead and motioning him to a chair across the booklined executive office. "You look as if you expected me."

Mr. Lippitt shrugged. "You picked the wrong man's brain. Vector Three left for France two days ago."

"Then why did you come?"

"May I have a cigarette?" Victor threw a pack of cigarettes across the room and Mr. Lippitt purposely let them fall to the carpet. He bent over, freeing the revolver. He was certain his speed was sufficient to draw and kill Rafferty before the other man could even pull the trigger. He sat back up in the chair and lighted the cigarette.

"I was curious," Mr. Lippitt said casually. "I don't think you meant to kill that man. If I did, I'd have had this place surrounded with troops. Why did you run?"

"I don't think I could make you understand."

"That's too bad. You see, having you around is like living with an H-bomb; whether it's ticking or not, it still makes you uncomfortable."

"Now you're beginning to understand."

Mr. Lippitt glanced around the room, fascinated by the many models of buildings Victor had designed, relying on the properties of the high-tension steel alloy developed by the foundry. Strange, he thought, how buildings had never interested me before. He rose and walked across the room to examine one of the models more closely; he could feel the gun aimed at the back of his neck.

"So, what are you going to do?" Mr. Lippitt asked.

"I've already been contacted and all the arrangements have been made. I leave for Russia tonight."

"That means you'll have to kill me."

"Yes."

Mr. Lippitt turned to face Victor. "Why? I mean, why defect?" He no longer made any effort to hide the emotion in his voice. "I wouldn't have thought you were a traitor."

Anger flickered in Victor's eyes, then quickly faded. "You forced me to do what I'm doing," Victor said. "An H-bomb! That's what you compared me to, right? To you and your people—"

"They're your people, too."

"All right, *people!* To people, I'm nothing more than a weapon! Did it ever occur to you I might want to lead my own life?"

"We've already been over that. Without us, you and your wife would either be killed or kidnapped. We wouldn't want you to be killed; we couldn't allow you to be kidnapped."

"Exactly. So it boils down to this: since my life is no longer my own anyway, the only thing I can do is choose the side which can best provide protection for Pat and myself. That means a communist country. By definition, a police state can provide more protection than a non-police state. Since I wouldn't be *free* in either country, I have to pick the country where I would be *safe*. Their very lack of freedom guarantees my life and Pat's."

"Very logical."

"Oh, there's money, too. I won't deny that. As long as I have to live out my life in virtual captivity, I may as well be comfortable.

I've been assured of . . . many things. You don't operate that way,
do you?"

Mr. Lippitt ground out his cigarette and immediately lighted another. He regretted not killing Rafferty when he had the chance.
"No, we don't. Unfortunately, our budget forces us to rely on patriotism."

Victor said nothing. Mr. Lippitt watched the other man rise and
walk toward him. He tensed, waiting for exactly the right moment
to drop to the floor and grab for his gun. He knew it would be very
difficult now, for Rafferty was close and the element of surprise was
gone. Yet, he knew he must not fail; he was the only remaining
barrier between Rafferty and the Russians.

"Out the door," Victor said, prodding Mr. Lippitt with the gun.
"Left and up the stairs. Walk slowly."

"Don't be melodramatic. Why not just shoot me here?"

"I want to show you something. If you prefer, I'll shoot you now."

There was something strange in the other man's voice, Mr. Lippitt
noted, an element that he could not identify. In any event, he realized
he would stand little chance if he made his move now. He walked
ahead and through the door. The barrel of Rafferty's pistol was
pressed against his spine, no more than an inch above the stock of
Lippitt's revolver.

The stairway led to a long, narrow corridor. Mr. Lippitt walked
slowly, the echo of his footsteps out of phase with those of the man
behind him. He said, "It's quiet. Where is everybody?"

"There's no shift on Saturday," Victor said tightly. "There's only
the watchman. I put him to sleep."

"You can do that?"

"You know I can."

"Just making conversation." Mr. Lippitt hesitated. "There is such
a thing as *lesser evil* in the world, Rafferty. We need you on our side.
Think about it."

"I'm sorry," Victor said. He reached out and grabbed Mr. Lippitt's
shoulder. "In there."

Mr. Lippitt pushed through the door on his left marked RE-
STRICTED. He found himself on a very narrow catwalk overlooking
a row of smelting furnaces. The cover hatches of the furnaces were
open, and Mr. Lippitt looked down into a liquid, metal sea that
moved with a life of its own, its silver-brown crust buckling and
bursting, belching huge bubbles of hot, acrid gas. The air was thick,
heavy with its burden of heat.

"You wanted to show me where you were going to dump my body,"
Mr. Lippitt said.

"Yes."

Mr. Lippitt watched Victor's eyes. He could not understand why
the other man had not been able to probe his thoughts and discover
the existence of the gun. Perhaps he had not felt the need; the reports
had mentioned the pain linked with the act. In any case, Mr. Lippitt
thought, Rafferty will be dead the moment he blinks or looks away
for even a fraction of a second. "You're going to do very well in your
chosen profession," Mr. Lippitt said, steeling himself for the move
he knew he would have only one chance to make. "People tend to
trust you, give you the benefit of the doubt. You have a very dis-
arming air about you."

"That's not all I wanted to show you," Victor said.

Lippitt's muscles tensed but his hand remained perfectly still.
When he did go for the gun it would be in one fluid, incredibly
explosive motion.

"I want to show you what might have been if things were different," Victor said.

Mr. Lippitt said nothing. It seemed to him that Rafferty was relaxing, letting down his guard. Also, he judged that the angle of the
gun would allow him to get off at least one shot, even if he were hit,
and one shot was all he needed. Still, he waited.

"You're cold," Victor said suddenly. "You can't even feel the heat
from those furnaces."

"What?"

"I said, you're cold. You're always cold. You've been cold for the
past twenty years. That's why your mind is so strong. You can't
block out the memories so you control and discipline yourself to the
point where they no longer make any difference, but still you can't
feel any warmth."

"Don't," Mr. Lippitt said, his voice scarcely a whisper.

"You can't forget the Nazis and their ice baths. They put you in
the water and they left you there for hours. You shook so much you
thought your bones would break. You remember how they laughed
at you when you cried; you remember how they laughed at you when
you begged them to kill you."

"You stay out of my mind! Stop it!" Mr. Lippitt's voice was quivering with rage.

"It takes enormous courage to keep going in the face of memories
like that," Victor continued easily. "All those coats, all those over-

heated rooms; none of it does any good. We're alike, you and I. Both of us suffer agony others can't begin to understand. That's why you broke all the rules and came here alone, even when you knew I'd be waiting for you; you were reluctant to see them kill me."

"You devil," Mr. Lippitt said through tightly clenched teeth. "You play with people, don't you?"

"There's nothing wrong with your body, you know. That healed long ago. The Nazis are gone. You don't have to be cold any more."

There was something soothing and hypnotic about Rafferty's voice. Mr. Lippitt struggled to clear his mind as he fought against the pervading warmth spreading through his body, fought it and yet embraced it as a father his dead child returned to life.

"It's a trick," the thin man said, startled to find his eyes brimming with tears.

"No," Victor said quietly, insistently. "I'm not putting the warmth in your body; it was always there. I'm simply helping you to feel it. Forget the water. All that happened a long time ago. You can be warm. Let yourself be warm."

"No!"

"Yes! Let me into your mind, Lippitt. Trust me. Let me convince you."

Mr. Lippitt closed his eyes, surrendering to the strange, golden warmth lighting the dark, frozen recesses of his soul. He thought of all the years he had spent in the prison of his memory, immersed in the water that was sucking away his life . . .

"You don't feel cold any more."

"No," Mr. Lippitt whispered. Now the tears were flowing freely down his cheeks. "I don't feel cold any more."

"Why don't you test it? Take off your coat."

Mr. Lippitt slowly removed his heavy overcoat. Now the revolver was within easy reach. "I'm sorry," he said. "I'm grateful to you, but no man should have that kind of power."

"Not unless he can use it wisely," Victor replied, raising the hand with the gun. The hammer clicked back with the soft, assured sound of finely-tooled metal. "The demonstration is over."

Mr. Lippitt dropped to his knees and rolled over on his side, clawing for the gun in his waistband. Years of experience and training had transformed him into a precision killing instrument, the movements of which must be measured in milliseconds. Still, inside Mr. Lippitt's mind, it was all slow motion, as in a nightmare; he drifted through the air and bounced on the concrete, the gun appearing miraculously in his hand and aimed at Victor Rafferty's heart, but there was something pulling at the gun, an invisible force that he could feel writhing like a snake in the metal. Steel bands had wrapped about his head and were squeezing, crushing his brain. He pulled the trigger twice, then peered through a mist of pain as Victor Rafferty threw out his arms and toppled over the guard rail, his body arching grotesquely as the pull of gravity snapped his legs over after his body and he fell through space to land with a muffled, crackling splash in the soft inferno below. It was the last thing Mr. Lippitt saw before sinking down into a black void laced with the smell of gunsmoke.

The barrel of the revolver was still warm, leading Mr. Lippitt to conclude that he couldn't have been unconscious more than a few minutes. He lurched to his feet and, supporting himself on the guard rail, stared down into the pit where Victor had fallen; the slag continued to belch and bubble. There was no trace of the other man, not even the smell of burnt flesh. So, he reflected, he had killed the man who had cured him. No matter that there was no choice; for the rest of his life, even as he savored the warmth of the sun on his body, he would remember this day and welcome his own approaching death; he had simply traded one nightmare for another.

He paused at the foot of the stairs and, after a moment's hesitation, entered one of the offices. He picked up a telephone and dialed one of the outside lines to the agency.

"Good afternoon," came the cheery voice, "this is—"

"This is Mr. Lippitt. The fox is dead."

There was a long silence on the other end of the line. When the woman spoke again, her voice was punctuated by heavy breathing.

"Sir, this is an outside line. If you'll wait for just a moment—"

"This is an emergency," Lippitt said slowly. "Fox is dead. Fox is *dead*."

He hung up before the frightened woman had time to reply. He reasoned that the others would be suspicious at first, at least until they'd had time to check their sources for the code words. Besides, he'd make sure that certain information was leaked. That, he decided, should keep them away from the woman. He lighted a cigarette, then picked up the phone again to call the Rafferty home.

*I'm here to see Mr. Thaag.*

The Civilized and the Savage. He'd been a guest of the General

Assembly the day Senator Thaag had made that speech. He'd never met the man. That should make things easier.

Some men would kill for a tattered tribal banner. Their imagination sets with the sun, their world ends at the horizon. Others travel the planet, whisper many tongues, and find only the face of their brother.

The Civilized and the Savage. How does one tell the difference? He could tell the difference.

*May I have your name, sir?*

*Nagel. John Nagel.*

Or any other name. It didn't make any difference. His real name had died with his old identity. It was all there in the two-column obituary in the *Times*. Everything in his past had died back in the foundry with the image he had planted in Mr. Lippitt's mind. Eventually, he would need a new appearance, a new manner and personality. For now, John Nagel would have to get along with tinted contact lenses, false beard, and an exaggerated limp.

He'd miss Pat; he'd ache for her. But his "death" had been her only guarantee of life.

*I'm sorry, sir, but your name is not on the appointment list. Are you expected?*

He would lean close, make contact with her mind. She must be convinced of his *importance*. The secretary would disappear for a few minutes, then reappear, smiling.

*The Secretary General will see you now.*

He was not sure what would happen next; he would have to wait until he could get close to Thaag and explore his mind. Even then, he was not sure what he would be looking for; perhaps, simply, a man he could trust.

Victor Rafferty went over his plan once more in his mind. Satisfied, he began walking slowly across the United Nations Plaza toward the massive glass and stone obelisk rising up from New York's East River. He stopped and looked up into the bright, sun-splashed day; a breeze was blowing and the multitude of flags strained against their stanchions, painting a line across the sky.

# Sweet Remembrance

## by Betty Ren Wright

"I blame those dreadful books for his death," Miss Mackey told the sergeant. "Indirectly, of course. I'm liberal in my thinking, I assure you, but I do think that publishers have a responsibility. Have you *seen* the kind of trash being sold in every drugstore and supermarket at this very moment?"

She didn't look like a liberal. The sergeant watched her thin white hands, expert among the tea things, and felt nostalgia for an age he had never known. In the short hours of their acquaintance he had become very fond of Miss Mackey, and he could not understand why. Certainly she was nothing like his mother—his noisy, moody, cheerfully vulgar ma—nor like any of his noisy, cheerful, vulgar sisters and aunts. Perhaps that was it, he decided, forgetting for a moment the dreary purpose of his visit in the pleasure of watching her pour tea into pearly cups. Perhaps he loved her because she was the other side of his moon, the unresolved, even unrecognized dream of what a female should be.

"Now, about Mr. Higgins," she said with endearing directness, after he had taken his first sip of tea. "He is a simply heartbreaking example of what I mean. If he didn't read those books—if he didn't think those thoughts!—I venture to say he would be alive at this moment."

The sergeant set his cup back on its saucer. "I don't see—" he began gently, but she was quite ready to explain her theory.

"He always had one of those dreadful books in his overalls pocket," she said. "You know, the ones with the *covers*. He was always snatching a moment to read them—I've seen him—and all that nastiness aroused his prurient curiosity. Prurient curiosity, young man." She passed him a plate of tiny cookies, which he refused. "Why else would he have been lurking behind my draperies?"

"Robbery, perhaps," the sergeant suggested, but Miss Mackey would have none of it.

"Nonsense! As the janitor of this building, he had keys to every apartment, and he knew that I go to my book club every Tuesday afternoon without fail, and buy my groceries every Friday morning,

188

so he had plenty of opportunity to come in if he simply wanted to take something." She shook her little white head decisively. "No, sergeant, carnal appetite was his problem, and guilt was what did him in. When I saw him and screamed, he turned and climbed out of the window as though he had taken leave of his senses. He was the very picture of a guilt-ridden man."

It was one more delight that Miss Mackey saw nothing strange in Mr. Higgins' choosing to spy on her instead of on one of the younger women who lived in the building, the sergeant decided. He put aside the tea regretfully. "Well, I won't bother you any longer," he said. "You've been very kind and helpful, and I'm sure you're tired after your bad experience. Thank you for the tea."

She followed him to the door. "You are not at all the way one usually imagines a detective to be," she said. "You're very young. And you have a certain—grace."

The sergeant stiffened for a moment. How his parents would have roared at that, how his brothers and sisters would have jeered! *Grace,* he thought, and then decided he liked the sound of it as long as no one else had heard.

Westerberg was waiting in the lobby. "Well?" he asked.

"An elegant old lady."

"Who pushes janitors out of windows."

The sergeant led to the way to the car, feeling very much on the defensive. "So a few people heard her scolding him for reading dirty books," he said grumpily. "So this makes her a killer? She admits she spoke to him about it—for his own good. She thought she was doing her duty."

"She threatened him," Westerberg said patiently. "He told people in the apartment house about it, thought it was a joke. She told him he'd be punished if he kept up his sinful ways, that his evil thoughts were showing in his face. She sounds like a nut."

"She's a nice old lady trying to set the world straight," the sergeant told him. "Anybody who wants to magnify that into a criminal act is going to have his hands full."

He thought about Miss Mackey while he shaved, mentioned her guardedly to his date at dinner, and that night he dreamt he was fighting a duel under an oak tree that was festooned with Spanish moss.

In the morning there was a report on his desk at the station, and Westerberg was waiting in the chair by the window, a cup of coffee in his hands. When he had finished reading the report, the sergeant sat for a long time staring at the crack that marred the brown-egg wall in front of him.

"I was never as young as you are when I was as young as you are," Westerberg said finally, when the coffee was gone and the silence had become too oppressive to be borne. "Do you want me to go get the old lady while you patch up your shattered illusions?"

"Go get her!" the sergeant repeated sharply. "Why should you get her? You want to send her to the chair because this damn sheet says someone died in the last apartment she lived in, too?"

"Not just *someone*." Westerberg set the coffee cup on the window-sill, adjusting its position slightly to coincide with the stains already there. "A window washer; a wholesome, clean-living fellow who supported a wife, a mother, a sister, and the sister's two kids. Been washing windows for seventeen years, and there was never a complaint about him not minding his own business until Miss Mackey moved into the building. She reported him twice as a peeping Tom—and the third time he was doing her windows, he fell seven stories to the ground and broke his neck."

The sergeant slouched in his chair and thought of gallantry in the shade of a giant oak. "You can't arrest a nice old lady for being around when two people died," he said, "whether she happened to like them or not."

"Tell me one thing," Westerberg said with irritating gentleness. "Did the nice old lady mention the window washer to you? Did she tell you Mr. Higgins was the second man to leave her elegant presence in a great big hurry?"

The sergeant looked at him with something close to hate. "No," he said. "She didn't happen to mention it. She probably assumed we'd look at it the same way she did—as a nasty coincidence."

"Good grief!" Westerberg said, but he didn't go on with the discussion.

They spent the rest of the day talking to residents of the apartment building. Most of them had known Mr. Higgins casually; none of them had thought there was anything odd about him, though they all agreed that he had been seen with lurid paperbacks in his hands and was always well-informed about, and eager to discuss, the latest sensational murder. Three residents reported having received anonymous letters in the last couple of months; a bachelor who had had a painting of a nude delivered to his apartment; a model who had posed in a bikini for a slick magazine; and a young actress who had been accused in her letter of letting a man stay overnight in her apartment. Each of the letters had been a warning of punishment to come; none of them had been taken seriously. The recipients remembered that they were written on pale gray, tissue-thin paper in fine script.

As he looked over his notes, the sergeant wondered why he found it impossible to believe anything bad of Miss Mackey. Who was to say, actually, that her righteous innocence did not become a twisted, perverted passion behind those bright blue eyes? His mind simply would not accept it. He moved angrily through the long day, and at the end of it he visited her again, wondering at his own sense of homecoming as he sat down in the parlor.

*Parlor,* he thought. The word prompted a picture of plush and velour and china figurines; a Seth Thomas clock; books bound in muted leather, stillness tucked protectively around every object. Then he remembered that when he was twelve he had asked his seventh grade teacher a question about Browning, and in an ecstasy of gratitude—how many seventh graders had ever asked her about Browning?—she had invited him to stop in at her home that evening and pick up a book.

The house was a treasure of towering gingerbread where she had lived first with her parents and then alone. The boy had entered into a dream when he stepped through its door. The crowded kitchen, center of life at home, had faded from his consciousness as if it had never been, and with it the bursts of laughter, the slaps, the curses, the tears that were the music he lived by. Dignity, dry wit, and most of all, orderliness were what he found in the teacher's old house, and he had gone back again and again, making mental lists of subjects to ask about the next time as his eyes moved over the ceiling-high shelves of books.

"You look tired, sergeant." There was a tiny crease of concern between Miss Mackey's eyes. "I don't think I'll offer you tea this time. I have a better idea." She crossed the room to a glass-doored cabinet and took from its glittering depths a crystal decanter and two glasses on a tray. The glass was like a small bubble in his hand; he held it gingerly and let the brandy restore him.

"How is your case developing?" she asked as he settled back in his chair. "Have you learned what you needed to know about that unfortunate man?" She might have been asking about the weather, or his indigestion, or where he was going to go on his vacation.

"Well," he said, "it seems to be getting more complicated instead of less so. We're beginning to wonder whether there's some connection between Mr. Higgins' death and another one that occurred some time ago."

She took a tiny sip from her glass. "I don't understand."

"Your theory," he told her, "may be the right one."

She leaned forward with a tiny smile of triumph. "Twisted thoughts," she said. "Evil influences lead men to do things they would not otherwise do."

"Twisted thoughts," the sergeant agreed. "Of the murderer's, however, rather than the victims'. There's someone living in this building, Miss Mackey, who is very mixed up indeed."

She watched alertly as he put down his glass and went to the window. "I hate to keep going over this," he said, "but I have to be very sure of the facts." He opened the window as far as it would go. "Now," he said, "when you came into the room you saw Mr. Higgins standing there, partly hidden by the drapery. You had no idea till then that he was in the apartment."

"That is correct," Miss Mackey said, and the sergeant seemed to hear again his seventh grade teacher's voice.

"You're sure you didn't call Mr. Higgins in to fix a window?" he went on. "Some of your neighbors report having heard voices in the hallway minutes before Mr. Higgins fell."

"Certainly not," Miss Mackey said.

"When you caught sight of him, you screamed and ordered him to leave," the sergeant went on.

"Exactly." Miss Mackey put down her glass and came over to the window. "He seemed to panic. He crawled out on the sill, looked back over his shoulder at me, and then he fell forward and was gone."

"Like this." The sergeant then climbed cautiously onto the sill and crouched there, balancing himself with his fingertips. He looked back in time to see her small, reproachful face close to his shoulder, and then he felt her hands on his back, pushing with great purpose, and he was hurtling out into space.

"Like that," he heard Miss Mackey say very close behind him.

It was an astonishingly long way down. The sergeant thought of his ma, and of the cheerful, sometimes ribald girls he had loved as he grew up. He saw, in kaleidoscope, the dark places of his life and the churning colors, the chronic grand disorder of being alive. When he landed, bouncing twice in the great lap of the safety net, it was as if he had resigned himself—committed himself—forever to the way things actually were.

Westerberg helped him down.

"You want to go up or should I?" he asked sympathetically.

"You go," the sergeant said.

He waited in the dark courtyard until Westerberg had disappeared into the building. Then he straightened his coat and went around the side of the building to where the patrol car was parked. He took out his pipe. He knew they wouldn't be down for a while. Miss Mackey would want to wash the brandy glass and put them away, powder her nose, and close the window before she went to the station.

# A Voice from the Leaves

## by Donald Olson

Looking back over these past few weeks I realize that I never intended this to be a permanent arrangement—Cobb living with me here in Chicago, I mean. Call it selfish, but I fully expected him to go back to Fairhill when the new school term began, assuming of course that Sam McAllister had not in the meantime been arrested for murder. Now, whenever I drop hints to this effect, Cobb blandly ignores them with that inwardly meditative smile of his, the smile that makes him look like a teenage Talleyrand or like his great hero, Lawrence of Arabia, palavering with sly Bedouins under an eastern moon.

For a lad of fourteen Cobb has remarkable aplomb and presence, and when I see him stalking about this big apartment with *The Seven Pillars of Wisdom* under his arm and a look of sober deliberation on his face, I get the creepiest feeling that he's making plans to take over this place—as if it were some strategic border area still in enemy hands; one of my more childish fantasies, since it implies that *I* am the enemy, which is absurd.

I first met Cobb McAllister when I returned to Fairhill for the first time in fourteen years in response to Sam's letter telling me that Cobb's mother was dead. Dead and buried, actually, and I thought it exactly like Sam to have been punctilious and feeling enough to inform me of Vinnie's death—but not in time for me to attend her funeral. Like most people who come from small rural towns, I'd cherished the illusion that nothing would have changed while I was away; the people, the quiet pace of life, the house where I was born, and especially that wilderness of heart-carved trees called Cobb's Woods, the enchanted playground of our youth. Yes, I clung to this last illusion despite common sense and Vinnie's last letter in which she'd reported that a midwestern firm had bought most of the acreage along the state road and planned to build a number of condominiums to be called Fairhill Farms.

As it was, trains no longer stopped at Fairhill and Sam had to drive all the way to Breezeford to meet me at the airport. Physically, he hadn't changed all that much, still wary-eyed and thin as whip-

cord, his manner as cool and self contained as when he and Vinnie
Cobb and I had been such close chums. He'd never been much of a
talker and the inhibiting sadness of the present reunion did not help
break the ice as we drove to the village.

I did ask him if Vinnie had been ill for long before she died, but
all he said was, "No, nothing like that," and I got the distinct feeling,
despite his reticence, that he had a great deal on his mind and sooner
or later would seek to unburden it.

We passed the Kidwell place and the livery stables, and as I had
mentally prepared myself for the devastation of those holy places
of my youth, not far up the road I was surprised and delighted when
we approached Cobb's Woods and all that came into view was a
single broken-window shell of a new apartment building, all brick
and half-timbering, rising out of the long grass which all but hid a
winding access road. Behind and around this solitary eyesore Cobb's
Woods lay undisturbed in the sunset, evoking a flush of enchantment
still strong enough to bring tears to my eyes—tears for Vinnie, for
myself, for the lost sweet wonders of childhood brought back so
vividly.

"They were going to put up a whole string of 'em," Sam explained,
without my asking.

"What happened?"

"Company pulled out. Bad luck and bankruptcy."

We slowed down, waited for a truck to pass us, then swung across
the road and into the drive of the old Cobb homestead where Sam
and Vinnie had lived ever since their marriage.

"Cobb!" Sam's voice rang with urgency as he walked into the front
parlor. "Where the devil's that kid got to?"

He went from room to room calling the boy, but no one answered.

"Relax," I said. "He'll show up."

"Kid's been told. Since all the trouble he knows he ain't supposed
to wander off this time of day."

"Trouble?"

"Shootings. Killings. Vinnie didn't tell you?"

So he knew that Vinnie wrote to me. But that would have been
like her, not to have deceived him about it.

"I haven't heard from Vinnie in months."

While another man might have reacted to this with dripping sat-
ire, Sam merely smiled his politely disbelieving and enigmatic smile.

"I mean it, Sam. I haven't."

He ignored the protest and told me about the "trouble." "All began with that infernal apartment project. Rumor said it was Mafia money. But they say that about everything nowadays, even in these parts. Anyway, they built one, the one you saw. Then one of the bricklayers was shot dead. Figured it was a hunter's stray bullet, but then another one got it. And there was a rash of vandalism, one kind or another. Finally got it up, though. Couple of tenants moved in. One of 'em was shot dead, right through her bedroom window. Other was wounded. Paralyzed. Couldn't trace who did it. Figured they were shot with a rifle stolen from the Kidwell place when they were in Florida. High-powered job with a fancy Bushnell scope. Johnny Kidwell let me use it once when we went hunting together. Well, that put the lid on the project. Really spooked the deal. Nobody'd touch the place. Then the firm got into money troubles and that was the end. Everybody steers clear of there now. Even the kids. Except Cobb, of course. You can't keep him out of those woods. You remember how we were. He ain't no different."

Sam stood at the window looking across the state road at the fringe of trees in front of which you could just make out the faint golden wash of the setting sun on the brook where it straggled out of the glade and lost itself in the pastures of the outlying farms.

"It's that damned tree house," he muttered. "I swear I've thought more than once of chopping it down out of there."

*"Our* tree house? It's still there?"

He gave me a rueful glance. "We built it to last forever, remember?"

The tree house. The heart of it all, the center of our activities, the symbol of all my happiest memories where golden summers cast their endless spells. I thought of it and I thought of Vinnie as she had looked at seventeen, clad only in green shadows up there among the leaves, smiling as she kissed me . . . that last perfect summer.

"You think Cobb's there now?"

Sam frowned. "I'll skin him alive if he is."

"I'll go look."

He protested, said I must be tired and would want to unpack and shower, but these were only excuses, I knew, and what really bothered him was that he wanted to talk about it, whatever it was, and here I was already rushing out of the house before I'd really got there; but I couldn't help it. More than anything else at that moment I wanted to see the tree house, the way it would look up there in the setting sun, which was so often the way it appeared in my Chicago reveries.

I crossed the road and the pasture into the shadows of the deep glade, following the brook to the big rock where forget-me-nots and shiny yellow cowslips grew as thickly as when I had waded upstream as a boy. I didn't try to scale the bank as I would have then, but followed the brook to the glade's end, then circled back toward the tree from behind.

I stopped under the branches and looked up. "Cobb? Cobb McAllister? You up there?"

Silence. Even the birds grew still, while all around me the smell of the woods and the textured pattern of the sunlight on the leaves were like keys that opened long-shut doors of memory.

I told him my name, whether or not it would mean anything to him, and said I'd helped build the tree house, and then I added: "Let me come up and I won't tell your dad you were here."

A voice came down to me out of the leaves: "Watch out below."

A thick knotted rope dropped at my feet. It appeared to be the same old rope. I gripped it and managed to scale the trunk to the lower branches, then clambered through them to the green-painted trapdoor, hauling myself through it to sprawl panting on the platform outside the one sizable room crammed with sleeping gear, candle stubs, ropes, knives, books, binoculars, tin plates and cups, all the essentials of tree housekeeping which hadn't changed since I'd spent so many happy hours there.

Vinnie had sent me pictures of Cobb at various stages of his development so I was not surprised to find him such a sturdy, handsome youth, big for his age and with an even more adult gravity of manner. He gave my hand a brief, unembarrassed shake. I offered my condolences. We chatted easily enough and presently I asked him if his mother had ever talked about me. He said. "Oh, sure. About all of you. All the fun you had. Heck, yes."

Surprising how many things hadn't changed. It might almost have been a shrine furnished with sacred relics. I reached out to the shelf for the Pyle *Robin Hood,* showing Cobb my name scribbled on the flyleaf. He smiled politely and I wondered if my excitement must strike him as silly in a grown man, for there was something about the watchful remoteness of his attitude that disconcerted me. I tried to act my age as I studied the view from the one small window facing west, straight across the treetops to the windows of the abandoned condominium.

"When I was last up here you could see all the way to the Overhead Bridge."

"Yeah, I know. Till they built that stupid apartment building. But we lucked out. They *were* going to build a whole mess of 'em."

Though the horizon was streaked with red, the glade below us was already thick with night shadows. "Your dad told me about the shootings. Aren't you scared being out here alone this time of day?"

He was quietly amused. "Why? Who'd want to kill me? Sometimes Vinnie and I'd stay here till after midnight, watching the stars."

*Vinnie.* I didn't like that. Children calling their parents by their Christian names is a modernism that always offends me.

On our way back to the house I asked him the same question I'd asked Sam: if Vinnie had been sick before she died.

Cobb's tone was tart, as if something smarted on his tongue. "He say she was sick?"

"Who?"

"Sam. Did he tell you that?"

"Not exactly."

"She wasn't ever sick. She fell. From the upstairs porch."

His words, or the quiet, offhand way he spoke them, chilled me as we passed out of the woods and along the brook flowing dark as mercury through the gray-lit stubbly pasture.

"I hadn't heard from her for months."

His voice quickened. "She wrote to you?"

"Occasionally."

"What about?"

"Her painting. Things like that. You."

"What'd she say about me?"

"How proud she was of you. Mother stuff. You know."

"She sure did love the tree house," he said with a faraway, gentle conviction. "We used to spend an awful lot of time there." He kicked a branch out of the path. *"He* didn't like it." This last he said with an obscure but trenchant emphasis, and though I knew he was talking about Sam, I couldn't tell if he meant that Sam didn't like the tree house or didn't like their spending so much time there. Not for the first time in my life I felt a profound pity for Sam; it seemed his destiny always to be a third wheel.

"You don't blame him, do you, Cobb?" I felt impelled to ask him. "For what?"

"For feeling that way about the tree house."

"Heck, no. I guess he's got a right."

We came to the barbed-wire fence along the road; he climbed over,

I crawled under. Before crossing the road he turned to look at me. "Tell me something, will you? Did he say she killed herself?"

"Good heavens, no."

"Because she didn't. My father killed her."

I couldn't have been more shocked, he said it with such utter authority. "You can't be serious, Cobb."

"No one could prove it, even if they tried. But just the same, he did. And he's going to pay for it. I'll see to that."

He opened the door for me. As I passed by him into the house, he added in a low voice, "Just thought you ought to know. In case something happens."

After supper Cobb disappeared to his room and Sam and I sat in the kitchen drinking beer and talking about the past, only now I wasn't so sure I wanted to hear whatever it was he was having such a hard time getting off his shoulders. I didn't believe what Cobb had said, but neither could I forget the shock of those words.

The clock struck midnight. I'd lost count of the number of beers Sam had drunk. At one point I asked him if I could look at Vinnie's old albums, all those snapshots of us as kids. He said he hadn't laid eyes on them for years, not since Cobb was a baby, that Vinnie must have stuck them away someplace. I said it didn't matter, but he insisted on looking for them and when he finally brought them to me he suggested I keep them. "I never look at them any more," he said.

As I turned the pages I began to notice something very odd: there wasn't a single picture in which I appeared; they had all been removed. I looked up at Sam but he wasn't paying any attention; in fact, his eyes were shut, and I was afraid he might fall asleep before imbibing enough courage to speak his mind.

"So Vinnie wasn't sick," I said rather sharply, and his eyes came open.

"No."

"Then how . . . ?"

"Killed herself."

I seemed to go on rocking involuntarily, as if the steady rhythm would soothe my pounding heart. "You can't mean that."

"Hell, I don't *know*. Not for sure."

He told me the story without my urging, how he'd gone looking for Vinnie one day just before dusk. She had gone for a walk and when it began to thunder and she hadn't come back he started to worry and walked up and down the state road looking for her. Then he'd taken it into his head that she might have gone to the tree house. She had a thing about that tree house, he said, with just a trace of bitterness. Both her and the kid.

"It was just about dark when I got there. I called but she didn't answer. There was no reason to think she was up there, but I was sure she was. Don't ask me why. You live with someone fourteen years you get like that, reading each other's minds, sensing things. I kept calling. Then it hit me. I got to thinking maybe she was up there, but not alone. With somebody, you know what I mean? I said, 'I'm coming up there, Vinnie.' That's when she spoke out. 'No!' she said, real scared like. 'Don't come up here! I'm coming down.' And the *way* she said it, you know . . . I never kidded myself about Vinnie. She was honest about it. Never once in them fourteen years did she say she loved me. She was always honest. That's what made it work for us. Honesty, I mean. It can be stronger than love. It holds up, you know. And when I heard her voice, scared like that, telling me not to come up there, I got this awful sick feeling that maybe she *hadn't* been all that honest. And lately, last few weeks, she'd been acting sort of funny, like she had something on her mind. Maybe all those years . . .

"I lost my fool head. I never get mad, not very often. You know that. But, hell, I'd been so damned *good* to Vinnie. So damned fair. I'd done things for her no man in his right mind would have done. I said, 'I'm coming up there, Vinnie,' and I grabbed the rope and started pulling myself up when all of a sudden she fell. Or jumped. Without a word, without a cry. She was dead, that quick. And I still had to *know,* don't you see? I couldn't go through the rest of my life not ever being sure. So I left her there, wasn't nothing I could do for her, and I climbed to the tree house. . . . There was no one there."

He tilted his glass and emptied it in one long draft. "Well, I carried her home and made it look like she'd fallen from the porch up there. Don't ask me why. It just seemed more . . . fitting."

"Did anyone see you?"

"You mean Cobb? No. He was asleep in his room at the time."

"You sure?"

"Of course. Why? Did he say something?"

I couldn't bring myself to say it. "It's just his attitude."

"I know what you mean. He doesn't take to me. More like his mother. Books and stuff. That damned tree house. Ivory tower, that's what it was. For both of them. Cobb, he don't know one end of a fishing rod from the other. And he'd never go hunting with me unless

I practically forced him." His head sank lower, chin almost on his chest. He was quite drunk. "I'll never stop wondering. I'll always hear her voice coming down out of the leaves like that. Like rain, like birds in pain, or panic." After what seemed like a very long time he looked up at me, eye to eye. "I loved Vinnie. You know that. I couldn't show it, not with words. But I always loved her. I did what I could to prove it. She knew that."

I was touched, impressed, but more than anything else, confused. I felt so positive that he was leaving something out, or lacked the courage to tell me why it was so important to him that *I* should hear all this—and I would never find out, not that night. He was so drunk by then I had to put him to bed without knowing the full story.

The following day, a Saturday, I went up to the cemetery on Pine Ridge Road and laid some fresh forget-me-nots among the withering funeral bouquets on Vinnie's grave. Below me the village drowsed, the traffic hummed no louder than bees along the state road, the green mystery of Cobb's Woods looked in the near distance like one of Vinnie's delicate, sun-washed pastels. Heading in that direction, I skirted the condominium and seeing no one about I found an un- locked door and went inside. It was the usual sleazily built structure, small rooms, fake marble baths, miniature kitchens in shades of cocoa brown and avocado. From one of the top rooms I looked out across the long grass and undergrowth to Cobb's Woods, but it was impossible to pinpoint the tree house.

I found Cobb there, of course, at the tree house, his nose in a book. I offered him a candy bar, conscious as I did so that it was with almost the identical feeling I had placed those forget-me-nots on Vinnie's grave. As if it were a bribe, an apology, a plea for under- standing if not forgiveness, and Cobb accepted the offering as if he knew this—which of course he could not.

We talked, among other things, about the aborted building project, Cobb explaining that the entire area had been scheduled for leveling and speaking proudly but not boastfully of his role in fighting the plan. "I helped circulate the petition against rezoning. Vinnie com- posed it. It was a real beaut. Lawyer couldn't have done a better job. It *was* against the law, you know, building that apartment house. The neighborhood had to be rezoned first. We got over a hundred names against it. But they had the money. They bought off the mayor and his cronies. Vinnie was really broken up about it. This tree house meant everything to her. She always said everyone ought to have a secret place where they could store their dreams and memories and know they'd always be there when they wanted them."

Such talk made me uneasy. I said. "Do you think they'll ever catch whoever did the shootings?"

"I sure hope not."

He laughed at my surprise. "Well, heck, look at it this way. Whoever pulled the trigger, it was the mayor and his pals who were responsible. They didn't have any right rezoning this area."

Sam's words came back to me: *I'd done things for her no man in his right mind would have done. . . . I always loved her. I did what I could to prove it.* I tried to believe that I was giving those words an arbitrary meaning.

"Was your mother pleased?"

Cobb's expression faltered, as if the candy bar he was munching had turned bitter in his mouth. "It saved the tree house, didn't it?"

"I asked you if she was pleased?"

"Look!" he suddenly cried. "There's McNutt, my pet squirrel. I'll bet he smelled my candy bar."

That afternoon, knowing I had to get back to Chicago by the following day, I was determined to bring things to a head, and when Sam and I were alone, I mentioned what Cobb had said about the rezoning business. "I guess Vinnie did all she could to preserve that tree house."

His lower lip jerked forward. "Vinnie was a dreamer. I could have told her it wouldn't do no good."

"But violence did."

His eyes were wide open but giving nothing away. "Sometimes that's what it takes."

"Yet it was all for nothing. She didn't live to enjoy it." I was prompting him as boldly as I dared, but perhaps he'd changed his mind; perhaps he'd decided he couldn't trust me after all. This possibility made me angry enough to prod him even more bluntly.

"Listen, Sam. Don't think I'm not aware of what I owe you. I've never forgotten. I'm willing to repay you any way I can. If you need help all you have to do is ask. If you've done something and it's bothering you and you want to talk about it, I'm ready to listen. And I give you my word. It'll go no further."

He looked at me rather strangely as I said this, and then, dropping his gaze, he loudly cleared his throat.

"You got somebody with you? In Chicago?"

"You mean living with me?" I grinned. "Not at the moment, as it happens."

"Take him with you."

It caught me unprepared, maybe because I was expecting, if anything, a more explicit confession.

"Please," he said. "Just for a while, anyway. At least till school starts."

"Why, Sam?"

"Better for him. All this moping and brooding ain't good for him. He needs a change."

The reticence of the man went too deep; he wasn't the confessing sort, and I had no right to badger him.

Nevertheless, I said, "He thinks you killed Vinnie."

"That's a lie."

"I know that. Maybe you'd have done anything *for* her. . . . I know you wouldn't have done anything *to* her."

His voice was blade sharp. "That's not what I meant. I meant it's not true he thinks I killed Vinnie."

"It's what he told me."

"You're wrong. You must have misunderstood him." He backed away, and I realized that we'd been standing toe to toe, like boxers. "What the hell, it don't matter. Will you take him away? Or will you run true to form and do your damnedest to avoid responsibility?"

I deserved that. I let it pass. "Will he come?"

"Only one reason he wouldn't. That damned tree house."

Our eyes met, and I knew what I must do. It was true, of course. If Sam was in danger of being exposed, the boy would be better off out of it all, away from him.

It took me less time than I thought, even though I probably worked harder than necessary knowing that I had to get it done before Cobb finished his chores and headed for the tree house. My emotions while I was doing it were as confused as my motives. It seemed to me that when I would pause in my exertions it was Vinnie's voice I could hear in the leaves around me, crying out against what I was doing, and I would be struck by a terrible sense of loss and shame and betrayal, and would have to whisper to myself: "It's only the wind in the leaves; it's only the wind."

Later, at the house, I didn't hear Cobb when he came in because I was upstairs packing, and it wasn't until I heard their voices ripping into each other that I went to the door and listened, and when I went down I found them squared off and furious in the middle of the kitchen.

"You're lying!" Cobb screamed. "I know you did it. You always said you'd tear it down. You hated it!"

If he'd been dead Sam's face couldn't have looked more like a corpse's.

Cobb turned to me in a frenzy. "He did! He destroyed the tree house! Vinnie's tree house. Our secret place. He said he would and now he's gone and done it. He was always jealous!"

"Not of you, boy," Sam murmured. "Never of you."

When there was nothing left between them but a bitter residue of hostility I took my cue and spoke quietly, reasonably, setting forth my proposition that maybe Cobb would like to come to Chicago with me for a while, an invitation to which he promptly agreed, without a moment's forethought, almost as if he had expected it, and Sam's eyes met mine in a secret smile of victory.

I had made up my mind to say nothing to Cobb about the past, with one exception, which my conscience insisted be made. On the plane I told him that I was sure he was mistaken about his father.

"What do you mean?" he said.

"He didn't kill your mother. You mustn't believe that."

"Oh, yes. He killed her."

"That's simply not true, Cobb."

His voice was as reasonable and patient as if he were explaining algebra to a poet. "I don't mean that *he* pushed her off the porch. But that doesn't mean he didn't kill her. Like those other people that were killed. The mayor and his buddies didn't actually shoot them, but it was still their fault. My father's an evil man. He never did the right thing by Vinnie or me. But he'll be sorry. He's going to pay for it. You wait and see."

Neither of us made any further reference to that conference and for a while I thought that bringing Cobb to Chicago had been an excellent idea, that all he had really needed was to get away from Fairhill and the tree house, and Sam. Naturally, I wondered if Cobb could suspect that Sam had shot all those people, but I've come to believe that he does not. Cobb has been with me nearly a month now, and when I mention Sam's name to see if his hostility toward him has diminished, he seems hardly to remember whom I'm talking about—or so he pretends, at least. I think that if he did suspect Sam he would have dropped some hint to that effect, even if he condoned and admired Sam for it. After all, he had been quick enough to accuse Sam of killing his mother.

Strike that last sentence. As it happens, I was wrong even about that. Two weeks have passed since I wrote those words and much has happened, so much that I'm almost too stunned to grasp its full significance. The evidence is there, I've seen it with my own eyes, so what else *can* I believe? Yet it's all so grotesque, so appalling, I find myself refusing to accept it, for though I believe in the *existence* of evil—it's all around us, I'm sure—this particular manifestation of it is simply too horrendous to conceive.

First, I'd better explain that on the surface nothing happened to disturb my peace of mind during the first week or so that Cobb was here. I'd let him do pretty much as he pleased and we seemed to take pleasure in each other's company. I'd told him to treat the apartment as his home, although I hadn't quite that degree of independence in mind that he gradually appropriated. I didn't mind his making a point of always locking his bedroom door whether he was in there or not—boys can often be funny about that sort of thing—but I did think he might have been more heedful of my warnings about wandering around Chicago after dark. After all, I told him, it isn't exactly Fairhill, and that he looks so much older than he is would, if anything, increase the risk he might be taking. All he said in reply was that he was looking for something, something he had to find as soon as possible, and yet he refused to tell me what it was, saying only that it would be a surprise.

As to the evidence I mentioned, this is how it came to light: Cobb had gone out for the afternoon, locking his bedroom door behind him as usual, and I was in my study working on a report when I discovered I needed to refer to some data packed away in the closet in Cobb's room. I'd never bothered to mention that I had a duplicate key to his door—I think he knew I would respect his privacy even if I had—and I unlocked the door and was rummaging about in the closet looking for the particular file I needed when I noticed a shirt on the floor in the corner. Thinking it must have fallen from a hanger I started to pick it up when I found that it was wrapped carefully around a small wooden box.

Not meaning to pry, but simply curious, I opened the box and found two things inside: a small package wrapped in brown paper, and an expensive Bushnell rifle scope. Call it memory, call it instinct, call it anything you want, I knew at once, and infallibly, that it was the scope stolen from the Kidwell place and used in the shootings at Fairhill Farms.

At the same time I knew that I was wrong about Sam, as if by holding that scope to my eye I could see what actually happened, could see Vinnie, tormented by suspicion, going to the tree house alone at dusk and finding the rifle and scope hidden there, and suddenly Sam was there, threatening to come up, and I could picture her terror and panic, her fear of having Sam discover what Cobb had done. In such blind distress she would have done anything to stop Sam—yes, I think she would even have jumped—but Sam had climbed to the tree house anyway, not looking for a gun, which he might not have noticed even if it was there, but for a man, a rival.

Yes, it all could have happened like that, or if not exactly like that, then in some way not so very different. There was, of course, another possibility, one which I refused even to let myself consider, for after all Cobb is only a boy, he's not a monster. He might have been capable of stealing a rifle and shooting strangers in one mad last resort to preserve his beloved tree house, but if his mother had somehow discovered what he had done and reacted in a way that had angered or displeased him, he still would not have been capable of harming her himself. That idea is unthinkable.

Four more days have passed, giving me time to reflect on my discoveries, and more of the pattern has become clear, almost all of it, and I'm beginning to understand how totally I've deceived myself. Sam knows the truth, of that I'm almost certain; nothing else would explain his behavior, or the things he said which I was so quick to misconstrue. His single purpose in calling me to Fairhill must have been to persuade me to take Cobb away from there, not only because that whole bad scene only nourished the boy's paranoia, or whatever one wished to call it, but because sooner or later he might be driven to some other act that would ultimately expose him to the authorities. Why Sam had not been more frank with me I can't be sure. Perhaps he doesn't trust me; after all, he never did.

Something else now: that other item in the box. When I unwrapped that small package I found what in some ways was an even greater shock to me than the gun scope—a collection of all those snapshots from Vinnie's album, the ones in which I was pictured. Now, Sam would never have told Cobb the truth about me, at least I don't think he would have, and I'm even more sure that the boy would never have learned anything from Vinnie; in fact, she must have hidden those albums away to be sure he would never come across those pictures and guess the truth. Obviously, he *had* found them. Then what? Had he faced Vinnie with them, one day up there in the tree house? Vinnie would not have lied, I'm sure of that. Later on, needing someone on whom to place the burden of guilt for his mother's death, regardless how it had happened, what could be more logical than to have chosen his father, just as he had blamed the other deaths on the "mayor and his buddies."

For you see, Cobb never did accuse *Sam* of killing his mother. What he'd said, with such curious emphasis and precision, with such diabolical candor and subtle duplicity was that his *father* had killed Vinnie; and on the plane he'd been so careful to say, "My *father's* an evil man. He never did right by Vinnie and me. But he'll be sorry. He's going to pay for it. You wait and see."

*You* wait and see. Even then I should have seen through his grim little joke.

I should have realized what he was telling me when he referred to his *father* both those times, for he never called Sam his father, any more than he called Vinnie by anything but her Christian name. He was talking about the person in those snapshots, the person who looked so startlingly like himself.

He was talking about his real father. About me.

Cobb came in a few minutes ago, stuck his head in the study door and waved a small package, announcing very gaily that he'd found what he was looking for—finally.

"What is it?" I asked.

He only laughed. "I told you. A surprise." Then, as if it were the biggest joke in the world, he added: "Actually, it's for my father. He'll really get a charge out of it."

With that he disappeared into his room, locking the door behind him, of course, and I've been sitting here trying to make myself believe that my reasoning about all this is absurd, way off the track, preposterous, and for all I know maybe it is. I certainly don't want to panic myself into the blunder of opening my mouth and saying a lot of things I'd later regret. There's no point in trying to excuse my past behavior if I don't have to, of trying to make him understand that it wasn't that I didn't *want* to marry Vinnie when she became pregnant with my child. I simply wasn't ready for all that. I had dreams, plans, ambitions. Vinnie understood. She never blamed me.

She never stopped loving me, either, which is probably why they hate me.

If they do hate me, both Sam and Cobb, is it remotely, wildly conceivable that they've been acting together in all this? That they have, for their own madly inscrutable reasons, *set me up?*

No, I must be mistaken. How could there possibly have been a gun in that package he waved in front of me? Just because he may have succeeded in stealing a rifle and scope in Fairhill doesn't mean he would have the skill to swipe a handgun in Chicago. He's clever, yes, but hardly that clever.

I've given up on the report; I can't possibly concentrate with that rock music blasting through the wall of Cobb's room. I can't imagine what's got into the kid, he never had it that loud before. He's always been the soul of courtesy and thoughtfulness.

I really must do something about it, but for some reason I have the strongest reluctance to get up and walk to his door and tell him to please turn it down. Not that it would do any good; he'd never hear me. Not even a cannon could be heard over that frightful din.

Now his door is opening, very, very slowly. And would you believe it? He's turned that volume up even *higher!*

# This Day's Evil

## by Jonathan Craig

It had been a near thing. It had been so near that even now, as he crouched there in the bushes behind the small frame house of the man he had come to kill, there was still a taut queasiness in his stomach, and the sweat that laved his ribs was chill.

Half an hour ago, he had been five minutes away from murder. He had stood at the back door of the house, one hand on the heavy automatic in his pocket, the other raised to knock. Then, through the barred but open window, he had heard the hollow pound of heavy boots across the front porch, the hammering of a big man's fist on the door, and the lazy rise and fall of Sheriff Fred Stratton's sing-song voice calling out a greeting to the man inside.

"Charlie!" Stratton had said in that fond, bantering tone he always used with Charlie Tate, "Charlie, you no-good rascal, your time has come. Open the door before I break it down."

He hadn't heard Charlie's reply. He had already been running toward the bushes in the back yard, his knees rubbery and his stomach knotting spasmodically with the realization that if the sheriff had come five minutes later he would have caught him in the house with a dead man.

Now, hidden from the house by the bushes, his fear-sharpened senses acutely aware of the incessant drone of insects and the sickening sweetness of lilacs, Earl Munger shifted his weight very slowly and carefully, trying to still the tremor in his legs.

To have been caught in the act by that lazy, fat slob of a sheriff would have been just his luck, he reflected. Sheriff Fred Stratton was the laziest, slowest man in the county, with a maddening, syrupy drawl that made you want to jam your hand down his throat and pull the words out for him.

They made a good pair, Fred Stratton and Charlie Tate. Stratton had lots of fat, and Tate had lots of money. Not that Tate would have the money long; just as soon as the sheriff left, Tate would have neither the money nor his life.

There were sure some strange ducks in this world, Earl thought sourly. Take Charlie, now. Here he was, seventy if he was a day, with nobody knew how much money hidden in his house, and living like a pauper. He didn't trust anybody or anything, unless maybe it was the sheriff, and he especially didn't trust banks. If all the cash money he'd collected in rent from the property he owned all over the county was in the house, as it almost had to be, there'd be something pretty close to fifty thousand dollars. Charlie never spent a dime. He was a crazy old miser, with bars and bolts on every door and window, just like in the story books, and for all the good his money did him, he might just as well be dead.

And he would be, Earl promised himself again. The money might not do any good for Charlie, but it would sure do a lot of good for him. At twenty-three, he owned the clothes he had on, and another outfit just like them, and nothing more. But after today things would be different. There'd be no more conversations like that one night before last with Lois Kimble, when he'd asked her to go for a drive with him.

"A drive?" Lois had said, the perfect doll's face as innocent as a child's. "A drive in *what*, Earl?"

"The truck," he had said. "It's more comfortable than it looks."

"You mean that old thing you haul fertilizer around in all day?"

"It doesn't smell," he said. "If it did, I wouldn't ask you."

"I'll bet."

"It doesn't. And it rides real good, Lois. You'd be surprised."

She looked at him for a long moment, the wide grey eyes inscrutable. "I'd be ashamed," she said. "I really would, Earl."

"You figure you're too good to ride in a truck? Is that it?"

She started to turn away. "I meant I'd be ashamed if I were you," she said. "I'd be ashamed to ask a girl to . . . Oh, it doesn't matter anyhow. I've got to be going, Earl."

"Sure, it matters. Listen—"

"Not to me," she said, walking away from him. "Goodbye, Earl."

And an hour later he had seen her pass the feed store where he worked, beautiful in her thin summer dress, wide grey eyes fixed attentively on the well-dressed young man beside her, the low-slung red sports car growling arrogantly through the town as if it were affronted by the big unwashed sedans at the curbs, impatient to be back with its own kind in the city where the bright lights and the life and the pleasure were, where there were places that charged more for a dinner than Earl made in a week.

But after today, all that would be changed. He'd have to wait a cautious time, of course, and then he could leave the stink of the feed store and the town far behind, and the young man in the sharp clothes and the red sports car with the beautiful girl on the seat beside him would be none other than Earl Munger.

This afternoon, he had rushed his deliveries so that he would have a full hour to kill and rob Charlie Tate before his boss at the feed store would begin to wonder where he was. He had hidden the small panel truck in the woods back of Charlie's place and then approached the house by a zigzag course through brush and trees, certain that no one had seen him, and that he could return to the truck the same way.

He wondered now why he hadn't robbed Charlie before, why he'd waited so long. And yet, with another part of his mind, he knew why. To rob Charlie, it would be necessary to kill him. The only way to get into his house was to have Charlie unlock the door, and Charlie couldn't be left alive to tell what had happened.

Then he heard the muffled slam of Charlie's front door, and a few moments later the sudden cough and roar of a car engine on the street out in front, and he knew that Sheriff Stratton had left.

Now! Earl thought as he left the bushes and moved swiftly to the back door. I can still do it and be back at the store before anybody starts getting his suspicions up. Once again he closed one hand over the automatic in his pocket and raised the other to knock.

Charlie Tate's footsteps shuffled slowly across the floor, and a moment later his seamed, rheumy-eyed face peered out at Earl through the barred opening in the upper half of the door.

"Hello, Earl," he said. "What is it?"

"The boss asked me to bring you something, Mr. Tate," Earl said, glancing down as if at something beyond Charlie's angle of vision.

"That so?" Charlie said. "What?"

"I don't know," Earl said. "It's wrapped up."

"I didn't order anything," Charlie said.

"It's too big to stick through those bars, Mr. Tate," Earl said. "If you'll open the door, I'll just shove it inside."

Charlie's eyes studied Earl unblinkingly for a full ten seconds; then there was a grating sound from inside, and the door opened slowly, and not very far.

But it was far enough. Earl put his hip against it, forced it back another foot, and slipped inside, the gun out of his pocket now and held up high enough for Charlie to see it at once.

There was surprise on Charlie's face, but no fear. "What do you think you're doing?" he asked.

"I'm taking your money," Earl said. "Wherever it is, get it, and get it now."

Charlie took a slow step backward. "Don't be a fool, son," he said.

"Don't you," Earl said. "It's your money or your life, Charlie. Which'll it be?"

"Son, I—"

Earl raised the gun a little higher. "Get it," he said softly. "You understand me, Charlie? I'm not asking you again."

Charlie hesitated for a moment, then turned and moved on uncertain feet to the dining room table. "It's in there," he said, his breathy, old-man's voice almost inaudible. There was a bottle of whisky on the table, but no glasses.

"In the table?" Earl said. "I'm telling you, Charlie. Don't try to pull—"

"Under the extra leaves," Charlie said. "But listen, son—"

"Shut up," Earl said, lifting one of the two extra leaves from the middle of the table. "I'll be damned."

There were two flat steel document cases wedged into the shallow opening formed by the framework beneath the leaves.

Earl pulled the other leaf away and nodded to Charlie. "Open them," he said.

"You can still change your mind," Charlie said. "You can walk out of here right now, and I'll never say any—"

"Open them, I said!"

Charlie sighed heavily, fumbled two small keys from his pocket, and opened the document cases.

It was there, all right, all in neat, banded packages of twenties and fifties, each of the packages a little over two inches thick.

The size of his haul stunned him, and it was several seconds before he could take his eyes from it. Then he remembered what else had to be done and he looked questioningly at the wall just over Charlie Tate's left shoulder.

"What's that?" he asked. "What've you got *there,* Charlie?"

His face puzzled, Charlie turned to look. "What are you talking . . . ?" he began, and then broke off with an explosive gasp as the butt of Earl's automatic, with the full strength of Earl's muscular arm and shoulder behind it, crashed against his skull just two inches behind his right ear.

He fell to the floor without a sound, all of a piece, the way a bag of old clothes held at arm's length would fall, in a limp heap.

Earl knelt down beside him, raising the gun again. Then he lowered it and shoved it back into his pocket. Nobody would ever have to hit Charlie Tate again.

He started to rise, then sank back, the sudden nervous tightening of the muscles across his stomach so painful that he winced. It was all he could do to drag himself to the table. He uncapped the bottle of whisky and raised it to his lips, shaking so badly that a little of the liquor sloshed out onto the table. It was a big drink, and it seemed to help almost at once. He took another one, just as big, and put the bottle back down on the table.

It was then that he heard the car door slam shut out front, and saw, above the sill of the front window, the dome light and roof-mounted antenna of Sheriff Fred Stratton's cruiser.

A moment before, Earl Munger would have sworn he could not move at all, but he would have been wrong. He moved too quickly to think, too quickly to feel. It took him less than five seconds to close the document cases and shove them under his arm, and it took him even less time than that to reach the back door and close it soundlessly behind him. Returning to the truck by the roundabout route that would prevent his being seen took the better part of ten minutes, every second of it a desperate fight against an almost over-powering urge simply to cut and run.

He'd left the truck on an incline, so that he would be able to get it under way again without using the starter. Now he pushed the shift lever into the slot for second gear, shoved in the clutch, released the hand brake, waited until the truck had rolled almost to the bottom of the incline, and then let the clutch out. The engine caught, stuttered, died, then caught again, and he drove away as slowly, and therefore as quietly, as he could without stalling the engine again.

Half a mile farther on, he turned off onto a rutted side road that led to a small but deep lake known locally as Hobbs Pond. There he shoved the gun and the packages of money into a half-empty feed sack, making sure they were well covered with feed, and then sent the metal document cases arcing as far toward the center of the lake as he could throw them.

Then, after burying the bag under half a dozen other bags of feed and fertilizer in the truck, he started back toward the store. The money would probably be safe in the truck for as long as he wanted to leave it there, but there was no sense in taking any chances. Tonight or tomorrow he would bury it somewhere, and then leave it there until the day when he could pick a fight with his boss, quit his job, and leave the area for good without raising any questions.

Back at the store, Burt Hornbeck came out on the front loading platform and eyed him narrowly.

"Didn't I see you gassing up that truck at Gurney's this morning?" he asked.

"That's right," Earl said.

"Well, how come? You ever know Gurney to buy anything from this store?"

"No."

"You bet, 'no.' What Gurney buys, he buys at Ortman's. Next time, gas it up at Cooper's, like I told you. Coop buys here, and so I buy from Coop. Got it?"

"The tires needed air," Earl said. "Coop hasn't got any air hose."

"Never mind the air hose. After this, gas that truck up at Coop's. I'm beginning to wonder how many times I got to tell you."

Not too many times, Earl thought as he walked back to the washroom to throw cold water on his face. Another couple or three weeks, a month at the most, and he'd be buying gas for a sassy red sports car, not a battered old delivery truck.

The whisky had begun to churn in his stomach a little. But it would be all right, he knew. From now on, everything would be all right. For a man with thousands of dollars everything had to be. That was the way of the world.

When he came back out to the loading platform, Sheriff Stratton's car was there, and the sheriff was talking with a fair-sized knot of men. The sheriff was sitting on the old kitchen chair Hornbeck kept out on the platform, his enormous bulk dwarfing it, making it seem like something from a child's playroom.

Trust the fat slob not to stand up when he can sit down, Earl thought as he edged a bit closer. The laziest man in the county, if not in the state. If Stratton was on one side of the street and wanted to get to the other, he would climb in his car, drive to the corner, make a U-turn, and come back, all to save walking a lousy forty feet. And talk about fat. The county could save money by buying a tub of lard and nailing a star on it. They'd have just as good a sheriff, and it wouldn't cost them a fraction of what they had to pay Stratton.

"What happened?" Earl asked George Dill, who had wandered over from his grocery store.

"It's old Charlie Tate," George said. "He's done took poison."

"He *what?*" Earl said.

"Poison," George said. "He killed himself."

The sheriff glanced up at Earl and nodded. "Howdy, Earl," he said, making about six syllables out of it. "Yes, that's what he did, all right. Lord only knows why, but he did." Beneath his immaculate white Stetson, the sheriff's round, pink-skinned face was troubled, and the small, almost effeminate hands drummed nervously on his knees.

"He—poisoned himself?" Earl said.

"I always said he was crazy, and now I know it," Norm Hightower, who owned the creamery, said. "He'd have to be."

There were a dozen questions Earl wanted to ask, but he could ask none of them. He wet his lips and waited.

The sheriff took a small ivory-colored envelope from the breast pocket of his shirt, looked at it, shook his head wonderingly, and slipped it back into his pocket.

"Charlie gave me that about half an hour before I found him dead," he said. "He told me not to open it until after supper. But there was something about the way he said it that bothered me. He tried to make it sound like maybe he was playing a little joke on somebody, maybe me. But he didn't bring it off. I had this feeling, and so as soon as I got around the corner I stopped the car and read it."

"And it said he was going to kill himself?" Joe Kirk, who carried the Rural Route One, said.

"That's what it said, all right," the sheriff said.

"But he didn't say why?" Frank Dorn, the barber, asked.

"No," Stratton said. "All he said was, he was going to do it, and what with." He reached into his right-hand trouser pocket and drew out a small blue and yellow tin about the size of a package of cigarettes. "And that's another thing I can't understand, boys. It's bad enough he would want to kill himself. But why would he do it with a thing like this?"

"What is it?" Sam Collins, from the lumberyard, asked.

"Trioxide of arsenic," the sheriff said, putting the tin back in his pocket. "I found it on the floor beneath the table."

"How's that again, sheriff?" Sam Collins asked.

"Ratsbane, Sam," Stratton said. "Arsenic. I reckon there isn't a more horrible death in this world than that. It must be the worst agony there is."

"Why'd he want to take such a thing, then?" Jim Ryerson, the mechanic from Meckle's Garage asked.

"It's like I told you," Norm Hightower said. "He was crazy. I always said so, and now I know it."

The sheriff got to his feet, ponderously, looking at the now badly-sprung kitchen chair regretfully, as if he hated to leave it. "Well," he drawled in that slow, slow singsong of his, "I reckon maybe I'd better call the coroner and the others. At least Charlie didn't have any kin. It seems like kinfolks just can't stand the idea of somebody killing himself. They always carry on something fierce. I've even had them try to get me to make out they died a natural death or got killed somehow. Anything but suicide. They can't stand it at all."

"I fed arsenic to some rats once," Tom Martin, the druggist, said. "I'd never do it again. When I saw what it did to those rats, I . . . well, I'd never do it again. Even rats don't deserve to die like that. It was the most awful thing I ever saw."

"Like I said before," the sheriff said. "I just can't understand old Charlie killing himself that way."

"Maybe he didn't know exactly what it would do to him," Tom Martin said.

"Maybe not," the sheriff said. "I don't see how he could know, and still take half a box of ratsbane and dump it in a bottle of whisky and drain almost half of it. There must have been enough arsenic in that bottle to kill everybody here and half the other folks in town besides." He moved off slowly in the direction of his car, picking his way carefully, as if to complete the short trip in the fewest steps possible. "I'd better be seeing about those phone calls," he said. "There's always a big to-do with a thing like this. Of course, Charlie's not having any kin is a help, but there'll still be a lot of work."

On the loading platform, Earl Munger tried to fight back the mounting terror inside him. No wonder the sheriff had taken one look at Charlie Tate lying there on the floor and thought he had died of posion. Why should he have looked for wounds or anything else? And how long would it be, Earl wondered, before the ratsbane really did to him what the sheriff had thought it had done to Charlie Tate? It was already killing him, he knew; he would feel the first horrible clutch of agony at any moment.

He forced himself to walk with reasonable steadiness to the truck, and although the door felt as heavy as the door of a bank vault, he managed to open it somehow and get in and drive away slowly.

Once on the highway that led to Belleville, he mashed the gas pedal to the floorboard and kept it there. He had to get to a doctor, and in this forsaken area doctors were few and very far between.

The nearest was Doc Whittaker, four miles this side of Belleville. Whittaker might be a drunk but he knew his business, at least when he was sober.

But when he reached Whittaker's place, Mrs. Whittaker told him her husband was out on a house call. He half ran back to the truck, already stabbing with the ignition key as he jumped inside, and took off with a scorch of rubber that left Mrs. Whittaker staring after him with amazement.

The next nearest doctor was Courtney Hampton, six miles east of Belleville on Coachman Road.

He was beginning to feel it now, the first stab of pain deep in the pit of his stomach. It wasn't like the other pains, the ones he had felt earlier when he was scared; it wasn't as acute, but it was growing stronger, and it was deep, deep inside him. It was the arsenic, and it was going to kill him.

There was a red light ahead. The Belleville cutoff. He kept the gas pedal on the floor, and when he reached the intersection, he shut his eyes for a moment, waiting for the collision that was almost sure to come. Brakes screamed and tires squealed on both sides of him, but no one crashed into him, and he started down the long, straight stretch of highway that would bring him to Coachman Road.

Eighteen minutes later, Earl Munger sat on Dr. Hampton's operating table, a rubber tube in his stomach, while the doctor filled a hypodermic needle, and then, without Earl's feeling it at all, inserted it in the back of his upper arm.

"And so you spread your lunch out right there where the insect spray could get to it," Hampton said, almost with amusement. "And sat there eating sandwiches garnished with arsenic, without even knowing it."

He glanced at Earl as if he expected him to say something, tube in his stomach or not. "Well," he went on, "you wouldn't be able to tell, of course. That's the insidious thing about arsenic. There's no smell or taste. That's why it's been a poisoner's favorite all through the ages."

"You want me to come back again, doc?" Earl asked when Hampton had removed the tube.

"Not unless you feel ill again," Hampton said. "That will be ten dollars, please."

On his way home, Earl Munger, for the first time in his life, knew the meaning of pure elation. It was a strange feeling, one he couldn't quite trust at first; but with every mile the feeling grew, and the happiness that flooded through him was the kind of happiness he had known as a child when things and people were the way they seemed to be, and not, as he had learned all too soon, the way they really were.

He took the long curve above the old Haverman place almost flat out, feeding more gas the farther he went into it, the way he had read that sports car drivers did. Even the old delivery truck seemed to handle like a sports car, and it amused him to think that, with the way he and the truck felt just now, he could show those fancy Ferrari and Lotus and Porsche drivers a thing or two.

He felt like singing, and he did. He felt like a fool; he felt as if he were drunk, but he sang at the top of his voice, and he was still singing when he braked the truck to a stop in front of the feed store and got out.

He would take the long way home, he decided. It was the better part of two miles that way, but he felt like walking, something he hadn't felt like doing in more years than he could remember.

He began to sing again, walking slowly, enjoying himself to an extent he would once have believed impossible. He sang all the way to his rooming house, and then, just as happily but a bit more quietly, continued to sing as he climbed the stairs to his room on the second floor and opened the door.

Sheriff Fred Stratton sat there in Earl's only chair, the pink moon-face as expressionless as so much suet, the small hands lying quietly on the brim of the spotless white Stetson in his lap.

Earl stared at him for a moment, then closed the door and sat down on the side of the bed. "What are you doing here, sheriff?" he asked.

"We were waiting for you at the store," Stratton said. "My deputy and me."

"I didn't see anybody," Earl said. "Why would you be wait—?"

"We didn't mean for you to see us," Stratton said. "It didn't take us long to find that money, Earl. And the gun too, of course."

"Money?" Earl said. "What money? I don't know anything about any money. Or any gun, either."

Stratton reached up and took the small, ivory-colored envelope from the breast pocket of his shirt. "Letter from my youngest daughter," he said. "Looks like she's bound and determined to make me a proud granddaddy again."

"That's the same letter you told everybody Charlie Tate gave you just before he—" Earl began, then broke off abruptly.

"That's right," Stratton said, putting the envelope back in his pocket and taking out the small blue and yellow tin. "Just like I told them this little box of throat lozenges was ratsbane."

Earl felt his mouth go dry. "Not poison?" he heard himself say. "Not arsenic?"

"No," Stratton said. "And even if Charlie *had* been meaning to poison himself, he wouldn't have put the poison in a bottle of whisky. He never took a drink in his life. That bottle on the table was mine, son. Charlie always kept a bottle on hand for me, because he knew I was a man that liked a little nip now and then."

Stratton glanced down at the tin.

"I dropped this at Charlie's house when I was there the first time, and so I went back to get it. When I saw what had happened, and that Charlie had opened his back door to somebody, I knew the killer had to be a man he knew pretty well. Otherwise, Charlie would never have let him in the house."

"But why?" Earl asked. "Why did you. . . ?"

"Why'd I make up all that about the letter and the lozenges?" Stratton said. "Well, I got the idea when I noticed the killer had helped himself to the whisky. I'd had a drink myself, the first time I was there, and I could see that somebody had taken it down another couple of inches, not to mention spilling some on the table. I figured the killing must have rawed somebody's nerves so much he'd had to take a couple of strong jolts to straighten himself out."

Stratton paused, studying Earl with tired, sleepy eyes that told him nothing at all. Earl waited until he could wait no longer. "And then?" he asked.

"Well," Stratton said, "there's one sure thing in this world, son. A man that thinks he's been poisoned is going to get himself to a doctor, and get there fast. And since there're only four doctors within thirty miles of here, all I had to do was call them and ask them to let me know who showed up."

"But I had the symptoms," Earl said. "I was in pain, and I—"

"Sometimes if a man *thinks* a thing is so, then it *is* so," Stratton said. "You were dead certain you'd been poisoned, and so naturally you had the symptoms."

He got to his feet, put the big white hat on his head very carefully, and gestured toward the door. "Well, Earl, I reckon we'd better head over toward the jail."

"A trap," Earl said bitterly. "A dirty, lousy trap. I guess you figure you're pretty smart, don't you?"

Stratton looked surprised.

"No such thing," he said. "Just pretty lazy. I saw a chance to make your guilty conscience do my work for me, and I took it. That's how it is with us lazy folks, son. If there's a way to save ourselves some work, we'll find it."

# The Forgiving Ghost

## by C. B. Gilford

The murder—although Claude Crispin, the murderer, was the only one who knew that that's what it was—occurred in broad daylight, in bright sunshine. But not, of course, within view of any casual spectators. Nobody saw it; so everybody took it for what Claude Crispin said it was, an accident.

The first that any outsiders knew of it was when Claude Crispin raced his motorboat in from the center of the lake, and started shouting and waving his arms at the nearby joyriders and water skiers. He told them something about his wife's falling in the water and his not being able to find her.

Immediately, all the boats—some with their skiers still dangling behind them—raced for the spot. They found it when they found the swimming dog. Momo was the belligerent little Pekingese which had belonged to Mrs. Crispin. Claude babbled something to the searchers about how the dog had fallen into the water, and Mrs. Crispin had jumped in to save her. Here was the dog still swimming, of course, but there was no sign of the mistress.

Somebody apparently thought that as long as they were there, they might as well save the dog. So Momo was pulled aboard one of the boats, where she showed her gratitude by shaking the water out of her fur rather indiscriminately and snarling at her rescuers. Claude looked especially askance at that part of the operation. Now that the Pekingese had provided the visible reason why Mrs. Crispin, a poor swimmer, had been in the water at all, he would really have preferred to let her drown.

Meanwhile, nearly all the other occupants of the boats had jumped into the water and were doing a lot of diving and splashing around. Claude, watching them, wrung his hands, wore an anguished expression, and generally gave the appearance of an anxious, worrying, tragic husband.

They were at it for some twenty minutes. But at the end of that time everyone was pretty well exhausted, and even the most enthusiastic divers were ready to admit that they weren't going to find Mrs. Crispin either dead or alive. When they related this fact to

Claude, he burst into tears and started to shake so violently that a stranger had to climb into his boat and steer it back to shore for him.

Thereafter, it became an official matter. The sheriff was summoned and he came out to the lake with a couple of his deputies. Preparations got underway for a dragging operation. The sheriff himself, a kindly, sympathetic man, sat down with Claude and got the whole story from him.

Yes, the Crispins were city folks, Claude said, and they'd vacationed for several summers at this lake. One of their favorite pastimes had been to rent a motorboat and cruise aimlessly around. Claude was a pretty fair swimmer, though he didn't get much practice these days. Mrs. Crispin wasn't afraid of the water, but she'd been a very poor swimmer.

"Why didn't she wear a life jacket, like the rules say?" the sheriff demanded, but without too much harshness.

Claude shrugged his shoulders helplessly. "You know how women are," he answered. "My wife had a very good figure, looked fine in a bathing suit. So she was always interested in getting a tan. If she'd worn one of those jackets, it would have covered her up and she wouldn't have gotten the tan. So she just left the jacket in the bottom of the boat. Vanity, I guess you'd call it."

The sheriff nodded sagely. "And you say she jumped in on account of the dog?"

Claude let himself sound bitter. "She loved that dog as much as if it had been a kid. Took it with her everywhere. Don't ask me how the dog fell overboard, though. Usually my wife carried it around in her arms. But this time she was letting it ride up front by itself. I don't know whether it fell or jumped. The thing never seemed to have much sense. But there it was in the water suddenly, and my wife started screaming. Now, I'd have stopped the boat and jumped in after it myself, but my wife didn't wait even to ask me. The next thing I knew, she was gone, too. I slowed the boat down and did a U-turn, but by the time I got back to the place, my wife had already disappeared. I cut the motor and went in after her, but I never did see her. I don't know what happened. She was just gone."

The sheriff seemed to understand. "Sometimes," he said, "when a poor swimmer jumps into deep water, gets a cramp or something, he just sinks to the bottom and never does come up. I guess it was one of those cases."

And that was the verdict. Probably because the idea never once crossed his mind, the sheriff didn't even mention murder.

Though he'd gotten rid of his wife, Claude Crispin still had his wife's prized possession, Momo. Sometime later that same afternoon Momo's rescuer returned her to Claude, clean, dry, but in no better humor.

The instant the dog was brought into the one-room cottage, she began an immediate sniffing search for her mistress. When the mistress couldn't be found, she set up a mournful, yelping wail. Claude, alone now and able to vent his true feelings, aimed a kick which almost landed, and which was close enough to send the animal scurrying into a safe corner to cogitate upon what had gone wrong with the world.

"Alvina is dead," Claude explained happily and maliciously.

The dog blinked and stared.

"I guess for the moment," Claude went on, "I've got to endure you. I'm supposed to be so broken up about the accident that I've got to pretend that I'm cherishing you as my remembrance of my poor, dead wife. It won't last, though, I can promise you that. Your days are numbered."

Momo whined softly and seemed to be looking around for a route of escape.

Claude smiled. He felt good, very satisfied with himself. "Ought to be grateful to you, though, oughtn't I, Momo? You were a very convenient gimmick. But don't think that's going to do you any good once we're away from this place. You swim too well, Momo, so I won't try a lake on you. Some little something in your hamburger, maybe, and then you can fertilize my garden. As soon as we get home, Momo."

The dog cringed and lay down with her head between her paws. She'd endured unkind remarks from Claude before, and now the threat in his tone was unmistakable.

Claude lay back on the bed and closed his eyes. He had really and truly had a hard day. There'd been the strain and excitement of planning, the deed itself, and then the display of grief all afternoon. It had been rewarding, but quite wearing, too. He felt like sleep.

That was when the dog yelped. Claude had begun to drift off, and the noise woke him. Cursing, he sat up and looked toward the corner where he'd last seen Momo. The dog was still there, but not cringing any longer. Instead, Momo was standing up shakily on her hind legs, her tail wagging, her eyes shining. In fact, she was the very picture of canine ecstasy.

"Hello, Claude."

The voice was a familiar one. Alvina's voice. At first he was sure that he was either dreaming or imagining. He blinked his eyes, striving to come fully awake. But then he knew somehow that he was already awake, and he looked in the direction the dog was looking.

Alvina was standing there!

Not all wet and dripping, her hair tangled with seaweed. Not even in the bathing suit and bandana she'd last worn. This Alvina was quite dry, lipsticked and powdered, and in a gay little flowered frock he'd never even seen before. Her blue eyes were bright; her blonde hair was shining; and she stood just inside the door of the cottage, although Claude was quite sure that the door had neither opened nor closed.

"Claude, I said hello, and you haven't even answered me." Then she smiled, as if she'd suddenly remembered something. "Oh, of course. You're dreadfully surprised. You hadn't expected to see me ever again."

Claude stated the incredible. "You're alive!"

"Oh, no, Claude, I'm a ghost."

Instinctively he looked to Momo for confirmation. She wasn't, however, howling with fear as dogs are supposed to do in the presence of the supernatural. Instead, she was still wagging her tail, quite as if she too saw and recognized Alvina. But the strangest fact of all was that, although Momo obviously was aware of the presence of her mistress, and would normally have run to Alvina to be picked up and petted, now she seemed to realize that this visitor was not the sort who could pick up and pet even the smallest dog. In other words, Claude reflected as he tried to sort out his thoughts—Momo knew it was Alvina and yet wasn't Alvina, a friendly spirit but a spirit nevertheless.

But Claude still found this hard to believe. "Are you sure you're a ghost? I mean . . . "

"Of course I'm a real ghost. I'd have to be, wouldn't I? I'm certainly not alive. Because you killed me. Remember, Claude?"

"It was an accident," he started to say automatically.

"Oh, for pity's sake, Claude," she interrupted him. "I should know, shouldn't I? I was there. It was murder. You pushed me in, dear, and then you held my head under water."

It wasn't till then that Claude began to wonder, not whether this was really Alvina's ghost, but more as to what Alvina's ghost was doing here. And with the curiosity came just a little tingle of fear.

"I swear to you, Alvina," he began again.

"Darling, I know it was murder, and everybody where I came from knows it was murder. Only people who've been murdered get to come back as ghosts. Or didn't you know that?"

"No, I didn't know that," he admitted.

She threw back her head and laughed. It was Alvina's old laugh, tinkling and silvery. Momo barked in happy accompaniment to it. "Maybe you wouldn't have murdered me if you'd known that, eh, Claude?"

He decided he'd better be frank and honest. There wasn't much choice. "You are rather frightening," he said.

She crossed the room and sat down on the corner of the bed. Appropriately enough, he noticed, she seemed utterly weightless, and the corner didn't sag at all under her.

"Poor Claude," she said. "I didn't mean to frighten you. But as I said, murdered people do have the privilege of coming back, and I just couldn't resist the opportunity."

He was beginning to take little courage now from her mild manner. "Why did you come back, Alvina?"

"We parted so suddenly, dear. There wasn't time to discuss anything."

"What is there to discuss?"

"Well, Momo, for instance." At the mention of her name, the Pekingese wagged her tail. "Claude darling, I know you had reason to hate me, but I hope that feeling of yours doesn't extend to that innocent little dog."

Remembering his conversation with Momo of just a few minutes past, Claude felt himself blushing guiltily. "Momo really will never be happy with you gone, Alvina," he evaded.

"She can be happy if you'll try to make her happy. I know how you two have always been enemies, but it was your fault, Claude, not Momo's. Promise me you'll try to make friends with her. Promise me you'll take good care of her. She's an orphan now, you know, thanks to you. Will you promise me, Claude?"

Claude grabbed at the chance of getting off so easy. "I promise, I solemnly promise," he said.

"Thank you, Claude," she answered, and she seemed very sincere. They sat in silence for a moment then. Alvina's ghostly eyes gazed on Claude almost affectionately. He tried to reciprocate, but found the situation a bit strained.

"Well, was that all you wanted?" he asked finally. "I mean, now that we've agreed about the dog, I suppose that puts your spirit at rest, Alvina, and now you'll be content to . . ."

He stopped, fumbling. What he wanted to say, of course, was that ghosts—even apparently friendly ones—made him nervous, and he'd prefer that she return to her watery grave and stay there. Saying it would have been impolite, however, and perhaps—he still wasn't sure of her attitude—a trifle dangerous.

"You've been very sweet, Claude," she said. "And I do feel a lot better now that I know Momo will be well taken care of. I'm so grateful to you."

If she was going to become so polite and sentimental and easy to get along with, he could afford to be decent himself. "Look, Alvina, I'm sorry . . . "

She leaned a little closer to him, and a little ghostly frown creased her brow. "Oh no, don't say that, darling. You have no reason to be sorry. I deserved what I got."

"You think so?" Surprise was building on surprise.

"I know so. I deserved to be murdered. I was simply an awful wife to you."

"Oh, I wouldn't say that, Alvina."

"But it's true. I'd become quite a witch. I didn't realize it when I was alive, but I see it all clearly now. I was selfish and headstrong and quarrelsome. I always wanted my own way, and I made a scene if I didn't get it. And worst of all, I wasn't loving enough. Don't you completely agree on my little catalogue, dear?"

"Well, yes . . ."

"So you were quite justified in doing what you did, Claude. Isn't that so?"

"Alvina!"

"I mean it, Claude. I mean it absolutely. I deserved to get murdered."

"Well, now, I wouldn't go so far as to say that."

"It's the truth. So I want to tell you this, darling. And I mean it from the bottom of my heart. I forgive you completely."

He stared at her incredulously. There was a little tingling in him again. Not from incipient fear as before. From what then? He wasn't quite sure. But when someone is so generous and tolerant . . . well, it just gives one a funny feeling, that's all.

"Gee, Alvina . . ." he started to say.

But she was gone. Momo was whining piteously, and frantically running about the room from wall to wall, searching for something that was surely no longer there.

"Don't bring that dog in my apartment," Elise said. She was in purple toreador trousers today and stood with her hands on her hips barring the passage. Her dark hair waved behind her as she shook her head.

"But, angel," Claude Crispin said, "it's my wife's dog."

"I know that," Elise snapped. "But I don't like dogs, and I liked your former wife even less."

"But, angel, I couldn't leave the dog at home alone. And I've got to take care of it."

"Why?" The electricity in Elise's dark eyes crackled. "Why don't you just get rid of it?"

"I promised . . ."

"You what?"

"Well, I sort of made a secret promise after my wife died. It was the least I could do. After all, I owed her something. Try to understand, angel. Don't be cruel. We have gained quite a bit, you know. There'll be no more interference. I'm free. Just the two of us . . ."

"Three," she corrected him. "You and me and the dog."

"But we're better off than before, aren't we? We've made progress. Please let me in, angel."

She hesitated for another long moment, scorning him with her eyes. Then, abruptly, she turned and walked away, leaving the passage free for him to enter. He slipped in, bringing Momo on her leash, and closed the door behind him.

Gaining admittance didn't make Momo happy. She lay down just inside the door, watching Claude reproachfully, and making small glum sounds. But Claude ignored the dog, and followed Elise to the sofa, where he sat down close but without touching her.

"You took your sweet time coming to see me," Elise said viciously.

"Angel, I had to be discreet. I'm a widower. I'm supposed to be in mourning. I explained that to you."

"Three whole months. Did it have to be that long?"

"Maybe I was trying to be too cautious."

"You certainly were."

"Forgive me, angel." He put his arms out for her, but she squirmed away. "Won't you forgive me? I was torn between caution and passion, believe me, angel."

"And the caution won."

"All right. But it's over now. Let's make up for lost time."

"I'm afraid I'm not in the mood, Claude."

"Elise, I went through an awful lot for you. I took big chances.
Seems you ought to forgive me a little caution in a case like this."

"I'll forgive you nothing. You'll have to learn you can't toy with
my affections this way, Claude Crispin. You can't leave me dangling
for three whole months . . ."

Elise's bitter speech was interrupted suddenly by a sharp bark
from Momo. Distracted, Claude looked at the dog. He found her
sitting up, eyes bright, tail wagging. And Alvina was sitting in the
chair opposite them.

"So this is the woman you murdered me for, Claude," she said.

"Alvina!" he breathed.

"Did you call me Alvina?" Elise demanded.

"Darling," Alvina explained, "she can't see me. So don't make her
think you've gone crazy by talking to someone she doesn't know is
here. I'll be very quiet. You just go ahead with what you were doing."

"Claude, what's the matter with you?" Elise wanted to know.

"Nothing. I'm just a little upset, I guess."

"She's very pretty, Claude," Alvina commented. "Much prettier
than I was. Different type, too. More exciting and romantic."

"Look, Elise," Claude said, hastily rising from the sofa, "I think
I'd better go home. I don't feel well."

"Go home? You just got here and I haven't seen you for three
months."

Alvina sighed audibly. "She's the demanding sort, isn't she,
Claude? I guess that makes women more desirable. I wish I could
have been more that way."

"Elise." Claude was confusedly fumbling now. "Maybe some other
time . . ."

"Claude, you stay here, or it's all over with us."

"But you don't want me, Elise. You're angry with me."

"You're so right. And I'm going to keep on being angry with you
till you apologize."

"All right, I apologize."

"That's better."

"Am I forgiven then?"

"That will take some time. You'll have to make it up to me. I've sat around here waiting for you for three long months, and you'll have to make that up to me."

"She's very demanding, isn't she?" Alvina said. "Is that what makes her so interesting, Claude?"

"That doesn't make her interesting!" Claude shouted.

"Claude," Elise screamed, "don't shout at me! And besides, I don't know what you're talking about." Then she stood up, too, facing Claude angrily. "You don't show up for three months. Then you come here without a decent explanation and you talk gibberish."

"Angel . . ."

"Don't angel me!"

"Is it presents you want, Elise? What can I do? Just tell me. I want to take up where we left off. I went through so much. You know what I did."

"I know nothing of the sort, Claude. Don't try to implicate me."

"But you're in it as much as I am."

"Oh no, I'm not. It was your idea, and you went through with it all alone."

"But you approved, angel. You wanted me to do it."

"Claude, if that's what you came here for, to tell me I'm just as guilty as you are, then you can leave."

Without waiting for him to accept her invitation, she turned from him and walked away, through the bedroom door, which she slammed behind her. Claude stood open-mouthed in the center of the living room, and Momo barked joyously.

"Poor girl," Alvina said, "she feels guilty. That's what's upsetting her so. I'm sure she's not like this normally. Claude, I want you to tell her that I've not only forgiven you, but I've forgiven her, too."

Claude sat down on the sofa again, heavily, wearily. "Thanks, Alvina. That's mighty decent of you."

"I'm sure the impression I just got of her is inaccurate."

"I'm afraid it isn't," Claude admitted with a frown. "She's headstrong. She's quarrelsome. She's tremendously selfish."

"But, darling, those are the very things that were wrong with me. Oh, I wish there was something I could do. The trouble is, you see, that ghosts can haunt only their murderers, and strictly speaking, Elise isn't even an accomplice. But I wish I could talk to her, and tell her everything I've learned. Because basically I think she must be a very nice girl. When are you going to get married, Claude?"

"Married?" The word startled him somehow.

"You did intend to marry her, didn't you?"

"Oh yes, she's always insisted on it. On her own terms, of course. The trouble is that now I don't know what her terms are."

"That makes her mysterious, darling. And mystery is so attractive."

"Look here, Alvina." He rose from the sofa again, greatly disturbed. "Are you trying to encourage me?"

"Darling," she remonstrated, "you went to an awful lot of trouble murdering me. I think you should get your reward. And if Elise is what you want, then I want her for you. You see, Claude, I still have your interests at heart. And, well, I must confess . . ."

"What, Alvina?"

"A little soft spot, I guess you'd call it."

"Really? That's very generous of you."

"Oh, no, it's still selfish, I'm afraid," she answered softly. "Sometimes, Claude, I have the very selfish yearning for another chance. If I could just get another body or something and come back to you, I'm sure I could do a much better job of making you happy than I did before."

He felt terribly embarrassed, felt he ought to do something or say something, but he didn't know what. Poor Alvina . . . but he didn't want to say that.

She was gazing tenderly up at him. "Oh darn," she said, "I'm afraid I'm going to cry. Goodbye, darling. Good luck, too."

Then once again, and as suddenly as before, she was gone. Momo began to whine pitifully and lonesomely. And Claude Crispin felt pretty much the same.

Alvina was home waiting for him, when he returned from one of his many unsatisfactory visits to Elise's apartment. He'd left Elise in a rage, but here was Alvina placidly curled up in her favorite old chair and giving him a smile of welcome. He felt almost glad to see her. It had been over two weeks.

"How's Elise, darling? I didn't want to be a busybody and poke my nose in there, but I am concerned."

"Well, she still can't stand the dog."

Momo barked in confirmation.

"And even though I've gone to see her every day since, she still hasn't forgiven me for staying away for three months."

"Darling, she's just as unreasonable as I was, isn't she? That's too bad. I wish you could find someone more suitable. You know, it's too bad you can't murder Elise. Then she'd learn her lesson like I have." She paused, crestfallen. "Oh darn, that wouldn't work either, would it? The dead and the living can't get together very well."

He crossed the room and sat down on the hassock in front of Alvina's chair. Momo followed him and hopped up onto his lap. He petted the dog.

"You know something, Alvina?" he said. "If murder were the proper way of managing a woman, I wouldn't have to bother with Elise at all. Because I would have already found the perfect woman in you."

"That's sweet of you, Claude." Her smile was radiant. "Isn't it too bad that things have to work out this way? That we couldn't reach our perfect understanding until it was too late? Oh, I wish there were some way. I've asked about borrowing another body somewhere, but they say it can't be done."

"Yes, I wish there were some way, too, Alvina," he said.

Momo agreed, barking enthusiastically.

"You know," Claude said suddenly, "I've just had a happy thought."

"What, darling?" Alvina's ghostly eyes lighted with hope.

"Well, though you can't join me, I could join you."

"Claude!"

"Yes, it's rather drastic, I know."

"What about Elise?"

"I don't think she'd mourn more than a day or two."

"But there are other things to consider, too. You're still a young man, Claude. You have so much to live for."

"What? Just tell me what? I lost everything when I lost you."

"Claude, darling. Oh, I wish I could kiss you."

"Can't you? Have you really tried?"

"I know I can't. I've been told. There's a barrier between us."

"Then if you can't cross it, I certainly shall!"

"Oh, Claude, do you mean it?"

"Of course I mean it. There must be something appropriate in that medicine cabinet. I'd go up to that lake again and use it, darling, for sentimental reasons. But that would mean an awful delay. And I'm impatient to be with you again."

"Claude, dearest . . ."

He stood up. "I'll go see what's in the medicine cabinet right now."

He rushed off, but her voice stopped him. He turned back.

"Claude, get something for Momo, too, will you?"

"Certainly. I don't want to be separated from Momo, darling, any more than I want to be separated from you."

When they met on the other side, Momo jumped down from Claude's arms and went running to Alvina. She leaped into her mistress's arms and cuddled there, giving off small, ecstatic squeaks.

"That's a lucky dog," Claude said. "When do I get my welcome kiss?"

But for the moment, Alvina and Momo were lost in the contemplation of each other, hugging and squealing and kissing. Claude was patient. He spent the time glancing around at his new surroundings.

"I never thought to ask you, darling," he said, "but what kind of place is this anyway?"

What prompted the question was the fact that a couple of strangers were approaching. They were wearing a sort of uniform, like doormen, or perhaps guards. The uniforms had a red and black motif.

"Claude Crispin?" one of them asked.

"That's me," Claude said.

"Come with us, Mr. Crispin."

"I'm afraid you don't understand," Claude objected. "This is my wife here. I intend to stay with her."

It was Alvina who explained the difficulty. "Claude darling, Momo and I really would like to have you stay with us. But there are those old rules, darling. You're a murderer, you know. You'll have to go to the other place."

And Alvina and Momo went back to hugging and kissing.

# The Crazy

## by Pauline C. Smith

**M**rs. Sedonia Naughton, his stepmother, did not introduce him to her guest. She simply threw open his door and the two women stood there observing him as if he were a disturbingly unique but harmless animal in a zoo.

He seemed to be constructing something on a long, bare wooden table placed in the center of the many-windowed room. The room, while crowded, still gave the appearance of studied organization. Exquisitely executed sailboats floated within narrow-necked bottles, precision-model automobiles rode the shelves; oil paintings, watercolors, grotesquely beautiful masks climbed the walls between windows, and booklined cases rose to the ceiling; a restive room at rest only upon the corner bedstead, pristine and smooth, but with two bed pillows alertly vigilant at its head.

He acknowledged the presence of the women by raising smoky eyes for only an instant, then he returned to his work. With a probing forefinger, he rolled invisible tools on the bare table. Selecting one, he picked it up delicately, scrutinized it attentively; then, bending with absorption over the table, he used it with finical exaction upon a nonexistent object.

The women stood there for some minutes watching this extraordinary pantomime, which was conducted with such scrupulous authenticity that the guest leaned forward, slanted from the hips, squinting tiny eyes in an endeavor to see that which could not be seen. She caught herself in the act and straightened indignantly when he looked up for a moment, his eyes filled with derisive amusement.

Sedonia tapped her shoulder, drew her back into the hall, closed the door to his room and the two went on downstairs.

"Well, I never," gasped the visitor, safe once more in the living room. She sank to a chair, breathed heavily, and fanning herself with a limp hand, gasped again. "In all my born days, I never!"

Sedonia was satisfied. She smoothed her armored hips with small, soft, well-manicured hands, sat down, and poured.

The visitor took a sip of coffee, which seemed to revive her. Patting her lips daintily, she asked politely, "What is he making?"

"What is he *making?*" cried Sedonia. "Well, for heaven's sake, he's not making anything. I mean, not anything except a fool of himself." Sedonia was annoyed because her guest had not stated an obvious fact. So she stated it herself. "He's crazy, of course. He's been fiddling around with nothing on that bare table of his ever since his father died. Six months now!"

"My goodness. Maybe he *thinks* there's something there," observed her guest.

"Of course he thinks there's something there. He's crazy."

The guest leaned forward and dropped her voice to a whisper. "Have you ever looked?"

*"Looked?"*

"I mean, gone in and felt around . . ."

"On the *table?* Oh, for heaven's sake, of course not. Anyway, I never go in there. I don't clean in there or make the bed or anything. He does that. He wants it that way. His father told me so. Well, that's all right." She shrugged. "That's fine with me."

"Maybe it was his father's death that—"

"That made him crazy? No, it just changed his craziness. Before that, he used to break out of his shell once in a while. Oh, not much and not with me, but with his father. His father'd go in his room and they'd talk up a storm, all about what he was making on that table, and he really made things then. He made all those models and painted the pictures and stuff."

"Well, my stars!" said the guest.

"When I used to tell his father I thought he was crazy, he'd say no he wasn't, he was a warped genuis, or an unconventional artisan, or if he was crazy, he was an idiot savant, whatever that is, and laugh."

The visitor clucked a sympathetic tongue. Then she said, "He certainly doesn't look crazy."

"No, I suppose he doesn't. He looks like his mother. There's a picture of her around here somewhere. She died when he was twelve or thirteen, that's ten—eleven years ago. . . ."

"Maybe it was her dying that made him—"

"All I know is he never went to school. From the very first, he never went to school, and you know they make kids go to school unless they're either dumb or crazy. You know that."

Her guest nodded.

"Well, he's not dumb because he reads all those heavy books in there, and besides, he keeps getting new ones. And his father said he wasn't crazy because he had tutors for him all those years—teachers that came to the house—and he said he learned more than the tutors could teach him. But I still say he's crazy because he acts crazy."

Sedonia retreated into a short brooding silence, during which her guest tried not to clink her coffee cup nor to become obtrusive as she surreptitiously slid curious eyes about the room.

"I thought somebody ought to see him," Sedonia said, startling her guest. "I just thought somebody ought to see how crazy he acts, somebody who wasn't in glove with him and his father and the will. Somebody who'd say, 'He's crazy,'—somebody like you."

The guest, on cue, eager to please, answered, "He certainly *seems* to be crazy, working like that on something that isn't even there. He certainly does seem to be *some* kind of crazy, anyway," she repeated thoughtfully, remembering the mathematical precision of the busily skillful fingers, the frowningly intelligent face so keenly intent upon an invention that only he could touch and see.

"Well, sure he is," announced Sedonia. "I told his father he was crazy . . . that was a while after we were married, of course, and I came to this house. Oh, this house!" With a crimson-tipped gesture of contempt, she waved away not only the lush Victorian elegance, but her guest's timid interjection as to its grandeur.

"After three years in it, I can't breathe any more. I thought, when we got married, with him retired and all, he'd take me places—to Mexico, Canada, England, France. Around the world even. Wouldn't you think—?" She withdrew once more into sullen refuge to dwell upon a cosmopolitan future she had been sure would be hers. . . . "Well, he wouldn't budge. He was older than I. Oh, much older," she said, fluffing unbelievably golden hair, "set in his ways, I suppose. And all hung up on his crazy son. Wouldn't leave him for a minute. 'So you won't leave him,' I yelled; 'that proves he's crazy and you're scared to go away.' Then he died and went away after all."

"What did he die of?" asked her guest.

"He fell down the steps." Sedonia pointed toward the steep, open stairway in the hall. "Right down those steps. I was watching from the top, and he hit each post and didn't move a muscle after he landed. So he died right away. The doctor said it was a heart attack."

"Tch tch," observed her guest.

"I never saw *him*," she said as she pointed at the ceiling, "move so fast. He was out of his room in nothing flat, pushed me away and

leaped down the steps three at a time. But did he call the doctor or
do any of the things a sane person would do, like see if his heart
was beating or feel his pulse? No way. He just sat there on the floor
in the hall by his father's body and looked up at *me* at the top of the
stairs! At me, not his father! So I went and called the doctor from
the upstairs phone. And I didn't go down until the doctor got here.
Then I *had* to go down to let him in because *he*," again pointing at
the ceiling, "wouldn't budge. Just sat there on the floor, not moving
except for his head, his eyes on me every second, as I went around
the body and walked to the door to let the doctor in the house. Even
when he helped carry the body in to the sofa and all the while the
doctor examined him, those eyes were on me, not on his father, the
doctor, or anything else . . . and it was like that all during the funeral, too. . . ."

The guest shuddered.

"Well, I was scared enough to tell the doctor about it, and the
doctor said oh, pooh, pooh, that he'd known him all his life and,
being a pundit, whatever that is, he'd probably react that way during
shock and didn't even know what his eyes were looking at."

"My, my," breathed the guest.

"Then, after the funeral, he kept his eyes on me all the time the
lawyer read the will. And as soon as the will was read, he got up
and went upstairs and closed his door, and that's when I told the
lawyer how he watched me all the time and how crazy he was and
that I was afraid he'd go violent any minute. The lawyer said something about ah, no, he wasn't crazy or violent or any of those things,
he was a sophist, whatever a sophist is. Then he patted me on the
shoulder and told me not to worry, that I was now comfortably well
off as long as I sat tight and let *him*—" pointing at the ceiling "—
do his own thing."

"Well!" said the guest.

"At least one thing. Right after that, he got all wrapped up in that
nothing on his table and he hasn't looked at me since."

"That's one thing," agreed the guest.

"But the will won't be probated for a year—well, six months now."

"What's probated?" asked the guest.

"It means everything will be legally mine. The money, house, and
*him*," nudging her shoulder ceilingward. "That's the way the will
goes. Like I'm kind of his keeper. So I said to the lawyer, 'If I'm his
keeper, it means he's crazy. Right?' 'Wrong,' said the lawyer, 'it
means you're a mentor,' whatever that is."

"Goodness!" said the guest.

"And it means I'm stuck in this house, with enough money to travel anywhere . . ."

"That's wonderful!" cried the guest.

"But I can't go. Not, at least, until the will is probated."

Sedonia leaned forward and poured a fresh cup of coffee for her guest, who gulped it down in one swallow, and asked, "Yes?" with a gasp.

"Well, you see," said Sedonia in a tone of confidence, "once that will is probated, it means I can *do* something."

"What?" asked the guest.  ·

"It means I can get somebody in here—a doctor who is not hung up on pundits and a lawyer who hasn't got a sophist routine, and have these new ones, who aren't hand in glove with the family, look over that crazy you-know-who," as she pointed on high, "and I bet I can get him committed in nothing flat."

The guest clapped her hands.

"Because he's crazy. You saw how he is."

"My goodness, yes," affirmed the guest, remembering the derisive smile and smiling now in happy retaliation.

Sedonia sat back in her chair and folded her arms across stiffly ample breasts. "Then," she said, "once I get him put away, maybe I can sell this house and live a little."

Sedonia moved into her slim and golden, youthful, exciting, cosmopolitan world of fancy, and the guest sensed the visit to be over.

She rose with a vague murmur as to duties involving grandchildren home from school and thought, momentarily, as she rose, of the crazy young man upstairs; entertaining a flash of comprehension that he might be—he just might be—working on something with true substance, something real. . . . "Well," she said, and moved across the flowers of the carpet.

Sedonia ushered her out the door, promising brightly, "We'll see each other again. . . . On the park bench sometime?"

"Oh my, yes," agreed the guest. She started down the broad cement steps, then turned as the door began to close. "You know," she offered timidly, "maybe you ought to feel around on that table—just feel around, you know . . ." but the door was now shut and she walked across the park toward the reality of a cramped apartment, swarming with hungry, disrespectful grandchildren whom she must feed and suffer, and wished she lived back there in the old house on this side of the park with a crazy stepson bent studiously over a bare table. . . . One thing, though, if she did, she most certainly would feel around on that table to learn, to really learn, if there was something there.

Sedonia felt the vindication of proof. Someone else, a stranger, an unbiased outsider, one without ties or guilt, had attested to the craziness of her stepson.

After pouring herself a half cup of fresh coffee, she walked to the kitchen and filled the cup with brandy. Then she climbed the stairs, unconsciously avoiding the banister side down which her late husband had toppled, striking every post of each tread along the way.

She reached the hall above, turned, and opened the door of her stepson's room. She stood there, sipping her coffee and brandy, watching him.

He appeared to pick up something from the table and wind it around something else.

Sedonia shook her head, smiled, and took a drink of coffee.

He crouched, squinted through a nothing-object along the top of the table, then he drew back his arm, inserted what he thought he had into what he thought he was looking through and rammed it back and forth, with vigor yet with delicacy and a certain grace.

Sedonia continued to sip her coffee.

He was in no hurry. He withdrew what he was using, unwound whatever had been around it, and laid the two on the bare table. Then he bent over, snapped his thumb, picked up something from the apparently bare table with his left hand and plucked, with his right thumb and forefinger, from the palm of his left hand, six small nonexistent objects, dropping them, one by one, into a nonexistent receptacle.

Sedonia drooped skeptical lips, leaned against the side of the doorway, and sipped her coffee.

He pressed something shut with his thumb and cocked another open with his forefinger. He picked up one object in empty arms. He swung around then, looking at and through Sedonia.

She lounged against the doorframe, languidly sipping coffee, whispering, "Crazy," through the liquid.

He raised his cradled arms and seemed to adjust a featherweight. His left hand curved emptily before him, his right grasped air alongside his hunched shoulder, and the right forefinger, stiffly outright, curled slowly and with purpose.

He moved his head an infinitesimal distance, closed his left eye, squinted his right, and the forefinger closed in.

Sedonia jerked, the cup and saucer sounding a velvet clatter against the carpet, her fool's-gold hair blowing gently. She crumpled in slow motion, sliding softly down the doorjamb while she faced the forefinger that stiffened and closed five more times before she reached the flowers of the floor.

He laid the cradled object down on the bare table. Then he watched, but did not move toward, Sedonia's body that showed no mark of violence and finally settled peacefully.

He bent over the table and, with quick flicks of his fingers, pushed unobservable and no longer needed tools aside into a small invisible pile. He walked to a window and opened it wide, returned to the table, bent his knees, and swept them all into his arms. He took them to the window, heaved them forth onto the shrubbery below.

He closed the window, glanced impassively at Sedonia on his doorsill, crossed the room, stepped over her body and to the phone in the upper hallway.

He dialed the doctor, and then the lawyer, explaining in his pundit voice, with sophist phraseology, that his erstwhile stepmother, wife of his murdered father, was now dead of a heart attack, probably caused by virulent imagination.

He hung up the phone, crossed the hall, stepped over dead Sedonia, and deliberated at his bare table before lifting something from it. He held the object lightly in a curved hand and walked with it toward his bed in the corner.

There, he lifted the top bed pillow and laid the object gently on the other where one might imagine a vaguely outlined indentation of a shotgun, stock and barrel hazily defined on the soft, white surface.

He placed the top bed pillow over the hiding place and smoothed it with care.

# Police Calls

## by Carroll Mayers

I am rather agitated when I phone police headquarters that first evening, but the officer I draw certainly is not. "What was that address again, Mr. Waters?"

"Walters. The Creston Arms. Apartment 4D."

"And this man in the hall, he was trying to open your apartment door?"

"That's what it looked like," I say. "He was picking at the lock with something—"

"Just like on TV, huh?"

"I don't see what—"

"No offense, sir. Can you give a description of the guy?"

"Nothing definite," I say. "He spun around, ran down the fire stairs when I yelled."

"That wasn't very smart, Mr. Waters."

"Look—"

"I mean, you should've quietly backed away, called us from another phone. He could've gotten violent."

I draw a breath. "So I didn't think," I say. "I was startled, just coming off the elevator—"

"Yeah . . . well, that's water over the dam," he says philosophically. "Anything special you'd like us to do?"

I blink, wondering if I am hearing okay. "I beg pardon?"

"I've made a record. Glen Waters. The Creston Arms. Apartment 4B."

"Walters. 4D."

"Oh. Thanks. Like I say, I've got it all down . . ."

"And you're not going to do anything about it?"

He is very patient. "You've got to understand, Mr. Walters," he explains. "This's a busy department, we can't hightail all over town on every petty sneak-thief call. Especially with no specific description . . ."

I sigh again. "Thank you, officer," I say. "I only thought I should call." And I hang up, trusting I will never have to call again.

But I do, three nights later. The voice which takes my call tells me it is the same officer. I am not enthusiastic.

"This is Glen Walters at the Creston Arms, Apartment 4D," I say. "I want to report a break-in."

"Yes, sir."

"There was a man in my apartment when I came back from visiting down the hall—"

"What time was this, Mr. Waters?"

"Walters. Just now; only a couple of minutes ago. As I said, when I came back—"

"Just a second, sir. You say Walters. Didn't you call in a few nights back? Something about a guy picking your lock?"

I am conscious my chest is beginning to tighten. "That's correct," I say. "It appears burglars are getting to consider my apartment some kind of windfall, but I can't help that—"

"Mr. Walters, do you realize how many crank calls this department gets in a week?"

I control myself admirably. "This is not a crank call, officer," I say stiffly. "My other contact was not a crank call. I am only reporting an attempted robbery—"

"No offense intended, sir. I only want you to appreciate our position."

"And I'm trying to make you appreciate mine," I say. "There was a man in my apartment when I got back to it. I surprised him in the living room. He must've only just gotten in because nothing was disturbed yet. When he heard me behind him—"

"How had he gotten in, Mr. Walters? I mean, were there marks on the doorjamb? Maybe you've heard: they're called jimmy marks, professionally."

A buzzing in my head begins to complement the constriction in my chest. "I didn't notice any," I tell him. "Probably I didn't fully close the apartment door when I left, and the latch didn't catch."

"Why had you gone down the hall, Mr. Walters?"

"Dammit, officer, what difference does that make?"

"Only for the record, sir."

The buzzing is stronger now. "Well, for the record," I say distinctly, "I had gone down to visit a new tenant to borrow a cup of sugar."

"Aha!" he chuckles into the phone. "The old cup of sugar dodge, huh? What is she, Mr. Walters, a blonde? Or a redhead?"

(In fact, the lady in question is neither, being a most toothsome brunette with whom I am very anxious to become acquainted

on—ah—intimate terms. The acquisition of and involvement with
such luscious fillies is a particular hobby of mine. Unfortunately,
in this instance my bright smiles and nods in lobby and elevator are
being pointedly ignored, and tonight my sugar ploy has fallen flat.)

I lace sarcasm into my rejoinder. "For the record, I assume?"

His chuckling dies a bit. "Sorry, sir. You know how it is, a little
levity now and then. So—what happened when you surprised your
intruder?"

"He whirled, swung at me, and knocked me down," I say simply.
"By the time I'd regained my feet, he'd bolted out the door and was
gone."

"You get a good look at him?"

"No. Chunky. Dark features. Dark sweater and slacks. That's
about all."

"He get away with anything?"

"I don't think so," I say. "I haven't made a thorough check, but
I believe I came back sooner than he'd expected. I imagine he's been
watching various apartments, mine included, and when he saw me
step out and the door didn't latch, he grabbed the opportunity."

"Most likely," he agrees. "We get a lot of squeals like that. Well,
anything special you'd like us to do?"

I close my eyes. Counting to one hundred would have been silly,
but I do make it to ten. Then I say deliberately, "You asked me that
the other time."

He's contrite. "I probably did, Mr. Waters, but—"

"Walters, dammit!"

"Sorry. But you've got to understand—"

What with my tight chest and buzzing head, I guess I am truly
agitated now. "I know," I cut in. "I can't give you any good description; and the man likely didn't take anything anyhow; and I can't
expect you to be chasing around town—so let's forget the whole
thing." And I hang up.

When I have to call the police once more the following week, I
make up my mind there will be no nonsense if a certain officer
happens to draw my "squeal." He does, and there isn't.

"This is Glen Walters again," I tell him firmly. "The Creston
Arms. Apartment 4D. I have been out for the evening and have just
returned. I went to the movies. It's now eleven thirty-two. The bedroom window of my apartment, on the fire escape, has been broken
open; I can see the jimmy marks. There was no money on the prem-

ises, but the rooms have been ransacked. I want you to send someone over here right away—"

"No money loss, you say, Mr. Walters?"

"Dammit, man, that's not the point."

"We're awful busy tonight. There's a Shriners' convention and the traffic problem's something fierce—"

Chest, head, the works are starting up again. I almost yell into the phone. "Don't you understand?" I plead. "Thieves keep breaking into this apartment! I demand an investigation."

"But—"

"No buts, officer! I want a detective over here. I want him over here immediately." This time, when I hang up, I hope it rattles his teeth.

For all my belligerence, I am not actually holding my breath waiting for said detective. It is just as well; nobody ever comes. I guess my citing no actual financial loss has something to do with it. That, and maybe the fact that there is a considerable number of Shriners in the country.

In any event, all the foregoing is a preamble to tonight. I am in quite an anticipatory state because the schedule calls for the company of a delectable redhead named Felicity (propitious omen?) I happened to meet in an intimate singles bar the evening before. Under my subtle blandishments, luscious Felicity has agreed to visit me tonight for cool cocktails, warm stereo, and whatever.Thought of the whatever is especially enthralling; the unexpected smooch Felicity bestowed on me in the bar promises much.

She is due shortly after eight. I have a few errands about town, but I get back to the apartment at seven thirty. And walk in on disaster. Once again the rooms have been ransacked—plus.

Naturally, I am sick; my evening is zilch. But I am not too sick to formulate my impending call to the authorities. This time there will be no yelling, no cursing—and no putoffs.

Accordingly, when I phone I am restrained but emphatic. My luck being what it is, I get the same officer, but even this does not deter me. I review all the pertinent facts crisply and then I conclude. "This is my fourth call in the past two weeks. I admit I suffered no previous losses, probably because those thieves were primarily interested in cash and I keep no loose cash on hand—"

"I should've told you before, sir. If they're looking just for money, it's likely amateurs. The professionals, you understand, will take anything . . ."

"I do understand," I say coldly, "and this time they did. A clock radio is missing, and two suits of clothes, and a portable TV—"

"Say, that's a shame! Was it a color TV?"

"—and a set of gold cufflinks. Now *you* understand something, officer. I definitely, positively expect a police investigation this time. I expect a detective—a real live, flesh-and-blood detective—to come here tonight. Within the hour. Failing that, I'll go to the city commission. I'll go to the mayor. I'll go to the governor."

"I can appreciate how upset and all you are, Mr. Waters, but—"

He is talking into a dead phone because, my resolution holding, I quietly break the connection. I am confident that my firm ultimatum will at last result in official action.

In the meantime, though, my exhilarating evening is ruined. I begin to half-straighten up the apartment, then reflect I should leave everything for the detective to witness. It also occurs to me to telephone Felicity (we'd exchanged numbers at the bar) to temporarily cancel her visitation. I try to reach her but nobody answers; unfortunately, she's probably already under way. Well, she'll understand. . . .

The detective who comes is lean and tired-looking, with mournful brown eyes like a beagle's. He stands in the middle of the living room, looks around, and shakes his head.

"It's a mess all right, Mr. Waters. You wonder how they know, eh?"

"Walters. Know what?"

"Where's a good place to hit. You take my aunt, over in Capitol City. She was hit just the past month. Lot of valuable antiques."

"This isn't the first time," I tell him grimly. "Counting tonight, I've called you people four times."

He shakes his head again. "Is that a fact? But then, I guess you've got insurance?"

My chest twinges. I say, "Look, officer—" and then I break off as the door buzzer echoes. I move to answer, expecting it will be Felicity.

It is. She stops in the doorway with a bright, tantalizing smile on her wet lips, and then she tilts forward from her spike heels and gives me a big kiss. "Hi, lover boy!"

I am a trifle embarrassed under the circumstances, but I assume the detective is a man of the world. I start to usher Felicity inside and then I stop, principally because said detective is abruptly making funny noises.

I swing back, surprised. The detective is looking—no, glaring—at

Felicity, and now he is mouthing words. "So," he tells her furiously, "my ever-loving wife really gets around, doesn't she? I've been suspecting as much!"

After that, the action gets hectic as the detective's tired blood perks up miraculously and he closes in on me, smashes my nose, knocks out two teeth, blacks one eye. Through it all, I vaguely appreciate you don't have to be single to patronize a singles bar. I also deplore footloose wives, particularly when they're married to cops. . . .

So be a good citizen. Curb your dog, don't litter the sidewalk, and obey traffic regulations. But be a bit hesitant about calling the police, demanding action. Eventually, you just might get the wrong kind.

For myself, I plan two steps as soon as they release me from this hospital:

First, I'll move to another apartment—with triple locks.

Then I'll have the phone disconnected.

# Funeral in a Small Town

## by Stephen Wasylyk

**B**arrett drove grimly, the speedometer needle well above sixty-five until he left the turnpike and headed east on the Fox River Road, a twisting, turning blacktop through the mountains that still held patches of ice and snow where the tall pines had blocked out the sun.

There was no sun this morning. The sky was gray and low, like the mood that had settled on Barrett when the phone had rung in the cool darkness of his bedroom long before dawn.

"Page," his Aunt Edna had said softly, "you'll have to come up here. Lou is dead."

The question stuck in Barrett's throat. "How?"

He sensed from the silence that his aunt didn't want to put it into words, as if not saying it would make it not true. "Killed," she said finally. "Someone went into the newspaper office last night and shot him."

Barrett let the words sink in, not wanting to believe them any more than she did.

"I'll be there," he said. "As fast as I can make it."

He flicked on the lamp between the twin beds, to be confronted by the annoyance in his wife's eyes as she blinked away the sudden brilliance. Phone calls at odd hours were nothing new for Barrett, but Deb had never become used to or accepted them. It was only one of the points of friction between them lately. It wasn't the major one.

For months, his aunt and uncle had been asking him to come back to the small town in the mountains where he had been born, where his uncle was the editor and publisher of the small weekly newspaper, so that his uncle could retire and turn the paper over to Barrett. Barrett, feeling hemmed in by the city and wanting to turn back the pages of his life to what he knew was a more free, unhurried existence, was in favor of the move, but his wife had announced firmly she had no intention of living in a small town.

His wife brushed back her long blonde hair. "Another crisis at the agency?"

"Far more serious," Barrett said. "Lou was killed last night."

She swung out of bed and into a robe in one fluid motion, a graceful woman almost as tall as Barrett, with a slim, well-proportioned body that never failed to stir him, even now. She accepted the announcement without shock or curiosity, which didn't surprise Barrett. As long as his uncle was alive, the decision to move or not to move could be postponed indefinitely. Now that he was dead, the decision would have to be made soon, and that was uppermost in her mind. "I assume you are going up there?"

He nodded. "You'll come with me, of course."

"No," she said. "He was your uncle, not mine."

Barrett felt a familiar touch of frustration and anger. There were times when he didn't understand her, couldn't understand her. "It would only be common courtesy."

"No," she said again. "I won't go. I have always felt out of place there." There was an inflection in her voice that said if he wanted to argue, she was prepared.

*Not this time,* Page Barrett thought wearily. *There are more important things to do.* He dialed Elmdorf, who headed the advertising agency where Barrett was a well-paid account executive, and explained the situation to him.

"Take as much time as you like," Elmdorf had said. "We'll talk when you get back."

Barrett knew what he meant. Elmdorf was aware of his uncle's offer and sided with Barrett's wife in thinking he should turn it down. His reasons were as self-centered as hers. Barrett controlled a large amount of business that the agency would probably lose if he left.

A patch of ice forced Barrett's thoughts to the immediate present. The car started to skid and Barrett twisted the wheel sharply and then he was back on the roadway, topping a small rise, a snow-covered valley spread before him. The Fox River bisected the whiteness like a piece of dark blue, twisted yarn, making a slight bend below, where a bridge took the road across and into a small town.

Barrett slowed. He always enjoyed this particular moment, summer or winter, when the valley unfolded suddenly and his long trip was almost ended.

A bright red VW, skis strapped to its rear deck, horn raucous, flashed by and cut back too quickly, forcing Barrett off the road and into the snow, inches away from the guard barrier and the long steep slope to the river. Barrett fought the car back onto the road and stopped. He took a deep breath. If he had been going just a little faster . . .

He looked down the slope. Except for a few scattered trees, there was nothing to have kept him from tumbling into the river.

He curbed an impulse to take out after the VW, but the little car was already halfway to the bridge, a small red speck speeding down the curving roadway. If it belongs around here, we'll meet again, Barrett reflected grimly as he set the car in motion.

Fox River looked no different from usual when he drove through, and Barrett was conscious of a slight surprise. He didn't know exactly what he had expected from the town because his uncle had been killed, but business as usual wasn't part of it, not with his uncle's position in the community.

Lou Beck and his newspaper had been the guiding light and the conscience of Fox River and the surrounding county for almost forty years, ever since he woke one morning tired of the push and the odor of the big city and the pressure of working for a metropolitan daily. Within a week he and Edna Beck had been headed for his home town, his bank savings in his pocket after a phone call had confirmed the weekly was for sale.

He had grown old there, surrounded by the dusty, dry smell of the newspaper office, of printing ink and hot lead, of the oil-soaked old press in the back room. He had made Barrett his reporter at sixteen, during high school summer vacation, hammering at his copy until Barrett knew what he meant when he said, "Write the facts, boy, and keep it short. Opinions are for the editorial page and I write that. You stay at it long enough and I'll make you a good newspaperman."

Barrett smiled, remembering his uncle's disapproval when he had gone into advertising. His opinion had been expressed in one healthy snort of disgust and he thereafter referred to Barrett's work only as that job of yours."

Barrett swung the car into his aunt's driveway. Waiting and watching for him, she opened the door, her silver hair neatly set, her small figure erect and already dressed in black, her arms outstretched, and Barrett had the feeling he had come home after a long absence.

Sometime later, he curled his fingers around a cup of coffee in the warm kitchen, examining the fine porcelain as if he were seeing it for the first time, wondering how to ask the questions that had to be asked. He sipped the coffee. "Tell me about it."

"I have very little to tell. Lou came home last night for dinner, took a short nap, and went back to the office. You know he always worked late the night before they started printing the paper. He was usually home by ten. At eleven, I called the office but there was no answer. I became worried, so I called Grant Rhodes and asked him to look into it."

Barrett nodded. Grant Rhodes was the chief of the three-man police force, and he and Lou had been friends for years.

"About an hour later, Grant came to the door. I knew something was wrong, but I never dreamed of anything like this. Grant said it looked like someone had just walked up behind Lou and shot him. Why, Page? Why should anyone shoot him?"

Barrett avoided the tear-filled eyes. "I don't know. All we can do now is try to find out. I'll go speak to Grant."

He slipped into his coat, knowing she hadn't asked yet why his wife wasn't with him, dreading the question because there was really no answer. She watched him affectionately, reaching out to turn up his coat collar. Barrett smiled. She had done that often when he was a boy, when he had come to live with them after his parents had died.

"Deb won't be coming?" she asked suddenly.

Embarrassed, Barrett shook his head.

"Well," said his aunt, "I suppose she has her reasons."

"You should have someone to stay with you," Barrett suggested.

"I do. Cindy Neal. You probably don't remember her. She was a little girl when you went off to college. She teaches English now at the high school and helped Lou at the paper with the women's pages. She's down at the office with Tom Cottrell."

Cottrell had been his uncle's combination typesetter, makeup man, and pressman, had been with the paper since the day Lou had bought it, and Barrett wondered what he would do now that the old man was dead.

"I'll stop by and see them," said Barrett.

He decided to walk. The town wasn't that big and, while it was cold, it wasn't the bitter dampness winter brought to the city. He found Grant Rhodes in his office, a thin man in a tan uniform, with a hook nose, skin that had the patina of well-cared-for leather, and a mouth bracketed by deep creases.

Rhodes motioned him to a chair. "I was expecting you, Page."

"Anything to tell me?"

"We are investigating, but we have very little to go on. Your uncle was alone in the office, sitting at his desk. Someone came up behind him and shot him in the back of the head with a small-caliber gun. There must be hundreds of those in the county, so we have nothing there. It had to be between nine, when Cottrell left as usual, and eleven, when I found him."

"Robbery?"

"In a town where people don't even lock their doors? His wallet was in his pocket. Nothing was missing from the office. Nothing there worth stealing, really."

"No motive at all?"

"None that is apparent. I can't think of one person who would want to kill Lou. To tell you the truth, Page, I'm a little out of my depth with this one, just as I was with the other."

Barrett sat a little straighter. "The other?"

"You wouldn't have heard about it in the city, but one of the local kids, a sixteen-year-old girl, was found raped and strangled in the woods about a week ago. The poor kid had been on the way home from school when someone caught her." He shook his head. "There is nothing yet on that one, either. Just some tracks in the snow that mean nothing. No one saw or heard anything." He sighed. "Peaceful county like this goes on for years with no trouble, then two killings within a week."

"Maybe there is a connection."

"The kind of man who would attack a young girl is not the same who would shoot an old man. At least, in my opinion."

Barrett nodded and rose. "I'll go over to the office and look around. Maybe I can find something that will help."

"If you need me, I'll be here." Rhodes pulled a long black cigar from his pocket and lit it, eyeing Barrett through the smoke. "I suppose you'll be taking over the paper now?"

Barrett shrugged and walked out. He had forgotten there were no personal affairs in this town.

He came across the red VW at the curb in front of the drugstore across the street from the newspaper office, the skis still in the rack. Lips tight, he walked around the car. Dents in the right side showed that his hadn't been the only car forced off the road.

Barrett entered the drugstore, eyes searching. Several young men and women dressed in ski clothes were seated at the soda fountain, others occupying the booths. It was impossible to tell which was the driver of the VW.

Behind the prescription counter at the rear of the store, a short, heavyset man with a bald head smiled and beckoned. He held out his hand as Barrett approached. "Glad to see you back, Page. Sorry about Lou, but still good to see you again."

A widower, Allen Carey had been the town pharmacist for almost as long as Lou had owned the paper, and he was a good one. He filled prescriptions cheerfully, even in the small hours of the morning, and did a little emergency *sub rosa* prescribing on his own.

Barrett jerked a thumb over his shoulder. "I don't suppose you know who owns the red VW with the ski rack that's parked out front?"

"I certainly do. It belongs to my boy Pete. He's a real ski nut. Spends almost all his time over at the ski resort on Big Bear Mountain." He winked at Barrett. "Don't know how much skiing he gets done, though. I think he goes for the company more than anything else. What's wrong?"

"That car almost ran me off the road this morning," said Barrett.

"Pete did that? Are you sure?"

"You don't forget a car that color," said Barrett. "Where is he now?"

"Asleep. I told you he went for this *aprés ski* stuff. He was out all night." He winked at Barrett again. "You know a lot of these kids come up from the city to ski. Some of them are real lookers, too. I can't blame him. Sometimes I wish I wasn't so old. Some of these young girls . . . "

Barrett felt a sense of distaste, as if Carey had said something obscene. "How old is he?"

"Turned twenty-one last summer."

"I thought he'd be in college."

Carey's eyes shifted, flicking around the store. "Well, he's not much interested in that. He helps me out occasionally."

Barrett didn't need it spelled out any further. The apologetic tone admitted that Pete Carey was a ski bum. Barrett decided to let the incident go. Carey had enough trouble. "Tell him to drive more carefully," he said. "I'll see you later."

"I guess you'll be around here a lot more, now that Lou is gone."

Barrett couldn't tell if that made Carey happy or not. "That remains to be seen," he said. Evidently there was no one in town who didn't expect him to take over the paper.

Carey, reaching for Barrett's hand, brushed a small prescription bottle from the counter. It splattered on the marble floor with a small crash. Carey grinned weakly. "Part of the profits gone."

Wondering if Carey became nervous every time he talked about his son, Barrett shook his hand and stepped out into the cold afternoon.

The newspaper office was a former store, fronted with a plate glass window and a door tucked away in a little vestibule. The shades were drawn. Overhead, a sign in Old English lettering said: FOX RIVER TRIBUNE, LOU BECK, EDITOR-PUBLISHER. The sign was weather-beaten and old. *Like Lou,* thought Barrett.

He pushed the door open and stepped inside. A rail and a waist-high counter separated the office from the door, not enough of a barrier to keep the cold draft from reaching a young woman at a desk in the corner. She stood up.

She was dark-haired and tall, wearing a turtleneck jersey over a plaid skirt, white boots almost reaching her knees. Her nose was small and upturned, giving her a pleasantly aggressive look, and her eyes were widely spaced above a generous mouth. It was the kind of face that would wear well through the years, Barrett decided.

"I'm Page Barrett," he said, pushing his way through a swinging gate in the office itself. "You must be Cindy Neal."

She nodded. "We've been expecting you." She indicated the back room and Barrett was aware of the soft hum of a motor, the spaced *whump* and the familiar staccato tinkle of brass mats dropping that told him someone was operating a Linotype machine. "Tom Cottrell is here."

Barrett wondered what Cottrell would be working on. He slipped off his coat and moved to the back room.

Cottrell looked up over the copy board and shifted a pipe from one side of his mouth to the other. "Page. Wondered when you'd get here."

"Working on the paper?" Barrett was puzzled. "I would think—"

"Figured Lou would want it this way. Paper is almost complete and would be a waste not to print it. I was thinking that if you showed up you could write a story about Lou. I can fit it in on page one by dropping something."

"That's what a good newspaperman would do," Barrett said dryly.

Cottrell removed the pipe and studied it. "Lou would do it. He'd expect you to do the same. The people in this county buy the paper to read the news and no matter how he died, Lou's death is news. You can't deny that."

"No," said Barrett. "I can't deny that, but I'm more interested in finding out who killed him and why. What do you know?"

"Nothing." He drew on the pipe reflectively. "Nothing you can ask me that I haven't already asked myself, Page, and I've got no answers."

He sat behind the Linotype machine, a thin, narrow-chested man dressed in blue work clothes, his sleeves rolled up on sinewy arms, metal-rimmed spectacles pushed up into his gray hair. Barrett was sure that Cottrell was working, not because he didn't care what had happened to Lou, but because he cared a great deal and preferred to keep busy rather than think about it.

"I guess I can still write a story," Barrett said gently. "Not as well as Lou, but good enough."

He stepped into the office. To his left were a half dozen steel filing cabinets; to his right a small heavy iron safe that Barrett knew held nothing but bookkeeping records. Along one wall was Cindy Neal's desk, and an ancient, massive typewriter on a wheeled stand flanked Lou Beck's rolltop desk and chair. Opposite the desk, a large drawing table held a pad of newspaper layout sheets that Lou used to guide Cottrell in making up the pages, filling in the blank columns with the ads and the stories as they developed. There would be a set of those for this issue in the back room and Cottrell would require no help from Barrett there.

Rhodes had been right. There was absolutely nothing in the office worth stealing.

The top of the desk was raised, the pigeonholes exposed and filled with projecting papers, but the working area of the desk was clean. Barrett frowned. That was unusual. He could not recall a time when Lou did not have papers scattered about, limiting himself to a small area in which to work.

"Who cleaned the desk?" he asked Cindy.

"I don't know," she said. "It was like that when I came in early this morning. Instead of going to the high school, I went to your aunt's house. I stayed with her for a few hours before coming here."

"Lou was working at the desk when you left last night?"

"As usual. He had papers scattered—" She stopped, realizing what Barrett was implying. "They're gone," she said. "Whatever he was working on is gone. There were some photographs, too," she added circumspectly.

"Photographs?"

She nodded. "I didn't look at them but I know they were there."

Barrett picked up the phone. Automatic dialing for Fox River was still a year away, and the operator's voice asked him for his number. "I want Chief Rhodes," he said.

He wasted no time when Rhodes answered. "Grant, did you clean off Lou's desk when you removed the body?"

There was a silence. "No," said Rhodes finally. "As near as I can remember, the desk was clean. You onto something?"

"I think I know what the killer took from the office."

"Something valuable?"

"I can't see how," said Barrett. "It was just a story and some photos." He cradled the phone gently, wondering what there could possibly be about a news item in a small town weekly that would be worth stealing.

Cindy Neal had moved closer to him and he caught the faint scent of an indefinable perfume. It was a pleasing scent, a bright, fresh fragrance very much different from anything his wife would wear.

"You have any idea of what Lou was writing?" he asked.

"Not exactly. I know he had been spending some time at the Big Bear Mountain Ski Resort. He'd been over there often the last few days."

"Do you know who he was seeing?"

"A man named Horn, I believe. You could talk to him."

He slipped into his coat. "I'll need my car."

She dangled keys before him. "No need. We'll take mine."

Barrett couldn't say no. He had to admit he would enjoy her company.

She made the thirty miles to Big Bear Mountain in a half hour, handling the car expertly, downshifting smoothly on the occasionally slippery road without losing speed. The ski resort was off the main highway on a back road that seemed to wind halfway around the mountain. Before they pulled into the parking lot, Barrett could see the two chair lifts operating to capacity, carrying brightly dressed skiers to the top of the long slopes.

The lodge at the foot of the chair lifts was low and rambling, bigger than Barrett remembered, and he realized that several additions had been built since he had last been here. They found Horn in a walnut-paneled office, a pale gnome of a man wearing ski boots and casual clothes that Barrett would have bet had never seen a ski slope.

"I'm sorry to hear about Mr. Beck," he said, "but I don't see how I can help."

"He'd been to see you several times in connection with a story on which he was working," said Barrett. "Can you tell us what it was?"

"Of course. I had been thinking of producing a brochure. We get many inquiries about our facilities and the one I'm using now is rather out of date. Mr. Beck and I were cooperating on a new one. I had provided him with the details and some photographs and he was going to print it."

It sounded logical. Lou had run a little job-printing business to fill in between issues of the paper, drawing most of it from local businessmen.

"Nothing more than that?"

Horn frowned. "I fail to understand."

"Whoever killed my uncle took both the photographs and the copy for your brochure. Would you know why?"

"Fantastic," murmured Horn. "I would have no idea or even what purpose it would serve. I do have additional photos, so the thief would really accomplish nothing. As far as the copy is concerned, that is easily rewritten.

Barrett stared. "You have *duplicate* photos?"

"I always order extras for publicity uses. I do regret, however, that I also gave your uncle the negatives. He did not consider the prints I gave him suitable for reproduction purposes, and he intended to have some made that would meet his standards."

"So the thief would have been under the impression there were no other prints and there could be none since he had the negatives?"

"I imagine he would, but I still fail to see why he would bother. The photos were routine shots of the lodge, the slopes, the lifts, all our facilities. There could be absolutely nothing in them that would be of value. If anyone had asked, I would have been happy to present him a set. Furthermore, even if they had all been completely destroyed, it would present no big problem to have them retaken."

"Obviously the killer was interested only in those particular photos," said Cindy.

Barrett appealed to Horn. "May we see the duplicates?"

Horn swung around to a filing cabinet and fingered his way through a sheaf of papers until he found an envelope. He handed it to Barrett.

"I regret they are not in color," he said. "Your uncle had no facilities for that type of printing."

Barrett spread the 8 x 10 prints on Horn's desk. There were more than a dozen, taken in and around the lodge and slopes, as Horn had said, most featuring laughing people in ski clothing. Several were almost stock shots of skiers plummeting down the slopes, trailing plumes of snow.

Cindy picked up a couple of breathtaking views of the snow-covered valley, taken from the chair lift as it descended the mountain, showing the valley spread out, the roads dark slices through the snow, the lodge at the foot of the lift, the parking lot full.

"When were they taken?" she asked.

"Just last week," said Horn. "They are the most recent ones we have. I had them made especially for this brochure." He indicated the photos in her hand. "I think these are particularly well done. They show the size of the lodge so well."

The phrase *last week* jarred Barrett. Rhodes had used the same words about the girl who had been killed. "The girl who was murdered," he said to Cindy. "What day was it?"

"Last Tuesday," she said.

He looked at Horn. "And when were the photos taken?"

"The same day. It was originally scheduled for the weekend, but clouds prevented that. Luckily, we had a rather healthy crowd on Tuesday, so it was decided to do it then."

Barrett and Cindy looked at each other, each having the same thought: there might be a connection between the photos and the murder of the girl. *But what?* Barrett flipped through the photos again, seeing nothing that could possibly be relevant. "May we borrow these?" he asked Horn.

"Certainly." Horn placed the photos in an envelope and handed them to Cindy. "I will need them for my brochure eventually."

"We'll take good care of them," promised Barrett. He held the door open for Cindy, feeling that she was carrying something valuable, even though he didn't know what it was.

They were crossing the parking lot when the red VW flashed by, dangerously close, and Barrett felt a quick surge of anger. He followed the car into a parking slot just as a young man with long brown hair, dressed in a dark green ski parka, stepped out.

"Are you Pete Carey?" asked Barrett.

"Do I know you?"

"You should. You cut me off this morning and forced me off the road, then you came a little too close to us now to suit me. I don't like the way you drive."

"Drop dead," said Pete nastily.

It wasn't the words as much as the tone that made Barrett's hand flash out, viciously backhanding Pete across the face, driving him into the side of the VW. Barrett regretted the move the moment he made it and stepped back, ready to apologize, but Pete came off the car, a knife suddenly in his hand, his face transformed, no longer young and smooth but somehow old, ancient with hate and hurt, animalistic with a growling fury that made Barrett step back, confronted with something dark and primitive and frightening.

Barrett's breath froze in his chest and a phrase he had once read popped into his mind. *The face of madness,* he thought, and then the knife was flashing toward him and Barrett reached out, seized the arm and twisted desperately, smashing the hand against the cold steel of the car until the fingers released the knife, while Pete clawed at his face and eyes with his free hand, spitting obscenities.

Barrett pivoted, throwing Pete over his shoulder and pinning him to the ground, feeling a touch of panic because he knew that losing the knife wouldn't let Pete end it; that Pete was determined to kill him, with his bare hands if necessary; and Barrett held him there, one knee on his chest, the other on his arm, still clasping Pete's other arm with both hands, not wanting to face the thought that the fight wouldn't end until one of them was dead, when Pete suddenly became quiet and his face smoothed over and Barrett was holding an ordinary-looking young man who looked up at him with a hurt expression as if questioning what Barrett was doing.

Barrett released him and stood up. Pete lay there, staring up at him.

Barrett turned away, feeling the after-fight reaction setting in, his stomach muscles knotting and unknotting, nausea gagging him, his arms and legs trembling. He made his way to the car and collapsed into the front seat. Cindy followed, silent and almost as shaken as he was. She stared straight ahead.

Barrett breathed deeply, forcing his body to stop quivering, knowing that for the second time that day Pete Carey had pushed him to the edge of death.

"He could have killed you," whispered Cindy.

"He *would* have," said Barrett, "but it's over now and you can bet I'll stay clear of him from now on. Someday he's going to hurt someone very badly. I don't want it to be me."

"What do we do now?"

Early winter dark was setting in as Barrett reached across the seat and took the photographs from her. "Back to the office. After

Pete Carey, I need a change of pace. I'll work up the story on Lou so Cottrell can have it in the morning."

"I'll leave you there," she said. "I want to check on your aunt."

"Good," said Barrett. "Come back later and we'll go over the photos."

She dropped him off in front of the newspaper office. A headache that had been dull and quiet all day had matured into a fierce throbbing that threatened to split Barrett's head open. He crossed the street to the drugstore. It was empty now except for an elderly woman just turning away from the prescription counter and Allen Carey. Barrett decided it would be wise not to mention his fight with Carey's son.

"I need something that will work fast on a headache," he told Carey.

Carey nodded sympathetically. "Just the thing for you, Page." He poured some white pills into a small envelope and handed them to Barrett. "I find these a little better than plain aspirin. Let me get you a glass of water."

Barrett followed him to the soda fountain and gulped down two of the pills.

"Anything develop about your uncle?" asked Carey.

"Possibly." Barrett tapped the envelope. "I may have something in here that will help."

Carey craned his head to read the return address. "You picked up something at Big Bear?"

Barrett slipped the envelope under his arm. "Some publicity photos."

"Photos?" There was an odd note in Carey's voice.

"Yeah. Want to check them before turning them over to Grant Rhodes. How much do I owe you for the pills?"

Carey waved. "On the house. I hope they work for you."

Barrett had the impression he had suddenly lost Carey, that Carey's mind had fled elsewhere, that Carey never even noticed his departure.

Cottrell heard him come in and appeared in the doorway to the rear room, wiping his hand on a rag. "Nothing left for me to do. She's all locked up and ready to be put to bed, except for page one. Found an old cut of Lou I can use. All I need is the story. You going to write that?"

"Right now," Barrett told him. "It will be waiting for you in the morning."

"Make any progress?"

"We have a lead, but it's too soon to tell." He slipped out of his coat and rubbed his cold hands together. "You've had a long day, Tom. You might as well go, I'll finish the story and lock up. We'll start printing tomorrow."

"Lou would like that." Cottrell hesitated. "Just want to say, Page, that whatever you decide to do about the paper is all right with me. A man has to do what he has to do. When do you think you'll decide?"

Barrett pulled the typewriter table toward him and rolled in a sheet of copy paper. "Soon, I guess, Tom. There are many people who expect an answer."

After Cottrell left, Barrett sat staring at the keys. *Many people,* he thought; *his wife, Elmdorf, Aunt Edna, Cottrell, and even Cindy Neal, all of their small worlds temporarily orbiting around Barrett.* Wishing that the responsibility belonged to someone else, he shook his head and then began to type:

Lou G. Beck, editor and publisher of the Fox River *Tribune,* was found shot to death in his office late in the evening of . . ."

The words didn't come easily. It had been a long time since he had sat at a typewriter and put into practice the things that Lou had taught him. It had never been easy, he realized. Lou had just made it seem that way. He finished with a short biographical sketch of Lou and pulled the paper from the typewriter. He scanned it, made a few pencil corrections and set it aside, reaching for the photographs taken at Big Bear.

One by one, he studied them, seeing nothing that meant anything, knowing he was overlooking a detail that was important to someone else, knowing, too, that it would have had significance to his uncle; but there was no way Barrett could put himself in the old man's place, know what he knew, think his thoughts, draw the same conclusions.

*No way?* His uncle had a method of looking at photographs that Barrett had almost forgotten, a trick he used to be certain that some obscure background detail he didn't want couldn't slip by him.

Barrett took a blank sheet of paper and tore a hole in it about an inch square, then took the photographs in turn, placing his makeshift mask over each and sliding it across the surface, concentrating his attention only on what appeared in the ragged window. He saw things in the photographs that he hadn't noticed before, but none triggered an idea until he was sliding his mask across one of the views of the valley taken from the chair lift. As closely as he was watching, he still almost missed it, a somehow familiar bug-shaped spot against a background of snow.

He slipped the mask away and searched his uncle's desk until he found his magnifying glass and focused it on the spot.

There was no question now. Enlarged, it was a VW with skis strapped to its rear deck. Seeing one at this time of the year in the valley was ordinary enough. There were many, including Pete Carey's. What intrigued Barrett was that this one didn't seem to be traveling along any of the snow-covered back roads. Instead, it was some distance from the nearest one, evidently following a service track through the snow that some farmer used to reach the back sections of his property in winter. The thought struck Barrett that the car was parked, but why in such an out-of-the-way spot? If there were an answer, he didn't know what it was.

Barrett tossed the picture aside and picked up another to find he could no longer concentrate on what he was doing. That VW in the middle of nowhere bothered him. Maybe Cindy would have an explanation for it when she came back. He closed his eyes and leaned back in the chair, thinking that he was more tired than he realized. Carey's pills had eliminated the headache but they also must have contained some sort of sedative. Barrett felt a warm lassitude creeping upward from his legs.

He hadn't heard the door open, but a cold draft made him look up as Allen Carey came through the swinging gate.

"Pete told me what happened," said Carey.

"I apologize for that. I was sorry I lost my temper."

Carey waved away his apology. "Pete gave you a lot of trouble, didn't he?"

"You could say that. In my opinion, he needs some sort of psychiatric attention before he hurts someone."

"I don't think it's that bad. He's just a confused young boy. He'll grow out of it."

He was no longer a boy and there was no chance he would grow out of it, Barrett knew, but then it wasn't his concern. He had problems of his own. He merely nodded, saying nothing.

Carey had been edging forward into the office. Barrett realized he was staring at the photos on the desk.

"May I see those?" There was a strange note in Carey's voice.

"I think not. They are the only set and I'm responsible for them."

"Lou had photos of Big Bear yesterday. I suppose these are different?"

Barrett was no longer tired. As far as he knew, only Cindy, Horn, and himself were aware that the killer had taken the original set. "No," he said cautiously. "These are the same. Horn had duplicates."

Carey's face was the color of Camembert that had aged too long. "You looked at them?"

"Of course," said Barrett.

"Ah," said Carey, sounding as if he were gagging. "Let me see the pictures."

"What for?"

Carey's hand went under his coat and came out with a gun, the kind that almost every kid in the county used for small game and target practice. Barrett froze. Carey's hand might be trembling, but at this range he wasn't shaking enough to miss.

"I didn't want this to happen. I never thought it would happen." Carey sounded as if he might start weeping at any moment. Perspiration glistened on his forehead. His eyes flicked around the room as if driven by tumbling thoughts.

"You'll have to tell me," Barrett said. "Give me a reason for the gun."

"Lou brought a picture to me yesterday. There was something he wanted to ask about."

Barrett, his mind half-numbed by the gun, was trying to sort it all out when it became clear; beautifully clear. "A Volkswagen," he said. "Parked where it had no right to be. Near where the girl was killed. Lou wanted to know if it was Pete's car, where Pete had been that day."

Carey nodded. "I see you think the same as Lou. He said he was going to have Grant Rhodes ask Pete about it. I couldn't allow that."

"Because you knew that Pete had killed the girl. Once Grant Rhodes started to question him—"

"No," Carey interrupted. "Pete didn't kill the girl."

Barrett thought of the secret Pete Carey he had glimpsed that afternoon. Someone like that could have easily raped and strangled.

"Yes," he said. "Pete killed her. So you came in here last night, killed Lou, one of your best friends, and took the photos and the negatives to protect a son you know should be locked up somewhere."

"That wasn't the way it was," cried Carey. "That's not how it was at all. There is nothing wrong with Pete. Nothing, you hear me? All Pete could have told Rhodes was that he didn't have the car that afternoon, that someone had borrowed it."

"Then you're a fool, Allen. Who borrowed the car?"

"Don't you understand?" Carey's voice was almost a wail. "It was *me!*"

The only sound in the room was Carey's labored breathing. *Ah, now,* thought Barrett, *not Carey himself. Not Carey, the pharmacist who had helped so many people, responsible now for two killings and intent on a third.*

"Why, Allen?" he asked gently. "I can see that you felt you had to kill Lou to get the pictures, but why the girl in the first place?"

"You just don't know what it's like in this town, seeing your life slip away. The years go and suddenly you're old and you haven't done anything."

"What does that have to do with it?"

Carey passed a hand over his face. "She made me feel young again. For just a minute . . . Then it happened. She was going to tell." He straightened suddenly, eyes no longer shifting, no longer trembling. "It doesn't matter now." The gun leveled at Barrett's head. "I have to do this, Page. I can't let anyone find out. You shouldn't have interfered. You don't belong here any more."

Barrett realized that talking would do no good. There was a set to Carey's expression and a light in his eyes that reminded Barrett of Pete Carey holding a knife. Carey was far beyond listening. He would hear only what he wanted to hear.

Barrett picked up the photograph and held it out. "This is what you want, Allen. Why not take it and go?"

"No. There would be nothing to keep you from telling Grant Rhodes."

Barrett casually placed his feet on the cross-brace of the heavy typewriter table. He tossed the photo at Carey and as Carey's eyes followed it, he violently pushed the typewriter stand toward him, using both feet and hands. If Carey had been a professional, he would have killed Barrett before the photo fluttered to the floor, but Carey was an overwrought, confused pharmacist. The typewriter stand, heavy machine tottering, catapulted across the office and smashed Carey across the thighs, doubling him up, the pistol falling as Carey dropped his hands to protect himself.

Barrett dived across the office and scooped up the pistol. Carey, bent over the stand, looked at him pleadingly, lips moving in some sort of silent entreaty. Barrett almost felt sorry for the crazed druggist.

They were standing like that when Rhodes and Cindy Neal came through the door. Rhodes looked at the pistol in Barrett's hands.

"What's that thing for? Allen charge you too much for a prescription?"

Barrett handed it to him. "Save the jokes. I think you'll find this killed Lou." He indicated Carey. "He pulled the trigger. He'll tell you why, but if he doesn't, you'll still develop enough to hold him on two counts of murder."

"Two counts?"

"He also killed the girl last week."

Rhodes had been a police officer too long to let any emotion show, but Barrett knew the news must have jolted him clear down to his polished shoes.

"I thought I was coming here to look at some photos," Rhodes said slowly. "Cindy called me and said you might have something. I didn't expect this. Suppose you start at the beginning."

Barrett explained while Carey stood there, a small, putty-faced fat man who didn't look dangerous at all, and Cindy leaned on the counter, eyes fixed on Barrett.

"That's the third time today you almost got yourself killed," said Cindy wonderingly when he had finished.

"I seem to have that trouble with the Carey family," said Barrett dryly. "But he showed the gun too soon. Lou turned his back on him before he knew Carey had one. We should have guessed that Lou knew the man who killed him, knew him well enough to let him get behind him without suspecting anything."

Rhodes placed a hand on Carey's arm. "I'll take him over to the station. You stop by later and we'll talk some more." He led Carey out.

Cindy sighed. "At least it is all over now."

"Almost," said Barrett. "There is still the paper to print and Lou's funeral to be attended."

"And then?" There was an unsaid hope in her voice, a hope that the paper wouldn't die as Lou had died, a hope that Barrett would stay.

She looked young, exceedingly beautiful, and very vulnerable. It was a look that Barrett hadn't seen on a woman's face in a long time.

Instead of being tempted, he merely felt old.

Allen Carey had been right on two counts when he said, "You don't belong here, Page."

The first was that Barrett was a different breed from a different age, from a faster moving, entirely different world, and he was no

Lou Beck, with little of the old man's talent and skill. Barrett couldn't run the paper, not the way the old man had run it.

The second was that Barrett's problem wasn't with his wife but with himself. He had clung too long to the dream that many men had; that it was possible to go back, to erase the years that brought him to this time and place. He had carved out an existence that might not be all he hoped it would be, but in many ways it was satisfying and, above all, it belonged to him and was no poor imitation of someone else.

Carey's words echoed: "You don't belong here, Page."

Barrett sighed. When they buried Lou Beck, they would bury part of Page Barrett, too: the part that had grown up here and developed here, though that part had been dead a long time, much longer than Lou Beck. Barrett had simply never realized it.

He looked at Cindy, smiled, and said, "And then I'll go home."

# Hit or Miss

## by Edward Wellen

**F**inley Crowe stepped into the Hotel Granville, cased the lobby, went to the phone booth at the far end, and riffled his right hand through the pages of the Manhattan directory as his left hand reached below to remove a slip of paper taped to the underside of the shelf.

Still pretending to be hunting a number and using his body as a shield, he brought up the paper, unfolded it, and read it. All it said was *819*. Finley Crowe now knew that the man he had to kill was staying in Room 819 of the Hotel Granville.

He balled the slip of paper and tossed it at the first sand urn he passed. Too sure of his aim, he failed to see that he had missed the desert waste. The ball hit the rim and bounded to the carpet.

Carefully watching carelessly to make sure that no one noticed him, Finley Crowe gained the stairs and started up.

Leroy Moore bent to pick up the ball of paper. He straightened slowly, silently cursing his aching back. He started to drop the crumple of paper into the sand urn, then something moved him to stay his hand.

He unwadded the paper and smoothed it out enough to read it. All it said was *618*. Leroy Moore made up his mind to hurry and play 618 and play it big. It would have been a sin to overlook this sign.

Clifford Fant, in Room 618, had a hangup hangup. His hand shook so that it took him three stabs before he hung up the phone.

The girl had disguised her voice, but he knew who it had to be. Making time with her, though she was hardly his type, was paying off now. It wasn't luck but forethought that had given him a pair of ears in syndicate headquarters—and now a voice.

"There's a contract out on you. You'd better hurry out of there. The hit man knows where you are."

Then, before he could ask questions or even frame questions to ask, *click!*

It was new to him to be on the same side of the law—the wrong side—as his clients. He had always managed to stay on the right side while advancing the fortunes of those on the wrong side. A syndicate mouthpiece, he had lately begun practicing the art of avoiding subpoenas.

Now it seemed that his former clients were taking no chances on the privileged communications between client and lawyer remaining privileged. They were not trusting to the canon of ethics alone to seal his lips, and since syndicate headquarters itself had put out the contract, it meant there was no appeal.

He tried to pull himself together, but the walls of the room closed in like a trap. *You'd better hurry out of there. The hit man knows where you are.* He didn't dare check out. He would just disappear. He would carry what effects he could on his person and sneak out. He looked around.

His gun, of course; he had started packing a gun these past few weeks, sensing that something like this might happen. It was one more thing putting him on the wrong side of the law because in his fugitive state he could hardly have openly sought a permit. Even as he stuck the gun in his waistband he knew it would avail little against the skilled hit man they would have sent after him. Still, its solid weight was some comfort.

Now to fill his pockets with razor, toothbrush, socks, shorts; really not much else worth taking or risking taking. *You'd better hurry out of there.* Quick. Otherwise, dead.

Murray Lenox, in Room 819, shot too much lather out of the can of shaving foam. His finger had been too heavy on the valve because he had been thinking savage thoughts about Ms. Missy.

Ms. Missy; he had invented the name so that she might ride the wave of women's lib. He had plucked her out of a nothing rock group going nowhere. Did she guess why he had picked her? Her voice and delivery were nothing special. Did she know he loved her?

He had spent months on the road, hitting every radio station with a disc jockey having a halfway decent following. It took a lot of buttering—and a lot of bread—but he had publicized and payola'd her recording into a hit number. Now that she was high on the charts and had hit the Big Apple, Ms. Missy had a swelled head.

She had come right out and said that maybe Murray's cut of the take was too much, that maybe for the same amount she could get a big-time agent-manager who would make her more than a one-shot.

He had just looked at her, turned, and walked away. Walked away with stiff dignity, though expecting her to call after him and say she was sorry and beg him to come back.

She hadn't called after him, and she hadn't rung up yet, but give her time. She would miss him, realize how much she owed him and how much she still needed him.

He slapped the foam on his face. He had enough to build a Santa Claus beard. He looked in the mirror, he looked in his heart. Some Santa Claus. He reached for his razor, stopped at a knocking.

Missy!

He limped eagerly to the door.

Finley Crowe rapped again on the door of Room 819. He had waited a few minutes on the landing before venturing into the eighth-floor corridor. That was as much to get his breath back after the climb as to screw the silencer onto his gun.

The years of being a hit man were telling on him. No, it was just the years. The hit stuff didn't bother him.

The door of Room 819 opened.

Crowe stared, but it was only the lather that had taken him aback. The right build, the right color hair, and the right color eyes; this was Clifford Fant, all right.

He and Cliff went back to the old days, but he had never let sentiment get in the way of his work.

The man's head jerked at the sight of the gun. His hands went up to push the sight away.

The man had time to say, "No."

Yes.

Just as Clifford Fant eased past the last doorway on the sixth floor and silently made it onto the stairs, he came face to face with Finley Crowe coming as silently down.

In Crowe, the feeling that he was seeing a ghost prompted the motor reflex of his gun hand. If it was the knowledge that he had already done his number that slowed Crowe, it was the knowledge that his hit man had found him that sped Fant.

It was a draw. They held each other at gunpoint.

Fant said, without hope, "Let's talk this over."

Crowe's reply was a real shocker. "Sure."

\* \* \*

Crowe's credit card let them into Room 819.

They looked down at the stiff just inside the door. Fant shivered. But for the 618-819 mixup, which he and Crowe had figured out together, that shattered, spattered face would be his. He shivered again. He could still wind up a corpse if Crowe should decide they couldn't pull it off. He edged away and inched his hand toward the gun in his waistband.

Crowe, turning to face him, smiled at what he plainly took to be Fant's squeamishness. "You registered here under another name, didn't you?"

Fant nodded.

Crowe nodded. "So it don't matter if the cops never find out who the stiff is, as long as the mob thinks it's you. Only problem might be the stiff's fingerprints. If I thought I had to, I'd scrape the guy's fingers raw. But look at his feet."

Fant frowned puzzledly. "Are you talking about *toe*prints?"

Crowe permitted himself a flash of irritation. "No. I mean, look at his shoes. One shoe's built up a bit. Means he was never in the armed services. That, together with the odds he's a square john, means his fingerprints won't be on file. I'll just check his I.D., make sure." He went through the stiff's pockets. "The guy's legit—if being a talent representative's legit. Now, change shoes with him." He handed Fant the stiff's wallet and keys.

Fant stared at Crowe. "What?"

"Change shoes with him. That'll be good enough; who's going to notice the inch difference when they lay him out?"

Fant grimaced as he walked back and forth in the dead man's shoes. The stiff's shoes fitted Fant fine, but they gave him a limp. Still, that would prove a plus worth getting used to when he went forth in his new incarnation.

Crowe got up from tying the shoestrings on Fant's shoes on Lenox's feet in neat bows.

"Okay, Fant. Now we're all set for the switch."

Fant stole out into the corridor, found a linen cart in the service closet, and sneaked it back to Room 819. He and Crowe wrapped Lenox in a sheet. When Fant bent to pick up his end of Lenox, his gun fell out of his waistband. Crowe picked it up and politely handed it to Fant. They stuffed Lenox into the linen cart, rolled the cart to the service elevator, and took it down to the sixth floor. Fant found he had kept his key; he let the three of them into Room 618.

Fant and Crowe lifted Lenox out of the cart, unwrapped him, and arranged him on the floor.

Crowe fitted the silencer onto his gun again. For a moment Fant felt faint, but Crowe simply drove another bullet through the body to pin the killing to this room. Crowe unscrewed the silencer and pocketed it and the gun. Then he fiddled with the air conditioner till it stopped working. This gave him the excuse to open the window. The open window took care of the missing first bullet.

Together, Crowe and Fant went over 618, wiping all surfaces that might have taken fingerprints.

Before leaving Room 618 for the last time, Clifford Fant looked down at the body of Murray Lènox, and felt a sudden sympathy for Clifford Fant.

Fant and Crowe went out with the linen cart and hung the DO NOT DISTURB sign outside the door of Room 618.

They got the linen cart safely back in its eighth-floor closet and Fant let them into Room 819 with Lenox's key. Crowe helped Fant clean up the mess in the room. Crowe found the bullet embedded in the wall. He gouged it out and pocketed it, then looked around and sighed. Fant echoed the sigh. There seemed nothing more to do but part.

This working out of their mutual bind suited both; Fant, because it meant he stayed alive but passed for dead—which would help him stay alive under a new name and in a new place; Crowe, because it meant he kept his name for always making a clean hit.

Before leaving, Crowe rested his eyes on Fant's face, the look saying that his eyes had better not ever rest on Fant's face again.

Fant took no chances on Crowe's changing his mind. He quickly packed Lenox's bags, then phoned the desk to say he—Murray Lenox—was checking out. He worried as he signed the tab with Lenox's name, but none of the Hotel Granville's personnel—desk clerk, bellhop, or doorman—focused on anything but the formalities and the gratuities.

He changed cabs several times, winding up at the Port Authority Bus Terminal. His gun would force him to forego planes and to go by bus, train, and rented car, but that made it all the easier to lose himself. He would travel on Lenox's credit cards till it became dangerous to do so; the monthly billing date would be the deadline. Then Murray Lenox would disappear, say while out boating or swimming in very deep waters.

At which point Clifford Fant would take on a new identity and

live out his borrowed life above one border or below the other as best
he might.

Ms. Missy used the Hotel Granville's courtesy phone to call Room
819. Room 819 did not answer. Ms. Missy's rocker platforms carried
her to the desk clerk. She was not too worried to give him her best
smile. Mr. Lenox? Sorry, Mr. Lenox had just checked out; she had
missed him by minutes. Sorry, Mr. Lenox left no forwarding address.
Ms. Missy's smile died.

It was Leroy Moore's lucky day. Number 618 hit.
He told his boss that he was quitting, and there were hard feelings
when he told the man what he thought of him.
Leroy Moore made big plans to spend his big money, but when it
came time for him to collect his winnings, he found that the runner
with whom he had placed the bet had kept his twenty dollars instead
of passing it on to the policy bank. The runner had figured 618 would
not come out. It had, and the runner had decided his best bet was
to be among the missing.

The syndicate boss's words came out wrapped in cigar smoke.
"We only got this Leroy Moore's word he played twenty bucks on
618. Be good public relations, though, to give him his twenty bucks
back. If that don't suit him, maybe he'd like a few broken bones
better. Now, about the runner that took off: quick as we find him
we finish him. Get Finley Crowe to do the job. There's a guy that
don't never mess up a hit."

# Murder in Miniature

## by Nora Caplan

A nn waited eagerly for her husband's response, but he said nothing for a long while. He remained standing, his face speculative as he looked down at the large dollhouse in the basement closet. It was pure Victorian ... a three storied wooden structure painted dark green with a mansard roof centered by a cupola and white gingerbread scrollwork ornamenting the front porch. Finally, he commented, "I thought you said Holly wanted a microscope for her birthday."

"Oh, Phil." Both annoyance and amusement were in her voice. "A microscope for an eight-year-old girl? *This* is what she needs. Have you ever seen anything like it?" Ann's delight was obvious as she pointed out the rooms, furnished to the last detail in authentic period pieces. "And when I saw the dolls ... look, there's even a maid." She sighed, "Well, I couldn't resist it."

Phil shrugged. "Maybe she'll like it. You know more about that than I do. I just don't want her to be disappointed, that's all. She's never cared much about dolls before, has she?"

"This is different," his wife said defensively. "Besides, Holly needs something unusual like this to stimulate her imagination. That's the whole trouble, Phil. She's never been given a chance to pretend anything. We've just always gone along with that matter-of-fact side of her."

"But that *is* Holly." As if to end the discussion, Phil walked over to the hot water heater. "This thing's leaking again. You'd better give the company a call before long. The warranty's up in a couple of months."

Ann was determined to justify her reason for buying the dollhouse, so disregarding his last remarks, she said, "I've never been able to share anything much with Holly. She's not the way I was at her age or like any other child I grew up with. She's never known the fun of pretending the way we did, and she's growing up so fast." Ann bent over the dollhouse and very gently fingered a miniature steamer trunk in the attic. "I've been looking for something the two of us could enjoy together. I knew this was it the minute I saw it."

271

Phil returned to her, and patted her on the shoulder. "Okay, if you think it'll make her happy. Come on upstairs now, honey. It's cold down here."

With his saying it, she shivered. Suddenly she felt depressed. Tomorrow was Holly's birthday. It was too late to get her anything else. She wondered if Phil could be right in doubting that Holly would like the dollhouse. No, Ann concluded shortly. It must appeal to her. It simply wasn't possible for a daughter of hers to be totally lacking a sense of imagination.

The next morning after Holly left for school, Phil and Ann moved the dollhouse upstairs to their daughter's room. "Should I try to keep her downstairs until you get home?" Ann asked her husband.

"The suspense would kill you," Phil grinned. He kissed the tip of her nose. "Don't wait for me. Go ahead and show it to her the minute she gets home."

Holly looked exactly like Phil, Ann thought that afternoon as she watched her daughter scrutinize the dollhouse for the first time. She had the same even expression in her deep-set brown eyes, the identical composed shape of her mouth. And as her mother had expected, Holly made a thorough inspection of each room before she stated an opinion. "This is different from Sara's. It's supposed to be in the olden days, isn't it?"

Ann smiled and stooped beside her. "The style is called Victorian. It's about eighty or ninety years old. Things were very different then. Look at the kitchen pump. It really works, too." She showed Holly how the handle moved up and down.

"I see," Holly nodded.

Ann couldn't wait any longer. "Do you like it, darling? Isn't it lots better than a microscope?"

Holly noted the elation in her mother's vivid blue eyes. "Well," she answered carefully, "it'll give me lots to learn about."

Some hours later when Ann went into Holly's room to see if she was reading in semi-darkness as usual, she found Holly lying on her side, staring at the dollhouse. The small tole lamp shining opposite it almost spotlighted the rooms, so that they gave the impression of stage settings for an Ibsen play. Ann reached to turn off the light.

"Please leave it on," Holly said without turning her head.

Ann smiled, and answered lightly but with purpose, "You know, you're keeping the Joneses from retiring."

Holly looked up at her mother. A puzzled frown wrinkled her

forehead at first, then it disappeared. "Oh, you mean *them*." She faced the dollhouse again. "Their name is Pettingill." She yawned. "The Bartholomew J. Pettingills. And the maid's name is Clara Fisher."

Though the following day was Saturday, Phil went to his office at the Bureau of Standards. Before he left, he murmured something about having to get the notes for his next lecture, but Ann was too preoccupied to pay much attention. Holly had already finished breakfast, and had gone back up to her room. On a pretext of starting the upstairs cleaning, Ann took a dust cloth to Holly's bedroom. Her daughter was sitting quietly in a rocker before the dollhouse. "Do you suppose," she asked her mother, "you could make them some new clothes?"

"I'd love to." Ann bent down and started to pick up Mrs. Pettingill.

"Don't, Mommy!" Holly's voice was sharp. "She hates to be touched."

Ann hastily withdrew her hand. "Oh, really?" The tiny figure's china face was rather proud and stern. Then Ann studied the father. "Mr. Pettingill seems pleasant enough."

"He is." Holly removed him from a Lincoln rocker in the parlor. She rubbed her finger over his black painted mustache. "That's the trouble."

"What do you mean . . . trouble?" Ann sat down on the floor, completely enthralled.

"Well, you see," Holly explained very seriously, "she thinks he's not strict enough with Charlie, for one thing."

"Their little boy?" Ann pointed to the doll in a sailor suit astride a hobby horse in the second floor nursery.

"Mm-hmm," Holly nodded. "He's really a nice little boy, but he does things that make his mother mad."

"For instance?"

"Oh, just little things. Getting his shoes muddy and forgetting to put his things away."

Ann's eyes twinkled. "What's so wrong with that? As a matter of fact, she doesn't sound very different from me, or any other mother."

Holly continued in the same earnest manner, "But she won't let him alone. She always wants him to do what she thinks is best for him and not what he'd really like to do at all. And another thing, she can't stand a bit of dust anywhere. She really works poor Clara . . . the maid . . . terribly hard. I think Clara would've left a long time ago if it hadn't been for Mr. Pettingill and Charlie." She stroked Clara's blonde pompadour. "I want you to make Clara a beautiful dress with a parasol to match."

Ann's mouth turned up. "But, darling, she's the maid."

Holly said stubbornly, "I don't care. Besides, she doesn't have to work on Sundays, and she always takes Charlie for a walk in the park after church. Sometimes Mr. Pettingill goes along with them, too. So she needs a pretty dress."

"And what about the new clothes for Mrs. Pettingill?"

Holly was indifferent. "Oh, you don't have to bother with her. What she has on is all right."

Ann felt curiously defensive about the mother doll. She couldn't understand Holly's hostile attitude toward Mrs. Pettingill. More to herself than to her daughter, Ann replied, "The mother's dress could be dark blue . . . taffeta, I think. With a white lace collar."

"I think I'll read for a while." Holly rose and went over to the bookcase under the dormer window.

Ann knew that she was being dismissed. She got to her feet and started to leave when Holly added, "I'd like Clara's dress to be pink with a real full skirt and ruffles around the bottom. Charlie and Mr. Pettingill would like that, too."

As Ann changed the linens on the bed in Phil's and her room, she kept thinking about her conversation with Holly. She was pleased, naturally, that her daughter's imagination had apparently begun to emerge. And yet, it had taken such a strange turn. There was something so . . . real about the Pettingills. They weren't at all like the improbably good, pretend families she remembered from her own childhood. Still, they were far more intriguing, and evidently real to Holly.

She went over to a chest and pulled out the bottom drawer. She rummaged through it and finally came up with a scrap of Alençon lace. There was more than enough of it for a collar, but the taffeta . . . She found a piece of dark blue satin. That would do even better. Mrs. Pettingill would be a model of good taste compared with the frilled pink organdy flounces of Clara, with matching parasol.

The following Monday afternoon Ann was in the kitchen making seven-minute frosting when she heard Holly come home from school. Her daughter called from the living room, "Mommy, Sara's here. Her mother said she could stay till five o'clock."

Ann raised her voice over the clatter of the beater. "Hang up your things in the hall closet." She expected the girls to come into the kitchen, but shortly she heard them run upstairs. Abruptly she turned off the mixer. Sara was such a helter-skelter sort of child, there was no telling what she might do to the dollhouse. And there were the new clothes on the Pettingills and Clara. She'd planned to surprise Holly with them, but it wouldn't be the same now with Sara around. Her face hardened. She would go upstairs anyway.

The two girls didn't notice her when she came to the doorway. "It's sort of funny looking," Sara was saying. "I like my dollhouse better. Mine's got electric lights, too." She seized Mrs. Pettingill by one arm, crushing the leg o'mutton sleeve that Ann had struggled over.

"Put her down," Ann commanded. The girls stared. Ann removed the doll from Sara's sticky fingers, and as she tried to fluff the sleeve into fullness again, she said coldly, "You'd better play down in the recreation room."

"But, Mommy," Holly protested.

"Go ahead. Do as I say." They left, subdued and silent, but she stayed by the dollhouse for a time. Finally she returned to the kitchen. Thanks to Sara, the frosting was ruined. She dumped it into the sink, and turned on the water with such force that it soaked her apron.

Holly was so constrained at dinner that night that Phil asked her, "What's the matter? Something happen at school today?"

"No." She avoided looking at her mother and addressed Phil, "Can I be excused now?"

He glanced at her plate. She'd hardly touched her food.

"It's all right." Ann made the decision for him. As soon as Holly slipped from the dining room, Ann explained, "Sara was over this afternoon. She always overstimulates Holly."

"I've never noticed it before," he said.

"Well, she does." Ann pushed back her chair, and began stacking the plates.

"You think Holly might be coming down with something? She's seemed pretty quiet the last couple of days."

"I don't think so. She's just tired, that's all."

After she'd finished the dishes, Ann carried a cup of coffee into the living room. Phil was watching a news report on TV. She drank the coffee thoughtfully. Maybe she had been a little too sharp with Holly this afternoon, but Sara had grated on her nerves so. She didn't see what there was about that child that attracted Holly to her. Then Ann remembered that she hadn't had a chance to discuss the new doll clothes with Holly. By now she'd probably got over her moodiness.

She found Holly stretched out on her bed, face down. Ann smoothed the child's hair. "You're not asleep, are you, baby?"

"No."

Ann sat down beside her. "I forgot to ask you what you think of the Pettingills' and Clara's new outfits."

"They're okay," Holly replied in a monotone.

"I had a terrible time with Mrs. Pettingill's dress. The sleeves still don't fit quite right below the elbows, but it's so hard to work on anything that small." Ann questioned gently, "Do you suppose she'll mind?" Holly didn't answer. Ann supposed that she was still resentful about not being allowed to play in her room. "I've been thinking that maybe we should fix up Mr. and Mrs. Pettingill's room. It's so drab compared with the rest of the house. I have some lovely pale green silk that I could make into draperies and a bedspread, and . . ."

"I don't want you to," Holly interrupted shrilly, and sat up on the edge of the bed. Her shoulders were rigid.

"But why not, sweetie?" There was a soft insistence in Ann's voice.

Holly repeated uneasily, "I don't want you . . ." She swallowed. "I mean, I don't think Mrs. Pettingill would like that."

"Of course she would," Ann argued more firmly. "Pastel green was just the sort of color that was fashionable in those days, and it would do a lot more for that dark walnut bed and highboy than that dingy lace."

Holly picked at one of the yarn ties on her comforter. "But it would make Clara feel bad."

"What's she got to do with it? She's only the maid." Ann glanced with annoyance at the uniformed figure in the kitchen. Clara's blue eyes stared back at her. At that moment there seemed to be something challenging about her vapid smile.

Holly misinterpreted her mother's silence as interest. "Clara's so much nicer than Mrs. Pettingill. She understands Charlie and Mr. Pettingill. I think they really like her better."

Ann was rather shocked. "But, Holly, that's not natural."

"I want to go to bed now." Holly untied one shoe slowly, then placed it on the floor beside her bed.

"All right, chicken." Ann kissed her daughter's cheek.

Holly kept her eyes on the floor. "Don't do anything more to the dollhouse. Please, Mother."

"We'll talk about it later, dear. You're tired now. Go to sleep."

For the next week the Pettingills weren't mentioned. Holly played at Sara's house every afternoon until dinnertime. Afterwards, she did her homework, read, or watched TV until bedtime. Phil was having Ann type a draft of his lecture, and she didn't have time to talk much to her daughter. She grew increasingly keyed-up, with Phil's demands that the copy be absolutely accurate, in spite of her having to decipher his illegible handwriting. And all the time she was bothered by Holly's strange reaction that last particular night.

She finished Phil's report Friday morning. At lunch she said to Holly, "I'm all through with Daddy's work now. Let's do something special this afternoon."

Holly captured a bit of carrot from her spoonful of vegetable soup, and put it aside on a plate. "I promised Sara I'd go over to her house. She told me she has a surprise for me."

Ann felt that she had to make a compromise in order not to estrange her daughter further. With resignation she said. "Well, bring Sara here then." When Holly hesitated, Ann added. "You've been at her place so much lately, I'm sure her mother needs a rest by now."

"Okay," Holly agreed. She glanced at the clock over the refrigerator. "I'd better go now. Sara said she'd meet me at the corner at twelve thirty."

Ann resolved to be as pleasant as possible to Sara that afternoon. She baked some brownies, and made a pitcher of lemonade. She set the kitchen table for a tea party. Holly would like this. Ann went upstairs to the spare bedroom, took from the closet a box of clothes to be mended, and sat down at the sewing machine.

"Mommy," Holly called from the foyer an hour or so later, "we're here. Come and see what Sara gave me."

Ann smiled at the two of them as she came down the stairs. Holly held out her hand. In it was a tiny circlet of white fur.

Sara's freckled face was exuberant. "It's a muff for Clara. I made it all by myself." She stopped abruptly as she saw the change of expression in Ann's eyes. She looked down. "Well, my mother did help a little. She showed me . . ."

"Why did you do it?" Ann's smile was fixed.

"Well, I . . ." Sara stammered.

"She wanted to, Mommy," Holly spoke up. "What's wrong?"

Ann was gripping the newel post so hard that her knuckes had turned white. "But why *Clara?*" The two girls registered nothing but bewilderment, and soon Ann said tonelessly, "There's a snack for you in the kitchen. I have to finish the mending."

But when she returned to the spare bedroom, she replaced the box of clothes in the closet. She went to her own room to get the remnant of pale green silk.

Ann timed the surprise perfectly. While Holly was taking her bath that night, Ann tiptoed into her room and knelt beside the dollhouse. What a difference the new curtains and bedspread made in Mrs. Pettingill's room. And the moss green velvet pillow on the slipper chair was an inspiration. As her final touch, Ann slipped a minute string of pearls around Mrs. Pettingill's throat.

"What're you doing?" Holly had entered with a towel draped around her shoulders, and water was still trickling down her legs.

Ann stood up. "Oh, I just made a little surprise for the dollhouse." She saw her daughter was trembling. "Dry yourself off first, dear. You can see it after you've put on your pajamas."

Holly remained near the door, shivering. "But I didn't want you to, Mommy," she said tearfully. "I told you not to do anything more to the dollhouse."

"You'll catch cold like that. Here, let me help you." Ann began rubbing Holly down briskly with the towel. "Now put on your pajamas quick." Holly was so slow about it that Ann finished buttoning the top herself. "There, now," her mother said. "Let's go see the surprise."

"No," Holly shuddered. "I'm still cold. I just want to go to bed and get warm."

Ann's disappointment changed to concern. "Do you feel sick, darling?"

Holly hunched herself under the covers. "My stomach feels funny."

"It's from all those brownies and lemonade this afternoon. I know Sara makes a habit of stuffing herself, but you should know better." Ann frowned. "Maybe some milk of magnesia . . ."

"I'll be all right."

"You're sure?"

Holly nodded.

Ann kissed her. "Call me if you should start to feel sick." She turned to look at Holly once more before she went downstairs. The child lay absolutely still, her eyes fixed on the dollhouse.

\* \* \*

The cry in the middle of the night was unrecognizable at first, but Phil and Ann awoke to full consciousness. Then from Holly's room came a terrified, "Daddy . . . Daddy."

Ann flung back the sheet and blanket. "Stay here," she said tersely to her husband. "I'll go to her."

Holly was huddled against her pillow. She wouldn't look up when Ann bent over her, murmuring, "What's wrong, baby?"

"Take it away," Holly gasped.

"Take what away?"

"The dollhouse. Take it away . . . now," Holly pleaded.

"In the middle of the night? But why, darling? Did you have a bad dream?"

"Just take it away . . . please. Right now." Holly's voice rose, shrill to the verge of hysteria.

Phil appeared in the doorway. He'd apparently heard what she'd said, for he commented smoothly, reasonably, "But we can't move it out at this hour, honey. All the stuff inside has to be taken out so nothing will get broken. We'll take care of it the first thing in the morning."

But Holly was unassuaged. She kept crying, "No . . . take it away . . . now."

"Tell you what," Phil said after a moment's deliberation. "Suppose we put something over the dollhouse so you can't see it." He motioned to Ann to get the extra blanket at the foot of Holly's bed.

"What do you suppose frightened her so?" Ann whispered to Phil as he stepped over to her.

"Never mind that now," he muttered. "The poor kid's upset enough already." Then he raised his voice to the same unruffled tone as before. "Holly, remember that time when you were about four or five, and you kept seeing those shadows from your tree swing on this wall . . ."

Ann unfolded the blanket. She was about to drape it over the dollhouse. But she sensed that something was terribly wrong. *Mrs. Pettingill. Where was she?* Ann searched every room in the dollhouse with mounting tension. Clara and Charlie and Mr. Pettingill were seated in the parlor, their china faces placid and content. The scene was entirely too innocent.

Ann found the clue she was looking for. The pearl necklace. *Clara was wearing Mrs. Pettingill's pearl necklace.*

Almost instinctively now, Ann knew where she would find Mrs. Pettingill. She reached up to the storage room in the attic. Her fingers felt numb as she unlocked and opened the steamer trunk. Mrs. Pettingill was inside . . . *crushed* . . . her neck broken.

Ann slowly turned around. With the trunk between her thumb and forefinger, she held it up for Holly to see. "Why did you let them do it?"

Holly leaned toward her father. "It . . . it was an accident." She pressed closer to Phil. "I didn't mean to. Honest."

Phil tightened his arm around the child. "For God's sake, Ann," he began angrily. Then he stopped. He'd never before seen the kind of emotion that was now darkening his wife's eyes.

Deadly calm, Ann said, "No, Holly. It wasn't an accident." She replaced the trunk in the attic, with poor Mrs. Pettingill still inside. "It was no accident," she confronted Clara and Mr. Pettingill. *"You* murdered her."

# Smuggler's Island

## by Bill Pronzini

The first I heard that somebody had bought Smuggler's Island was late on a cold foggy morning in May. Handy Manners and Davey and I had just brought the *Jennie Too* into the Camaroon Bay wharf, loaded with the day's limit in salmon—silvers mostly, with a few big kings—and Handy had gone inside the processing shed at Bay Fisheries to call for the tally clerk and the portable scales. I was helping Davey hoist up the hatch covers, and I was thinking that he handled himself fine on the boat and what a shame it'd be if he decided eventually that he didn't want to go into commercial fishing as his livelihood. A man likes to see his only son take up his chosen profession. But Davey was always talking about traveling around Europe, seeing some of the world, maybe finding a career he liked better than fishing. Well, he was only nineteen. Decisions don't come quick or easy at that age.

Anyhow, we were working on the hatch covers when I heard somebody call my name. I glanced up, and Pa and Abner Frawley were coming toward us from down-wharf, where the cafe was. I was a little surprised to see Pa out on a day like this; he usually stayed home with Jennie when it was overcast and windy because the fog and cold air aggravated his lumbago.

The two of them came up and stopped, Pa puffing on one of his home-carved meerschaum pipes. They were both seventy-two and long-retired—Abner from a manager's job at the cannery a mile up the coast, Pa from running the general store in the village—and they'd been cronies for at least half their lives. But that was where all resemblance between them ended. Abner was short and round and white-haired, and always had a smile and a joke for everybody. Pa, on the other hand, was tall and thin and dour; if he'd smiled any more than four times in the forty-seven years since I was born I can't remember it. Abner had come up from San Francisco during the Depression, but Pa was a second-generation native of Camaroon Bay, his father having emigrated from Ireland during the short-lived potato boom in the early 1900's. He was a good man and a

281

decent father, which was why I'd given him a room in our house
when Ma died six years ago, but I'd never felt close to him.

He said to me, "Looks like a good catch, Verne."

"Pretty good," I said. "How come you're out in this weather?"

"Abner's idea. He dragged me out of the house."

I looked at Abner. His eyes were bright, the way they always got
when he had a choice bit of news or gossip to tell. He said, "Fella
from Los Angeles went and bought Smuggler's Island. Can you beat
that?"

"Bought it?" I said. "You mean outright?"

"Yep. Paid the county a hundred thousand cash."

"How'd you hear about it?"

"Jack Kewin, over to the real estate office."

"Who's the fellow who bought it?"

"Name's Roger Vauclain," Abner said. "Jack don't know any more
about him. Did the buying through an agent."

Davey said, "Wonder what he wants with it?"

"Maybe he's got ideas of hunting treasure," Abner said, and
winked at him. "Maybe he heard about what's hidden in those
caves."

Pa gave him a look. "Old fool," he said.

Davey grinned, and I smiled a little and turned to look to where
Smuggler's Island sat wreathed in fog half a mile straight out across
the choppy harbor. It wasn't much to look at, from a distance or up
close. Just one big oblong chunk of eroded rock about an acre and
a half in size surrounded by a lot of little islets. It had a few stunted
trees and shrubs, and a long headland where gulls built their nests,
and a sheltered cove on the lee shore where you could put in a small
boat. That was about all there was to it—except for those caves
Abner had spoken of.

They were located near the lee cove and you could only get into
them at low tide. Some said caves honeycombed the whole underbelly
of the island, but those of us who'd ignored warnings from our parents as kids and gone exploring in them knew that this wasn't so.
There were three caves and two of them had branches that led deep
into the rock, but all of the tunnels were dead ends.

This business of treasure being hidden in one of those caves was
just so much nonsense, of course—sort of a local legend that nobody
took seriously. What the treasure was supposed to be was two million
dollars in greenbacks that had been hidden by a rackets courier
during Prohibition, when he'd been chased to the island by a team

of Revenue agents. There was also supposed to be fifty cases of high-grade moonshine secreted there.

The bootlegging part of it had a good deal of truth, though. This section of the Northern California coast was a hotbed of illegal liquor traffic in the days of the Volstead Act, and the scene of several confrontations between smugglers and Revenue agents; half a dozen men on both sides had been killed, or had turned up missing and presumed dead. The way the bootleggers worked was to bring ships down from Canada outfitted as distilleries—big stills in their holds, bottling equipment, labels for a dozen different kinds of Canadian whisky—and anchor them twenty-five miles offshore. Then local fishermen and imported hirelings would go out in their boats and carry the liquor to places along the shore, where trucks would be waiting to pick it up and transport it down to San Francisco or east into Nevada. Smuggler's Island was supposed to have been a short-term storage point for whisky that couldn't be trucked out right away, which may or may not have been a true fact. At any rate, that was how the island got its name.

Just as I turned back to Pa and Abner, Handy came out of the processing shed with the tally clerk and the scales. He was a big, thick-necked man, Handy, with red hair and a temper to match; he was also one of the best mates around and knew as much about salmon trolling and diesel engines as anybody in Camaroon Bay. He'd been working for me eight years, but he wouldn't be much longer. He was saving up to buy a boat of his own and only needed another thousand or so to swing the down payment.

Abner told him right away about this Roger Vauclain buying Smuggler's Island. Handy grunted and said, "Anybody that'd want those rocks out there has to have rocks in his head."

"Who do you imagine he is?" Davey asked.

"One of those damn-fool rich people probably," Pa said. "Buy something for no good reason except that it's there and they want it."

"But why Smuggler's Island in particular?"

"Got a fancy name, that's why. Now he can say to his friends, why look here, I own a place up north called Smuggler's Island, supposed to have treasure hidden on it."

I said, "Well, whoever he is and whyever he bought it, we'll find out eventually. Right now we've got a catch to unload."

"Sure is a puzzler though, ain't it, Verne?" Abner said.

"It is that," I admitted. "It's a puzzler, all right."

\* \* \*

If you live in a small town or village, you know how it is when something happens that has no immediate explanation. Rumors start flying, based on few or no facts, and every time one of them is retold to somebody else it gets exaggerated. Nothing much goes on in a place like Camaroon Bay anyhow—conversation is pretty much limited to the weather and the actions of tourists and how the salmon are running or how the crabs seem to be thinning out a little more every year. So this Roger Vauclain buying Smuggler's Island got a lot more lip service paid to it than it would have someplace else.

Jack Kewin didn't find out much about Vauclain, just that he was some kind of wealthy resident of Southern California. But that was enough for the speculations and the rumors to build on. During the next week I heard from different people that Vauclain was a real estate speculator who was going to construct a small private club on the island; that he was a retired bootlegger who'd worked the coast during Prohibition and had bought the island for nostalgic reasons; that he was a front man for a movie company that was going to film a big spectacular in Camaroon Bay and blow up the island in the final scene. None of these rumors made much sense, but that didn't stop people from spreading them and half-believing in them.

Then, one night while we were eating supper, Abner came knocking at the front door of our house on the hill above the village. Davey went and let him in, and he sat down at the table next to Pa. One look at him was enough to tell us that he'd come with news.

"Just been talking to Lloyd Simms," he said as Jennie poured him a cup of coffee. "Who do you reckon just made a reservation at the Camaroon Inn?"

"Who?" I asked.

"Roger Vauclain himself. Lloyd talked to him on the phone less than an hour ago, says he sounded pretty hard-nosed. Booked a single room for a week, be here on Thursday."

"Only a single room?" Jennie said. "Why, I'm disappointed, Abner. I expected he'd be traveling with an entourage." She's a practical woman and when it comes to things she considers nonsense, like all the hoopla over Vauclain and Smuggler's Island, her sense of humor sharpens into sarcasm.

"Might be others coming up later," Abner said seriously.

Davey said, "Week's a long time for a rich man to spend in a place like Camaroon Bay. I wonder what he figures to do all that time?"

"Tend to his island, probably," I said.

"Tend to it?" Pa said. "Tend to what? You can walk over the whole thing in two hours."

"Well, there's always the caves, Pa."

He snorted. "Grown man'd have to be a fool to go wandering in those caves. Tide comes in while he's inside, he'll drown for sure."

"What time's he due in on Thursday?" Davey asked Abner.

"Around noon, Lloyd says. Reckon we'll find out then what he's planning to do with the island."

"Not planning to do anything with it, I tell you," Pa said. "Just wants to *own* it."

"We'll see," Abner said. "We'll see."

Thursday was clear and warm, and it should have been a good day for salmon; but maybe the run had started to peter out because it took us until almost noon to make the limit. It was after two o'clock before we got the catch unloaded and weighed in at Bay Fisheries. Davey had some errands to run and Handy had logged enough extra time, so I took the *Jennie Too* over to the commercial slips myself and stayed aboard her to hose down the decks. When I was through with that, I set about replacing the port outrigger line because it had started to weaken and we'd been having trouble with it.

I was doing that when a tall man came down the ramp from the quay and stood just off the bow, watching me. I didn't pay much attention to him; tourists stop by to rubberneck now and then, and if you encourage them they sometimes hang around so you can't get any work done. But then this fellow slapped a hand against his leg, as if he were annoyed, and called out in a loud voice, "Hey, you there. Fisherman."

I looked at him then, frowning. I'd heard that tone before: sharp, full of self-granted authority. Some city people are like that; to them, anybody who lives in a rural village is a low-class hick. I didn't like it and I let him see that in my face. "You talking to me?"

"Who else would I be talking to?"

I didn't say anything. He was in his forties, smooth-looking, and dressed in white ducks and a crisp blue windbreaker. If nothing else, his eyes were enough to make you dislike him immediately; they were hard and unfriendly and said that he was used to getting his own way.

He said, "Where can I rent a boat?"

"What kind of boat? To go sportfishing?"

"No, not to go sportfishing. A small cruiser."

"There ain't any cruisers for rent here."

He made a disgusted sound, as if he'd expected that. "A big outboard then," he said. "Something seaworthy."

"It's not a good idea to take a small boat out of the harbor," I said. "The ocean along here is pretty rough—"

"I don't want advice," he said. "I want a boat big enough to get me out to Smuggler's Island and back. Now who do I see about it?"

"Smuggler's Island?" I looked at him more closely. "Your name happen to be Roger Vauclain, by any chance?"

"That's right. You heard about me buying the island, I suppose. Along with everybody else in this place."

"News gets around," I said mildly.

"About that boat," he said.

"Talk to Ed Hawkins at Bay Marine on the wharf. He'll find something for you."

Vauclain gave me a curt nod and started to turn away.

I said, "Mind if I ask *you* a question now?"

He turned back. "What is it?"

"People don't go buying islands very often," I said, "particularly one like Smuggler's. I'd be interested to know your plans for it."

"You and every other damned person in Camaroon Bay."

I held my temper. "I was just asking. You don't have to give me an answer."

He was silent for a moment. Then he said, "What the hell, it's no secret. I've always wanted to live on an island, and that one out there is the only one around I can afford."

I stared at him. "You mean you're going to *build* on it?"

"That surprises you, does it?"

"It does," I said. "There's nothing on Smuggler's Island but rocks and a few trees and a couple of thousand nesting gulls. It's fogbound most of the time, and even when it's not, the wind blows at thirty knots or better."

"I like fog and wind and ocean," Vauclain said. "I like isolation. I don't like people much. That satisfy you?"

I shrugged. "To each his own."

"Exactly," he said, and went away up the ramp.

I worked on the *Jennie Too* another hour, then I went over to the Wharf Cafe for a cup of coffee and a piece of pie. When I came inside

I saw Pa, Abner, and Handy sitting at one of the copper-topped tables. I walked over to them.

They already knew that Vauclain had arrived in Camaroon Bay. Handy was saying, "Hell, he's about as friendly as a shark. I was over to Ed Hawkins' place shooting the breeze when he came in and demanded Ed get him a boat. Threw his weight around for fifteen minutes until Ed agreed to rent him his own Chris-Craft. Then he paid for the rental in cash, slammed two fifties on Ed's desk like they were singles and Ed was a beggar."

I sat down. "He's an eccentric, all right," I said. "I talked to him for a few minutes myself about an hour ago."

"Eccentric?" Abner said, and snorted. "That's just a name they give to people who never learned manners or good sense."

Pa said to me, "He tell you what he's fixing to do with Smuggler's Island, Verne?"

"He did, yep."

"Told Abner too, over to the Inn." Pa shook his head, glowering, and lighted a pipe. "Craziest damned thing I ever heard. Build a house on that mess of rock, live out there. Crazy, that's all."

"That's a fact," Handy said. "I'd give him more credit if he was planning to hunt for that bootlegger's treasure."

"Well, I'm sure not going to relish having him for a neighbor," Abner said. "Don't guess anybody else will, either."

None of us disagreed with that. A man likes to be able to get along with his neighbors, rich or poor. Getting along with Vauclain, it seemed, was going to be a chore for everybody.

In the next couple of days Vauclain didn't do much to improve his standing with the residents of Camaroon Bay. He snapped at merchants and waitresses, ignored anybody who tried to strike up a conversation with him, and complained twice to Lloyd Simms about the service at the Inn. The only good thing about him, most people were saying, was that he spent the better part of his days on Smuggler's Island—doing what, nobody knew exactly—and his nights locked in his room. Might have been he was drawing up plans there for the house he intended to build on the island.

Rumor now had it that Vauclain was an architect, one of these independents who'd built up a reputation, like Frank Lloyd Wright in the old days, and who only worked for private individuals and companies. This was probably true since it originated with Jack Kewin; he'd spent a little time with Vauclain and wasn't one to spread unfounded gossip. According to Jack, Vauclain had learned that the island was for sale more than six months ago and had been up twice before by helicopter from San Francisco to get an aerial view of it.

That was the way things stood on Sunday morning, when Jennie and I left for church at ten. Afterward we had lunch at a place up the coast, and then, because the weather was cool but still clear, we went for a drive through the redwood country. It was almost five when we got back home.

Pa was in bed—his lumbago was bothering him, he said—and Davey was gone somewhere. I went into our bedroom to change out of my suit. While I was in there, the telephone rang, and Jennie called out that it was for me.

When I picked up the receiver Lloyd Simms's voice said, "Sorry to bother you, Verne, but if you're not busy I need a favor."

"I'm not busy, Lloyd. What is it?"

"Well, it's Roger Vauclain. He went out to the island this morning like usual, and he was supposed to be back at three to take a telephone call. Told me to make sure I was around then, the call was important—you know the way he talks. The call came in right on schedule, but Vauclain didn't. He's still not back, and the party calling him has been ringing me up every half hour, demanding I get hold of him. Something about a bid that has to be delivered first thing tomorrow morning."

"You want me to go out to the island, Lloyd?"

"If you wouldn't mind," he said. "I don't much care about Vauclain, the way he's been acting, but this caller is driving me up a wall. And it could be something's the matter with Vauclain's boat; can't get it started or something. Seems kind of funny he didn't come back when he said he would."

I hesitated. I didn't much want to take the time to go out to Smuggler's Island; but then if there was a chance Vauclain was in trouble I couldn't very well refuse to help.

"All right," I said. "I'll see what I can do."

We rang off, and I explained to Jennie where I was going and why. Then I drove down to the basin where the pleasure-boat slips were and took the tarp off Davey's sixteen-foot Sportliner inboard. I'd bought it for him on his sixteenth birthday, when I figured he was old enough to handle a small boat of his own, but I used it as much as he did. We're not so well off that we can afford to keep more than one pleasure craft.

The engine started right up for a change—usually you have to choke it several times on cool days—and I took her out of the slips and into the harbor. The sun was hidden by overcast now and the wind was up, building small whitecaps, running fogbanks in from the ocean but shredding them before they reached the shore. I followed the south jetty out past the breakwater and into open sea. The water was choppier there, the color of gunmetal, and the wind was pretty cold; I pulled the collar of my jacket up and put on my gloves to keep my hands from numbing on the wheel.

When I neared the island, I swung around to the north shore and into the lee cove. Ed Hawkins' Chris-Craft was tied up there all right, bow and stern lines made fast to outcroppings on a long, natural stone dock. I took the Sportliner in behind it, climbed out onto the bare rock, and made her fast. On my right, waves broke over and into the mouths of the three caves, hissing long fans of spray. Gulls wheeled screeching above the headland; farther in, scrub oak and cypress danced like line bobbers in the wind. It all made you feel as though you were standing on the edge of the world.

There was no sign of Vauclain anywhere at the cove, so I went up through a tangle of artichoke plants toward the center of the island. The area there was rocky but mostly flat, dotted with undergrowth and patches of sandy earth. I stopped beside a gnarled cypress and scanned from left to right. Nothing but emptiness. Then I walked out toward the headland, hunched over against the pull of the wind. But I didn't find him there, either.

A sudden thought came to me as I started back and the hairs prickled on my neck. What if he'd gone into the caves and been trapped there when the tide began to flood? If that was what had happened, it was too late for me to do anything—but I started to run anyway, my eyes on the ground so I wouldn't trip over a bush or a rock.

I was almost back to the cove, coming at a different angle from before, when I saw him.

It was so unexpected that I pulled up short and almost lost my footing on loose rock. The pit of my stomach went hollow. He was lying on his back in a bed of artichokes, one arm flung out and the other wrapped across his chest. There was blood under his arm, and blood spread across the front of his windbreaker. One long look was all I needed to tell me he'd been shot and that he was dead.

Shock and an eerie sense of unreality kept me standing there another few seconds. My thoughts were jumbled; you don't think too

clearly when you stumble on a dead man, a murdered man. And it
*was* murder, I knew that well enough. There was no gun anywhere
near the body, and no way it could have been an accident.

Then I turned, shivering, and ran down to the cove and took the
Sportliner away from there at full throttle to call for the county
sheriff.

Vauclain's death was the biggest event that had happened in
Camaroon Bay in forty years, and Sunday night and Monday nobody
talked about anything else. As soon as word got around that I was
the one who'd discovered the body, the doorbell and the telephone
didn't stop ringing—friends and neighbors, newspaper people, in-
vestigators. The only place I had any peace was on the *Jennie Too*
Monday morning, and not much there because Davey and Handy
wouldn't let the subject alone while we fished.

By late that afternoon the authorities had questioned just about
everyone in the area. It didn't appear they'd found out anything,
though. Vauclain had been alone when he'd left for the island early
Sunday; Abner had been down at the slips then and swore to the
fact. A couple of tourists had rented boats from Ed Hawkins during
the day, since the weather was pretty good, and a lot of locals were
out in the harbor on pleasure craft. But whoever it was who had
gone to Smuggler's Island after Vauclain, he hadn't been noticed.

As to a motive for the shooting, there were all sorts of wild speculations. Vauclain had wronged somebody in Los Angeles and that
person had followed him here to take revenge. He'd treated a local
citizen badly enough to trigger a murderous rage. He'd gotten in
bad with organized crime and a contract had been put out on him.
And the most farfetched theory of all: he'd actually uncovered some
sort of treasure on Smuggler's Island and somebody'd learned about
it and killed him for it. But the simple truth was, nobody had *any*
idea why Vauclain was murdered. If the sheriff's department had
found any clues on the island or anywhere else, they weren't talking—but they weren't making any arrests, either.

There was a lot of excitement, all right. Only, underneath it all
people were nervous and a little scared. A killer seemed to be loose
in Camaroon Bay, and if he'd murdered once, who was to say he
wouldn't do it again? A mystery is all well and good when it's happening someplace else, but when it's right on your doorstep you can't
help but feel threatened and apprehensive.

I'd had about all the pestering I could stand by four o'clock, so I got into the car and drove up the coast to Shelter Cove. That gave me an hour's worth of freedom. But no sooner did I get back to Camaroon Bay, with the intention of going home and locking myself in my basement workshop, than a sheriff's cruiser pulled up behind me at a stop sign and its horn started honking. I sighed and pulled over to the curb.

It was Harry Swenson, one of the deputies who'd questioned me the day before, after I'd reported finding Vauclain's body. We knew each other well enough to be on a first name basis. He said, "Verne, the sheriff asked me to talk to you again, see if there's anything you might have overlooked yesterday. You mind?"

"No, I don't mind," I said tiredly.

We went into the Inn and took a table at the back of the dining room. A couple of people stared at us, and I could see Lloyd Simms hovering around out by the front desk. I wondered how long it would be before I'd stop being the center of attention every time I went someplace in the village.

Over coffee, I repeated everything that had happened Sunday afternoon. Harry checked what I said with notes he'd taken; then he shook his head and closed the notebook.

"Didn't really expect you to remember anything else," he said, "but we had to make sure. Truth is, Verne, we're up against it on this thing. Damnedest case I ever saw."

"Guess that means you haven't found out anything positive."

"Not much. If we could figure a motive, we might be able to get a handle on it from that. But we just can't find one."

I decided to give voice to one of my own theories. "What about robbery, Harry?" I asked. "Seems I heard Vauclain was carrying a lot of cash with him and throwing it around pretty freely."

"We thought of that first thing," he said. "No good, though. His wallet was on the body, and there was three hundred dollars in it and a couple of blank checks."

I frowned down at my coffee. "I don't like to say this, but you don't suppose it could be one of these thrill killings we're always reading about?"

"Man, I hope not. That's the worst kind of homicide there is."

We were silent for a minute or so. Then I said, "You find anything at all on the island? Any clues?"

He hesitated. "Well," he said finally, "I probably shouldn't discuss it—but then, you're not the sort to break a confidence. We did find one thing near the body. Might not mean anything, but it's not the kind of item you'd expect to come across out there."

"What is it?"

"A cake of white beeswax," he said.

"Beeswax?"

"Right. Small cake of it. Suggest anything to you?"

"No," I said. "No, nothing."

"Not to us either. Aside from that, we haven't got a thing. Like I said, we're up against it. Unless we get a break in the next couple of days, I'm afraid the whole business will end up in the unsolved file—that's unofficial, now."

"Sure," I said.

Harry finished his coffee. "I'd better get moving," he said. "Thanks for your time, Verne."

I nodded, and he stood up and walked out across the dining room. As soon as he was gone, Lloyd came over and wanted to know what we'd been talking about. But I'd begun to feel oddly nervous all of a sudden, and there was something tickling at the edge of my mind. I cut him off short, saying, "Let me be, will you, Lloyd? Just let me be for a minute."

When he drifted off, looking hurt, I sat there and rotated my cup on the table. Beeswax, I thought. I'd told Harry that it didn't suggest anything to me, and yet it did, vaguely. Beeswax. White beeswax . . .

It came to me then—and along with it a couple of other things, little things, like missing figures in an arithmetic problem. I went cold all over, as if somebody had opened a window and let the wind inside the room. I told myself I was wrong, that it couldn't be. But I wasn't wrong. It made me sick inside, but I wasn't wrong.

I knew who had murdered Roger Vauclain.

When I came into the house I saw him sitting out on the sun deck, just sitting there motionless with his hands flat on his knees, staring out to sea. Or out to where Smuggler's Island sat shining hard and ugly in the glare of the dying sun.

I didn't go out there right away. First I went into the other rooms to see if anybody else was home, but nobody was. Then, when I couldn't put it off any longer, I got myself ready to face it and walked onto the deck.

He glanced at me as I leaned back against the railing. I hadn't seen much of him since finding the body, or paid much attention to him when I had; but now I saw that his eyes looked different. They didn't blink. They looked at me, they looked past me, but they didn't blink.

"Why'd you do it, Pa?" I said. "Why'd you kill Vauclain?"

I don't know what I expected his reaction to be. But there wasn't any reaction. He wasn't startled, he wasn't frightened, he wasn't anything. He just looked away from me again and sat there like a man who has expected to hear the words for a long time.

I kept waiting for him to say something, to move, to blink his eyes. For one full minute and half of another, he did nothing. Then he sighed, soft and tired, and he said, "I knew somebody'd find out this time." His voice was steady, calm. "I'm sorry it had to be you, Verne."

"So am I."

"How'd you know?"

"You left a cake of white beeswax out there," I said. "Fell out of your pocket when you pulled the gun, I guess. You're just the only person around here who'd be likely to have white beeswax in his pocket, Pa, because you're the only person who hand-carves his own meerschaum pipes. Took me a time to remember that you use wax like that to seal the bowls and give them a luster finish."

He didn't say anything.

"Couple of other things, too," I said. "You in bed yesterday when Jennie and I got home. It was a clear day, no early fog, nothing to aggravate your lumbago. Unless you'd been out someplace where you weren't protected from the wind—someplace like in a boat on open water. Then there was Davey's Sportliner starting right up for me. Almost never does that on cool days unless it's been run recently, and the only person besides Davey and me who has a key is you."

He nodded. "It's usually the little things," he said. "I always figured it'd be some little thing that'd finally do it."

"Pa," I said, "why'd you kill him?"

"He had to go and buy the island. Then he had to decide to build a house on it. I couldn't let him do that. I went out there to talk to him, try to get him to change his mind. Took my revolver along, but only just in case; wasn't intending to use it. Only he wouldn't listen to me. Called me an old fool and worse, and then he give me a shove. He was dead before I knew it, seems like."

"What'd him building a house have to do with you?"

"He'd have brought men and equipment out there, wouldn't he? They'd have dug up everything, wouldn't they? They'd have sure dug up the Revenue man."

I thought he was rambling. "Pa . . . "

"You got a right to know about that, too," he said. He blinked then, four times fast. "In 1929 a fella named Frank Eberle and me went to work for the bootleggers. Hauling whisky. We'd go out maybe once a month in Frank's boat, me acting as shotgun, and we'd bring in a load of shine—mostly to Shelter Cove, but sometimes we'd be told to drop it off on Smuggler's for a day or two. It was easy money, and your ma and me needed it, what with you happening along, and what the hell, Frank always said, we were only helping to give the people what they wanted.

"But then one night in 1932 it all went bust. We brought a shipment to the island and just after we started unloading it this man run out of the trees waving a gun and yelling that we were under arrest. A Revenue agent, been lying up there in ambush. Lying alone because he didn't figure to have much trouble, I reckon—and I found out later the government people had bigger fish to fry up to Shelter Cove that night.

"Soon as the agent showed himself, Frank panicked and started to run. Agent put a shot over his head, and before I could think on it, I cut loose with the rifle I always carried. I killed him, Verne, I shot that man dead."

He paused, his face twisting with memory. I wanted to say something—but what was there to say?

Pa said, "Frank and me buried him on the island, under a couple of rocks on the center flat. Then we got out of there. I quit the bootleggers right away, but Frank, he kept on with it and got himself killed in a big shootout up by Eureka just before Repeal. I knew they were going to get me too someday. Only time kept passing and somehow it never happened, and I almost had myself believing it never would. Then this Vauclain came along. You see now why I couldn't let him build his house?"

"Pa," I said thickly, "it's been forty-five years since all that happened. All anybody'd have dug up was bones. Maybe there's something there to identify the Revenue agent, but there couldn't be anything that'd point to you."

"Yes, there could," he said. "Just like there was something this time—the beeswax and all. There'd have been something, all right, and they'd have come for me."

He stopped talking then, abruptly, like a machine that had been turned off, and swiveled his head away and just sat staring again.

There in the sun, I still felt cold. He believed what he'd just said; he honestly believed it.

I knew now why he'd been so dour and moody for most of my life, why he almost never smiled, why he'd never let me get close to him. And I knew something else, too: I wasn't going to tell the sheriff any of this. He was my father and he was seventy-two years old; and I'd see to it that he didn't hurt anybody else. But the main reason was, if I let it happen that they really did come for him he wouldn't last a month. In an awful kind of way the only thing that'd been holding him together all these years was his certainty they *would* come someday.

Besides, it didn't matter anyway. He hadn't actually gotten away with anything. He hadn't committed one unpunished murder, or now two unpunished murders, because there is no such thing. There's just no such thing as the perfect crime.

I walked over and took the chair beside him, and together we sat quiet and looked out at Smuggler's Island. Only I didn't see it very well because my eyes were full of tears.

# Monkey King

## by James Holding

I've always loved jade. Green jade refreshes me like the cool crisp taste of mint in my mouth. Pink jade reminds me of sunset cloud that's been carved from the sky with a soft knife. And white jade makes delicious icicles of pleasure parade down my back like tiger tracks in snow.

Indeed, I'm hardly normal when it comes to jade; unfortunately, I've never had the means to indulge my feeling for it. If I'd been a millionaire, I'd have assembled a private collection. If I'd had an adequate education, I might have become an expert on the subject, serving on the staff of a distinguished museum. But as it is, forced since childhood to scratch desperately for a living, I'm a thief.

Not a common thief, however; I specialize in jade. And by "jade" I mean not only jadeite, nephrite and chlormelanite, the true jade minerals, but all their beautiful blood brothers, too, from saussearite to quartz.

That's what I was doing in Bangkok.

Bangkok is the home of the Green Monkey, an image of Hanuman, the ancient monkey king, lovingly carved five hundred years ago from a single block of flawless green Chanthaburi jasper. The head is thirty-five centimeters tall, the body gowned in rich vestments, seated on a golden pyramid-shaped throne twelve feet high, and proudly displayed in an exquisite temple-museum building of its own, just off the Royal Plaza. It's one of the loveliest jades in Asia.

I intended to steal it.

The round the world cruise ship, on which I'd been a minimum rate passenger since San Francisco, anchored at dawn off the mouth of the Chao Phraya River in the Gulf of Siam. A huge flat-bottom barge met it there to carry three hundred of us, American tourists all, across the sand bar blocking the river's mouth and upstream to Bangkok for two days of sightseeing, then back downstream to our cruise ship again the next evening.

Incredibly, there was no customs inspection for two-day cruise touring of our kind, either coming or going from Bangkok. That's why I chose to enter the city, and leave it, as such a tourist. For the excursion, I carried with me from the ship only my large holdall camera bag, toothbrush and razor, and my umbrella.

Arriving in Bangkok, I left my fellow tourists to their own devices and took a taxi to the Ratanokosin Hotel where I registered. It's only two blocks from the Royal Plaza and the Abode of the Green Monkey. When the boy showed me to my room, I took off my jacket and tie, switched on the air conditioner to full, and ordered a gin sling sent up.

Sipping it in a positive glow of anticipation and pleasure, I went over my plans once more, carefully and professionally. They were simple in the extreme. I'd reconnoitered the job several months before, you understand. I knew what I was up against. No one would question my camera case, I was sure. In a city whose temples, canals and towers are so infinitely photogenic, photographers are as common as cockroaches in China. And certainly no one would suspect my umbrella, a common sight on the streets of Bangkok at the beginning of the rainy season.

This was Saturday afternoon. My real work didn't start until Sunday, since the Abode of the Green Monkey is open to the public only on Sundays.

On Sunday, I arose late to a muggy, overcast day threatening rain. I felt fresh, confident, and strong. After a hearty breakfast at my hotel, I listened contentedly for an hour or so to the Sunday concert of music played on the *ranad ek,* or bamboo xylophone, by three Thais in the hotel lobby. Then I went to my room, secured my camera bag and umbrella, and checking the time carefully, set off for the Abode of the Green Monkey.

Under the wide overhang of its gracefully curved roof, the Abode's double doors are high and broad, beautifully inlaid with mother-of-pearl. They are guarded by an imposing pair of glazed tile demons, one on either side, and more effectively, perhaps, by half a dozen slightly-built Thai guards with ingratiating ways and fineboned faces, who patrol the platform outside while the Abode is open to the public.

The sweet tinkling notes of temple bells filled Bangkok's air, but I had ears and eyes for nothing save my immediate goal. And there it was. Dimly through the open doors I could see the Monkey King squatting crosslegged, wrinkled and benign atop his gold throne.

Scores of Bangkok residents and foreign tourists were streaming in and out of the great doors, even though it was now only five minutes until noon, when the Abode of the Green Monkey would be closed for the siesta hours. Casually I joined a spate of ingoing tourists, my camera draped around my neck in approved shutterbug style, my camera case hanging by its stout strap over my shoulder, my furled umbrella in my right hand. Soon I formed a part of a knot of sightseers who stood at the foot of the pyramidal throne and gazed upward, enthralled at the simian jade features of the Green Mountain which sat serenely above our heads on the pyramid's truncated top.

Unnoticed, I edged out of the cluster and around to the side of the throne, where I began to examine with spurious interest one of the lifesize golden statues that flank it. Shielded by this statue, I unslung my camera case and put it down as though to rest a moment. When no one was looking, I shoved the case out of sight with my foot under the trailing skirt of gold brocade that hangs down to the floor on all sides of the throne to mask the lower beams of its inner framework. It was the place I had selected, after much observation on my previous visit.

Nobody took any notice of me. I wandered farther toward the rear of the throne, glancing at my watch. A moment later I heard the voices of the guards outside the doors calling out that it was closing time; the tourists and sightseers rapidly began to depart. When I felt safe from observation, one minute before the noon closing hour by my watch, I lay down on the floor behind the throne, lifting its brocade skirt, and rolled under the platform with my umbrella, all in one smooth uninterrupted flow of silent motion. I dropped the brocade skirt back in place, and grinned with delight.

I was completely concealed. Seconds later, two guards made a circuit of the Abode's interior to check that all visitors had left before they locked the massive doors. I could hear their heels clicking on the floor. And although their inspection of the premises was superficial at best, I was glad I was well hidden. If I could get past this tense moment without discovery, if the guards who saw me come in had not remarked my absence in the flow of departing visitors, I was home free. The guards were changed for the afternoon shift, I knew. There would be new men outside when I left with the Green Monkey.

With my ear to the marble floor, I heard the jarring thuds that told me the massive doors had been swung shut. Darkness and silence descended on me as the dim lights were switched off from outside.

I waited several minutes. Then I rolled out from under the throne, groped in the blackness until I located my camera case, and drew it forth. From it, I took a flashlight which I lit and set upon the floor to work by. I unscrewed the cap from the end of my umbrella's fat, straight, outsized handle, and shook out of it a heavy cylinder of short, hollow, paper-thin steel tubes, nested one inside the other for storage, but capable of being screwed together like the sections of a fishing rod to form a light, strong ladder. I was proud of that ladder when it stood assembled less than fifteen minutes later. I'd designed it myself, and the oversized umbrella shaft and handle, too.

I was prouder still of the next object I lifted from my camera holdall bag. It was the heart and soul of my plan for stealing the Green Monkey.

Have you ever been in a glass factory? And seen the solid, rough-hewn chunks of broken green glass called "cullet" that they take out of the bed of a glass furnace when they shut the furnace down to reline it with new fire brick? Maybe you haven't. But what I took from my case in the Abode of the Green Monkey that day was just such a chunk of cullet, roughly pyramidal in shape, and like no other chunk of cullet in one respect: its upper section had been crudely carved and ground into a recognizable monkey's head.

It was, indeed, my first attempt at sculpture and not too badly done, I told myself. I had stolen the chunk of cullet from the waste pile of a California factory; I had lovingly worked on it in my cabin for five long weeks of cruising, chipping, carving, rubbing it with fine sand to kill the gleam of glass.

I set it gently on the floor. I leaned on the ladder against the high throne of the Monkey King and flashlight in hand, climbed carefully upward. When I was high enough to reach the image, I took the flashlight between my teeth and used both hands to lift the Green Monkey from his pedestal. Then I carried him, still wearing his rich vestments, down the ladder to the floor, rung by precarious rung. There, I stripped his raiment from him, a royal headdress and a jewel-studded, stolelike cloak that entirely covered his body. I placed the headdress on my glass monkey's head, the concealing cloak around the shapeless torso of my chunk of cullet.

Examining the result in my flashlight's beam, I smiled to myself, not unsatisfied. Swathed as it was in cloak and headdress, the cullet looked enough like the Green Monkey to be his cousin, certainly enough to escape detection almost indefinitely in the anemic light of the Abode, perched so high above its viewers' heads.

Now I mounted my ladder once again and placed the glass statue

on the Green Monkey's throne. I dismantled and restowed the ladder
in my umbrella shaft. Then and only then, I turned the flashlight
on the genuine jade image, now resting naked on the floor.

I caught my breath at its beauty. I devoured it with my eyes. I
stroked it with tender fingertips. I rubbed my cheek against it. I did
a slow blind dance with it in my arms, fondling it. The Green Monkey
was mine.

At last, regretfully, I slid him out of sight into my camera bag
where the chunk of cullet had nested until now. I zipped the case
closed, then sat down to wait behind the throne in the darkness
until the Abode of the Green Monkey should reopen for the afternoon.

I had much to think about. The time passed quickly. About ten
minutes before the Abode reopened, a drumming, rushing sound
began on the roof above me, and I correctly deduced it had begun
to rain outside. Soon the lights inside my sanctum flashed on and
the doors were thrown wide to the afternoon visitors.

Despite the rain, they arrived and entered in impressive numbers,
quieting the only small worry I had—that if the shrine were sparsely
patronized, I might have trouble departing it inconspicuously. I
drifted aimlessly from the back of the throne, and managed to melt
unnoticed into a group of tourists. I accompanied them when they
left, secretly smiling to hear them enthuse over the piece of broken
glass they thought was the Green Monkey.

Outside the doors under the roof's overhang, I saw it was raining
very hard. All the better, I thought with delight. I raised my umbrella, like most of my companion tourists, and prepared to step out
into the rain, the jade image of Hanuman, the Monkey King, safe
in my camera bag, which was now all but concealed from view by
my opened umbrella.

The Thai museum guards, clad in oilskin rain gear, still patrolled
before the entrance doors, keeping a sharp eye on the crowd. They
were different men from the morning's guard. I was safe.

During the brief moment I paused under the Abode's eaves, while
I was opening my umbrella and savoring my triumph, I found time
to pity those guards. They saw the statue of the Green Monkey every
Sunday of their lives, true. But had they ever seen the Green Monkey
unclothed, as I had, the glory of the jade unhidden? Had they ever
felt the cool, faintly oily tenderness of the stone? Had they ever seen
the unbelievable beauty of a flashlight's beam shining through the
green translucence of the loveliest carved wonder in Asia? No. Poor

bodyguards to the Monkey King, they were bodyguards only, and nothing more.

At the moment, the eyes of one of them scanned me, poised to step out into the rain, and the weird conviction swept through me that he was reading my thoughts across twenty feet of space.

For he frowned suddenly, and began to walk toward me, his intent gaze never leaving me for an instant. At the same time, he made a sign to two other guards nearby who immediately began to converge upon me. Within the space of a single breath, all three stood confronting me, looking ridiculously petite in their little oilskins but somehow threatening, too, with the rain dripping from their hats, noses, and chins.

"*Kho apia*," said the first one, politely. Then he switched to English. "Pardon, sir. Will you come with us, please?"

I gaped at him, utterly confounded. "Why?"

"Cannot talk in rain," he said. "Kindly accompany us in car, yes?" He was very apologetic, but also very stern, very sincere.

"Accompany you? In a car? Are you crazy?" I bleated. A spasm of genuine alarm squeezed my heart. I peered at him under the rim of my umbrella.

The other two guards stepped close and placed delicate hands gently on each of my arms. "Come," said my thought-reader, and led the way toward the car park beside the street.

My heart dropped into my shoes. As I followed between my captors, the camera bag over my shoulder suddenly seemed intolerably heavy, as though the Monkey King weighed a million pounds.

They took me to police headquarters, where a doll-like magistrate listened to a rapid flood of Thai from my guards, punctuated with thumb-jerking in my direction. Then, at a crisp command from the magistrate, I was relieved of my passport, camera case, and umbrella. They found the Monkey King within seconds.

I was locked into a cell, still dazed and uncomprehending. I had been promptly arrested after a single casual glance from the guard. Why? Everything had gone so smoothly, so swimmingly. Nothing, I told myself stubbornly, *nothing* could possibly have given me away, so it must have been thought-reading or some other occult art that had brought the gendarmes down on me. Orientals sometimes possess strange mental powers, they say.

Through the bars of my cell door, I said to the English-speaking guard who was locking me in, "Tell me, please, how did you know

I had stolen the Monkey King?" I had been caught with the goods—there was no use pretending innocence.

He looked at me, smiling. "You inside Abode of Hanuman alone during siesta," he lisped. "This very suspicious, no?"

"Very suspicious, yes. But how did you *know* I'd been inside during siesta, just by looking at me?"

He shrugged daintily. "Rain," he said.

"Rain? What's that got to do with it?"

"Rain begin before opening of Abode for afternoon, yes?"

I nodded.

"That explain mystery, sir," he said. "Very sorry." He went away.

Belatedly, then, the light dawned on me.

My umbrella had been *dry* when I raised it to leave the Abode of the Monkey King.

# Nice Work If You Can Get It

## by Donald Honig

The threat of competition, an ugly noise that generally starts when your back is turned, can waken a man's pride and arouse his self-respect until it glitters like the eye of a tiger. Competition is a disease that sooner or later infects every trade and profession and makes it take a long step forward. Still, it remains the obligation of every honorable man to oppose it with all his skills.

As a matter of record, me and my associates, Jack and Buck, have long been the leading exponents of the delicate art of scoop-'em-up, which is the art of abduction fined down to a science whereby not a footprint, fingerprint, howl, yelp, or regret is left behind. Perfection is the only formula for success in this tricky profession. Tyros have long studied our techniques and have tried, with no luck, to emulate them.

So I was quite surprised to hear one day that another organization had scraped up the men, the courage, and the resources to go into competition with us. I met the captain of the crew one afternoon while paying my semi-annual visit to my aged father (a retired second story man who had developed vertigo) at the Home for Retired Vikings, which is a fine old institution maintained by the trade, catering to sore-footed footpads, conscience-stricken swindlers, abstemious rum runners, arthritic forgers, and cattle thieves turned vegetarian.

On the way back to the bus I chanced to run into Barney Blue, an old friend from bars both legal and alcoholic. Barney had been visiting his father, an old safecracker who had been forced into premature retirement after developing an unaccountable fear of the dark.

"Bush," said Barney to me as we headed for the bus, "I have long admired your organization. You and your boys have stood pre-eminent and par-excellent in the field for years. Your capers have captured the hearts of bold men everywhere and become veritable textbooks on the art. I know all this because I've been studying them for years. Now, having learned the craft from the master, I've or-

303

ganized a little group of my own and we're going into competition with you."

"We're a nation of free enterprise, Barney," I said. "There's nothing wrong with you going into business for yourself, but I ought to warn you that you'll be doing yourself a severe disservice by announcing yourself as a competitor. You're encroaching on very, very private ground. Why try and buck perfection? Why don't you take your boys and go into something that calls for initiative, like holding up stagecoaches or selling protection to the vendors on the Oregon Trail?"

He laughed; but it was a terse sound.

"Don't like the idea of somebody coming into your pasture, eh, Bush?" he said. "Well, maybe the profession can stand a little more dash and daring. The talk is that you and your boys have become a bit smug and conservative lately. The grapes are withering on your vine, old boy," he said.

Well, I laughed him off gently. But when I returned home I found myself brooding a bit. Perhaps it *was* true that we had been doing some laurel-resting of late. I felt that we were on top and could afford to coast. But now this threat of competition cast a new light on everything. It was just possible that Barney Blue and his boys could score some tremendous coup and put us in the background. I decided there was but one thing to do: give my career a fresh crown. So I gathered together the boys and let them know.

"In order to repel this dreary threat," I said to Buck and Jack, "we have to perform a job which for skill and audacity, will belittle anything that Barney Blue and his boys can conceive, as well as make all our previous efforts look like blueprints. We have to swing a job that will gladden every heart in the Home for Retired Vikings, give inspiration to novices and hope to failures, as well as teach an enduring lesson to Barney Blue and his boys." And I meant *enduring*.

"It sounds big," said Jack.

"It will have to be big," I said. "It can be nothing less than the greatest scoop job in history. I want a job of such magnitude that it will bathe our competitors in shame, of such brilliance that historians the world over will skip a hundred pages in their manuscripts and begin recording us in the next century."

Jack beamed happily; the boys had an ardent and spirited attitude in these matters. Big Buck remained sullen, but I could tell that even he was inspired.

"Who do you have in mind as a subject, Bush?" Jack asked.

"See if you can guess: who is the richest man in the world?"

"Not him," said Jack, shocked.

"Yes, him," I said.

"But it's practically impossible to get near him," Jack said. "He's only too well aware of people like us. His car is a tank and his bodyguards are Neanderthals."

"Those are his achievements," I said. "He also has his weak points. He's impressed and disarmed by millionaires and other dubious celebrities."

"Who are we talking about?" Buck asked, making a rare utterance. He was strictly brawn.

"J. J. Griggen, the bilious billionaire," I said.

"The oil man," Jack said.

"Yes," I said, "oil. Whenever any thing in the world stops, stalls, or squeaks, it's another windfall for J. J. Griggen."

"He sounds likely," Buck said.

"We can ask five million for him," I said. "And get it. We'd be depriving him of a week's salary, but what of it. He'll buy up a few congressmen, have them put through a ransom-is-deductible law, and then forget about the whole thing."

"But how do you make the scoop?" Jack asked.

"I've got that worked out," I said. "Barney Blue's audacious intrusion upon our personal domain has inspired me to conceive the noblest attempt of our career. J. J. Griggen is going to attend a Charity Ball for Overprivileged Children two weeks from tonight. The ball is being held in order to raise funds to build mosaic handball courts for these kids in their Adirondack summer retreats. And the enchanting thing is it's going to be a masquerade ball. It was in the papers today. Boys," I said, "pick out your costumes, unbutton your alter egos, and let your hearts sing out—for we're going to a ball!"

From Handy Harry, the corner forger, we obtained our invitations to the ball. It was being primed as the social event of the season, and little did the primers know how eventful it was going to be. The affair was going to be held at one of those commodious Long Island mansions where they play polo in the living room on rainy days. We drove out there several times to inspect the premises, then back to the city to formulate the plan, which, as it took shape, was by turn feasible, infallible, ingenious, and diabolical.

I chose the costumes for my entourage. Buck was going to go as a caveman, *Homo extinctus,* with loincloth, club, and scowl. Jack was going to be Lord Byron, with frills and ruffles and pithy couplets. I was going to be Millard Fillmore, dignified and undistinguished. And with us we were bringing an added, unannounced guest who was going to play an important role later in the evening.

We arrived at the ball at about nine thirty. The place was ablaze with lights and jewels. They were all there, dukes and duchesses and princes and princesses from places that are remembered today only by stamp collectors and retired map-makers; and all the playboys and tycoons and titans, and the men who live in Wall Street's shadow and the women who shadow Wall Street's men. All of them in costume. The grand ballroom was a whirl of bizarre celebrities. I shook hands with Oliver Cromwell, Talleyrand, William McKinley (there were three of them), Julius Caesar, Beau Brummel, Marie Antoinette, Madame Du Barry and dozens of others.

After an hour or so of calculated mingling, I finally caught sight of J. J. Griggen. Humble man that he was, he had come as Moses; not Michelangelo's Moses, but Griggen's Moses, short and paunchy and ferret-eyed. He might have been the real article, the way everyone stepped aside for him and stared after him.

I jostled him at the punch table.

"Excuse me, Moses," I said, and he laughed. He liked that.

"So you recognized me, eh?" he said.

"It was easy."

"And who might you be?" he asked.

"President Millard Fillmore," I said.

"President of what? G.M.?"

"U.S."

"Ah, Steel!" he said and graciously patted me on the back. "Always a pleasure, always a pleasure. Are you really in steel, sir?"

"In a way, if you want to say it's a play on words."

We talked, and while I beguiled the old boy with anecdotes, I was maneuvering him out onto a balcony. Outside, on the balcony, out of sight, we met a caveman. With a club.

"Ah," said Griggen with a laugh, "a representative of Organized Labor!" He offered to shake hands. But this caveman was not one for social niceties. One tap with the club and J. J. Griggen was stretched out on the balcony.

Then we went to work. Buck retrieved the parcel we had cached there, containing the unannounced guest—a bearskin which we had bought from a store that sells bearskins and halberds and morions and shrunken heads and Minié balls from the Gettysburg battlefield.

While I propped up old J. J., Buck fitted him into the bearskin and zipped him up. Then Buck hefted the bear into his arms and I led them back into the ballroom.

"Thomas Jefferson," I announced to all the smiling, costumed guests, "leading behind me the symbolic brawn and brute strength of America." Several men, Lewis and Clark particularly, cheered, while a woman said how cunning it was.

I led the symbols out the front door and down the path to the parking lot. There I found Lord Byron at the wheel of our car, the motor running, the back door open. Buck dropped the bear onto the back seat and got in beside it. Then we took off down the driveway and through the gate where the special police in charge there for the evening saluted us nicely; after all, it wasn't every night they saw Millard Fillmore, Lord Byron, a caveman and the world's richest bear.

We sped along the dark, woodsy Long Island lanes, towards the little cabin I had prepared, up a dirt road, perfectly secluded. While it wasn't one of the great mansions that Griggen was accustomed to, he was going to have to call it home for the next few days.

By the time we pulled up to the place in dark, warm, crickety night, Griggen was beginning to stir. I don't suppose he had any idea what he was wearing (I think there is hardly a man anywhere who can conceive of himself waking up in a bearskin), but he began to yell for us to get the horrid thing off of him, and in a voice that bespoke authority, hurrying subordinates, scurrying waiters, scuttling doormen, and gushing oil wells. But we were having none of his impertinence. Buck—Buck, who was rich only in brawn and friends—Buck told him to shut up. Griggen almost gagged on that.

We led him into the cabin and then removed the bearskin. Griggen looked with amazement at the thing, then peered at us in our costumes, and I guess the knock on the head made him lose his bearings for a moment, as he said:

"What have I fallen into—a time machine or a lunatic asylum?"

"Neither, Mr. Griggen," I said. "We're all fugitives from the charity ball and you're our guest. In the spirit of the evening I might say that we're masquerading as your abductors and you as our victim, but don't believe it—the ball is over and this is the real thing."

"This is an outrage!" he howled.

"Agreed," I said. "But we haven't brought you here because we needed a fourth for bridge. I warn you, we're desperate men who will stop at nothing to achieve our aims. So please sit down and make yourself comfortable. This whole outrageous business won't take more than a day or two, depending upon what cooperation we receive from you."

"Cooperation? What are you talking about?" he demanded, cutting quite an indignant figure in his toga.

"We're going to trade you for five million dollars, and at the same time make you famous not only in the world of high finance and low dealings, but in the history books, too. You are now a key figure in the greatest scoop-up caper of all time. Welcome to the history books, Mr. Griggen. You've risen this evening from the footnotes to a chapter-heading." He was perversely unimpressed, however.

"You'll never get away with this, Mr. . . . Mr. . . . ."

"Fillmore."

"Damn you, Fillmore. You can't do this to me. It's an outrage, and besides, I can't stand notoriety."

"It's already half done, Mr. Griggen. Now, we've got beer and baloney in the icebox. Not very substantial, but homey. Won't you join us?"

Later we changed clothes, and Moses, Byron, Fillmore, and the nameless caveman vanished. As befitted a man of his economic stature, Griggen proved quite a nuisance. He was forever demanding a battery of telephones with which to call his lawyers. Only when we threatened to put him back into the bearskin and train him to ride a bicycle did he finally desist and go to sleep. Buck sat watch over him while Jack and I sat in the kitchen and drank beer and congratulated ourselves.

"Let Blue and his boys top this one," I said with pardonable pride. "Once they hear about it, they'll pull in their nets and close shop and leave the field to the professionals."

"I have to hand it to you, Bush," said Jack. "You've got genius. But do you really think we'll get five million for him?"

"No question about it," I said. "Now you could never get five million for the king of England or for a billionaire's grandson; but for somebody like J. J. Griggen, yes, absolutely—because he's still capable of making that a hundred times over; that's why whoever we contact will be only too eager to dish it out and get him back. Griggen can go right back to his desk, roll up his sleeves, and start making money again. Get it?"

"What a theory," Jack said admiringly. "Pure genius." It was a conservative estimate at best, but I blushed nevertheless.

The next morning we jostled Griggen out of bed, treated him to a free breakfast, and then got down to brass facts, as my old grandpa used to say.

"Whom do we contact for the payment?" I asked.

"I'm not saying a word," Griggen said.

"Mr. Griggen," I said, giving him my darkest and deadliest look, "we have in the basement of this cabin a medieval torture chamber, replete with racks, whips, vises, and long playing records of television commercials. If you don't prove to be an amenable client, you'll find yourself subjected to the more barbaric side of human nature. Now—answer the question."

He sighed. He was beaten and, shrewd businessman that he was, saw it. But he made the best of it.

"You contact my wife, Mrs. Hildegarde Griggen." He gave us the number. "She's the only one who can do anything. She has the key to my vault."

"Is she an hysterical woman?"

"Cold as ice."

"She'll follow my instructions?"

"If she knows my welfare depends on it, certainly."

"Excellent."

That afternoon I drove into town and stepped into a phone booth, about to make a thin dime turn into five million dollars. I dialed the number J. J. had given me, and waited. The phone rang and rang, and rang and rang. After five minutes I decided there wasn't going to be an answer. I returned to the cabin.

"What did you give me here, boy," I asked Griggen. "Custer's number on the Little Big Horn?"

"What do you mean?" he asked. "That's Mrs. Griggen's private phone."

"It's so private that nobody answered."

"That's not so odd. Mrs. Griggen is very active."

"Won't she be sort of alarmed at your being missing?"

"Not yet she won't. I often spend the night away from home. My interests are far-flung, Mr. Fillmore; they demand constant attention, day and night; as you'll soon learn."

I tried again, later that afternoon, then that evening again. No answer. I was beginning to get nervous about things. A man like J. J. Griggen does not remain missing for long without about a thousand people starting to miss him. Once somebody caught wise to what was going on, there would be enough heat put on to fry every egg in New Jersey.

"Didn't your wife accompany you to the ball?" I asked this creature of opulence.

"No," said Griggen. "She doesn't like those things. I wish you would get hold of her and consummate this deal. I'm getting damned sick of this place."

That night passed and then it was morning again.

"This has to be it," I said to Jack. "We either contact the old lady today or we have to let him go. By tonight he'll be so thoroughly missed that I wouldn't be surprised if both Wall Street and the Wall of China collapsed. We'll have the army, navy, Marines, Air Force, Coast Guard, and a reactivated CCC looking for us."

So I drove back to town, thinking again about the thin dime that stood between me and five million dollars. I would tell Mrs. Griggen not to be panicky, not to tell a soul, merely to go into the vault with a shovel and a barrel and she could have her husband back.

But I didn't tell her anything. Because she wasn't there. All I got for my dime was a soft, constant ringing of a telephone. Then I had to hang up and go back to the cabin.

"Mr. Griggen," I said to him, "you're a free man. Go back to your oil wells."

"Are you getting the five million?" he asked with a certain fascinated interest.

"Go home, Mr. Griggen," I said. I couldn't wait to get him out of my sight. It hurt me to look at him.

We watched him walk through the door, down the path, and out into the road.

"There goes five million dollars, tax-free," I said to my tragic-faced associates. "Lost for want of a woman's voice. All she had to do was come home from the beauty parlor or the tea at Mrs. Vanderfeller's or wherever she was, and say hello into the phone, and we had five million."

"This will become a day of mourning for me," said Jack.

Buck grunted.

Being an odd fellow, not wanting notoriety, J. J. Griggen said nothing to the police of what had happened. And I, of course, was not about to go mentioning it to people. For one thing, I didn't want our abysmal competitors, the Barney Blue boys, to hear about how I had to let five million dollars pass through the door. It would have cast a tarnish on my reputation that not even the latest detergent could have gotten out.

As it was, I ran across Barney Blue some weeks later at a downtown tavern where gentlemen of a certain stripe generally converged.

"How is my competitor?" I asked him.

Instead of the bright smile and flippant remark, all I got from him was a glum look.

"We're out of it, Bush," he said. "The field is all yours again. And believe me, after getting my feet wet in the profession and seeing what a complicated business it is, you have all my esteem and admiration."

"Well, thank you, Barney, thank you very much. You're giving up?"

"We tried something big, but it didn't work out. I guess we just didn't have your know-how. Do you know who we scooped up, Bush?"

"Tell me."

"The wife of the richest man in the world—Mrs. J. J. Griggen. It worked out perfect, except we couldn't get the old man on the phone to hold him up."

"This was about three weeks ago?" I asked, trying to maintain my composure as the blood left my body.

"Exactly. How did you know?"

"There are no secrets in this business, Barney. None at all," I said. And for the first time I could see myself sitting on a rocking chair on the porch of the Home for Retired Vikings, discussing burglar alarms, alert policemen, eyewitnesses, and all the other pitfalls of the profession.

# The Weapon

## by John Lutz

"**Y**ou came here to do *what?*"

"Blackmail you," the little man said calmly. He sat on the edge of the sofa, in a comfortable but prim position. Dan Ogdon had been behind the house sifting leaves from the swimming pool when the little man had let himself in through the gate. Ogdon had assumed at once that he was the mutual fund salesman who was due to call, though he didn't look like a mutual fund salesman, with his rather correct air and his contrasting polka dot bow tie.

"Blackmail?" Ogdon blinked his eyes, trying to think of some mistake he'd made in the past that wasn't common knowledge. "I don't get it," he said at last.

"Of course not." The little man smiled above the bow tie. "I get it—ten thousand dollars in cash."

"This is some kind of sales gimmick," Ogdon said. "I have nothing at all to fear about my past."

"Ah," the little man said enthusiastically, "but what about your future?"

"You're an insurance salesman!" Ogdon said triumphantly.

His visitor seemed amused. "In a manner of speaking, by golly, I am!"

"What kind of insurance?" Ogdon asked.

"Life," the little man answered without a moment's hesitation.

Ogdon rested his hands on his bare knees. Suddenly he felt oddly vulnerable sitting there in the cool leather easy chair in his bright Bermuda shorts. "I have more than enough insurance," he said, hoping against hope that the man would leave.

"But you don't," the man said. "I know almost everything about you, Mr. Ogdon. I've researched you very carefully indeed. You're forty years old, separated from your wife and children, and last year your income was thirty-five thousand dollars from your Ogdon Auto Agency."

"That's very thorough, Mr. . . . .?"

"Oh, I didn't give my name."

312

"Well, anyway, I'm pretty busy, so if you don't mind. . ." Ogdon stood and moved toward the front door.

"If I leave now, Mr. Ogdon, you'll be dead within a month."

Ogdon sat back down. "Just what company do you work for?"

"Self-employed."

"A self-employed insurance salesman?"

"Self-employed blackmailer."

Ogdon felt himself flush, then he sighed. "All right, Mr. Whatis-name, just what is it you want?"

"As I said, ten thousand dollars in cash."

"Now, why should I give you ten thousand dollars, I ask you?"

"Because I'll kill you if you don't."

Ogdon was stunned for a second. "But why would you want to kill me?"

"Oh, heavens, I don't *want* to kill you, but I'll have to if you don't pay me the money. It's my business, you see."

"I don't see," Ogdon said. "Why pick on me?"

"Simply because you have money, Mr. Ogdon. At frequent intervals I choose someone like yourself and charge them a nominal fee for not killing them. If you hadn't been home today, I might have gone on to an alternate client. I'm a very busy man."

"You're insane!"

"Yes, but soon I'll have enough money to be merely eccentric."

"Get out," Ogdon said, "before I call the police."

"If you did that, Mr. Ogdon, I'd simply leave, and the police, helpless at any rate, probably wouldn't believe you. Then, when the time was right, I'd kill you. Not that I hold a grudge, but I can't make any exceptions. Not only could it be bad for business, but I'm afraid I'm something of a perfectionist."

"Suppose I throw you out myself?" Ogdon asked in an angry voice.

"Why, then I'd kill you right here," the little man said quietly.

"With what?"

The little man pulled a red fountain pen from an inside pocket of his conservative, dark sport coat and smiled at Ogdon. "With my fountain pen."

"Your fountain pen!"

"Well," the little man chuckled, "not really a fountain pen." There was a sharp, low report, like a man spitting angrily, and the lamp on the table beside Ogdon shattered.

"It's a two-shot," the little man said, casually rotating the pen-gun in his hand. "Quite untraceable and reliable. They say they'll even fire under water."

Fear closed in on Ogdon. Fear and disbelief that this could actually be happening on an otherwise ordinary Saturday afternoon.

"Ten thousand is a little steep," he said in a shaking voice.

"Make it $9,999 then," the little man said amiably, "like one of your cars."

Ogdon looked at the shattered lamp and tried to control his breathing. All he wanted now was for this maniac to get out of the house. He was ready to agree to any terms. "How shall I get you the money?"

"Send it in a brown envelope to B. M. Enterprises, Post Office Box 19. Make it a week from today, if that's convenient for you."

"That will be fine," Ogdon said. He was afraid to move from his chair.

The little man stood and carefully smoothed the wrinkles from his trousers. "Of course," he said, "you're thinking that you can inform the police of all this after I leave and they can arrest me when I attempt to pick up the money at the post office." He smiled cockily. "Let me tell you that you'll have a very weak case. The only fact will be that you mailed me some money—no real evidence of blackmail. You won't be able to prove my visit here." He buttoned the second button of his sport coat. "Then, after things die down, I'll kill you anyway."

"I see," Ogdon said softly, and he did see.

The little man walked to the front door and slipped his fountain pen back into his pocket. He glanced around briefly before leaving. "Nice place you've got here." Then he was gone.

Ogdon sat in a state of shock. Had the weird visit really taken place? What should he do? What *could* he do?

The first thing he did was get up and mix himself a drink. Then he sat out on the patio to try to think things out.

He couldn't give that oddball the ten thousand dollars. Not only was it a lot of money, but what was to prevent him from being tapped for future payments? Ogdon tried to convince himself that he should simply forget about the whole thing, pass it off as just some kind of odd, crackpot occurrence, but then he remembered the casual, accurate shot and the shattered porcelain lamp.

Well, he had a week to think about it. He set his glass on the metal outdoor table and walked across the yard toward the three-car garage to lose himself in tinkering with his antique automobiles. That never failed to soothe him. . . .

Ogdon decided to call the police, and a detective sergeant came out to see him. Sergeant Mortimus was a short, stout man in his early sixties, with thick white hair, a red, bulbous nose and watery eyes.

"Ahh, my legs!" Mortimus said painfully as he sat down on the sofa. "Too many years on the beat."

The sergeant refused a beer in the line of duty and sat silently listening to Ogdon's story.

"That's unbelievable," he said when Ogdon had finished.

"I was afraid you'd say that."

"Oh, I believe it," the sergeant said. "You're lucky they sent me. I've seen many a strange thing during my time on the force, but those days are dead and gone." He shook his head sadly. "I retire in six months, Mr. Ogdon. My legs."

"That's nice," Ogdon said.

"Nice? No, I enjoy my work, Mr. Ogdon."

"Well, then *that's* nice. But what do you intend to do about this blackmail problem?"

"Do? Why, we'll pick up this character at the post office when he shows up for the money."

Ogdon sighed inwardly. "That's what he said you'd do."

"You mean that's what he was afraid we'd do. Don't you worry, Mr. Ogdon, nobody goes around extorting money from honest citizens in this city and gets by with it."

"Look what he did to my lamp," Ogdon said. "Don't take him too lightly; he's a crack shot."

"Crackshot crackpot," Sergeant Mortimus said. "They won't give him a gun at the state funnyfarm!"

"Should I mail the money like he said to?" Ogdon asked.

"We'll mark the bills and you mail them, then we'll close in on him and pick him up. Ahh!" Sergeant Mortimus stood and limped toward the door. "Don't you fret, Mr. Ogdon, he's in the web."

Saturday afternoon Ogdon was called down to the police station. Sergeant Mortimus met him there, a Lieutenant Sifford introduced himself, and they led Ogdon over to a small window set high in a heavy wooden door.

"Is this the man?" the lieutenant asked.

Ogdon peered through the pane of one-way glass into the tiny room. The little man was sitting with his legs crossed in the room's only chair, an air of complete nonchalance about him. His hand went to the base of his throat casually to straighten his polka dot bow tie as Ogdon watched.

"It's him," Ogdon said, turning away from the window.

Sergeant Mortimus beamed.

"Are you absolutely positive?" the lieutenant asked.

"Absolutely."

"We'll have to let him go."

Ogdon stood for a moment in shocked silence. "You'll *what?*"

"Have to release him," the lieutenant said. "We have no real evidence on him. All we really can prove is that you mailed him some money."

"That's because we marked the bills," Sergeant Mortimus said proudly. "I apprehended him with them myself."

Ogdon felt his blood pressure spiral upward. "But if you knew you couldn't hold him, why did you bother to arrest him?"

"Had to check your story out, Mr. Ogdon," the lieutenant said, expertly igniting a book match with one hand, to light a cigarette. "You have to admit it was pretty wild. For all we knew, you might have been some kind of dangerous nut."

"But we believe you now," the sergeant said, "even though we can't prove anything."

"He's in our files now," the lieutenant said smugly.

Ogdon was striking crimson. "But what about me?" he almost screamed in anger. "What in the hell file am I going to wind up in? He said he'd kill me!"

"He's obviously unbalanced," the lieutenant said. "Probably he didn't really mean it. I'd say it was just a scare tactic."

"I'd say it worked!" Ogdon said, "I want some protection!"

"If it will make you feel better," the lieutenant said, "we'll send a man out tomorrow."

"But what about tonight? You said you were going to release him."

The lieutenant looked thoughtful. "I'm sure Tweeker wouldn't try anything so soon, but we'll detail a patrol car to watch your home nights until our man gets there in the mornings."

"Tweeker?"

"That's his name," the lieutenant said. "Tom Tweeker."

"That his *real* name?"

The lieutenant shrugged. "He says it is."

Ogdon clenched his fists. *"Nobody* has a name like Tom Tweeker!"

"Tweeker does," the sergeant said.

The lieutenant walked to a desk and poured a cup of coffee from a battered electric percolator. "There was no identification on him; we're checking on that name."

Ogdon breathed out through his nose very loudly and turned to leave.

"Don't you fret," Sergeant Mortimus said. "There'll be a squad car at your home every night and a man to stay with you during the day."

"Thanks," Ogdon said dryly as he reached for the doorknob.

"Oh, Mr. Ogdon." The lieutenant stopped him. "The ten thousand dollars has been returned to your bank."

"Very efficient," he said over his shoulder. He was sure he heard Sergeant Mortimus say thank you.

Ogdon wasn't really surprised when he opened his door the next morning to see Sergeant Mortimus. The sergeant was in uniform, summer blue with three huge stripes on each shirtsleeve.

"I'm detailed to stay with you, Mr. Ogdon," he said as he entered.

"It figures," Ogdon said.

The sergeant walked to the most comfortable looking chair in the living room and sat down. "Ahh!" He began to massage his legs through the dark blue material of his uniform pants. "If you want to go to work or something, go ahead," he said. "Just go on about your business like I wasn't around, only I will be."

"I'm going to take a few weeks off work," Ogdon said. "My nerves are bothering me."

"Whatever you say, Mr. Ogdon." The sergeant screwed up his lips. "This isn't usually my line of work. I'm more of a leg man." He shook his head. "But my legs gave out on me."

"I know," Ogdon said. "You retire in six months."

Sergeant Mortimus gave a short laugh with his mouth closed. "Old sergeants never die, Mr. Ogdon, they're just pensioned away."

Early as it was, Ogdon felt the need for a drink.

"I guess they don't think the old sarge is good enough for the tough details any more," Sergeant Mortimus was saying sadly, "so they send me out here to protect you."

*It's hard to believe,* Ogdon thought. *It's hard to believe it's really happening.*

The telephone rang.

Both men listened as it rang three, four, five times.

"Go ahead," Sergeant Mortimus said. "Answer it."

Ogdon crossed the room, snatched the receiver from its cradle, and pressed it to his ear. "Hello?"

"Mr. Dan Ogdon?"

"Yes."

"Your blackmailer here, Mr. Ogdon. It was an unfortunate thing you did, calling the police. They kept me four hours. I told you I was a busy man."

"Should I apologize?"

"You should, but I don't expect it. You think you're quite safe, Mr. Ogdon, with your squad car and your personal guard, but you aren't safe at all. I have a weapon to use on you, a most unusual weapon."

Ogdon felt his mouth go dry, remembering the fountain pen gun. "You seem to specialize in unusual weapons."

"Only when I must, Mr. Ogdon. Well, I have to hang up now. I wouldn't want them to be able to trace this call and prove it was really me you talked to. Good morning, sir."

"Wait!"

But the receiver was appropriately dead.

"Who was it?" the sergeant asked.

"Tweeker. He says he has some unusual weapon he's going to kill me with."

"Talk," Sergeant Mortimus said, "just talk."

"What are we going to do?"

The sergeant ran a hand through his thick white hair. "Do you play gin rummy?"

Ogdon cursed and began to pace. He paced for over an hour, his mind alive with wild speculations about plastic bombs and deadly laser beams. Finally he moaned in frustration. "Yes," he said, "I play gin rummy."

The sergeant looked up from the newspaper he'd been reading. "Penny a point?"

Ogdon nodded. "In the kitchen," he said. "There's only one window in there."

Sergeant Mortimus struggled to his feet. "Ahh! That's good thinking, Mr. Ogdon. You should have been a cop."

So it went for more than a week: day after endless day of gin rummy that proved profitable only for Sergeant Mortimus. His mind was on the game completely.

When the card game became intolerable, Ogdon would go out to the garage to work on his antique cars while the sergeant sat in a redwood lounge chair and watched with interest. Occasionally, he'd make some kind of remark: "I rode in many a one of those Model

T's, but I don't remember any that shade of black. . . . My old dad used to have a Hupmobile like that, only his was in lots better shape."

Ogdon was working on the suspension of the Hupmobile now, waiting for another of Sergeant Mortimus's illuminating comments, when he heard the sergeant groan and get up off the lounge chair. Ogdon turned his head slightly and from where he lay on the dolly beneath the car, he could see the sergeant's much talked about blue-trousered legs approaching.

"Too hot out there in the sun," the sergeant said.

Ogdon pushed himself farther under the car and resumed working on a tight nut.

After a few minutes of silence Ogdon glanced toward the front of the car again and saw that the sergeant was still there. "Why don't you move the chair into the shade?" he suggested. It always annoyed him to have someone watch him while he worked.

The sergeant didn't answer, and Ogdon suddenly noticed that the heavy iron head of a long-handled sledgehammer was resting alongside one of the sergeant's highly polished black shoes. The other end of the wooden handle must be in the sergeant's hands. Only a single metal jack was holding the car above the cement garage floor, and the sledgehammer head was dangerously close to it.

"Watch out for that jack," Ogdon said, starting to push with his heels so he could roll out from beneath the car.

The low dolly stopped. There was something jammed under one of the wheels.

"This isn't my idea," the sergeant said. Ogdon saw the polished black shoes widen their stance, as if their owner was readying to strike a blow with the hammer.

Ogden was suddenly frozen with claustrophobic terror. The wheels were off the front of the car. There was nothing to keep more than a ton of metal just inches above his face from falling to meet the cement floor. "Is this some kind of a joke?" His words wavered with fear.

The sergeant's voice was sympathetic. "I don't want to do this to you, Mr. Ogdon, really I don't. But I retire in six months because of my legs, and I think I have a right to enjoy that retirement. So you have to have an accident."

"I don't understand!" Ogdon almost sobbed. "What's that got to do with it?"

"He's making me do this," the sergeant said. "Tweeker is."

Now Ogdon did understand completely. He thrashed with his heels and tried desperately to roll the dolly, but it would not move either forward or backward.

"You know I don't want to do it, Mr. Ogdon, but he'll kill me if I don't. He'll kill me."

Ogdon saw the heavy hammerhead describe its deadly arc. He tried to scream.

"It's nothing personal," the sergeant said.

Metal struck metal.

# Dead Drunk

## by Arthur Porges

It takes a lot to stump an experienced pathologist, and even more to surprise him. Nor will any findings, no matter how grotesque, shock a man familiar with every possible use and abuse of the body.

But some weeks ago I was in at the finish of a case that made me dig deeper than is necessary in most of them, and had me tangled up in my own emotions like a kitten with a ball of yarn.

It was one of Lieutenant Ader's headaches. He and I have worked together, informally, for a number of years. Although I'm not officially connected with the Norfolk City Police, Pasteur Hospital is the only one around with a full time pathologist on the staff. That's me—Dr. Joel Hoffman, middle-aged, unmarried—possibly, because of my dedication to my work. And since the nearest adequate crime lab is a hundred and fifty miles away, Ader calls on me occasionally to carry out autopsies and other tests which the local coroner—a political hack—is unable to handle properly.

The case really began fifteen months ago, and oddly enough I was there, although without any idea of the ramifications to come later. At that time, the lieutenant was driving us back from a stabbing at the south end of town: a simple matter, with no subtleties, consisting of a steak knife driven into a lung. But on the way home, we heard a radio call about a traffic accident not too far off, and Ader decided to have a look. It never does any harm to barge in on your subordinates by surprise now and then; keeps them on their toes, Ader feels.

It turned out to be a typical and infuriating example of the genus legal murder. We found a huge, garish convertible, a shaky driver, and a dazed woman crouching over the body of her child, a boy about eight.

As we pulled up, the man responsible for the tragedy was protesting to all and sundry, but especially to the pair of stonyfaced officers from the prowl car.

"I'm not drunk," he insisted, his voice only slightly thick. "It's my diabetes; I need insulin. Sure, I had a couple, but I'm quite sober."

The man reeked of alcohol, but his actions were not those of a drunk. This is a familiar phenomenon. The shock of the accident had blasted the maggots from his nervous system, so that to the casual observer, he seemed in full command of himself.

I was busy with the child. There wasn't a hope. He died before the ambulance got there five minutes later. The mother, smartly dressed and attractive, knelt there pale and rigid, as if in a trance. It was that dangerous state before the blessed release of tears.

I never did learn the details of the accident. Apparently, mother and son, the latter leading a puppy, were waiting at the crosswalk, when the animal got away. Before the woman could stop him, the child had scampered into the street. He should have been safe in the crosswalk in any circumstances; the law is strict about that; but the car was moving too fast, and its driver was drunk. An old story.

Ader watched the interns put the pathetic little body into the ambulance. The heavy muscles of his jaw corded.

"I know this murderer and his convertible," Ader told me in a gritty voice. "He was sure to kill somebody sooner or later. A worthless guy if ever there was one. I wish we could nail him this time."

I took a good look at the man. Plump, expensively dressed, well tanned, sun-lamp style, not the kind you get out in the air. He had a jowly face with bags under the eyes. His earlier paleness was gone, but he seemed nervous, and yet arrogant, too, as if he anticipated a punch in the nose, and was ready to yell police brutality.

"You can't blame a man for diabetic coma, lieutenant," he said defiantly. "You've tried it before, and the jury didn't buy any. I'm Gordon Vance Whitman, remember, not some scared, friendless punk you can frame."

"You're drunk," Ader said. "And you forgot the 'third' at the end of your distinguished name."

"Like hell I am. Diabetic coma." There was a sly glint in his small eyes.

I glanced at the lieutenant. He shrugged in disgust.

"We've had this guy up several times for drunk driving; nobody was killed before—just maimed. He has diabetes, all right; and the symptoms are rather similar, as you know. A jury isn't competent to assess the difference, not with a gaggle of highpriced lawyers working on them."

"The juries are fine," Whitman grinned, swaying a little. "All I need is a pill." With deliberate ostentation he pulled a vial from one pocket, opened it, and popped a tablet into his mouth. I spotted the label; the stuff was one of those new drugs which, for people over forty, take the place of insulin. "Just a matter of excess blood sugar," he said, making sure the scene went on record.

"You don't seem much concerned about the child you killed," I told him, feeling a strong urge to mash a handul of knuckles against his beautifully capped teeth.

"Naturally, I'm very sorry," he replied in a solemn voice. "But it wasn't my fault; the kid ran out after that fool pup all of a sudden."

"That's no excuse," Ader snapped. "If you hadn't been soused and speeding, you could have stopped in plenty of time. You hit him in a crosswalk."

"If I *was* going too fast," Whitman explained, "it happened after the coma dazed me. I blanked out for a minute, and may have stepped on the gas."

"You can at least see that he never drives again," I reminded Ader.

"Yeah," he said wearily. "That'll cheer the parents no end. You don't know the half of it, son. Let's get out of here: Briggs and Gerber can handle the details."

"Wait a minute," I said. "What about her?"

Ader jumped, as though startled. "You're right. I'm an idiot."

We both looked at the woman. She was still crouched there, but now she was cradling the puppy in her arms. A low, pathetic moaning came from her throat, and the little animal, tightly gripped and unhappy, joined in with a shrill whimper.

"Look," Ader said. "You and Briggs take her home in the cruiser. Get her husband, and call the family doctor."

It seemed a good idea. I managed to get her on her feet, and over to the police car. Briggs climbed in, and we were off. The low moaning became louder; suddenly she was weeping with passionate intensity. That was all to the good, though there are limits.

It's been at least ten years since I had a patient to treat. All of mine are just bodies to be studied. Nevertheless, I always carry a minimum emergency kit, and it came in handy now. I had a devil of a time, but finally managed to give her a sedative. I'll never forget the ride: the woman, her dainty dress all smeared from the gutter; her carefully made up face a mask of grief; and that pitiful puppy's whimpering, incessant and at times shrill.

Twice the woman pulled away from me and tried to jump out of the moving car. "I want to go back!" she cried. "Where did they take Derry? Let me go; let me go!"

Well, we got her home at last, and called her husband, a college professor. He picked up the family doctor on the way, and I was relieved from duty. Briggs dropped me off at the hospital, where I found hours of work already piled up. Yet busy as I was, I couldn't get the incident off my mind. Do doctors ever get used to that sort of thing, I wondered. More than ever, I felt I'd been wise in avoiding general practice. It was too easy to get involved. For days I winced every time I thought of that poor woman and her loss.

Sometime later, Ader gave me the whole sad story of Gordon Vance Whitman III. This character was a playboy of fifty plus and almost as many millions. One of the most sued people in the country. He'd never been any good, and the chief thing of interest about him was the foresight of his father, a canny old pirate of an earlier generation, when financial morals were even lower than now. He had put the boy's inheritance in the form of an unbreakable trust, of which Gordon enjoyed only the income. Such arrangements, which unfairly protect irresponsibles like Whitman against legitimate claims, are barred in most states, but not, alas, in mine. The income, of course, was enormous by ordinary standards, and cleverly designed to make tracing and attaching any portion of it as tricky as legally possible.

Whitman had married the usual series of showgirls, all of whom were collecting large slices of his assorted dividends; but other judgments, totalling millions, were unenforceable because of the machinations of the late Whitman, Senior.

In short, Ader saw little hope of convicting Whitman this time, either.

Well, I was too busy to keep track of one more social injustice—the needless death of a child—among many. I seem to recall that Whitman's license was revoked for a long time, and another large judgment added to the list. He beat the drunk charge, since blood tests are barred here. The old diabetes story was good again. As for transportation, there are chauffeurs available for a price, and after enough high-toned specialists had testified that his diabetes was under control, this model citizen may even have recovered his maiming rights.

Occasionally I saw an item about him—he was always news. Another marriage, a startlet this time. Apparently he favored petite redheads; this was the fourth to become Mrs. Whitman.

"A few more marriages," Ader remarked sourly once, "and maybe the guy'll be too worn out to drive around killing children!"

The accident happened over a year ago, and seemed to be past history, but last month saw a new phase of the Whitman story, and it was a lulu.

Ader phoned me late on a Tuesday afternoon. The body of a man had just been found inside a locked third floor apartment. No marks of violence; no sign of any other party's having been present, even. The victim had apparently enjoyed a lone binge behind a bolted door. He had then stretched out on the divan, and instead of awakening with a size twelve head and lepidoptera in his stomach, never came to at all.

"And the dear departed," Ader told me with ghoulish satisfaction, "is none other than our old friend, Gordon Vance Whitman III."

"Good," I remarked. "But where do I fit in?"

"We have a curious policy here at headquarters. We'd like to know what this crumb died of."

"You'd better take the usual pictures, and then bring me the body," I told him. "I can't possibly leave the hospital today. In any case, it certainly sounds like a stroke or coronary."

"Very likely," Ader agreed. "But I have an instinct in these matters, and let's be sure, okay?"

"Fair enough. Bring me the remains, and I'll do the P. M. this evening."

At that stage, of course, there was no indication of murder, what with the locked door and all. There aren't many John Dickson Carr puzzles in real life.

The police brought me the body about five, and I got all the details and photos. It was a matter of luck that Whitman had been found so promptly. One of his numerous lady friends, unable to rouse him by leaning on the buzzer, had finally called the manager, who in turn notified the police. They had broken in, seen that the man was dead, and now it was up to me. We all expected that the cause of death was something quick, massive, and natural. I would have bet on it myself. Hence my first real surprise in years.

Now, an autopsy, when properly done, is a long and involved chore. The "gross" part, actually carried out on the table, is almost identical with a series of major operations, and performed with the same care and precision as if the person were still alive and under anaesthesia. No sloppy hacking will do; the job takes from three to six hours with a conscientious pathologist. The microscopic phase, completed in the laboratory, may go on for weeks, and could include work in chemistry, bacteriology, toxicology, and any other specialty you'd care to name.

My preliminary examination seemed to confirm the existence of some sort of respiratory failure, for the face was gray and the lips bluish—a condition called cyanosis. Nevertheless, there is a standard routine for a post mortem, so I began with the skull. The brain tissue was quite normal; no sign of a bloodclot there, which ruled out one kind of stroke.

Next, working by the book, I explored the chest cavity, and found pay dirt immediately. The appearance of the lungs—the edema and signs of severe irritation—caught my eye at once. I bent over for a better look with a 3X magnifier, and as my face came close, noted an odd odor—the faint, musty smell of new-mown hay, along with the sharper, unmistakable reek of hydrochloric acid.

It was a clue I might easily have missed. That would have meant many hours of lab work to discover the obvious. You see, nobody who served in the army would forget that scent of moldy hay. In the early months of 1942, when gas warfare seemed highly probable, every soldier, and particularly those of us in the Medical Corps, was taught to recognize the main types of poison gas. This unique smell meant phosgene, a deadly stuff invented during World War I. A few good whiffs, and the victim, beyond a little coughing and chest congestion, might go about his business unworried, only to collapse and die later, without warning. It's tricky and variable, forming hydrochloric acid in the lungs. Real nasty, that vapor.

I told you it was a puzzler—a man dead of phosgene in a locked room. The case was no longer one of death by natural causes or accident—not with the victim's lungs full of poison gas.

Now don't misunderstand me; I'm a pathologist, not a detective. Theoretically, when I completed the rest of the autopsy, my job was done. But when something this intriguing comes along, which is seldom, and they can spare me at the hospital, I like to tag along with the lieutenant. Sometimes I've been helpful; at worst, I'm a useful sounding board.

Well, he took me to the apartment, where I got another jolt. I'd assumed, reasonably enough, that somebody had pumped phosgene into the room; there didn't seem to be any other explanation. But I was wrong. A few simple tests showed that no such wholesale release of gas had occurred. Fantastic as it seemed, the stuff must have been introduced directly into the man's lungs—and only there.

That seemed to imply a tank of phosgene, along with a tube or mask. It was a sticker, all right.

But Ader skipped that point for the moment. Instead we concentrated on the source, thinking that would be easier. You don't just pick up a tank of war gas at the corner drugstore. It's not too hard to make a little of it, chemically, but not in any form that would permit its being pumped into a person's lungs.

The lieutenant checked all the nearby army camps. We weren't too surprised to find that none of them stocked the stuff. Gas warfare is nearly passé. All they had were those recognition kits which teach rookies the characteristic odors. Harmless samples. The one big chemical warfare depot was able to state positively that no phosgene—stored in big tanks—was missing.

That left the question of motive, which gave us both a grim chuckle. It was obvious that Gordon Vance Whitman III had plenty of enemies. Not as many as the late Hitler, maybe, but quite a few.

The money angle was a flop. Whitman had no heirs. In the event of his death, the huge trust became a sort of foundation like the Ford or Rockefeller setup. Which meant that none of those judgments would be any better than they were now—in short, useless to the litigants.

Well, police work is mostly tiresome routine. Somebody had murdered, and how we still didn't know, the late Mr. Whitman. Therefore it was a matter of motive. Ader and his staff had to check out a list of more than twenty prime suspects, all people with good reasons for hating the victim. I withdrew from that part of the case; they were yelling for me at the hospital anyway. Instead, I continued to ponder the phosgene problem. I kept gnawing at it during the weeks Ader's crew was struggling with the legwork.

Their efforts finally paid off. Everybody was eliminated from the list but one woman. She was definitely It. Oddly enough, the lieutenant hadn't felt strongly about including her at the start; it was almost certain, he thought, that she had no connection with the case. But the principles of sound police work sink deep into a competent officer, and her name was added to the others. You see, she was merely the maid who cleaned the hallways and did similar odd jobs. The apartments themselves were the problem of the tenants.

She called herself Mrs. Talbot, but the first thorough check soon revealed that her right name was Eleanor Oldenburger. A college graduate, the widow of a distinguished professor, she had recently suffered a complete nervous collapse. She had taken this job a few weeks after leaving the hospital. On the off chance that her arriving at this particular building might be significant, Ader looked for a connection between Whitman and her. It didn't take long to find one. If anybody had a good reason to loathe the late playboy, Mrs. Oldenburger qualified in spades. We were brought back fifteen months to the killing of that little boy. His name was Derry, and he was the Oldenburgers' only child. Loss of the boy had undoubtedly hastened the professor's death. Their small amount of insurance went for the widow's medical expenses—nervous breakdowns come high. A damage suit initiated by the professor before his death had resulted in a judgment of three hundred thousand dollars, but there were dozens of others ahead of it, all uncollectible.

When Ader told me all this, I looked him in the eye, and said, "If she did kill him, more power to her. Why not drop the case now?"

He didn't lower his own stare for a moment.

"I'm a police officer. I can't do that. I'm no judge; you know that." A crooked little smile touched his lips. "I certainly want to know *how* she managed it, but if there isn't enough evidence to make a case, I won't be heartbroken." He paused. "Husband, child—all lost because of that stinker. You can't really blame her."

"What's she like?" I asked him.

"You saw her. Woman in her forties, I'd say. So far, I've seen her only at work, not in her home, in those shapeless things maids wear for dirty jobs. I've a hunch it was mostly protective coloration. I seem to remember a pair of electric blue eyes that didn't fit a common drudge at all. But I'm about to visit her at home. Why not come along?"

I jumped at the chance. Although I was no nearer to a solution of the phosgene puzzle, the woman began to interest me for herself. Whatever her plan, it showed a cool, keen intelligence, as well as the ruthless judgment of a Minerva.

She lived in a tiny but immaculate apartment in Orange Grove. I saw Ader blink at the sight of her. She wore well-tailored slacks of gray material, and a pale blue blouse; they emphasized a slender but rounded figure that suggested twenty-five rather than forty-five. Her hair was the sort Holmes called "positive blonde," that is, fair, but with highlights and subtle colors. She seemed quite relaxed.

With almost insolent coolness, she insisted on our having martinis. When we were settled with ours, she curled up catlike on a big sofa, and gave us a faint smile.

"Let the inquisition begin," she said lightly. On the surface she was hard, cold, and callous. As a doctor, trained to study people behind their pathetic facades, I knew that her nerves were stretched to an unbearable tension; that she was on the knife-edge of hysteria.

Ader was brusque. I think he too sensed her delicate balance and hoped to break her down.

"Why didn't you tell us your real name?"

Her smile deepened.

"Come, lieutenant. I was taking a menial job, under very distressing circumstances. Why should I parade my identity as a fallen woman?"

"You deliberately picked that building to work in. The manager testified that you phoned her repeatedly. Why did it have to be there? Wasn't it so you could get at Whitman?"

"You know, of course," she reminded him sweetly, "that I needn't answer any of these questions without a lawyer. But I've nothing to hide. I liked the location; as you see, it's near this apartment. I could walk; I'm too nervous these days to drive, and can't afford a car, anyway. And what makes you think I'd want to kill Whitman?"

"Look, Mrs. Oldenburger," Ader said. "We know about Derry. In case you've forgotten, Dr. Hoffman and I happened to be on the spot just after that swine Whitman—"

She was deathly pale now, but interrupted him in a even voice.

"You agree, then, that he was a swine."

"Of course. I sympathize with you in every way. But I can't condone murder."

"Neither can you prove it," she flashed. "I understand this apartment was bolted inside."

"The transom was partly open. Isn't it true that you use a small ladder to clean woodwork in the halls?"

"Yes. I'm only five feet six, you see."

"Were you using it that day?"

"Yes. Did I crawl through the transom and kill Whitman?"

Ader frowned. "No, it's too small even for you. I measured it."

She gave him a look of mock consternation. "Oh, dear. And me bragging about my slender build."

"We don't know how you did it—yet. But obviously you found out where he lived, and wangled this job as a maid. Somehow you managed to fill his lungs with poison gas—phosgene, to be exact. It's only a matter of time until we discover the method."

She raised her carefully pencilled brows, and squirmed deeper into the soft cushions. She seemed perfectly relaxed, but I could see a significantly throbbing vein by one ear.

"Phosgene? I doubt if I could spell it, in spite of my general chemistry in college. As for that job, I had a complete breakdown. Probably you know all about that, too. For weeks I was catatonic. When I recovered, any mental effort was still impossible. I had to find some simple physical work. That's all there is to it. I'm no scientific genius to make poison gas and get it into a locked room."

"What makes you think it had to be made?" Ader snapped. "Why not bought?"

She tightened visibly, aware of her mistake.

"Can you go out and buy poison gas?" she asked brightly. "I wouldn't know. But, in any case, gentlemen, it's getting late, and if you don't mind . . . "

We left then; there wasn't much else to do. She was under a terrific strain, but wouldn't crack. Yet I felt sure reaction and regrets were inevitable. And I didn't like the prospect.

But intellectual curiosity is a passion with me, so I couldn't quit. And the next day I made my first real advance. I placed the name Oldenburger. Surely I had seen some of his articles in the past. What had they covered? Then it came to me; the man had been a top physiological chemist, often consulted by the big poison centers.

I got in touch with the nearest one immediately, with highly significant results. The puzzle was solved now except for one small item. Ader supplied that, but didn't know it. It was the first time I held out on him. I merely asked for a list of cleaning agents available to the maids in Whitman's building. Among them, sure enough, was carbon tetrachloride, kept on hand to remove spots from upholstery. I decided to pay Mrs. Oldenburger a visit on my own.

This time she wore a simple dress, the kind that is tasteful-expensive-simple, if you know what I mean. It confirmed my suspicion that she was far from broke, and didn't actually need a job as maid.

Seeing her again, I realized what an attractive woman she really was. Without Ader there, she seemed to be more natural. As I'd suspected, the hardness and diamond sparkle had been at least partially assumed before—a shield.

My emotions were clawing me. I meant to prove I knew the solution, but after that—well, the way wasn't clear at all.

I accepted a drink, and for some minutes we made small talk. I began to lose hope of getting through because the woman was at peace with herself. Apparently her conscience had been stilled; perhaps she had finally rationalized the murder to the point of feeling no guilt.

Relaxed and warm, she had that rare facility of withholding the best part of her considerable beauty, and then in a dazzling stroke, flashing it like a weapon. I had no defense against it, and didn't seem to want one.

The small talk had to end sometime. I took the plunge.

"I know exactly how you did it," I told her.

A slight shadow passed over her face.

"I was more afraid of you than of the officer," she said. "My husband mentioned your work occasionally. A new test for morphine poisoning, I believe."

I may have blushed; this was, naturally, hardly what I expected as counter.

"Thank you. And I know about Professor Oldenburger. He had a very intriguing case once at the Poison Center. Maybe he discussed it with you. Whitman's addiction to liquor was the key. It's an odd fact of chemistry that if a man with plenty of alcohol in his system gets a few whiffs of carbon tetrachloride, the two compounds unite in the blood to form phosgene, one of the deadliest of the early war gases. Now I believe you soaked a rag in the spot remover, and using a mop handle or something, reached through the transom to hold the cloth over Whitman's nose and mouth. With the ladder it was a cinch. Two or three minutes would be enough time. If anybody had appeared, you could have pulled away from the transom and busied yourself with the moldings. Besides, who knows better than a maid how deserted those apartments are by day?" I looked at her pale, composed face. "Am I right? There are no witnesses here, so why not admit it?"

She sat there, a fragile figure, with that odd air of repose, and my heart went out to her.

"Not quite," she said shakily. "I used a fishing rod. Rufus—my husband—was a great one for trout. It was the rod," she added, with a catch in her voice, "he taught Derry on." She turned her head away for a moment.

"It's hardly a case to stand up in court," I told her. "I doubt if any jury—"

"No," she said passionately. "You mustn't say that. I've been mad, distracted. It was a terrible thing. I have nightmares when I think of putting that awful rag—a sleeping man, helpless . . . " She straightened in the chair. "I've signed a confession. I want you to call Lieutenant Ader."

To my surprise, I found myself protesting. The words came in a wild flood. I told her without my testimony, there was no case; that I wouldn't go to court. That Ader didn't know about the spot remover. She smiled as if I were a child.

She pled guilty, but by law a trial is still possible. I got the best lawyer in the state. I was now convinced she had been temporarily insane, and that was the line we held. The jury wouldn't convict.

During the long weeks of legal maneuvering, we grew closer together. I never dreamed I'd marry a murderess, but, as I said at the start, it's not easy to shock a pathologist.

# Jurisprudence

## by Leo P. Kelley

Sheriff Patrick Caldwell, leaning against one of the towering maples and smoking his cigarette, felt the vague discomfort of a man who has missed lunch and the distress of a man facing a decision he would rather not have to make.

Fifty feet below him lay the broken body of Tracy McBain, looking very much like an unwanted toy thrown carelessly down into the gaping mouth of the abandoned quarry.

Caldwell turned to study the retreating figures of his deputy, Clint Travers, and Kenny as they headed down the mountainside toward the town and the jail where Kenny would be held pending his trial. As Caldwell watched, they disappeared among the trees, and he turned back to stare again at the body of McBain as if it held the answer to a frustrating riddle which he felt compelled to solve.

Soon, he realized, the knowledge of what Kenny had done would become the common property of the small Vermont town. Heads would shake and tongues would cluck and everyone would say he had always expected something like this. Kenny would be tried, convicted, and sent to Graybriar, the state institution for the criminally insane.

Caldwell flung his cigarette away and promptly lit another. He forced himself to think of the present and to face the facts. Fact: Tracy McBain was dead. Fact: Kenny had confessed to murdering him. Fact: Kenny was Caldwell's friend.

It was this last fact that seemed most important to Caldwell now. He recalled how Kenny, at first as shy as any yearling, had learned to trust him and to turn to him for help and simple companionship, and how he had honored that trust with a patience and understanding that had brought warm smiles to the faces of many of the town's residents, although there were those who said Kenny ought to be put away "for his own good"—a kid like that could be "dangerous."

Kenny had come to Caldwell just as stray cats and people with problems had come to him for as long as he could remember. He guessed he was just that kind of man.

It should be simple, the facts being what they were, but he knew it was not simple at all. It was this disquieting knowledge that kept him standing on the rim of the quarry, smoking one tasteless cigarette after another and trying to decide whether to turn his idea into action or just to go on down the mountain and let things take their inevitable course.

Once again Caldwell went over the events of the day in his mind, thinking back to how it had all started a little more than two hours ago.

He had been sitting at the desk in the corner of his dusty office, not quite asleep and not quite awake, when he heard the sound of familiar footsteps on the porch. He lifted his feet to the scarred wooden desk, nodded to Kenny as he appeared in the doorway, and spoke a greeting.

Kenny made no answer.

"Come along in, boy," Caldwell said. "It's getting hot out there."

Kenny strode with measured steps across the room until he stood beside the desk, gazing down at his friend, his eyes even blanker than usual. He was many years younger than Caldwell, not more than twenty, with hair so blond it turned white under the sun. He was almost handsome, but his vague eyes contradicted his handsomeness, giving it something of the quality of a fresh coat of paint on an abandoned dwelling. One day in the past, Kenny's mind had just stopped developing, but his arms had continued pushing themselves beyond the edges of his shirtsleeves and his voice had cracked and then deepened.

"Sit down, Kenny," Caldwell said. "Nice day."

Kenny sat down stiffly, staring steadily at Caldwell, who was trying to ignore the pain in his fingers. Arthritis was an ignoble affliction, he had long ago decided. It robbed you of little things, a sly thief. It made you hate the spring rain and the sight of other men squeezing the triggers of their rifles without a twinge of pain or a thought to anything other than the game in their sights. It made you know you were growing old.

At last, Kenny spoke. "I've come to tell you that I shot Mr. McBain and he's dead as dust."

Caldwell swung his feet down from the desk and leaned over its cluttered surface. When he spoke, his voice was steady, betraying nothing of the sudden fear he felt. "You shot Tracy McBain?"

Kenny nodded.

"You aren't just telling stories, are you, boy?" Caldwell asked anxiously. "You are saying the truth?"

"Yes, the truth."

"And he's dead?"

"He don't move."

"Where is the—where is Mr. McBain?"

Kenny jerked a thumb over his shoulder. "Up at the quarry," he replied in a shaky voice. His hand returned to lie stolidly in his lap.

Caldwell saw the stains, unmistakably blood, on the boy's hands. But the boy had never even hunted, never had a gun in his hands! He hated hunting and guns! Caldwell let out his breath with a sound somewhere between a sigh and a groan. "Ah, Kenny," he said softly. "Why?"

Kenny shook his head slowly and said nothing.

"Where did you get the gun?"

The boy shrugged. "It was his."

"McBain's?"

"Yes, Mr. McBain's."

"It was an accident?" Desperately, hopefully.

Kenny shook his head again. "No, I meant to do it and I did it." He paused. "I guess I'm glad."

Caldwell yelled, "Clint!" He heard the sound of booted feet hurrying from the rear of the building. Clint Travers, Caldwell's deputy, came into the room, halted when he saw Kenny. Noting the dismayed expression on Caldwell's face, he elected to keep his mouth shut.

"Kenny," Caldwell began, "says he shot and killed Tracy McBain." He pointed to the dried blood on Kenny's hands.

Travers let out a low whistle. "When?"

Caldwell repeated the question to Kenny a little too loudly.

"Half an hour ago," Kenny answered. "I came right down to tell you," he said to Caldwell and then lapsed into silence, examining his hands.

"I'm sorry, Patrick," Travers said quietly. "You tried your best."

Caldwell, looking up, saw something in Travers' eyes that suggested Clint was sorry, too. Yes, he mused, I tried my best. I did what little I could. I taught the boy to shingle a roof and to cook his own meals. I tried to teach him self-respect and truth and love and a lot of other things I'm not at all sure I understand myself. I tried my best and now I see that my best was not enough.

Caldwell shifted his gaze to where Kenny sat, eyes cast down, shoulders hunched over in an attitude of defeat. He knew Kenny was really, in a way, not much more than a child. Everyone thought

of Kenny that way—just a child, really. You tended to forget the
brawny arms and the broad shoulders and remember only the bright
smile that burst into being at the sight of a brilliant butterfly or
the sound of an unseen someone laughing in the soft darkness of a
summer night. After his mother had run off almost fifteen years
ago, there was only an aging aunt left to look after him. When she
died, Kenny was left alone except for the dappled hound he loved
and who followed him everywhere—over the hills in the blaze of
autumn and across the snow-smothered fields in winter.

Caldwell forced himself to think of the here and now, of what
Kenny had just told him: I've come to tell you that I shot Mr. McBain
and he's dead as dust.

"Why did he do it, Patrick?" Travers asked. "Did he tell you why?"

Caldwell shook his head. "He only told me how," came his terse
reply. "He used McBain's gun, that's all I know. He wouldn't or
couldn't say why." The *how* was usually quite enough for most people, Caldwell thought with some bitterness. People always wanted
to know *how*. Did the killer use a knife, a gun, a rope—poison perhaps? The *why* was seldom as important and never as exciting.

"Maybe," Travers ventured tentatively, "maybe it was self-de-
fense."

Caldwell hoped so. His fingers felt like wood and he wondered if
the pain would ever stop or even lessen. He shoved the ten offenders
into his pockets as if he were ashamed of them. He stood up slowly.
"Will you take us up to the quarry and show us how it happened,
Kenny?" he asked gently.

Without a word, Kenny got up and started for the door. Caldwell
stepped around the desk and Travers followed them out into the
sunlight.

It took them forty minutes to reach the rim of the quarry. Kenny
stood off to the left where the trees thinned out and the land fell
away to form a plateau. They all stared down at the twisted body
of Tracy McBain.

"He paid me once to take him up the trail over there and show
him the salt licks," Kenny remarked absently.

Caldwell barely heard him. He was remembering Tracy Mc-
Bain—a fixer of parking tickets and a man overly fond of boasting
that he always paid his own way. Caldwell had heard him say as
much many times: "Money talks and I'm a guy who knows how to
listen." Such a remark would be followed by the slow parting of
McBain's lips and his disagreeable chuckle. It had always set Cald-

well's teeth on edge to note that McBain's eyes at such times remained like steel.

"You wait here," Caldwell instructed Kenny. To Travers, he said, "I'm going down to have a closer look. You stay here. Keep an eye on the boy."

As Caldwell began the treacherous descent, he asked himself why he was doing this. He knew the answer. Because he had to see for himself. He had to search for a pulse and find none. He had to seek a heartbeat and find only stillness. He had to know for certain that Kenny had killed McBain. Then maybe he would let himself believe something he did not want to believe.

Slow as his progress was, it seemed all too swift to Caldwell. Within minutes, he was bending over the body. He had seen violent death in that legendary war to end all wars. It was not merely the sight of death which sickened him now, not merely the terribly twisted limbs and the awful angle of the neck. It was because all this was Kenny's doing.

Caldwell's eyes examined every inch of McBain's body. The man was definitely dead. Then, thoughtfully, he rose and looked up from the corpse at his feet to where Travers and Kenny stood gazing down at him from the top of the quarry.

The ascent was more difficult than coming down had been. Loose rock slid away with every step. It seemed that for every step he took upward, he slid back two. At last he reached the top with the help of Travers' strong hands.

"He's dead all right," Caldwell told Travers. "Where's Kenny?" he asked, looking around, breathing heavily from the effort of his climb.

Travers said, "He was here a minute ago. I wonder if—"

"There he is," Caldwell said. He had spotted Kenny a dozen yards away, almost out of sight behind a sharp outcropping of rock. He was stooping down to something hidden from Caldwell's gaze. "Come on," he said.

If Kenny heard their approach, he gave no sign. It was not until Caldwell reached him and spoke his name a second time that he looked up and seemed to be really seeing them.

"What have you got there?" Caldwell inquired. The question was unnecessary because he had already seen and recognized the bundle in the boy's hands.

"It's Bess," Kenny replied, looking down at the bloody body of the hound. "She's dead."

"Tell me what happened," Caldwell commanded tonelessly.

"She was always full of ginger, Bess was," Kenny said, with the trace of his former smile. "She didn't mean no harm but she ran on ahead of me and Mr. McBain and he got mad because Bess chased the doe he'd been about to drop from up there on the rise. He started yelling and Bess ran up and jumped on him, barking and all, and he swung his gun and sent her spinning. You should have heard her scream!"

Caldwell looked down at the limp body of the dog in Kenny's arms. "What happened then?" he prodded, unable to look away from the dead dog, afraid that if he did he might have to meet Kenny's eyes.

"I ran up here but Bess was almost dead already. There was something wrong with her back, you could tell. Mr. McBain said how he was sorry about losing his temper and he—"

"He offered to pay for the damage he'd done," Kenny said, and there was a sense of wonder in his tone. "He was going to *pay!*" His breath came in short, shallow gasps now. "Bess was watching me and her eyes were only partway open. I grabbed Mr. McBain's gun from him and he backed off and started to run and then I fired it at him a couple of times and he went over the edge into the quarry. After I killed him, Bess died. I dropped the gun." Kenny drew a deep, obviously painful breath, looked up at the white clouds drifting unconcerned in the sky, and let his breath out before proceeding. "You see, Bess she was looking at me as if she was waiting to see what I would do and I—" He discovered that the words, whatever they were, wouldn't come.

Travers shifted position, pulled a clean handkerchief from his pocket, and leaned down, intending to pick up McBain's rifle from where Kenny had dropped it earlier.

Caldwell stepped forward. He spoke in a tone so low Travers almost failed to hear him. "I'll bring the gun," he said. He took the handkerchief from Travers' hand. "It would look bad, you and the boy and the gun walking into town. Take him down and let him bury Bess. I'll be along in a bit."

The better part of an hour had passed since Travers had led Kenny away, and, still leaning against the stout trunk of the maple, Sheriff Caldwell considered the facts for the final time.

Kenny was a born loser. That, it seemed, was one indisputable fact. The boy had come unweaponed to the war, betrayed by nature, his mother, his father, his aunt. Nature had betrayed him by her unfinished handiwork, his mother by her disappearance years earlier, his aunt by dying. His father, whom he had never known, had betrayed him by his absence and his silence. But Bess had never shown any sign of betrayal and Kenny, Caldwell calculated, meeting her dying eyes, had not been found wanting. He had sought to avenge her murder.

Now Caldwell knew that Kenny had failed in his endeavor. Having examined McBain's body at close range, and carefully, he knew that it held no bullets, no bullet wound. He had reconstructed the scene in his mind—Kenny seizing the unfamiliar rifle and firing wildly, McBain backing off in terror, slipping and falling to his death at the bottom of the quarry. The blood on Kenny's hands, Caldwell realized, had belonged to Bess.

Thus, Kenny would not stand trial for murder but on some lesser charge. He would learn that he had failed Bess, unless Caldwell saw to it that he stood trial for the crime he had intended—the crime uncommitted—murder. In either case, for Kenny, it was hopeless; he would wind up in Graybriar to wear for the rest of his life an invisible sign that said *criminally insane;* in either case.

Caldwell made his decision. He picked up McBain's rifle, using the handkerchief he had taken from Travers, and checked the magazine. Two bullets remained. He raised the rifle to his shoulder, took careful aim at the corpse fifty feet below him, and fired once, putting a bullet in the lifeless heart of Tracy McBain. The body lurched as the bullet struck.

Caldwell lowered the gun. The sun warmed him and he discovered with mild surprise that his fingers felt as strong as those of a man many years his junior. He hurried down the mountainside to see if Travers had remembered to give Kenny his lunch.

# My Daughter, the Murderer

## by Eleanor Boylan

**M**y daughter Pam, who lives in New York City because she says that's where theater is at, is always forgetting that the sun takes its sweet time about getting to California where her mother is at. My phone is forever ringing at times like six A.M. and she's telling me, "Mom—I got the part!" or, "Mom—I didn't get the part!" or, "Mom can you spare fifty bucks?"

But one day comes a call that's a beaut. The phone rings about nine o'clock Saturday morning when I'm trying to sleep late and I feel around for it and I hear Pam's voice: "Mom! They're saying I killed a man!"

Well, that lands me on my feet and I'm on a plane to New York at about the time I'd normally be plugging in my coffeepot and opening the paper to read juicy news about *other* people's daughters' troubles.

On the plane, in between worrying about my kid, I had time to think about how much I hate New York. I gave it the best years of my life and what did it give me? Dancing parts in a couple of forties' musicals and two husbands, both of whom I lost—the first, Pam's father, to a drunken driver in the Holland Tunnel and the second to a redhead in *Bloomer Girl*. Now I'm a fat middle-aged dame with a little apartment in Burbank, a part-time job in a dress shop, a bridge club, a nice old widower boyfriend, and life is perfect—or was. My poor Pam, my poor baby, they can't do this to her, I thought. Because she's got talent. *She'll* make it.

In the cab heading out of Kennedy Airport, I tried to make some sense of the twenty or so words I'd had with Pam on the phone. First I'd said, "Did you?" and she'd said, "Did I what?" And I'd said, "Did you kill him?" and she'd said, "Mom!"

Then I'd said, "Who was he?" and she'd said, "An actor I auditioned with this morning." I'd said, "Why suspect you?" and she'd started to say something and the operator butts in with the "time's up" bit, so I'd just yelled, "I'll come!"

I was still trying to adjust to the fact that it was five P.M. while the cabdriver was barging around downtown Manhattan looking for

12 Murphy Street in the Bowery (yes, my darling daughter lives in the Bowery—she says it's "in"). We finally found the dump and do you believe my child pays rent to live over a liquor store in a studio with one little window so high a monkey couldn't reach it in case of fire?

She was out on the sidewalk waving the third time we came around the block and she scrambled into the cab before it was half stopped and was crying and hugging me—I wish I may die before I ever feel my heart torn apart like that again. But I just hugged her back and patted that pretty, long brown hair and said, "My daughter, the murderer." That made her giggle because it's a joke we have: I've always introduced her as "my daughter, the actress," ever since she was little and started telling me she was going to be one.

On the sidewalk I tried not to gag at the sight of the crummy-looking neighborhood and I asked where the cops were if she was a murder suspect. Pam said she was on her honor not to leave the place and Sergeant Somebody was coming later to talk to both of us. That eased my mind and I followed her up the ratty stairs to the "apartment." She proudly showed me the furniture she'd bought at a flea market and pointed out how nice the rug I'd sent her looked. She told me the kitchen area was only a matter of pulling aside the curtain (God forgive the landlord for that stove) and that a mere twenty steps took you down the hall to the bathroom she shared. I asked her if she shared it with a herd of elephants and she said what I was hearing was some members of a ballet troupe who'd just moved in upstairs.

"Well, to business," I said and sat down at a rickety card table while Pam made tea. "Right from the beginning—go."

She stared down at a mug she was holding and said: "The poor old man died right here in this room."

"Old?" I was surprised. "He was old?"

"Yes, seventy, maybe eighty. Didn't I tell you?"

"You did not." Pam was squeezing lemon in my tea. "What the hell was he doing here?"

"I invited him. Mom, he was so pathetic. He knew he wasn't going to get the part and he wanted it so much. Do you remember the play—it's a revival—*Death Takes a Holiday?*"

Not only do I remember the old tearjerker, my roommate understudied the girl's part when it was revived back in the forties. I said: "Were you auditioning for Grazia?"

Pam nodded. "They said they'd let me know by tomorrow."

She'd be *perfect*. But it was creepy to think that the old guy had
died on the day he'd auditioned for a play which is about a mysterious
few days when nobody in the world can die—something about Death
taking the form of a man and falling in love. I dragged my mind
back to the present mess and said: "So what happened?"

Pam folded her hands on the table, but they shook anyway. She
said: "We walked out of the audition together—oh, God, I can't believe it was only this morning—and I said, 'I think you read Manuel
beautifully.' He said they'd just told him they weren't going to cast
him and he knew it was because of his drinking. I said that I was
going to walk home because it was such a nice day, real Indian
summer, and it was only fifteen blocks and that if he'd like to come
along we could have a bite of lunch at my place."

"You soft-hearted dope," I said, knowing I'd probably have done
the same thing.

"Mom, you probably would have done the same thing. He was
such a sweet old guy, a real old-time actor. His name was Lawrence
Canfield. We walked down Seventh Avenue and he was telling me
about when he played with people like Forbes Robertson and Walter
Hampden. When we got to 18th Street he said he lived a block away
and asked if I'd mind waiting while he went and got his coat in case
it turned chilly later. I said I'd wait in the bookstore on the corner.
I could tell he probably didn't want me to see the fleabag he lived
in."

*He* lived in a fleabag, I thought, looking around.

Pam went on, her voice getting shaky. "I waited about twenty
minutes—I thought maybe he wasn't coming back—but he did and
he had the coat and we walked on down here. I opened a can of soup
and I had some banana bread and we sat here and talked about the
theater. Then Ruth Pearlman—she's an artist, she lives across the
hall—Ruth knocked on the door to say I had a phone call from the
Morris Francis office. I don't have a phone and Ruth lets me take
calls on hers. So I went over to her studio and they told me about
an audition I could go to tomorrow. I wasn't gone five minutes and
when I got back"—Pam started to cry—"he was lying dead on the
floor. The police said it was cyanide."

It took me a while to get her calmed down but I felt better already.
The thing was so obvious I was even getting sore at the police for
being dense.

"Honey," I said, "drink that tea and listen. What could be more obvious? Has-been actor takes powder after bum audition. It's the classic story—"

"But his wallet was missing," sobbed Pam.

"His wallet?" I was getting more aggravated by the minute. "His *wallet?* Who knew he had one with him?"

"I did." Pam wiped her eyes.

I was beginning to feel like my head wasn't screwed on tight. "How would you know?"

"He took it out while we were talking. He was showing me some clippings, old reviews of some good performances he'd given."

Oh, he'd given a good performance, all right. He'd given a *great* performance and landed my kid in the soup. Rave reviews for you, buster. But it still didn't make sense.

I said: "So his wallet was missing. Maybe an itchy-fingered cop took it. Who cares? An old down-and-outer like that—how much could have been in it?"

Pam said, "Five thousand dollars," and swallowed her tea.

It's a good thing I wasn't swallowing at the moment; I'd have choked. I stared at her and said: "You saw the money?"

"Not till they found the wallet."

"It's been *found?*"

"Yes. In that closet. In my coat pocket."

She began to cry again and I nearly joined her. But in spite of the craziness of it all, what had happened still stuck out like a sore thumb. The poor old gink had performed the last dramatic deed of his career. On the day he knew he was washed up, a lovely girl befriended him, he slipped her all his worldly goods, and took a powder.

But where'd he get the money? He didn't take it to the audition with him; they left the theater and started to walk downtown. Bingo!—he asks Pam to wait while he goes for his coat because the great and noble idea for the end of the act has just occurred to him.

Would he have that much cash stashed away? Not that it mattered—he could have robbed a bank yesterday for all I cared—the thing was to prove he'd planted it on Pam himself before he bowed out. Couldn't the dope have realized it might look like she knocked him over for it? Why didn't he just give it to her and then go home and croak there? But no, he had to expire at her feet. Actors!

There was a knock on the door which practically said open up, this is the law. The fellow who walked in wasn't too coppish, though. I liked the way he smiled at Pam and shook hands with me. He was middle-aged with sandy hair and glasses and Pam introduced him as Sergeant Whelan. I spoke right up and said look, sir, you must remember some of those old Grade B movies with Lewis Stone we could all guess the end of—this has got to be one of them. He said I know, I know, but he wished the dead man had left some positive evidence that Pam had not (a) killed him, and (b) robbed him.

We all sat down and looked at each other. By now it was almost seven o'clock and the sun had given up on the one lousy little window. The room was full of shadows, like Pam's face. She said in a tired way that she could fix us some supper but I just told her to stay put, that I wanted to ask the sergeant a few questions about what had happened from his point of view.

He said this is what had happened: at about noon a call had come into headquarters from a hysterical girl saying that a man had committed suicide in her studio. When they got there, she and a friend from across the hall were hanging onto each other and the old gent was stretched out dead as a haddock from—examination had shown—cyanide.

I said: "How does his wallet come into it?"

He and Pam looked at each other and she put a hand over her eyes. He said: "The body had just been taken away and a few of us were still here. My boss told Pam she'd better call a lawyer and she said she'd rather call her mother and she'd use the booth across the street. She opened that closet and took her coat out and I held it for her. I saw this wallet bulging in the pocket. I said she'd better carry her wallet in a safer place, especially in the Bowery, and I took it out and handed it to her. Then I saw the initials on it. L.C."

I said: "What was in it?"

He said: "Identification, some old newspaper clippings, and about five grand in hundred-dollar bills." Sergeant Whelan looked at Pam in a real kind way. "By the way, it was all his own money. We found a cancelled bankbook in his coat pocket. He closed out his savings account at the Provident Trust on 18th Street this morning."

While Pam waited for him in that bookstore, I thought, and wondered why he was taking so long.

There was another knock on the door and a straggly-haired girl put her head in to say that Pam had a phone call. Pam thanked her and looked at Whelan. He got up and said he'd go with her and that decided me. We all piled across the hall to another studio apartment worse than Pam's—hardly a stick of furniture, and with an awful statue of something or other in the middle of the floor.

Pam picked up the phone and listened for about half a minute. Then she began to cry. I grabbed the phone and said: "This is Pam's mother. She's very upset. A man killed himself in her place this morning."

A man's voice said: "My God, then he meant it. Was it Lawrence Canfield?" My heart jumped and I said yes, who was this, please?

The voice went on: "This is Jerry Pope at the 22nd Street Theater. We had auditions this morning for a play called *Death Takes a Holiday*. About an hour after everyone left, Canfield phoned to ask if Pam had gotten the part of Grazia. I said yes, we'd just decided because she was so great, and Canfield said he was on his way down to her studio with her and he'd like the pleasure of telling her himself since this was—I forget his exact words—something like 'the last happy thing he'd ever be able to do.' I knew he was depressed about not being cast and I started to tell him I was sorry but he said, and I remember this distinctly, 'Don't worry about me, Jerry, I won't be around to embarrass you after today.' I began to wonder if he'd even told Pam about the part, so I just told her myself."

I said, "Jerry, will you please repeat what you've just said to this police officer?" and I handed the phone to Sergeant Whelan.

Pam had already beat it back across the hall and I found her sitting on her bed holding her head in her hands. I said, "Honey, you got the part, how great," and she just nodded and said she hated herself for feeling happy. Then she lay back on the pillow, exhausted. There was a little pink afghan at the foot of the bed and I pulled it up over her and nearly burst out crying when I saw it was the one I'd made for her crib.

Whelan came in and closed the door behind him. I said, "Will that take care of it—the suicide, I mean?"

He said: "I think so. Now prove to me what we all know anyway: that Pam didn't take the money from his body."

Damn it, I knew he was going to say that. I looked at Pam but she just lay there with her eyes closed. I beckoned Whelan over to the kitchen area and said: "Hasn't she had enough for one day?" He looked upset and said she sure had but—

"But there's still this one point left." He nodded.

The room was getting chilly. I put my coat around my shoulders and turned on a few lights. Then I found a bottle of wine in one of the cupboards and the sergeant got two glasses and we sat down at the card table. I said: "You got any kids?" "Four," he said. "One of them is her age."

We didn't talk for a while. I was thinking that back in Burbank it was around five o'clock and I'd have been whipping up a chocolate cream pie for my bridge club and maybe trying on the new wig my boyfriend says makes me look like Claudette Colbert. But I was thinking about something else, too. I was thinking about actors, especially old ones like Canfield, and their vanity. (Him and his clippings!) He'd wanted to tell Pam she'd gotten the part, and he wanted her to know he was giving her his money. Then he *must* have told her—he *must* have left a message. There was no way he would give his final performance without getting credit in the program.

Sergeant Whelan seemed to be on the same wavelength. He'd gotten up and was poking around on Pam's desk. I went over to the bed and sat down. "Honey," I said, "what were you and Canfield talking about just before you got called to the phone?"

She didn't answer for a minute and I thought she was asleep. Then she said slowly, thinking hard, "We were talking about the play, about *Death Takes a Holiday.* He asked me what my favorite scene was and I said the last one, where Death tells Grazia who he really is and that he must give her up. Mr. Canfield asked me to read it for him and I went over to the closet to get the script out of my coat pocket. Then Ruth knocked—"

She sat up with a jerk and Whelan and I both froze. We all looked at the closet and Whelan started walking toward it like he was on eggs. He opened the door and on the hook inside it hung Pam's old blue raincoat—she'd had it in college—and there in the right-hand pocket was a thin paperback. He brought the coat over to the bed and we all three stared at it. I said: "Is that the pocket the wallet was in?"

Pam nodded and Whelan said: "I guess it's why the pocket looked so wide open but I never noticed the book or thought about it."

Pam said, "Neither did I."

Whelan pulled the book out, carefully by the corner, but if it was fingerprints he was worried about he needn't have bothered because later they were able to identify Canfield's scrawly writing from a lot of stuff in his flat. On the last page he had written:

"Grazia: This is all I have in the world. My holiday from death is over but I hope you live forever."

Well, the play was a success and Pam got terrific notices. Like I said, she's got the talent (if no common sense—she gave Canfield's money to the Actors' Relief Fund). And what have I got? I've got Burbank, bridge club, and boyfriend. Life is perfect again.